THE BUTTERFLY EFFECT

The stubby little child's fingers were wrapped firmly around the hilt of her largest kitchen knife. The blade caught the glitter of the morning sunshine and flickered it back at her. In her mind's eye, Andrea saw the drawing again: the shredded bodies and blood, the child with the knife and the hateful, inhuman eyes.

With great effort, she found her voice. "Evan? Wh-what are you doing with that?"

It was as if a switch was tripped inside the boy's head. One moment, he was inert and doll-like, and the next life suddenly filled him again, the sparkle of intelligence re-emerging. Evan dropped the knife in shock. The blade caught itself in a crack between two tiles and settled upright, buried in the putty.

THE BUTTERFLY EFFECT

NOVELIZATION BY
JAMES SWALLOW

BASED ON THE SCREENPLAY BY
J. MACKYE GRUBER & ERIC BRESS

BLACK **FLAME**

For all my friends on this timeline.

A Black Flame Publication
www.blackflame.com

First published in 2004 by BL Publishing, Games Workshop Ltd.,
Willow Road, Nottingham NG7 2WS, UK

Distributed in the US by Simon & Schuster, 1230 Avenue of the
Americas, New York,. NY 10020, USA

10 9 8 7 6 5 4 3 2 1

ISBN 1-84416-081-5

A CIP record for this book is available from the British Library.

Printed in the UK by Bookmarque, Surrey, UK.

"The time is out of joint –
O cursed spite, that ever I was born to set it right!"

Hamlet, Act I, Scene v

ONE

Summer is here now, and the garden outside my window is filled with a brilliant riot of colors, with the flowers blooming and turning their faces to the sun. I watch the insects dart in between them, the bees hard at work and the butterflies skimming across the petals like tiny kites. This seems like as good a time as any to begin.

As I try now to put it all down on paper after so many years, it's still difficult for me to draw the dividing line between what actually happened and what I think—or what I remember—happened. Even now, just trying to tie it all together makes me feel a little queasy, almost as if the memories hidden back in the depths of my head are somehow poisonous, that they're toxic enough to make me sick to my stomach just thinking about them.

For the longest time I couldn't even bring myself to talk about it—hell, I wouldn't even think about it, for fear that I'd trigger the whole damn thing all over again, upset the balance and pull everything crashing down around me. People always laughed and joked about that, they said that I was a man who lived for the here and now. I always looked to the future: they never knew that it was because I was afraid of the past.

It's hard to know where to start. At first, I thought it all began with Jason, but to begin with him would make this his story and to this day I still don't know all of what he went through. In truth, his father may have been party to it as well. Perhaps there's a long line of us, a lineage of men stretching back into history, all of us cursed with this terrible gift. I pray to God that I am the last.

So, then. This is about me, this is about what I did. The weird thing is, the memory I have that's the strongest—the one that's like a rock in among the shifting mess of all the rest—is of the one moment when I was willing to risk it all, when I was quite ready to toss my life away for one last chance. I suppose, at that point, I had crossed some sort of line, just stepped over from self-doubt, anger and fear, and into certainty. I wonder how many people can say that? How many of us can ever say with absolute honesty that there was a moment when we knew exactly what we had to do?

It's clear like crystal to me now. A summer night still dozy and clogged with the heat of the day, the sheetrock walls of Doctor Redfield's office holding the clammy warmth of the sun hours after nightfall. His room filled with unkempt piles of paper, the big desk with the dirty gray computer, the framed certificates on the walls, filing cabinets and rickety chairs. There's an alarm ringing out in the corridor, a two-tone warble that sings back and forth, back and forth. Through the marbled glass of the office door I can see the darting blinks of light from flashlights, flickering off Redfield's name on the pane. They're coming for me. They shout, they call and they run, their voices distant and foggy. From where I sit they could almost be the barks of dogs and not the sounds of men.

In my hands is the box. My name is written on the cardboard flaps in the doctor's hasty, imprecise style. Inside there are shapes, spools, indistinct objects. These things, these simple little things will save me. They will save everything.

Someone runs past and I glance up. In that moment I catch a glimpse of myself, reflected in the glass of a picture frame, lit in bars of light that peek through the blinds. I am haggard and weary, and my eyes are haunted by something terrible. Blood, black and oily in the dimness, streaks my face and chest. The pain seems oddly distant, as if it is happening to someone else. It's there, coils of it wrapped around my head, pressing into my skull.

I take the box and drag it into the space under Redfield's desk, pulling sheets of paper and a pen along with it. I can barely see what it is I'm scrawling as my hands start to move over the pages. It's a compulsion, driven by muscle memory more than conscious thought; I cannot do anything else but write.

The words escape my lips—saying them aloud seems to focus the agony. "If anyone finds this, then I guess my plan didn't work and I'm already dead…" With cold understanding, I realize that I am crafting my own epitaph. "But if I can just go back to the beginning of all this, I still might be able to save her—"

There would be more, but the pain does not allow me. Blood spots the paper as it trickles from my nose. I'm rooting through the box now, tugging at the contents, fear and panic rising up inside me like a dark fountainhead. And there I find the reels, Day-Glo plastic spools heavy with strips of film, hundreds of feet of footage all packed into tight discs, labeled with black letters on age-worn masking tape. A single word in Jason's writing. My father's writing. *Evan*.

The film rattles through the aged projector and stutters into life—the air tingles with ozone from the laboring lamp and motors—the hot, close texture of heated celluloid. It's the smell of movies.

On the screen, behind the camera, Dad fumbles at the controls of the old Bell & Howell, working to keep it in focus as he follows Mom's gurney down the hospital corridor. She moves in and out of frame as he runs after her. Her pretty face is streaked with sweat and she yells out, one hand straying to her swollen belly and the other flailing. Dad side-steps just in time as she slaps out at nothing and catches some poor guy's IV bottle. The glass whips into the wall and shatters, but we've already left him behind.

A juddering cut, a poor edit made with adhesive tape. Dad pulls back from Mom's pale, teary face to show the tiny bundle of life in her arms. The baby, pink and newborn, yawns and gives the camera a casual glance. "Say hello, Evan!" she smiles.

From out of frame, Dad's voice catches. "Welcome to the world, little man."

Snap-blink-cut.

The shutter jiggles as Dad tracks Mom. She turns and gives him a brilliant smile, revealing the baby in swaddling clothes. With infinite care, she places the child in a crib. The camera dithers for a moment—it's as if Dad cannot be sure where to look first: at the woman he loves so much, or the son he's just brought into the world.

The projector complains as another hasty edit whines through the sprockets.

"Jason, look this way!" Mom's words are warm and close to the camera's microphone. In the foreground, Dad lifts up a one year-old Evan and both of them wave to her. Jason deposits him on a shallow playground slide and the toddler gives a yelp of excitement.

The film stock changes to a brighter, less grainy grade, but still age-spotted and lined with cracks.

Lenny Kagan's backyard blurs into view: the swing set, tired old apple tree and the porch's peeling white paint over careworn pine. Even at the age of five, Lenny wears the aspect that will follow him his whole life, chubby and awkward, self-conscious in his cardboard 'Birthday Boy' hat among his few, few friends. Lenny's mother carries a scattering of boxes wrapped in gaudy paper, and he attacks them with gusto. The camera finds Mom as she gently prods a five year-old Evan toward Kayleigh, a pretty girl the same age. Evan shuffles past her scowling brother and gives her a clumsy handshake. Kayleigh smiles and kisses Evan on the cheek. As the adults laugh, Evan breaks away—the focus wavers as the camera finds him again, face red with blushes, hiding behind his mother's legs.

Evan's face fills the screen, and something his father says is stuttered into gibberish as the film suddenly judders, flickers and snaps out of the reel—

Evan Treborn shifted his weight from foot to foot in a careful rocking motion and he surveyed the driveway. A frisky cocker spaniel puppy ambled up and fixed him with what was, in his doggy way, a most serious look. Evan dropped to his haunches and tickled the dog's ears.

"Good boy, Crockett," Evan said. "I can't play with you now. We have to go soon."

The dog looked back at Evan, then down the drive to the white Toyota Celica parked a few feet away, then at Evan again.

"Soon," Evan repeated, as if that would some-how make his mother pick up the pace a little. He sighed and wandered over to her, with Crock-ett trailing at his heels.

Andrea Treborn drew herself out from under the Celica's hood and rubbed a thick film of oil from her hands with a greasy cloth. The com-plex snarl of components laid out before her seemed to be correct. She flipped a glance at the detached carburetor assembly and blew out a breath. Six weeks at an adult education center course on car maintenance, and she still found the mechanics of an engine to be somewhere between brain surgery and rocket science. Her eyes wandered to the house next door. She'd lost count of the number of times her neighbor Jerry had offered to help her out with this sort of thing, what he had labeled "Y'know, guy-stuff." She resented the implication that a single mother couldn't handle anything more complex than running a vacuum cleaner or a toaster oven—but there were times, and this was one of them, when she wished someone else could deal with this grease-laden monkey puzzle.

The sound of pounding footsteps drew her attention as another of her neighbors jogged along the sidewalk. Andrea waved and received a smile in return. Lisa Halpern was a newlywed and had just moved in to a big colonial-style house a few blocks away, with her handsome young husband and their massive 4x4. Even in a baggy sweat-suit and leggings, Lisa looked perky and radiant as she raced away, while Andrea felt shapeless and pallid in her oil-stained mechanic's overalls.

Yeah, she thought, but just let her have a kid and then we'll see how quickly she starts to sag…

She turned back to the engine. "Okay. Okay." She paused. "What now?"

Evan peered past her and studied the problem for a moment. Reaching into the open toolbox on the drive, he retrieved a 5/16" wrench and spun it around in his hand, like a gunfighter twirling a six-shooter. "We're gonna be late again."

She took the tool from him with a nod. "When did you ever care about getting to school on time?" she asked over her shoulder.

The boy looked away. "We're puttin' up pictures for Parent's Night."

Andrea turned a bolt, ignoring the underlying tone in Evan's voice for the moment.

Her son rose up on his tiptoes. "Remember, Mom, righty-tighty, lefty-lucy,"

She smiled. "Thanks, Evan. Don't worry, you'll have plenty of time…" Her voice trailed off as she examined the carburetor that sat wrongly out of its fitting. With a grimace, Andrea swiped it with the wrench. "Darn it!"

"Uh…." began Evan, and she knew his next question before he said it. "Can Dad come along this time?"

"You know the answer to that." Impatience colored her tone.

Evan tried and failed to keep a whine from his voice. "Can't he come out for just one day?"

She shook her head. "We've been over this a hundred times. It's too dangerous for him…"

"But Lenny said that his dad is coming." Evan stepped closer. "And Tommy and Kayleigh's dad—"

Andrea handed the wrench back to him. "Here, Ev. Finish this up for me." She felt a little bad for distracting her son by giving him the chore, but she was tired and she didn't have the answer he wanted. As Evan seated the component, she shrugged out of the overalls, revealing her clean, untouched nurse's uniform beneath it.

"All the dads are gonna be there." The hood muffled his voice.

"I get the point, kiddo, but I'm not so bad, am I?"

"No…"

"Good, because I've been waiting to see your art projects all week and I'd feel terrible if all you thought about was your father not being there."

"Done," replied Evan after a moment. "Try it." The boy's disappointment could have been written on his forehead.

Andrea slid into the driver's seat and worked the Toyota's ignition. With a throaty rumble, the engine turned over and a grin of pride broke out on Evan's face. Beaming, Andrea replied, "You're amazing, kiddo! Don't we make a great team, huh?"

"Yeah!"

And for that instant, nothing could spoil the moment they shared together.

The bell blared into life at the exact second they reached the school zone outside Huber Elementary. Racing at near-illegal speed into the drop-off space by the front gates, Andrea handled the Celica with all the focus and expertise of a world-class rally driver, pitching the car into place with a squeal of brakes. This was a drill that Evan had grown to be familiar with in the last few years: the rapid dash from home to school against the clock. Mom made being late an art form. He already had the passenger side door open, one hand ready on the seatbelt release, his backpack wrapped around the other. The car halted with a jerk and he leapt out, blowing his mother a kiss as he dashed over the quad to the main doors, disappearing into the milling throng of a hundred other school kids.

"Okay have a nice day I love you I'll pick you up later gotta go!" Andrea called after him in one breathless outburst. She was about to shift gears and accelerate away when a stern finger tap-tapped on her windshield.

"Mrs Treborn! I need to speak with you!"

Andrea recognized Evan's teacher Mrs Boswell from previous meetings of the Parent-Teacher Association and that one occasion when her son had fallen ill on a trip to the state capital. She was a little older than Andrea, and she always seemed to wear a tight, unhappy expression. "I'm sorry, but can't it wait until the Parent's Night tonight?" She waved at the clock on the dash, "I'm already late for work and—"

But the morbid look on Boswell's face stopped her in mid-sentence. "I think you really need to see this," said the teacher. "Now."

Mrs Boswell led Andrea into the classroom, into a sea of screaming, running, shouting children. She scanned the room automatically for Evan, and they caught each other's eyes right away. On the other side of the class, her son gave a half-wave, a flicker of surprise on his face at seeing her here. Andrea watched him turn away, returning to play with Kayleigh Miller. She suppressed a smile—the little girl was besotted with Evan, and had been since they had first met.

Mrs Boswell's voice barked out a warning. "Tommy!" she snapped. "Leave Lenny alone!"

Andrea turned to see Kayleigh's elder brother brandishing a whiffle-ball bat as if it were a club at Lenny's plump head. The portly boy sniffled and pouted, while Tommy made a sour grimace.

"Don't make me send you to Mr Voytek's office, young man!" the teacher added.

Andrea looked back at the teacher. Perhaps it was no surprise she always seemed unhappy, because dealing with little demons like Tommy Miller five days a week would be enough for any woman.

They reached her desk and Mrs Boswell recovered a large sheaf of folded construction paper from a drawer. "I was going to show this to the principal, but I wanted to talk to you about it first…" She removed a single page, but then held it to her chest.

Andrea felt her mouth go dry with sudden concern. "What is it?"

"Yesterday, I had all the children draw pictures of what they wanted to be when they grew up. Most of them made drawings of what their parents did, but this…" The teacher trailed off, and unfolded the page, her face troubled. "This is what Evan drew."

Something acidic twisted in Andrea's stomach as she looked at the picture, and her blood turned ice cold. The crude drawing was rendered in eye-searing color, and it depicted what seemed to be a child standing atop a hill of shattered, broken corpses. The face of the child was dark and angry, and in one of its hands was the unmistakable spear-point shape of a butcher knife. Rivers and pools of bright crimson blood were everywhere. Most of the bodies seemed to be wearing blue coveralls and some of the ones in the foreground displayed horrific wounds that sported recognizable internal organs and bone structure. It was a violent, hateful glorification of killing, an image drawn from some horrific, tortured place.

"The drawing is quite sophisticated for a seven year-old boy," Boswell said in a low voice, but Andrea could not look away from the picture. "As you are a nurse, I wondered if he copied some of these images from medical anatomy books you might have at home?"

Andrea finally snapped free from the awful composition of the drawing, and she shot a look at Evan. He sat with Lenny, the two boys laughing as they played with toy cars. It seemed impossible, utterly unbelievable that her son could have created something so macabre and hellish. "Thank you for showing it to me first," she managed, finding her voice once again. "I'll... I'll take care of it... Can I have the picture?"

"Of course." Mrs Boswell folded the paper and held it out to her. "There is one more thing, Mrs Treborn, and I feel bad even mentioning it—"

"What?" Andrea snapped.

"When I asked Evan about his drawing, about what it meant, well... He said he didn't even remember doing it."

The color drained from Andrea's face. "I have to go," she said, snatching the picture from the teacher's hand and darting out of the room.

Evan looked up in time to see her leave, his face a mask of childlike concern. When he glanced over at Mrs Boswell, he found the teacher studying him with a cold, measuring stare.

Andrea made it to the curb before her knees turned to jelly. She fumbled open the door to the Toyota and collapsed into the driver's seat, her heart hammering at the inside of her chest. Her mouth tasted of harsh metallic bile, and her hands would not stop trembling.

Oh dear God, no! Her mind reeled, terrible thoughts and long-ignored memories flooding back as an awful possibility rose to the surface. What if Evan is the same as his father? What if he's just as sick as Jason was? Andrea held the offending drawing tightly in her hands, the rough paper bunching into a knot. Muscles in her wrists spasmed. She wanted to dig her fingernails into the picture and rip it apart, shred and tear it into tiny flecks, anything to destroy what it might represent.

But what then, she asked herself? Even if she got rid of Evan's picture, the image of it would stay lodged in her mind, and so would the fear of what it could mean. As much as she wanted to, she couldn't wish it out of existence.

Andrea tried to insert the key in the ignition and failed, the sweat-slick dart of metal slipped from her fingers and fell into the footwell. She slowly placed both her hands on the steering wheel and willed them into steadiness.

It was a good ten minutes before she was calm enough to start the car and drive on.

TWO

By the lunchtime bell, Evan had forgotten all about his mother's impromptu visit to class, and as the afternoon period began, he launched himself into his art project with all the enthusiasm his seven years could muster. Parent's Night was just hours away, and as far as Evan was concerned, the clock was ticking on him making the most excellent picture for his Mom.

He paused, admiring the masterpiece coming together under his hands—multiple shades of construction paper, splashes of thick, gooey poster paint and dry curls of macaroni were turning into an idyllic, kid's-eye view of family life. Evan considered and then rejected the idea of using glitter. Nah, that was a touch that only girls would put on a picture.

He didn't see the look on Mrs Boswell's face as she passed by behind him, the narrow-eyed glance as she scanned him for the tell-tales that earmarked a troublemaker. Susan Boswell had been an elementary school teacher since she was twenty, and she was good at it. Early on, she'd learned the knack of being able to see a bad kid a mile off, like some kind of internal alarm that picked up on mischief before it had a chance to bloom. Some of her pupils, aggressive boys like Tommy Miller or screaming hair-pullers like Heidi Nixon, stood out in Boswell's vision like red flags, their need to misbehave constantly bubbling away just under the surface. Children like that, Boswell knew how to deal with them.

It was the ones like Evan who she worried about, the ones who slid right under her radar. He was a smart kid, attentive but not too outgoing, and the last one she suspected to go wrong on her. The image of Evan's horrible drawing passed through her mind and she suppressed a shudder. Without alerting him, Mrs Boswell peered over his shoulder at his latest creation and, inwardly, she relaxed a little. It was simplistic and happy, much more the creation of a boy his age than the appalling thing he'd made before. The teacher was well aware that Mrs Treborn was a single mother, that Evan's father had been absent from his life for many years, and she resolved to speak to Andrea alone at the meeting that night, perhaps in hopes of getting to the bottom of it. Perhaps the picture had been some sort of acting-out, she reasoned, or maybe something he saw in a movie? Whatever the cause, she hoped it would be the last shocker he saw fit to create. The teacher left Evan to his art, and carried on out of the room to fetch a few more pots of paste.

Evan cut at a slip of brown paper with a deft series of snips, the tip of his tongue protruding out of the side of his mouth as he did so. He blew on the paper to reveal a carefully made cut-out of a dog and, with a spot of glue, he stuck it down on the broad green hill that served as his picture's backdrop. It was finished. The hill was joined by a smiling yellow sun and two more cut-outs—one depicting Evan in his favorite Batman T-shirt, and another of his mother, her head a full mane of macaroni-hair.

A girlish giggle made him pause. "What?" he asked, looking up at Kayleigh.

She pointed at his face. "Your tongue."

"What about it?"

"You always stick it out like this," and she mimicked him, "when you're working. It's funny."

He gave a shrug. "I guess,"

Evan glanced over at Kayleigh's picture. Her brother was hard at work on his art at the same desk, with Lenny busy gluing at the far end. Tommy and Kayleigh's drawings were virtually identical. Each of them showed a boy and a girl with a taller father figure clustered at one end of the page, and a lone mother off on her own at the opposite side. Evan thought that the mother figure looked a little sad on her own, but said nothing. Mom had told him in no uncertain terms never to talk about the break-up of the Miller family.

Lenny beamed as he held up his drawing for the entire world to see. "I'm all finished. I made a new clear family,"

Tommy made a snorting sound. "A what? What does that mean?" He stabbed an accusing finger at the picture.

"My dad says that's what it's called. When you have a mom, a dad and a kid, it's a new clear family," Lenny's brow furrowed.

Evan smiled. "You mean nuclear, Lenny. Like the bomb."

Tommy laughed harshly. "Ha-ha, Lenny's gotta radioactive family!"

"I don't!" Lenny pouted. He looked down at Tommy's picture. "You put the mommy too far away. Mrs Boswell has macaroni and glue if you wanna fix it."

"You're such a retard!" Tommy snapped at him, his face clouded.

Kayleigh looked away. "Mommy lives far away from us, but she comes and visits some-times."

"If… if I'm so retarded," Lenny began, mus-tering all his courage against Tommy, "then why didn't my mommy move away from me?"

Kayleigh's brother went red and yelled out, sending a savage swipe at Lenny's picture. Tommy's fingers raked over the paper and tore his perfect family apart, shredding the macaroni figure of his mother. Instantly, Lenny's face flushed crimson and he began to wail.

"Hey!" Evan snapped. "What'd you do that for?"

"Fat little baby, crying for mommy!" Tommy shouted the words in sing-song fashion and stomped away.

Evan took up the ruined picture and walked over to Lenny, who sat heavily on the floor, wheezing out sobs in between gasping breaths of air. "Come on, Lenny," he began. "It's not that bad... You can still see your mom a little."

But the other boy didn't seem to be listening to him. Alarm rose in Evan's mind as Lenny began to shudder, his desperate panting for breath growing worse by the second, racing out of control.

Evan frantically looked around for Mrs Boswell, but the teacher was nowhere to be seen; only a growing ring of gawking kids and Tommy, looking on with callous disregard.

Evan saw a solution—he grabbed at his own picture and tore free the cut-out of his own mother in a single stroke, then laid it down on Lenny's ruined drawing. The family was whole again, and with that Lenny's fretful chugs of air began to slow, as the chubby little boy calmed himself.

After a moment, Lenny caught his breath and looked up at Evan with puffy eyes. "Can... can... can I keep this?"

Evan gave a smile of relief. "Sure thing. I was gonna make a new one anyway."

Tommy scowled and turned his back on them, annoyed that his amusement had been brought to an end. At the desk, Kayleigh handed Lenny the glue and helped him fix his new "mother" in place. She threw Evan a smile, and he nodded back at her.

Mrs Boswell knew something had happened the moment she returned to the classroom—what it was she couldn't be exactly sure, but the tension of spent childlike anguish hung in the air like a faint whiff of smoke. She took in all of the pupils at once, automatically spying Tommy Miller's closed fists and set jaw, and the flushed expression on Lenny Kagan's moon-like face. She set down the paste pots and circled the room without comment. Whatever had happened between the two boys had been and gone, and she had no desire to stir it up again.

Passing Evan Treborn again on her orbit, she glanced at his work, and a shiver ran through her. Whereas before, he'd had a picture of an ideal, happy family—all smiles and sunshine—the drawing had now been mutilated. Evan's mother had been physically ripped from the page and discarded. The grim symbolism of the action made her blood run cold. Mrs Boswell looked away from the butchered family portrait and moved on, pausing only to discreetly gather up the scissors from Evan's desk, just in case. For the rest of the day, she found herself watching Evan's every move, a steady churn of worry turning over and over in her stomach.

It had taken some serious string pulling, and the calling-in of a few favors, but Andrea had managed to convince Barbara to let her take the afternoon off. The senior nurse was a large, acerbic woman who had moved out of Chicago and brought all of her street smarts from the projects to Sunnyvale's upstate New York lifestyle. Barbara ruled her nurses at Mercy General with a rod of iron, but she had kids of her own and when Andrea had pleaded her case and concern over Evan, she'd let her off without comment.

Like most of the nurses at Mercy, Barbara knew about Jason—the broad strokes of what had happened to him, at least—and she sympathized. The hospital was only a few blocks away from the Sunnyvale Psychiatric Clinic, so many of the staff from both facilities knew one another, and they talked. Andrea remembered a time when she had thought it would be good that Jason had been placed somewhere so close— somewhere that she could visit at a moment's notice—but the truth was, it had been more than a year and a half since she'd last seen her husband. At their last meeting they had degenerated into an argument over Evan's future, and both of them had said things that hurt. Andrea had walked out and not looked back.

As she drove the short distance to the clinic this afternoon, she caught herself fiddling with

her wedding ring. For what had to be the millionth time, she asked herself why the hell she
was still wearing it. Sure, it was fine for warding
off assholes trawling for lonely divorcees, but the
reality of it was she was wife to Jason Treborn in
name alone. Jason's shrink, Doctor Redfield, had
told her on several occasions that no court in the
land would stand in her way if she wanted to
end her marriage, but it was a line she felt she
couldn't cross. At least, not yet. Damn him, but
she still loved her husband, and some small part
of her still held tight to the dream that, one day,
he would be healthy again.

Andrea's Celica drew to a halt in front of the
imposing Gothic face of the clinic. Local lore sug-
gested that it had been built back in the early
1900s as a poorhouse, picked up in later years by
a rich doctor type from Maine and made into an
insane asylum. She corrected herself as she
stepped out of the car. *Clinic*, she told herself,
not asylum. Or funny farm. Or psycho ward.
This was a place where sick people got well, just
like Mercy General.

But not all sick people. Not Jason.

She pushed the image of her husband back and
back into the darkest recesses of her mind; he
was the last thing she wanted to dwell on right
now. With a deep breath, she pushed her way
through the heavy oak doors and entered.

Doctor Harlon Redfield made a half-hearted
attempt to tidy his desk, finally giving up as he

tipped over a dozen *Psychology Digests* into an unkempt pile on the floor. Despite his best attempts, the room still looked like the debris from an explosion in a filing cabinet. Someone tutted from the doorway and he glanced up. His colleague Doctor Pulaski gave him an arch look.

"Why don't you put on some cologne while you're at it?" she smirked. "Set out some throw cushions and maybe a bottle of red wine?"

Redfield shook his head. "I'm sorry, Kate, did you want something?"

Pulaski made a face. "God, Harlon, you are so transparent! You never clean up your office when I come to visit."

"That's because you're a nasty old woman and I wouldn't want to encourage you to stay," he deadpanned. "Now go on, get out of here. I have an appointment."

Her manner became a little more serious. "You know, you're skating along the edge of the doctor-patient relationship here. Everyone knows you've got a thing for that Treborn woman."

"She's not my patient," Redfield snapped. "Her husband is."

"Uh-huh," drawled Pulaski, "And I suppose you agreed to give her an appointment at an hour's notice because you're such a nice guy, despite the fact she hasn't visited the poor schmuck in over a year? You're too old for her anyhow."

"Shut up, Kate. Go scare the paranoids or something. You bother me."

Pulaski was about to add something more, but a strident beep from Redfield's desk intercom sounded. "Mrs Andrea Treborn is here to see you, doctor," said his secretary.

He thumbed the "talk" key. "Thank you, Karen. Send her in." He gave Pulaski a hard stare. "And you, go away!"

The other doctor rolled her eyes and walked off. "Just remember," she called over her shoulder, "what would Hippocrates have said?"

Any answer he might have given was smothered as Andrea entered the office. Redfield swallowed hard, standing up and shaking her hand. "Mrs Treborn, how are you? You're looking well…"

"Call me Andrea, please."

"Of course. Andrea." He gave a weak smile, still a little put-off by how close to the truth Pulaski's comments had been. "Well, I don't really have anything new to say about Jason. His behavior—"

"This isn't about my husband," she interrupted. "It's about Evan."

"Your son?" The doctor was slightly surprised. "He's, what, six now?"

"Seven. I'm worried that… well…" Andrea paused, wringing her hands. "It's just that, he drew this." She handed him the folded picture. "He says he doesn't remember drawing any of it."

Doctor Redfield put on his reading glasses and studied the drawing. He was very careful

not to react. "Evan did this? It's extremely...
detailed."

Andrea nodded, her head bobbing like a bird's.
"According to his teacher. It just got me thinking
about Jason, and what if Evan's inherited his
father's condition—"

Redfield heard the panic building in Andrea's
voice and held up a hand to silence her. "Hold it
right there. Let's not jump to any conclusions. If
you want, I can run some preliminary tests on
Evan, just to see what we can rule out." He
glanced at a notepad on his desk. "Tell you what,
why don't you bring him here tonight and we'll
run a CAT-scan series?"

She gave him a brittle smile. "Thank you, doctor. I didn't know who else to turn to."

He returned the smile, doing his best to inject
as much warmth into it as he could. "Harlon,
please. My name's Harlon."

Evan was at the head of the wave of children as
they boiled out of the school gates, the end-of-
period bell singing them away from lessons and
work for another day. It hardly mattered that
he'd be coming back there in a few hours to face
his teachers with his mother in tow. For now,
school was well and truly out.

Kayleigh danced past him, heading toward her
father's parked car. "See you later, Evan!"

"Okay!" he waved, homing in on the white
Toyota idling at the curb. He was in and belted
before his mother said anything to him.

"We're not going to go straight home, Evan. We have to go see someone first."

Evan squirmed as the car pulled away. "But what about Parent's Night? Is this about why you came into class today?"

Andrea kept her eyes on the road. "Sort of. It's nothing to be worried about. You'll see."

The boy was silent for a moment, as the car wound its way out toward the clinic. Then, with a timbre of fear in his voice, he asked her, "Is this about that drawing that Mrs Boswell didn't like?" When his mother didn't answer straight away, he pressed on. "It is, isn't it? I told her, I didn't remember drawing it!"

She flashed him a false grin. "I know, kiddo, but we just have to speak to the doctor about it."

The rest of the ride took place in an awkward silence, both of them lost for words or for some way to get back into the conversation.

Evan said nothing until they were walking towards the oak doors. "I don't like this place, Mom," he said, eyeing the gloomy building. In the fading light of evening, the clinic looked even more sinister and forbidding than it did in the daytime. "It's creepy. Please can we go home? I promise I won't make any more bad pictures."

"You'll be fine," Andrea said, forcing a light-hearted tone into her voice. "Doctor Redfield just wants to give you some tests. You'll like him."

Redfield greeted them at the door of his office, and shook the boy's hand. He'd always found that children were more open to adults who treated them as if they were adults too. "Hello Evan, it's very nice to meet you." He smiled at Andrea. "He's as handsome as his father."

Evan's mouth dropped open. "You know my father?"

Andrea cut the doctor short before he could say any more. "That's why I brought you here, Evan. Doctor Redfield already has a background in problems with memory loss."

"My dad has a bad memory too?" Evan tried to assimilate this information, forming it into the vague picture he had of Jason Treborn.

Redfield took a cue from Andrea and began to usher Evan toward the door. "Uh, tell you what, Evan, if it's okay with your mother, I'd like to run some tests." He smiled again. "Nothing scary."

Evan gave the doctor a very mature look of disbelief that reminded him of Doctor Pulaski's arch expression.

"Well," he amended, "it might be a little scary."

Andrea's heart hammered as she watched Evan lie down on the platform before the massive CAT scanner. Behind a window, she and Redfield stood by a medical technician as he ran through the calibration of the massive machine. The doctor spoke into an intercom mic, his voice resonated into Evan's room.

"Are you comfortable, Evan? You have to make sure you don't move your head at all. We're going to take some pictures of you with this big camera. It won't hurt."

"I'm scared."

Evan's tiny voice cut through Andrea like a knife.

"Don't be," said Redfield. "Just do what I do, and pretend you're an astronaut in a space capsule, heading off to Mars. Can you do that?"

"Okay," he managed.

"We're ready to go," said the technician.

Redfield flipped off the intercom. "Spin it up."

The big device hummed into life and turned about its own axis, shifting into place around the boy's prostrate body. The scanner began to slowly rotate around Evan's head.

"Just tell me that my son doesn't have Jason's illness..." said Andrea, watching the machine do its work.

The doctor crossed his arms. "Look, Andrea, I'm sure he'll test negative for any brain disorders, but in the meantime there's something else you can try to monitor his memory. It's simple, no drugs or anything like that."

"Anything." The word held the sting of desperation that Redfield had heard a thousand times from the relatives of his patients.

"Get him to start writing a journal. Just have him write down everything he does."

"Why? What good would that do?"

He glanced back at the scanner as the machine rolled to a slow halt. "We've found in memory related problems that a diary, a record of events can be extremely useful to assist recall. You can use it to jog his memory, see if he remembers anything new the next day."

The technician shut the CAT scanner down and nodded to Redfield.

"That's it, we're done. I'll have the test results ready by the end of the week."

Andrea tried not to run as she stepped into the scanning room and went to Evan. Doctor Redfield helped him to his feet and patted him on the shoulder.

"So, how was your trip to Mars, spaceman?"

Evan shook his head, as if trying to ward off a bothersome flying insect. "Cold and dark. I like the Earth a lot better."

"Me too," said his mother, taking his hand. "How about we stop for some ice cream? I figure we could share a bowl before we go to Parent's Night?"

"Okay." Evan smiled a little, and for the moment, Andrea felt her tension ease.

THREE

The journal was covered with a card-stock colored like black marble. Evan ran his fingers over it experimentally. His mother had already christened it by writing 'Age 7' in thick black marker on the cover. She'd let him pick the color he liked best from the store, and the lines and whorls of the marble design had attracted him instantly. They were like little rivers, and for a moment he imagined himself in a tiny boat no bigger than a speck of dust, voyaging along them. In his hand he held a pen he'd fished out of his school bag, one end slightly chewed.

He took a deep breath—because what he was about to do would be very important—and opened the composition book to its first page. He began at the very top corner of the ruled paper, and with a steady, careful hand, Evan started to write. *My name is Evan Treborn. This is my journal.*

"It's like you'll be telling a story, but it will be all about you, and what you do," Mom had said.

At first, Evan had been suspicious of the whole thing. Writing reminded him too much of school, and he wondered if this was some kind of sneaky way for Mrs Boswell to get him to do more home-work, but his mother had brought him around as she explained things to him. "A journal is like a notebook of your life," she'd said, between spoonfuls of Rocky Road at the 31 Flavors, "and in the future, when you're very important, people will be able to look at it and know what you were like when you were younger."

Evan grinned—he liked the idea of leaving something for future people to read about him, something like the time capsule that he'd seen the PTA bury in the school grounds a few years earlier.

"Maybe my journal will be like dinosaur bones," he said, warming to it, "and hundreds of years from now someone will dig it up!"

Mom had pointed at him with a half-eaten wafer. "Now you're cookin'!"

Evan came to the end of his first entry and laid the book flat on the kitchen table amid the break-fast things. He glanced up at his mother, but her attention was elsewhere as she talked rapidly into a telephone. He looked back at the page and read his words back to himself, his lips moving silently.

Today Mommy is takeing me to play with Kay-ley and Tommy. I will mete there father and see what a real dad is like. Maybe one day I will mete my Dad.

Andrea wandered over to Evan and flashed him a quick smile, one hand pressing the phone to her ear, the other brandishing an open box of Lucky Charms. She waved the box at him and he held up an empty bowl.

"Yes. That's right," she was saying, careful to pour just enough without spilling the oats and marshmallow pieces all over the table. "Uh-uh. It's really good of you to do it at such short notice. I've got to make up the time and—" Evan heard an indistinct garble from the earpiece. A man's voice. "Thanks again, George. I really appreciate you watching him." She gave her son a wink. "He won't be any trouble at all."

Evan felt a rough tongue tickle the back of his foot and he giggled. Crockett's face peered up at him from inbetween the legs of the chair and gave Evan a curious look. With deliberate care, he fished all the green clover-shaped marshmallows from the cereal bowl and cupped them in his hand. Crockett licked his lips expectantly: this was a morning ritual the dog had become used to.

"Here," said Evan, dropping them one by one to the floor. "You should eat all of these. They'll bring you lots of good luck, Crockett."

Andrea cupped her hand over the telephone mouthpiece. "Evan!" she snapped. "What have I told you about feeding the dog at the table?" He shrugged, but her attention was already back on the voice at the other end of the line. "Yes. Great.

See you soon, then." She hung up and gave Evan a not-too-serious glare. "You're going to make Crockett fat, you know that?"

"But he likes them, Mom," he replied, pouring a generous splash of milk over his breakfast.

She shook her head. "Okay, okay. But don't give him any more. He'll be sick." Glancing around, Andrea's brow furrowed. "Evan, have you seen my pocketbook?"

"In the living room," he replied, through a mouthful of milk and cereal.

"Hurry up and eat your breakfast," she began, walking into the other room. "Get your shoes on and we'll be going." Andrea nodded to herself; her purse sat on the coffee table and she swept it up, rooting inside for her car keys. "Evan? Did you hear me?"

She looked up as she returned to the kitchen and gave a yelp of surprise—the purse and the keys fell from her hands in shock, clattering against the tiled floor.

Her son stood in the far doorway, staring at her. His face was a blank, expressionless mask, ugly and slack as if the skin had been hung wrongly across his skull. Evan's eyes, always bright and sharp, were now empty pools of darkness, flat and glassy like those of a shark.

She called out his name, but he gave no sign of hearing her speak, or even that he was aware she was in the room with him. Andrea felt the rush of cold over her cheeks as the color drained from her complexion. The stubby little child's fingers of his right hand were wrapped firmly around the hilt of her largest kitchen knife, the big stainless steel one that she used to cube beef and cut steaks. The blade caught the glitter of the morning sunshine and flickered it back at her. The coffee and bagel she'd eaten earlier suddenly churned in her gut, threatening to force their way back up. In her mind's eye, Andrea saw the drawing again, the shredded bodies and blood, the child with the knife and the hateful, inhuman eyes.

With great effort, she found her voice. "Evan? Wh-what are you doing with that?"

It was as if a switch was tripped inside the boy's head. One moment, he was inert and doll-like, and the next life suddenly filled him again, the sparkle of intelligence re-emerging. It happened with a jolt, and Evan dropped the knife in shock. The blade caught itself in a crack between two tiles and settled upright, buried in the putty.

"What happened?" Evan cried, tears of fear glistened in his eyes, confusion and raw terror swelling within them. "Mommy?"

Andrea took a tentative step toward him. "Honey?" She struggled to maintain an even tone to her voice. "What were you doing with that?"

Tears began to race down Evan's cheeks. "I… I don't remember…" He called out to her and dashed across the room, wrapping himself around his mother, desperate for her comfort.

It took every iota of Andrea's self-control to stop her muscles from going rigid as he touched her, to bend down and gather him up in her arms. As Evan wept into her shoulder, she watched Crockett take a wary sniff of the butcher knife. The dog made a low growl of alarm in the back of its throat.

They didn't speak until they reached the Miller house. In the way that only families can do, Evan and his mother agreed not to discuss the episode with the knife—at least for the moment.

Tommy and Kayleigh's home was a lot larger than the Treborn's, mostly because their father had made a pile on the stock market in the early part of the decade. He'd speculated on some computer companies in what was now the heart of Silicon Valley, and coined it in—which explained how he could have a decent lifestyle, handle two children and still pay his ex-wife's alimony. Compared to their two-bedroom house with its pokey little yard, the Miller's place was practically a mansion.

George Miller gave them a jaunty wave as Andrea pulled the Toyota around the drive in a tight turn. He'd invited her in for coffee once after giving the kids a lift back from soccer practice, but Andrea had demurred. She'd always thought he was a good-looking man, easy-going and quite the sporty type—just not her type—but the kind of guy a lot of women her age were interested in. Andrea had never been able to understand what broke up George's marriage with his wife Alice, but whatever it was, it had been enough to send her off to live in Florida and not take her kids with her. That didn't sit well with Andrea: for a mother to abandon her children was anathema. She glanced at Evan, who still seemed subdued, and felt a swell of love for him. Whatever is going on, she promised him in a silent oath, we'll deal with it.

George opened Evan's door with a flourish. "Hey, Andrea," he smiled, "and hello to you, little man."

Evan managed a mumbled "Hi" and got out.

"Thanks a lot, George," Andrea said, fumbling with a pen and a piece of paper. "Look, here's my work number, just in case there are any problems—"

George took the paper and chuckled. "What, are you kidding? We're going to have a great time today, right, Evan?"

The boy said nothing, mute and sullen.

"Okay…" Andrea blew a kiss to her son. "I gotta go. I'll see you later, Evan." She flashed a quick wave over her shoulder as the Toyota drove away, watching the two of them shrink in the distance of the rearview mirror.

Evan sighed and took a moment to study his surroundings. Mr Miller looked down at him and waggled his eyebrows. "Well, then. Come on."

By reflex, Evan walked up to Mr Miller and reached for his hand: it was something Evan did whenever he was in the company of a friendly adult. Their fingers touched for a split-second and Mr Miller jerked his hand away, as if he'd been stung. He broke the awkward moment of silence that followed with a false chuckle. "So, are you waiting for an invitation? The kids are inside."

Mr Miller's sudden rudeness confused Evan for an instant, even as the boy followed him into the house. He'd seen someone on TV talk about how some people didn't like to be touched because they were afraid of germs, and he decided that Mr Miller must be one of them. Evan wiped his hands on his jeans and entered the house. Perhaps if he was cleaner, Mr Miller might like him better.

The living room was almost as big as the entire bottom floor of Evan's house, and it had a big television dominating one corner. Around its base was a snarl of cables and a Nintendo, surrounded by dozens of the latest games. Normally, Evan's attention would have wandered straight to the videogame, but his gaze was caught and held as Kayleigh bounced into the room, twirling like a ballerina. She was wearing a child's party costume, a long pink gown that rolled off her shoulders and into a diaphanous train; on her head she had a tall, pointed hat tipped with a streamer of cloth.

"Wow!" he said. "You're like a princess from a storybook."

Kayleigh gave an elaborate curtsey. "Evan, guess what?" Excitement bubbled over in her voice, and it was infectious. "Dad got a brand new video camera and we're all going to be in a movie!" She held out a bag full of clothes. "We got you a special outfit and everything!"

Tommy entered behind her, also in costume. His was more basic, a Medieval-style getup with a plastic sword dangling from a cloth belt. "I don't think Evan gets to be in it—" he began, with subdued menace glinting in his eyes.

Kayleigh rounded on him and put her hands on her hips. "Quit it, Tommy," she said in her most Queenly voice. "Evan gets to be Robin Hood. I'm gonna be Maid Marian, and you're the Sheriff of Nottingham!"

"I thought I was going to be the bad guy!" Tommy growled.

His sister made a face. "You are, silly. He's a bad sheriff."

That seemed to please Tommy, and he whipped out his toy sword, making experimental slashes and stabs at the air with it.

With a clatter of dragging cables, Mr Miller ambled into the room with a heavy camera bag over one shoulder and a tall tripod in his right hand. In his other, he gripped a tumbler full of whiskey, clinking with ice. He quickly set the bag down, pausing for a swing of his drink. "Here we go."

Evan watched with interest as Kayleigh's father unpacked the bulky video camera and locked it into place, running cords to the power outlet and another to a large portable recording deck. "I've never seen a movie camera before," Evan began, extending a hand toward it.

"Don't touch!" Mr Miller snapped, and Evan drew his hand back in shock. "It's expensive." Behind him, Evan heard Tommy give a snide laugh.

Mr Miller slammed home a tape into the deck and grinned. "Lights, camera, action!"

"We're really going to be in a movie?" Evan asked.

The adult winked at him. "That's right, Evan, and you get to be the star!"

The boy's face split in a wide, beaming smile.

Tommy frowned, flicking his sword disconsolately. "But I thought I was the star..."

Mr Miller shot his son an acid look. "Shut up, moron," he grated. He turned back to Evan, and was all smiles once again. "Now, get in your costume, Evan. And you have to promise, your bestest super-duper promise, that this will be our little secret." Mr Miller drained his glass and stepped behind the camera's eyepiece. "Think you can do that?"

Kayleigh gave Evan an encouraging nod and he raised his hands in the air to signify a hearty yes. Mr Miller gave a predatory smirk as he put

aside the tumbler and began to help Evan off
with his clothes—

Suddenly Evan's stomach turned upside down
and he stumbled. Panic shot through him. A second ago, they had been standing in the living
room. Now, Evan found himself somewhere
unfamiliar. He was in a basement, a recreation
room like the kind Uncle Peter and his family
had in New Jersey.

"Where am I?" he bleated. "What happened?"

His eyes darted madly around the room.
Kayleigh was sitting on the floor close to the
inert fireplace, her Maid Marian dress half-on
and half-off her shoulders, the tall hat discarded by the staircase. Her face was haggard
and ashen. George Miller was a few feet away,
his hands clasping the video camera as if he
half-expected Evan to kick the tripod over.

Evan shook his head, as if that would clear
his bewilderment. "Where did we all go?" The
shock of the abrupt transition made his guts
knot with tension. "Mr Miller, please!" He
became aware that some of his clothes were
strewn about the room, and he scurried to and
fro, snatching them up and balling them to his
chest.

Kayleigh's father blinked. "Calm down, kid."
He appeared to be just as uneasy as the children
were. "Stand still."

"I was just somewhere else…" Evan paused,
panting. "How did I get here?"

Mr Miller's voice turned angry. "Quit acting like some damn retard," he snarled, "or I'll call your mother right now and tell her what a naughty little shit you've been!"

The threat was enough to stop Evan in his tracks, and he looked at Kayleigh. She hadn't moved, her eyes never leaving the ground. "Kayleigh, what happened?" he implored. The girl said nothing, slowly starting to inch her dress back over her bare skin.

Evan slumped on the bottom tread of the staircase and closed his eyes. Every part of his body was alive with tension, trembling like a struck chord.

Above, at the door to the basement, Tommy looked down. In his hands he held one of Kayleigh's dolls. With dull, thoughtless savagery, he twisted the head of it around and around, wringing the plastic toy's neck.

"Can I get you anything?" Redfield asked. "A cup of coffee? Or perhaps some herbal tea? I have a—"

Andrea shook her head. "No thanks. Unless you got a cigarette?"

Redfield paused. "Uh, no. No, I don't smoke. I'm sorry."

She tried, and failed, to smile. "Don't be. I don't smoke either, or at least I haven't since before Evan was born. But I've been so wound up after what happened, and after he had

another blackout at George's place, I just…"
She trailed off.

"It's hardly the best way to relieve anxiety,"
said the doctor, "and I know this must be hard
for you."

Andrea clasped her hands together to keep
them from fidgeting. "So, what do you have to
tell me?" Just saying the words took all the
effort out of her.

"I'll show you." Redfield led her to a light
box mounted on the wall of his office. "These
are the slides from Evan's CAT scans." He
flipped a switch and a series of oval images
came to life, blurry cross-sections of Evan's
brain rendered in shades of gray and black.
"The good news is that the test results are one
hundred per cent negative. They show
absolutely no evidence in the way of lesions,
hemorrhaging, tumors—"

"And the bad news?" she broke in. Suddenly,
all Andrea wanted was for it all to be over.

The doctor took a breath. "Unfortunately,
we've got nothing physical to work with,
which means the problem is purely psycholog-
ical. It's going to be much harder playing
detective now."

Andrea stared at the CAT scans, as if the
answer would suddenly leap out at her, like in
one of those weird three-dimensional pictures
they sold in the mall. "But, you must have
something to go on? A little boy can't just start
forgetting things for no reason!"

"If I had to make a guess, I'd say the most likely causes for Evan's blackouts are stress-related triggers."

"But he's seven years old!" Andrea said, her voice rising, "What kind of stress could he possibly have?"

"Plenty." Redfield replied. "Who knows? Maybe he's got severe coping problems that stem from not having a father-figure in his life. You did say that the last blackout occurred when he was with his friend's dad."

Andrea shook her head. "Come on now, doctor. I doubt the answer could be that simple."

Redfield gave a slight smile. "You'd be surprised how often the simple things are the answer."

"You really think so?" She hesitated for a moment. "You know, he has been pushing me to meet his father, but I've been putting it off. He hasn't seen Jason since he was four years old."

"When your husband was institutionalized," the doctor said with a nod. "I think this is worth a shot, Andrea. I can arrange a controlled meeting between Evan and his dad here at the clinic. A careful dose of some sedatives for Jason, and I'll call in some orderlies for extra security. You and I can monitor them from an observation room next door." He reached for a day planner and began thumbing through it. "You can bring Evan in for a quick visit, and with any luck, that will be the end of your son's missing father complex."

For the first time in days, Andrea felt a glim-
mer of hope. "How soon could we do this?"

"How about next week? The fifteenth?"

FOUR

The starched collar on Evan's shirt was scratchy and restrictive around his neck. He tugged at it and fidgeted in the Celica's passenger seat. He felt hot and flustered, even though the day was cool with a scent of rain from the night before. Andrea made a *tsk* noise at him and he frowned. They turned past the mall where they were building the new movie theater, up on to the highway toward the Sunnyvale Clinic, and he glanced out of the window. Evan saw himself reflected there, his hair combed and neat, dressed in his Sunday best. He hoped his Dad would be pleased at how well turned out he was.

Mom, by contrast, was in more casual attire; it was Evan who had insisted on dressing up to meet his father. He drummed his fingers on the cover of his journal, anxious to reach their destination. The book was becoming a constant companion to him now, and he used it not just to jot down a diary of his days, but also to make lists of things or scribble little drawings. Evan had taped an oak leaf in there, a saved bus ticket, stickers from packs of gum, placing them around sketches of interesting bugs or rocket-ships. Unlike the regimented pages of his school exercise books, Evan's journal was a reflection of a little boy's mind, poured out onto paper. He flipped the notebook open to the next clean page and took a pen from where it lay in the dashboard ashtray. He started to write, slowly and carefully, working hard not to let the bumps in the road jog his hands.

April 15. Today I get to mete my father. His name is Jason and he is crazy. I hope he lets me call him Dad.

He capped the pen and studied what he'd wrote, dwelling on his description of his father. Mom had all kinds of ways of talking about Jason—on the very rare occasions that she did—and each one had a different phrase for what was wrong with him. He wasn't mad, he was unwell. He wasn't a nut, he was sick, and so on. Evan remembered the time that Tommy had picked up on the story about Jason Treborn's mental illness and relentlessly provoked Evan about being "the crazy boy, the son of the loony". There had been strong words between Andrea and Alice Miller over that, but when Tommy's mother moved away the bigger boy suddenly found things to make fun of other than Evan's father. But Evan had never really found it difficult to get a handle on his dad's condition, and accepted it with innocent logic. He was crazy and that was why they kept him in a hospital all the time. It didn't mean that Evan loved him any less.

The Toyota ambled to a halt and Evan looked up. "We're here," he said.

His mother nodded. "Are you ready? If you don't want to go through with this, we can just turn around and go home. Whatever you decide, Evan, I won't be upset." She tried to keep her voice neutral, but Andrea felt anxiety creeping into her tone.

There was a long moment when she was sure that he was going to say no, but then he gave her a look, a mix of excitement and trepidation. "I want to meet him, Mom. I want to meet my Dad."

"Let's go, then."

Evan hesitated a moment, the journal in his hand. Should I bring this along to show him, he wondered? No, not yet. I'll wait until it's full. Then I can give it to him and he'll be able to read all about me.

They were taken into a wing of the building that neither of them had ever visited before. Andrea held her son's hand firmly as they walked along the halls of the clinic, with Doctor Redfield striding ahead of them, his white coat flapping like a cloak.

"Just through here," he said, gesturing forward.

She had thought that she had successfully compartmentalized her feelings for Jason, but now, as they drew ever closer to him, she felt her pulse start to race. Andrea realized that she wanted to see him, to speak and tell him that she still loved him very much. She wanted to tell Jason about the nights when she would cry herself to sleep, as she recalled how their life together had been snatched away from the three of them. She wanted to shout and rail at him—demand to know why he had been so weak, and why he had got sick and left her to raise Evan all alone. It was a wonder how one person could instill so much love and so much anger in her all at once.

But above all that, she was afraid. Andrea was terrified that her son would follow his father into madness, that somehow this meeting would be like the transmission of a virus, and Evan would be infected with Jason's delusions. The muscles in her legs bunched as her fight-or-flight reflex urged her to run. All these thoughts and emotions whirled around inside her in a hurricane of contradictions. With a near-physical effort, Andrea smothered the turmoil within and put on a cautious smile for Evan. She would be strong, for his sake.

Her son's enthusiasm was waning; she could feel it through the tightening of his fingers as they held hands. His head darted from side to side as they moved through another ward of the clinic. The scent of disinfectant hung in the air, barely covering the smell of urine and something else that was unidentifiable. There were a few patients who sparsely populated the corridor; a thin, drawn-out girl who sat at a window working on a Rubik's cube—eyes unfocussed and medicated; a middle-aged man walking in slow figure-of-eight and a rough-hewn guy with white stubble all over his chin who watched them pass as if they were his most hated enemies. Every few footsteps there were doors, and from behind some of them came wordless shouts, screams or babbling laughter.

Redfield gave them both a sheepish grin. "Normally we wouldn't come this way. The main corridor's being refurbished, we're stripping out the asbestos—"

A piercing shriek cut through his speech and Evan blinked. "What was that?"

"Some of our residents are a bit loud," the doctor said in an off-hand manner, as if he were discussing a noisy neighbor.

"Does... does Dad live here?" Fear was creeping into the boy's voice.

Redfield shook his head. "Not in this wing, no. This is where we look after the more, uh, special residents."

Andrea lent close to speak to Evan. "Now, your father may appear a little bit sleepy to you when you see him, but that's just because of his medicine, so don't worry, okay?"

"Okay," repeated Evan.

They moved through another passageway and Redfield led them into an anteroom with the word "Observation" stenciled on the door. One wall was a large picture window that looked into a visiting room beyond; the other room was sparsely decorated, with only a long rectangular table and a couple of gray metallic chairs. A clock, its face covered with a wire mesh, sat high on the far wall, watching over the empty chamber like a sentinel. It reminded Evan of the rooms he'd seen on television, where policemen put bad people to ask them questions.

The anteroom contained a desk and a box with some buttons on it. "What are those for?" Evan asked.

Redfield pulled out a chair for Andrea to sit. "That's just so I can call for someone, if we need help." He licked his lips. "You know, if someone was sick, or if they had a seizure."

"Oh." Evan seemed unconvinced.

Andrea glanced at the door that led to the observation room, then the proffered chair. "You want me to stay in here with you?"

"Yes," said Redfield. "At this stage, I think having you in there with Evan would be a bit disruptive. We'll let Jason speak to Evan alone to begin with."

She sat hesitantly. "All right then." On some level, Andrea was secretly grateful that she wouldn't have to look Jason in the eye, though she hated herself for thinking it.

The doctor opened the door and gestured to one of the metal seats. "Sit down, Evan. Your dad will be here in a moment."

He did as he was told, and turned to see the anteroom door swing shut with a solid thud. Evan looked back at the window; his side of the glass was dull and opaque. He leaned forward and tried to pull the chair closer to the table, but it would not budge. Every piece of furniture in the room was secured to the floor with heavy iron bolts.

Time seemed to drag itself out into interminably long seconds, and Evan listened to the steady tick-tick of the clock, his eyes never leaving the other door on the opposite side of the room. The glowing fluorescent light over his head cast a severe color over everything, making the featureless walls and fittings seem sharp-edged and cold. After what seemed like an age, a shadow moved behind the frosted glass window of the door and it opened.

Evan hadn't seen his father in years, and he knew Jason would look older, but nothing prepared him for the man that shuffled into the room. He was clad in a pair of light-blue pajamas and overlarge bedroom slippers, and he shambled closer with a slow, docile gait. Evan's memories of his father were of a wiry adult, a man full of life and zest, and the figure who stood before him was not the Jason Treborn that he remembered. He was not the man who had twirled him in the air or placed him on a rocking horse with strong, careful hands. Evan's father looked haggard and pasty, as if the vitality he'd shown his son so long ago had been drained away. There was almost a sparkle in his dark eyes, but not quite. Evan pondered Mom's comment about his father's "medicine", whatever it was, and if it had dulled Jason's manner. He seemed dreadfully old and tired.

Even though he appeared terribly fatigued, his father still radiated warmth. Jason sat opposite and gingerly touched Evan's hands. He twitched a little, making the cuffs around his dad's wrists clink together.

"Hello, Evan. It's so good to see you."

"Hello… D-dad."

"It's okay," his voice was cautious. "I won't bite." He then smiled, and Evan returned the gesture. "You've seen pictures of me, right? You do remember me?"

Evan nodded, his confidence building, eager to assuage any fears Jason might have had of being forgotten. "We have lots of pictures of you. Mom, she says that I have your eyes—"

And then, without warning, Evan's world was inverted and his lungs wheezed with pain. There was no transition or sensation of movement, but the room had suddenly rotated around him and he was staring upward at the observation room ceiling, the clock visible high above him. His vision was fogging, but clear enough for him to study the face that loomed over him in total detail.

Jason's soft, worn expression was gone, replaced with burning, livid anger. His monstrous frame twitched with rage as Evan choked and struggled for air. His father's hands squeezed Evan's throat in a vice-like grip, the metal chain between the cuffs pressing the starchy, scratchy collar into the soft skin of his neck. The enormity of it, the horror, was almost too much for Evan to comprehend.

Someone was scratching and banging at the door, and an alarm bell was ringing, echoing through a faraway tunnel. As Evan's sight constricted into a woolly gray cavern, he felt hot spots of spittle on his face as Jason snarled out a sentence through gritted teeth. "I... love... you..."

Then suddenly a white shape collided with Jason Treborn and he flew backwards, shoved into the far wall. Evan struggled to raise his head, but his neck had lost all its strength and he failed. He caught a whiff of Mom's perfume as she grabbed him, hauling him up from the tabletop.

"Muhhh..." he mumbled, as she pulled him into a corner.

The two orderlies were both twice Jason's size, but each of them knew from experience that the inmates held at Sunnyvale made up for their lack of strength with other things. One of them shoved a rubber-coated police baton under Jason's chin and pulled it back, trying to trap him, while the other tackled his waist.

Andrea's heart pounded furiously as Jason made eye contact with her; she could see panic and fear, not the black murderous intent she had expected.

"He has to die!" Jason shouted, his voice shrill and hysterical. "You don't understand! He'll destroy everything! It's the only way to stop it—"

With a jerk, Jason butted the first orderly in the head and grabbed the baton, tearing it out of his hands. Without slowing, he cracked the second orderly in the kneecap and downed him. Jason then turned and leapt at Evan, the nightstick coming up to strike at the boy's head. Andrea screamed.

The second orderly came after Jason and drove his baton into the small of his back. Jason cried out and the orderly struck him across the rear of the head with a glancing blow. Jason stumbled but he continued to launch himself forward at Evan.

"Stop him!" Redfield's voice cut through the air. "Stop him now!"

The orderly lashed out again, and this time the heavy baton hit Jason squarely on the crown of the skull. Bone shattered and tissue crumpled under the impact as Jason Treborn's knees buckled and he crashed to the floor like a felled tree.

Andrea pulled Evan as close as she could to herself, folding her coat around him, holding him tightly in her arms. She rocked him repeatedly back and forth, her voice keening, "I'm sorry, Evan... I'm so sorry..."

Through blurry, tear-clogged eyes, Evan saw his father between the gaps of his mother's fingers as she shielded Evan's face with her hand. Jason's eyes were wide open and unblinking, staring into space; from his nose and ears red ribbons of blood pooled into a shimmering halo around his head.

"I'm sorry," wept Andrea. "I'm sorry..."

Jason Treborn's death left no family members behind other than his wife and son, so the gathering at the cemetery was little more than a knot of people. Most of them had come, not because they knew Jason, but because they wanted to offer their support to Andrea and Evan through this difficult time.

Andrea was thankful for it. Although she'd had her disagreements with her neighbors over the years, they had all pitched in and had provided flowers, cards or other small gestures of kindness. She struggled to overcome her grief, placing one hand on Evan's shoulder as the casket descended below the grassy lawn, vanishing into the earth.

Evan looked at the box and tried to connect the blank rectangular shape with the man who had been his father. There appeared to be a strange disassociation going on around him. There was the man from his memories, his father—a crazy person he'd seen in the clinic—and now this coffin. As much as he tried, Evan's seven year-old world view could not compile all the pieces and understand. It seemed to him that his father had been gone a long, long time, and whoever that man was at the hospital, it had not been Jason Treborn.

The priest was reciting words from a book over the grave. "Ashes to ashes, dust to dust…" Evan looked away, catching a glimpse of Kayleigh behind him. She gave him a small, sympathetic smile, and for a moment the cold hollow in his chest warmed a little.

Mrs Halpern whispered to his mother and she nodded, pausing to dab at her eyes. Evan felt oddly distant from the whole experience; Doctor Redfield had spoken with him several times since the disastrous visit to the clinic and told him that it would be okay for him to cry, if he wanted to. Nobody would mind. But Evan shed no tears, and instead he watched the priest read out a few more things, until at last the funeral was over and the mourners began to drift away in twos and threes.

Kayleigh appeared by his shoulder and her hand found his. The warmth of her touch made some of the numbness inside him melt away, and he took in a shuddering breath through his bruised throat. "You're better off, anyway," she whispered in his ear.

"What do you mean?" he replied.

She shot a look at her father and Tommy, who stood impatiently by their car. "Fathers. You're

better off without them." Mr Miller irritably
stubbed out a cigarette and looked at his watch.

He hardly noticed when she released his grip
and slipped away; it was only the distant rumble
of an approaching thunderhead that shook Evan
from his reverie.

"Come on, kiddo," said his mother, her voice
still thick with sorrow. "Time to go."

Evan watched the tombstones flicker past as
they drove out of the cemetery, the gray mono-
liths and statuary catching the fading light of day
between them, forming it into a hypnotic pulse.
His father's open grave receded, vanishing
behind the forest of marble and stone, disappearing, fading from sight.

When Evan looked away, to the forbidding
skies ahead, he felt something give inside him.
Some tiny little piece of him had broken. Slowly,
without ceremony, a rain of unbidden tears
began to trickle down his face.

Childhood ended for me that day. Before, there
had always been some inkling of it in my life, an
innocence, a joy of sorts, I suppose you'd call it.
It was gone from then on, as sure as if they had
buried it there in the dirt with my father and his
casket.

I changed. We all did. Death changes everything for a family, even one like ours where Dad
had been so long gone that for all intents and
purposes, he might have well already been dead.
It was the cold certainty of it that made it hard

for Mom and me, the two of us having to watch him die right there on the floor of the observation room, the sickening crunch of his skull breaking echoing through the air. And the blood. I will never, as long as I live, forget the smell of my father's spilled blood.

Doctor Redfield advised my mother to have me visit him on regular occasions, and for a year or so that's what I did, dutifully doing as I was told; not because I wanted to, but because I knew with all the seriousness of a seven year-old boy that it was important to Mom that I did. Redfield asked me about my dreams. He asked about my pictures. And he asked about the journal. I didn't write a word for months and months, until one morning Kayleigh Miller gave me a Valentine's Day card and I realized I wanted to commit something that important to paper. I took up the book as if no time had passed and I kept on writing. I filled them up with everything that happened to me. Redfield told my mother it was a reaction to Dad's death, that I was trying to make sure that when I died, there would be something of me left. I'm not sure about that. Maybe he was right, but that's not why I wanted to do it. For me back then it seemed that if I hadn't written it down, then in some way it hadn't really happened to me.

I told my Mom that and she laughed, something that had become a rarer occurrence in those days. "You know what you're doing?" she said, "you're re-writing history. You're making up things the way that you want them." Then she turned a little more serious. "That's a nice idea, Evan, but it never really works. In the end, history will prevail. You can't alter it just because you don't like it."

We both knew what that meant, but I kept on writing, and the ghost of my father's memories— of those terrible moments in the clinic, grew fainter every year. I took comfort in knowing I would never see him like that again, as a broken, shattered parody of the man I loved.

I was wrong.

FIVE

The air inside the basement of the Miller's house was warm and still, baked by the heat of the bright, summer day and thick with thin wisps of cigarette smoke. Lenny found that if he stood on the worn armchair in the far corner and pushed up on tip-toe, he could just about peek out at the front lawn, where lush, freshly cut grass glistened under the artificial rain from a clicking, hissing sprinkler. He turned his head, looking over at the driveway strewn with cuttings and an upturned Toro lawnmower. "No sign of your dad out there," he said as the armchair wobbled a little beneath him.

"Good," grunted Tommy. "Now get down from there before you break the chair, fat ass."

Lenny frowned and turned, still standing on the seat. "You left the lawnmower out in the drive."

"I know!" Tommy gave him an irritable stare. "That way if Dad comes home, it'll slow him up and we'll hear him! What, are you stupid?"

Lenny got down and chewed his lip, looking away. Evan and Kayleigh were sat nearby, at opposite ends of the threadbare sofa by the fireplace. She was fishing in her bag for something, while Evan worked carefully at a drawing in one of his notebooks. Lenny smothered a pang of sad jealousy as he watched them, Evan was the coolest guy he knew. He was smart, mature, good-looking and most of all, Evan was the object of Kayleigh's undying affections. Even though Evan was his best and oldest friend, there was a faraway part of Lenny that resented, maybe even hated, him for it. Oh, for sure, Lenny knew that Kayleigh liked him too, but not in the way she liked Evan. Evan was Mr Cool and Lenny... Well, he was never ever going to be anything more than just Lenny. Fat Ass Lenny with his wheezy breath and his clumsy manner.

Kayleigh and Evan; it was plain as day, and it hurt Lenny a little bit more every time he thought about it. Sometimes he wished he could just run away, but the truth was, it wasn't as if he could just turn his back on them. They'd all grown up together—Lenny, Evan, Kayleigh and Tommy—and now they were thirteen, just starting to edge into adolescence, leaving childhood behind. Lenny was most afraid that one day soon, he would turn around and Kayleigh would be gone, gone with Evan, and that thought hurt him most of all. The worst part of it was that Evan had always been good to Lenny. He'd never made fun of him and had often stood up to other kids when they picked on him at school.

Sometimes, Lenny wondered if Kayleigh could see it in his eyes, how he felt about her, and all the dreams he had about her. Wasn't it obvious? Couldn't she see how devoted to her he was? Why else would he still be hanging out with them after all these years, enduring Tommy's constant stream of ridicule, if not to be near her? What other reason could there possibly be than to hover somewhere close to Kayleigh's orbit? He sighed and forced the thoughts away with a physical effort. "What are you drawing?" he asked Evan.

"Take a look." Evan exhaled a cloud of gray smoke and tapped ash off his cigarette into a Coke can. The picture was a rough sketch of Kayleigh, a smile on her face, a three-quarters on view. Her long hair, unkempt and stringy in reality, was lustrous and full on paper. "Gorgeous, ain't she?"

Kayleigh giggled a little, and Lenny fought down the urge to ask Evan if he could have the drawing.

"Here, hold this a second." Evan held out the book to Lenny, and he took it as if it were a sacred artifact.

Kayleigh had produced a slightly bent Marlboro from her bag, one she'd carefully stolen from George Miller's latest girlfriend, and raised it to her lips. In turn, Evan coolly ignited a strike-anywhere match with his thumb and lit her

cigarette with a flick of the wrist. Lenny handed
him back the journal and frowned. Evan liked to
use the strike-anywhere matches, because it
made him look a movie star.

Evan gave Kayleigh's brother a sideways glance.
"So, Tommy, I'm bored shitless over here. What's
up already?" He faked a yawn to underline his
point.

Tommy was half-buried in an old US Army footlocker that belonged to his father, rooting around
inside for something; he hadn't been exactly clear
on what it was he was after. Without looking up,
he gave Evan the finger. "Hold your horses, man.
It's in here, somewhere. I saw it when I was a
kid…"

Lenny caught a breath of Evan's smoke and
coughed. He couldn't stand cigarettes; the smell
of them always irritated his asthma and it was
another small indignity he suffered to be near
Kayleigh. Why the hell did she have to smoke the
stupid things, anyway? He knew the answer:
because Evan and Tommy did. Lenny turned to
look at her brother in time to have Tommy throw
something at him underhand. A thick magazine
slapped him in his face, and he caught it awkwardly. The glossy pages fell open in his hands to
reveal a pair of naked breasts.

"You like pictures of girls, huh? How about
that?" Tommy said mockingly. He barked out a
laugh, as Lenny blushed red at the photos in the
Playboy's centerfold. "Better than Evan's stupid
sketches."

"Put that thing away," Kayleigh snapped. "Those magazines are for perverts."

Lenny instantly threw the Playboy into a corner rather than upset her. "I... I was just, uh—" His cheeks glowed hot with embarrassment.

Kayleigh seemed to be unaware of Lenny's distress and pointed at Tommy with her cigarette, the glowing red tip dancing in the murky air like a firefly. "We should go soon. If Dad catches us smoking down here, we're dead."

"So let's go," said Evan, getting to his feet, "This place creeps me out, anyhow."

It wasn't something he could put his finger on, but Evan never really felt at ease at the Miller house. The basement bordered on the claustrophobic, with its bland walls and poor lighting. Every time they came down here, some vague, unpleasant feeling settled on him, like a half-recalled nightmare.

Kayleigh's brother continued to rummage through the container, dumping the rusted shape of a folding entrenching tool on the floor next to a pair of worn boots. "Shit, where is it?"

"Tommy?" asked Lenny, as they all stood.

"Just a damn minute, you moron!" Something clattered in the footlocker and Tommy emerged with a grin on his face and an olive drab cylinder in his hand. "Got it!" It was a battered, military-issue thermos flask, and it rattled as he shook it. "I knew it had something to do with the army..." Unscrewing the cap, Tommy emptied the contents into his hand. It was a small, fat tube, wrapped in discolored grease paper. He held it up between his thumb and forefinger, like a jeweler appraising a gemstone.

"What the hell is that?" Evan was unimpressed.

Tommy gestured theatrically. "This, ladies and germs, is a Blockbuster!"

"Like the video store?" asked Lenny.

"You're such a retard," Tommy snorted. "It's an explosive, get it? A quarter stick of dynamite. Light the fuse and kaboom!"

"That's dangerous, Tommy," said Kayleigh.

He rolled his eyes. "Gee, sorry, Mom. I'll just go play with my Hot Wheels instead, then..." He shook his head. "Don't be such a chicken shit."

Lenny peered at the device. "Can I see it?"

"Hands off!" A mischievous glint came into Tommy's eyes as the others were now hanging on his every word. "So," he chuckled, "let's blow the shit out of something!"

Tommy could barely contain his excitement as he led them through the woods behind the houses, laughing and insisting that they were on a secret mission, like a combat demolitions team out to blast an enemy fuel dump or blow up some important bigwig. Lenny trailed behind, his breath laboring.

"Hey!" he gasped. "Guys, slow up, would you?" He took out an inhaler from his coat pocket and drew a puff from it.

Tommy wanted to slap the thing from his hand and watch him squeal after it. He never could figure out why the fat ass kept hanging around like a bad smell and wondered if Lenny was one of those people that his dad called "gluttons for punishment". If he was, Tommy was happy to hand it out to Lenny in spades. He never got tired of making fun of the porky little dork.

Evan, though, he was a different story. Most of the time, he could get Evan to go along with what he wanted. The guy usually followed his sister, and Tommy could make her dance to his tune without even breaking a sweat. But they'd had fights in the past that had not always gone in Tommy's favor, and he knew that there was a line that he couldn't cross with Evan. At least, not yet. But what Tommy found the most offensive was how Kayleigh and Evan were together, always making eyes at each other and mooning like idiots. It sat very badly with her brother, and he disliked even the suggestion of the two of them having anything going on. He kept wondering when she was going to wake up and realize that Evan was just a wuss, like all the other kids. He certainly wasn't good enough to touch his sister. Deep down, Tommy was afraid that Kayleigh would turn out to be weak, just like his mother was.

A footstep or two behind him, Kayleigh and Evan walked side-by-side. "Evan, did I tell you? My Mom said I might be able to visit her this summer in Orlando, with her new family—"

Tommy turned around abruptly, his face taut with anger. "What did I say about mentioning that bitch?" He gripped the Blockbuster in his sweaty hands, suddenly thinking about how he'd like to plant it in Mom's fancy Florida house, with her fancy new kids and stupid husband. Yeah, that would teach her to toss them away like garbage...

"Just where the hell are you taking us, anyway?" Kayleigh ignored her brother's implied threat. "Just blow something up."

The odious smirk returned. "Just blow something up?" he mocked Kayleigh in a high singsong tone. "Are you nuts? There's an art to mass destruction. Would you 'just paint' the Mona Lisa? No!" He gestured around. "Besides, we're here already."

"Yeah, like you'd know who the Mona Lisa is," Kayleigh retorted in a low voice. "Not unless she had her boobies hanging out in some porno magazine."

Evan stifled a laugh and followed Tommy's direction to their "target".

"Hey!" Lenny came up behind them, panting. "This is Mrs Halpern's house."

Evan had never visited the Halpern's place, but they'd driven past it a million times on the way to school. It was situated in what Evan's mother referred as "the high end" of the district, where the houses turned from simple blue-collar places to the more luxurious homes where lawyers or doctors could afford to live.

The Halperns had a three-story colonial-style house, and at the far end of the short driveway was an ornate mailbox. It was an exact duplicate of the Halpern home, rendered in perfect miniature detail.

"We're gonna bring the house down!" Tommy laughed harshly. "Well, at least the little one!" He turned to Lenny and pressed the Blockbuster into his waiting hands. "Here you go, soldier!"

Lenny turned pale and recoiled, pushing it back at him. "What? No frigging way, man. I'm not touching that thing!"

Tommy stepped closer, towering over the smaller, chubbier teenager. "The hell you aren't. Anyone of us does it, you'll puss out and nark for sure." He waved a finger in front of Lenny's face, making him blink. "It's gotta be you."

"Ain't gonna work this time, buddy." Sweat was beading Lenny's brow. "Look how small that fuse is! I'll get killed."

"Not necessarily..." Evan interjected, as Tommy's hands began to ball into fists. Taking his lit cigarette, Evan pinched the filter tip and broke it off, then jammed the unlit end into the dynamite fuse. He brushed flakes of tobacco from his fingers. "There, that should buy you ten minutes at least."

"Gee, thanks friend," Lenny deadpanned. This was not the solution to the situation that he had been looking for. Tommy snatched the

makeshift bomb from Evan's hands and thrust
it at Lenny, jerking his head at the mailbox.

Lenny hesitated for a long moment, then took it.

Kayleigh found a good vantage point for them at
the edge of the wood, amid a snarl of brush. She
crouched there with Evan and her brother as
they watched Lenny pace back and forth in front
of the Halpern house.

"Will you look at that loser?" Tommy grated.
"What is he doing over there?"

Lenny was trying and failing to look noncha-
lant, making a pantomime out of noticing his
shoe was untied, then bending down to tie it
next to the mailbox.

"Oh, for Christ's sake, just do it, Lenny!"

Kayleigh elbowed her brother in the ribs. "Why
don't you go and plant it then?"

"Shut up," Tommy retorted. "Look, he's gonna
do it!"

Finally, Lenny drew up the courage and jerked
open the mailbox, thrusting the Blockbuster
inside. He slammed it shut and bounded away,
across the road toward them.

"Took you long enough," sneered Tommy, as
Lenny almost collapsed in a wheezing, panting
heap.

Kayleigh shook his inhaler with a rattle and
handed it to him. Lenny squeezed a deep
draught from the plastic device and choked back
a cough. "Thanks."

Evan patted him on the back, impressed with his performance. "You got balls, man."

The four teenagers fell silent as the seconds rolled by. Evan chewed his lip and tried not to look down at his wristwatch to see how much time had passed, afraid that he'd miss the moment of detonation. Lighting a fresh smoke, he clasped it between his teeth and leaned forward, cupping his hands over Kayleigh's ears to deaden the imminent noise of the blast. She smiled at his touch and pressed his palms to her head. From the corner of his eye, Evan saw Tommy shoot them a venomous look, but then Kayleigh's brother snapped back to staring at the mailbox like the rest of them.

Evan's heart was pounding in anticipation, and he started to speak—

He was suddenly running, his feet pounding out of control through the woods. The shock of the unexpected shift caught Evan unawares and his footing fell away from him, the grassy woodland carpet rising up to meet him as he tumbled over himself in a clumsy heap. Lenny, racing blindly a pace behind, clipped his legs and stumbled over him, dropping to his knees with a violent exhale of air.

Tommy's voice called from nearby, pitched with excitement and alarm. "Hurry, let's go! Get him up, Evan! Come on!"

It was all Evan could do not to give in to panic. "What happened? Where are we?" He was frantic and trembling. It had happened again, after six years of thinking that his terrifying blackouts had gone forever. Now with no warning they had come crashing back into his life. Evan felt queasy with the thought of it.

He dragged himself to his feet and ran, afraid that someone was chasing him, but after a few moments he realized there were no pursuers in the woodland. Behind him, Kayleigh and Tommy were dragging Lenny to his feet, and Evan met the boy's gaze. Lenny's face was milk-white, his eyes unfocussed and lifeless.

"Don't just stand there gawking, help us with this fat ass!" Tommy spat.

Evan doubled back and grabbed Lenny's free arm, taking the weight of him from Kayleigh. Lenny was mumbling something under his breath, but it was too low and indistinct for Evan to decipher. Together, the four of them shuffled through the woods as fast as they could, slipping and dragging Lenny Kagan with them.

Kayleigh's pretty face was twisted with racking sobs. "Oh God..." she whimpered. "What did we do?"

"Shut up!" Tommy shouted. "Shut your damn mouth!"

"But... but..." The words caught in her gasps. "What are we going to do with Lenny? Look at him!"

Evan gave his friend a rough shake. "Shit, Lenny, what happened to you?" For a moment,

Evan's own fear about his blackout was replaced with concern for the other boy. "We've gotta get him some help!"

"Take him home!" Kayleigh cried. "His mom will be there!"

"No way!" said Tommy. "What's she gonna say, you moron?"

"Hey!" Evan snapped. "We're not just going to dump him in the woods and run, okay Tommy? That's not gonna happen!"

Kayleigh pointed. "His house is just over there."

Tommy gave Evan a furious glare, but he helped them walk Lenny the remaining distance to the Kagan home.

Andrea almost drove her Toyota straight into the hood of the ambulance as she roared up into the Kagan's driveway, swerving at the last moment to halt inches from a flowerbed. She burst out of the car, heedless of her nurse's cap flying from her head and raced toward the front door. As she approached, two paramedics— guys she knew from the ER at Mercy General—were wheeling Lenny into the ambulance, with his mother at his side.

"Janet?" she asked, but all she got in reply was an ice-cold glower. Before Andrea could say anything else, Mrs Kagan slammed the door shut in her face, and the ambulance leapt away from the curb, the lights and sirens screaming into life.

She took a cautious step toward the other teenagers, her eyes catching her son on the front stoop, his shoulders hunched, his hands trembling. "What is it?" she demanded. "What happened?"

Tommy spoke first, quickly and sharply. "We were building a fort out in the woods when Lenny freaked out. One minute he was fine and then he just froze up." The Miller boy gave Evan and his sister a menacing look. "Right, guys?"

Kayleigh said nothing, her face puffy and flushed from crying.

"What happened, Evan?" Andrea asked, crouching to look him in the eye. "I want the truth."

He answered in a dead monotone. "I don't know. I don't remember."

"Something must have happened!" she snapped. "What set him off?"

"I…" Evan seemed to be laboring the words out, as if each one was like a lead weight in his chest. "I blacked it out."

Andrea shook her head with building frustration and anger. This would not have been the first time that Evan had pretended to have one of his "episodes" to avoid answering for something, but his mother had thought he'd outgrown it, and she'd never known him to lie about anything so serious. "Don't try to use your blackouts to get out of this one!"

But even as she said it, Andrea knew that he was being utterly truthful. He looked up at her

with an expression of total, absolute helplessness, tears swelling in his eyes as he searched for
an answer that wasn't there. She hadn't seen
him that vulnerable since he was seven, on the
day of his father's death, and it made her want
to hold him tightly and protect him from whatever darkness threatened. "Oh, Evan," she
breathed. "You're not making this up, are you?"

Her son shook his head slowly, almost as if he
were ashamed to admit that his memory had
failed him.

SIX

Andrea perched on the edge of the chair in Doctor Redfield's office and wrung her hands together. He was talking to her in his usual, calm and modulated tones, but she was only really getting a little of what he was saying—her mind was reeling back to the last time she'd been here, when Evan was a few days away from his ninth birthday. She had convinced herself that it would be the last time that she would see the inside of this despised building.

"You told me he wouldn't get these blackouts anymore." The words burst out of her in a rush.

Redfield blinked in surprise, pausing before he replied. "Uh, well, Andrea, that's not strictly true." He glanced at Evan's open file on his desk. "What I said was, he probably wouldn't get any more blackouts. You have to remember we assumed that his 'episodes' at age seven were linked to stress about his father. The fact that he's had this sudden recurrence may now mean some new anxiety has entered his life."

The doctor was graying at the temples now, and he wore a pair of thin oval glasses across a drawn face. Andrea found herself thinking that he hadn't aged well.

"What I find most interesting is that this happened at the same time as the incident with the Kagan boy. The two are good friends, so there's obviously some connection."

"Poor Lenny," she said. "How is he?"

"He's undergone a mild catatonic episode. Essentially, his mind shut down for a few hours. You could think of it as the mental equivalent of a fuse blowing. The brain switches off rather than deal with something it can't handle. It's something that I've seen before with people who witness accidents, or endure very frightening experiences. Fortunately for Lenny, he's responding well to treatment and we should be able to send him home in a few days." Redfield sighed. "He's tight-lipped about what happened in the woods, though."

"You don't think..." The words she was about to say made Andrea's stomach turn over. "Someone couldn't have... abused them?"

"We can't know for certain at this point, but of course that could be a possibility. What I'd like to do is try something with Evan that might unlock his blocked memories of the day in the woods. Would you be willing to let me try?"

"But what if the thing he's holding back is something awful? Wouldn't bringing it up make things worse?"

Redfield took off his glasses and gave her a level stare. "Andrea, six years ago Evan was having catastrophic, total blackouts related to one root cause—his father. If we don't nip this relapse in the bud, he could start all over again. It might even begin to manifest into a full-blown psychosis."

And then Evan would have to be sent to the clinic. The unspoken words hung in the air between them. More than anything, Andrea was afraid of losing her son the same way she had lost her husband. She nodded. "All right."

The doctor stabbed at his intercom. "Send Evan Treborn in, please."

Andrea gave her son's arm a friendly squeeze as he entered; his young face was haunted and devoid of color.

"Hello again, Evan. How are you?"

"Not happy about being here," he said in a dispirited voice. "No offense." He hesitated for a moment. "Is Lenny here? I was wondering, could I see him?"

Redfield shook his head. "I'm afraid not. Mrs Kagan was very insistent that he not be allowed any visitors other than family members."

"Oh. Okay. Will he get better?"

"In time." The psychologist indicated a couch. "But now I want you to lie down on there, Evan. We're going to have a talk about your memory problems."

The boy gingerly sat down. "Is this the part where you ask me about my mother?"

"No, no," Redfield forced a laugh. "We're going to put you into a restful trance, so we can tap into what you've forgotten. It won't hurt you. It's called regression hypnosis. Do you know what that is?"

Evan nodded. "Oh yeah, I've heard of that. They use that on people who are kidnapped by UFOs. I saw it on an episode of *The X-Files*."

"Uh, that's right. But we're going to use it to take you back to the woods, so we can find out what happened there, okay?"

Evan gave his mother a fearful look. "Mom?"

"It's okay, kiddo." She kept her voice even. "Just listen to the doctor. He's here to help you."

As Andrea watched from across the room, Redfield talked her son through a series of breathing exercises, slowly putting him at ease.

"I want you to imagine you are lying on a tropical beach somewhere. You're listening to the waves lapping on the shore. You can feel the soft sand against your back."

He began a measured count, and in time the rise and fall of Evan's chest settled into a steady, relaxed rhythm. "Five. Six. You're drifting off into a gentle sleep. Seven. Eight."

"With every breath you exhale, you can feel all of the tension draining from your body like water from a faucet." The doctor studied the teenager's peaceful, dreamy face. "Nine, ten, and you are completely asleep. Relaxed."

The room fell silent for a moment, with only the faint whisper of Evan's breathing to disturb it. Redfield gave Andrea a look that said: so far, so good.

"Now listen to me carefully, Evan. I want you to go back to the time you were in the woods with Lenny Kagan. Think of it as if you are watching a movie. You are outside your memories, watching it on a screen. You can pause, rewind, or slow down any details you wish. Do you understand?"

"Yes," Evan replied thickly.

"Where are you now?"

"Kayleigh," he began, in a languid voice. "I'm standing next to Kayleigh and I'm putting my hands over her ears."

The doctor's eyes narrowed. "Why are you doing that, Evan? Are you hurting her?"

"No. Protecting her."

Despite herself, Andrea couldn't help but give the tiniest of proud smiles.

"Okay. Now go forward a little bit in time. What do you see now?"

A nerve in Evan's jaw jumped. "I… see a car…" The words came slowly, as if he were drawing them out with great effort. His eyelids trembled, revealing slivers of white beneath them.

"Yes, tell me about the car. What color is it? Who is in the car?"

A dull moan like a low animal cry escaped Evan's lips and he began to shiver. Redfield leant closer to the boy. "Go on, Evan. Nothing can hurt you here, what you're seeing has already

happened. Remember that it's only a movie.
You're completely safe."

"I can't…" he groaned out the words. "The car
vanishes and all of a sudden I'm on the ground.
In the woods."

The doctor's voice became more insistent.
"The car doesn't vanish, Evan. The movie in
your head has broken, that's all. But now, I've
spliced it back together and I want you to tell me
all about the car. Try to visualize it in your mind.
Find the image of the car and freeze it."

"It's coming…" he made a choking sound, "I
can't…" Evan's shivering became a fierce shaking, his back arching as his muscles bunched
with tension.

Redfield laid a hand on his arm. "Don't be
afraid, Evan, fight it! Hurry, it's coming!"

In the depths of himself, Evan's thoughts
churned and bubbled in a dark undertow of
impressions, sounds, scents and images, merging
and mixing in chaotic disarray. The car! He
struggled to hold on to the fleeting glimpse of it,
so tiny and ephemeral that it was more the vague
idea of a vehicle than the actual sight of it. He
saw the car, but then beyond it was nothing but
a yawning blackness where memory should have
been. Evan tried desperately to trap the recollection, but it slipped away from him like mercury,
vanishing into the abyss in his mind. The void
within threatened to swallow him whole.

The doctor gasped in surprise as the teenager
let out a tortured, guttural sound from deep in

his chest, and a glistening rivulet of blood began to seep out from his nostrils. Redfield bolted upright in his chair and began to speak to Evan in urgent tones.

"Okay, Evan, listen to my voice! On the count of ten, you're going to wake up feeling refreshed and remembering everything we talked about—"

Andrea vaulted from her chair as her son moaned in distress. "What's happening to him? Make it stop!"

Redfield waved her away with a sharp, dismissive gesture. "One, you're feeling more awake now. Two, your eyes no longer feel heavy. Three. Four."

Her hands quivering, Evan's mother dragged a tissue from her pocket and tried to stem the flow of blood from her son's nose, that trickling down over his lips and chin. She lifted one of his lids and saw no pupils, just the white of the eyeball rolled back into his head.

"Five. Six," the doctor continued, anxious and tense. "Refreshed and awake! Seven. Eight, come on, Evan, wake up, damn it!"

The teenager suddenly went slack, his skin clammy to the touch. "Evan, wake up! Oh, please wake up!" Andrea repeated the words over and over, like a litany.

"Nine, ten, and you're awake!" Redfield shouted, "Open your eyes, damn it!" But Evan still did not respond. The doctor had a sudden flash of recollection back to Jason Treborn, his body laid out in the clinic morgue, his face showing the same dull cast as his son did now. Redfield pulled savagely at the drawer of his desk, tearing at the detritus inside, spilling spent pens and boxes of paper clips everywhere. His hand fell on a pill bottle and he tore it open, removing a tiny blue capsule.

Pushing Andrea to one side, Redfield pinched Evan's bloody nostrils closed and snapped the capsule in two, letting him inhale the acrid chemical stimulus of the smelling salts. Instantly, the boy choked on the vapor and jerked upward, knocking the two adults out of the way. He lurched forward on the couch and fell to the floor, one hand pressed to his nose.

"What, what happened?" he managed. "Did it work?" Evan looked up at his mother and the doctor. Their pale, panicked expressions were answer enough.

Redfield had one of the clinic's duty nurses take Evan to the infirmary to have his blood-streaked face cleaned up. Andrea seemed on the verge of screaming in rage or bursting into tears and Redfield himself was quite shaken. He coughed involuntarily; the stink of the smelling salts still lingered in the air.

"You... you've just made it worse!" Andrea spat. "What the hell happened to him?"

"I've never seen anyone respond like that before," he admitted. "I've treated firemen who saw their friends burned alive and veterans who were torn apart by shrapnel in Vietnam, but none of them had a reaction like Evan's. It's absolutely extraordinary."

"He's not one of your damned lunatics, he's my son!" she snapped. "What can I do? I don't want him in a place like this."

"No, of course not," said Redfield, for the moment keeping the idea of making Evan a patient to himself. "You have to realize that the human memory is a tricky thing. We still don't fully understand the inner workings of it. I told Evan his memories were like a strip of film, but really they're more like a hologram." She gave him a blank look. "A three-dimensional image. Memory has so many components, and sometimes the smallest one of them can set off a complete recall. It's not just sight and sound, it's also taste, touch, even smell. Like the way a certain perfume reminds a guy of an old girlfriend…"

"But are you saying you can't help him?"

"I'm saying we both have to try to help Evan. Look, just take your son home and try to go back to as normal a routine as you can. Let him go to school, hang out with his friends, whatever boys of thirteen do these days. If we're lucky, some trigger will hit the right mark and what he's repressing will start to return on its own." He scribbled an entry in Evan's file. "In the meantime, I'll set up an appointment for him in a couple of weeks, to check on his progress."

There was a weighty pause before Andrea spoke again. "Evan is not going to end up like Jason," she said with force.

"That's what we both want." replied the doctor, as he showed Andrea to the door. However, he wasn't so sure if Evan Treborn hadn't already started down the same road as his father.

Redfield was still turning over the events hours later, as the clinic's duty shift changed over. He looked up as Pulaski tapped on his door.

"Harlon? Leonard and I are going out for a drink, you wanna come? It's nickel beer night."

He shook his head. "Some other time. I don't think I'd be good company."

Pulaski eyed the file in front of him. "The Treborn kid again? Karen told me he got wheeled out of your office with a bloody nose this afternoon. You slapping your patients around now?"

Redfield waved her into the room and gave her a quick outline of what had happened. The other doctor made a face. "That's damned peculiar. A reaction like that, it's completely atypical for a subject with his history."

"You're telling me." Redfield blew out a breath. "I'm stumped, Kate, I really am."

Pulaski tapped a finger on her chin. "You know, if I didn't know any better, I'd say that the Treborn boy was physically incapable of accessing that memory. I mean, on a mechanical level."

"What, like someone who has lost bits of brain tissue? He hasn't had any head trauma, Evan's brain is perfectly intact."

She shrugged. "I didn't say it made any sense, Harlon, but whatever way you look at it, that memory you want him to access isn't blocked or repressed. It's just not there."

Andrea tried to maintain a false front of cheer for the rest of the day; she wore a plastic smile as she dropped off her son and the Miller kids at the multiplex movie theater that evening, as if all in her life was sunny and fine. As she drove the Celica, Andrea found herself hoping that Evan didn't see the tears that threatened to overwhelm her.

In the parking lot behind the Sunnyvale MegaCine, the three teenagers stood in silence for a moment. Evan's jaw worked; he wanted to say something, but every sentence in his mind fell apart half-formed. Kayleigh wouldn't meet his gaze, or anyone else's. As they began to follow Tommy toward the movie theater, Evan got a good look at her morose and dispirited expression.

"So, uh," Evan finally piped out a few words, "what are we gonna see? *Waterworld*?"

Tommy made a spitting sound. "I ain't gonna pay five bucks to watch some lame sci-fi crap. We're gonna see *Se7en*. It's a cop movie."

"We can't get in for that. It's R-rated."

"The ticket guy knows my Dad. Said he'd let us see any damn movies we want."

"I don't want to watch anything like that," Kayleigh said in small voice.

Tommy abruptly threw up his hands and blew out a loud breath, making Evan flinch. Ever since the woods, Kayleigh's brother was behaving differently, constantly overbearing and spoiling for an argument. He gave her a sneer. "What the hell are you bleating about? It's got that pretty boy film star in it you like, what's his name?" He poked a finger at Evan. "Or maybe you want another pretty boy, huh? You wanna sit in the back row and make kissy faces?"

"Tommy," Evan began. "Take it easy—"

"What?" He stepped a little closer to the pair of them. "Don't tell me what to do, Evan. And as for you," he prodded Kayleigh in the chest, "wipe that sad-assed look off your face before you get us all busted. You see the way that Evan's mom was looking at you?"

"I'm sorry," she mumbled.

"Would someone just tell me, what the hell happened with the mailbox?" Evan asked exasperated.

As the last word left his lips, Tommy suddenly snatched at the front of Evan's jacket and shoved him against the side of a parked car. The assault was totally unexpected and Evan folded with Tommy leaning into him. Kayleigh's hands flew to her mouth in shock.

Tommy flicked a quick glance left and right to see if anyone was in earshot, then he hissed a warning into Evan's face. "Don't you ever bring that shit up again." His words were heavy with malice. "Not ever. Not to me, not to Kayleigh, or even Lenny, the stupid fuck, if he ever learns to talk again. Understand?"

Evan nodded nervously; he'd never seen Tommy like this before, with a mean glint in his eyes that sparkled like a razor. "Ever." Tommy spat, then underlined his point by giving him a vicious final shove before releasing his grip. "Besides," he cast a careless nod at his sister, "she don't want to talk about it anyway, do you, Kayleigh?"

The girl said nothing.

Tommy strode boldly through the lobby to the box office and collected the tickets, leaving Evan with Kayleigh for a moment. Evan felt a swell of emotion inside him. Suddenly, all he wanted to do was to run away with Kayleigh—to leave Sunnyvale and his whole life behind, and take off and hold her. He wanted to protect her from everything; but most of all, he wanted to take her away from Tommy. "Kayleigh," he said gently. "Talk to me. Are you all right?"

She started to say something, but Tommy returned and smothered her words with his own brash snarl, brandishing the tickets. "I got them. Easy meat. Let's go."

Evan and Kayleigh followed him in, and as the lights dimmed, Evan plucked up courage to hold her hand, out of sight where Tommy couldn't see it.

"Man," Tommy crowed, shoveling a handful of popcorn into his mouth. "If I don't get to see a bunch of dead bodies in this flick, I'm going to ask for my damn money back!"

Without Evan in the house, the Treborn's modest home always seemed to be twice as big to Andrea. It was at moments like these that she felt the loneliness of her situation, a single mother now for almost a decade—and that alone made her feel old enough—with only her son to keep her company. She'd dated other guys since Jason, some of them more than once, but with a kid in tow it was hard to find men who had time for her, and there was always something she could be doing at home. George Miller had given up hitting on her; the better-looking single guys at Mercy General were out of her league and she'd politely declined Doctor Redfield when he'd made a discreet, well-mannered pass at her. That had been a few years ago, though.

She caught her reflection in the darkened glass of the kitchen window as she finished off cleaning the day's dishes, and for a second she felt every single bit of her thirty-eight years. It was killing her by inches, the gnawing slow dread about Evan and his blackouts, and the few years of relative peace they'd had thinking the problem had gone away now seemed like some fanciful dream. Until they had an end to all this, Andrea knew that it would chew her up inside. For Evan's sake as much as hers, she wanted him well. She loved him so dearly, and it made her heart go cold to imagine him like Jason, manacled and medicated, slowly rotting away in the bowels of the clinic.

"Not on my watch," she said aloud, with more determination than she really felt. The last of the dishes done, she turned off the water tap and caught the voice of the TV news anchor from the other room. Drying her hands, she wandered to the doorway, attracted by the sound.

A smartly presented woman in a blue power dress hosted a newsflash report with a deadpan expression. Over her shoulder, an inset image of police cars and cops stringing out strips of yellow crime scene tape was playing. "Earlier this week, this traumatic scene in suburban Sunnyvale was the grisly aftermath of what local police officials in upstate New York are calling 'a horrible act of vandalism gone awry'."

Andrea's mouth went dry. Something about the house was familiar to her, and her mind raced as she tried to place it. The inset picture expanded to fill the whole screen as the anchor continued. The handheld camera tracked past a 4x4 in the driveway, a sooty black discoloration over the hood and windscreen. "The powerful explosion that tore through this quiet neighborhood is believed to have been caused by a small quantity of dynamite placed inside a mailbox."

Lisa Halpern's house. Suddenly it was clear as day to Andrea and she paled. Shaking her head in terror, she grabbed for the remote control, desperate to silence the reporter's ceaseless voice.

"Advanced forensics testing at the New Jersey office of the Federal Bureau of Investigation will attempt to determine the make and manufacture of the explosive used in the crime."

She found the remote beneath a throw cushion on the sofa and grabbed it.

"Police thus far have no leads as to the suspects—"

Her trembling fingers found the power button and pressed it hard, silencing the woman in mid-speech.

SEVEN

In the dark, stale cavern of the movie theatre, Kayleigh found herself trembling slightly, her feet shifting in little jerks of muscle tension. The soles of her worn sneakers crackled quietly every time she moved; someone had spilled a cup of soft drink on the floor beneath her chair, and the sticky, half-dried patch pulled at her shoes where they touched the ground. In the row in front of her, Tommy was sat spread-eagled and indolent, his legs cocked on the seats before him, one hand rooting through an open bag of popcorn, the other dangling over an armrest. He hooted with laughter at something only he found funny; the rest of the sparse crowd in the auditorium was silently trying to watch the film, and a few of them threw Tommy dirty looks. If he noticed, he didn't care.

It seemed that Tommy's volatile attitude was on the increase, as if he didn't give a damn about what anyone else thought. The aftermath of the mailbox prank had brought his undiluted cruelty and arrogance to the surface.

Kayleigh felt Evan's hand slide on to her bare forearm and her heart skipped a beat. It was weird, the way that his touch could comfort her, the strange manner in which just being in the same room with him made Kayleigh feel a shade better. At least, it used to. Things were different now. Ever since that day in the woods, Kayleigh's world had gone through a sideways shift for the worse. It wasn't as if her life had been a bowl of cherries before—what with Tommy and Daddy and their constant belittling of her—but in the days since Lenny had been taken to the clinic, Kayleigh was starting to wish that things could just go back to the way they had been before. Anything was better than this, living in fear of Tommy lashing out at her and the constant worry of being implicated in the explosion.

Evan gave her hand a squeeze and she glanced at him. He wore a forced smile, like he was trying to be brave and strong for the both of them. There had been a time when that would have been more than enough for Kayleigh, but not any more. Now it felt like the darkness of the cinema was being replicated all through her life, a suffocating blanket of gloom closing in on her from all sides.

Up on the big movie screen, the two police detectives were penetrating the interior of a dingy apartment, and Tommy snorted as the

corpse of a massive, obese man came into view.
"Holy shit! Look at that fat fuck!" he bellowed,
snapping open a packet of chocolate-covered
peanuts with noisy abandon. "You'd have to
wipe his ass with a forklift!"

Someone down toward the front row called out
for silence, a view shared by a number of other
irritated adults who were hidden in the darkness.
Tommy emptied some of the candy into his hand
and threw it in the direction of the screen, ping-
ing pieces off seat backs and the heads of
audience members. "Shut up, faggot!" he called
out to nobody in particular. "No one's talkin' to
you!" His voice was boorish and loud, daring
anyone to argue with him.

Evan sighed heavily and shifted in his seat; he
didn't want to be here any more than Kayleigh
did. The girl felt her color rising, embarrassment
and revulsion flushing her cheeks bright pink.

On the screen, Brad Pitt leaned over a bucket-
ful of the dead man's rancid vomit and caught a
whiff, jerking backwards; the image made
Kayleigh's stomach suddenly constrict and she
felt the burn of hot bile in her throat. Before
Evan could react, she darted out of her chair and
into the aisle, turning and running for the door.
Behind her, she heard Tommy's bray of cruel
amusement call out again.

She took a dozen unsteady steps through the
lobby, gasping at air as she tried to stop herself
from throwing up. Kayleigh was aware of
someone at her side and she felt Evan's firm

but gentle grip on her wrist. "Are you okay?" he asked, walking her towards a small bench in an alcove. "Was it the movie?"

"Not just the movie…" Kayleigh managed. "I feel a bit sick." She realized the film's disturbing images had been a trigger. She had been balancing on the edge of collapse all day, wracked with fear and apprehension; this had finally pushed her over the top.

They shuffled unnoticed past a group of older teenagers clustered in front of the concession stand, high-school students kidding around and laughing among themselves. Kayleigh had to choke off a sour backwash in her mouth when she caught the mixed lukewarm stink of day-old hot dogs and too-sweet buttered popcorn in her nostrils. She gulped at a stream of water from a nearby fountain and then let Evan set her down on the bench. Kayleigh studied the worn pattern of the carpet, the cartoon motif of a film reel repeated over and over in an endless stream of circles. She just wanted the ground to open up and swallow her, leaving no trace that she had ever existed.

"I'm sorry, Kayleigh," Evan said after a moment. "I thought if we all went out together, we'd be able to relax, but this was a bad idea."

Her head tilted up and met his gaze. Kayleigh looked into the warm brown eyes she so often dreamed about. She spoke slowly. "You really don't remember anything that happened?"

A glint of frustration flared in Evan's steady glance as he shook his head. "No. Not a thing. It's just a huge, blank space in my head…"

Tears welled up at the corners of Kayleigh's vision, misting her sight. She had a swift, fierce surge of envy of him, jealous of his ignorance and wishing that she too could blot those terrible, indelible images from her mind forever. "You're so lucky." She began to cry softly. "Every time I close my eyes, I can see it…"

Evan looked around to make sure no one was staring at her, but the teenagers were in a world of their own, talking and joking, unaware of the emotional scene playing out behind them in the alcove. He gently stroked Kayleigh's unkempt hair. "It's going to be okay. Lenny will be fine. You'll see."

Kayleigh sniffed and gasped. She wanted to tell him that it wasn't Lenny she was afraid about, but the words would not come. Evan reached out a hand to her arm and an electric spark of pain shot through her. "Ouch."

"Oh, s-sorry!" Evan stuttered. "Did you hurt yourself in the woods?" Kayleigh was already pulling up her sleeve to examine the spot where he touched her. Evan's throat tightened as she revealed a livid bruise, a disc of gruesome purple-yellow marring her skin. He'd been in enough schoolyard fistfights to know that Kayleigh's wheal had come from a punch, not a casual injury.

"It's not your fault," she said, sniffing away the tears. "Mrs Kagan called Daddy and blamed us for what happened to Lenny."

Evan's jaw set in anger. "Damn, your dad did that to you?"

Kayleigh pulled back her shirt to expose another bruise, twice as big and darker in tone, along her collarbone. She wore it like some horrific rosette. "I deserve a lot worse," she added, and Evan's retort died on his lips. Kayleigh had been punished for her crime and she felt it was her just reward, whatever Evan's shocked expression said to the contrary. She looked morosely away.

"What are you talking about? You can't let yourself believe that, Kayleigh," he said. "What you deserve is a better father and brother. All they do is make you feel like shit. What you deserve is someone who really cares about you." Like me, he added silently.

The tender note in Evan's voice brought her eyes up to meet his again. When he spoke, his words tumbled out unbidden, spilled from some honest, open place inside him. "You really have no clue how beautiful you are, do you?" Her hand strayed to his face, tracing the curve of his cheek.

Kayleigh searched Evan's eyes for truth, for the light of sincerity, and she found it lingering there, heartfelt and real. They leaned closer together, their breath brushing each other's lips, and Kayleigh turned her face towards his, her eyes closing as she surrendered herself to the moment. Suddenly, everything she was afraid of, every fear and terror in her life was gone for a perfect, impossible instant.

But in the next second the kiss broke like shattered ice as Tommy's voice pitched into a roaring snarl across the lobby. "What the fuck are you doing?" He stood staring at them past the crowd of teenagers, from the cinema doorway.

Kayleigh and Evan jerked apart, repelled instantly like two opposed magnets. Evan gaped and fumbled for words as Kayleigh caught the look in her brother's eyes. Shock, betrayal and hate shone back at her.

The group by the concession stand all looked at Tommy, and a few boys and girls giggled at the stormy expression on the irate thirteen-year-old's face. Ignorant of Evan and Kayleigh's presence, the teenagers thought Tommy was talking to them. "What the fuck am I doing?" said one of them, an older boy in a denim jacket. "I'm buying some popcorn. What the fuck are you doing?"

Tommy seemed unaware of the jibe and rushed forward to shoulder his way through the group, his hands balling into fists. He was a few steps away from Evan and Kayleigh when a foot shot out from the crowd and looped around his ankle; Tommy tripped on it and fell hard, face-first to the monogrammed carpet. The other teenagers burst into a chorus of cackles and cat-calls.

"Watch your step!" said the girl who had tripped him.

"Aw," Denim Jacket put on a faux-concerned face and spoke in baby-talk singsong. "Little boy all fall down. There, there. We'll call your mommy for you."

Tommy got to his feet with exaggerated slowness, sparing the teenager who tripped up the most fleeting of glances before eyeing Evan. Kayleigh saw the raw, unfiltered spite in Tommy's face, all of it desperate to be turned on someone.

Every explanation Evan tried to give crumbled as he shook his head weakly, trying to find some way to mollify Tommy. "Hey, we were just… It's… it's not what you think…" he said lamely.

Without warning, Tommy suddenly lunged. But instead of diving at Evan, he turned on the teenager in the jacket, launching a frenzied flurry of punches at the elder boy. The other boy was a good foot taller than Kayleigh's brother, but Tommy attacked him undaunted and rained blow after blow upon him, catching the boy totally off-guard. As Tommy struck at the teenager's face, splitting his nose with one brutal punch, he eyed Evan and gritted his teeth. The message was clear: I want to do this to you.

The savagery of Tommy's assault made everyone step back and pause; it was only when two security guards dashed to the scene that anyone made an attempt to part the fighters. The older teenager had started to hit back, but his punches were wide and lacked co-ordination, while Tommy landed his with the pinpoint savagery of a prizefighter. For a second, he struggled against the grip of the adults, but when it became clear there was no way he could resist them, Tommy allowed himself go slack and be dragged away.

"Uhh!" The boy in the denim jacket had a puffy, bloody ruin where his face used to be, and his voice was thick with pain. "Thad liggle fugger! He broge my doze!"

As the guards pulled him toward the doors of the multiplex, Tommy gave Evan a final look of contempt, a sick smile etched across his face. In his own callous manner, Tommy had somehow scored a twisted victory over him.

"Come on, let's get out of here before they start asking questions," said Evan, tugging Kayleigh's arm. "We'll go out the back way."

"But what about Tommy?" she bleated.

"What about him?" said Evan. "You saw what he did, he's got a screw loose. He just started whaling on that guy for the slightest provocation, and if that hadn't happened, you can bet he would have tried to take it out on you and me."

"He's my brother," Kayleigh insisted. "And if he tells Daddy what happened here…" She trailed off.

Evan swallowed hard, his eyes drifting to Kayleigh's neck and the bruise, now covered once again by her blouse. "You can't let him hit you. That's against the law, you could tell someone…"

Her face tightened with anguish. "Evan, please. Just take me home." Kayleigh found herself almost believing the comfortable lie she was starting to spin in her head, that everything that was going wrong with her life would vanish, if she could just get home and hide from it all.

Finally, he nodded and fished in his pockets for a quarter. "Okay, I'll call my Mom to come and get us." He jerked his thumb at a payphone across the lobby. "If that's what you want."

She hesitated as the lie seemed to lose a little of its sheen.

"You could come stay with us," Evan said, with quiet desperation. "My Mom's a nurse, she could look after those bruises. We could talk to the police—"

"No," Kayleigh infused the single word with all the emotional fatigue that churned inside her, shutting him down hard. "I want to go home, Evan."

And because he couldn't find the words to tell her how he felt, Evan walked to the telephone and dialed his home.

"I'll be there in five minutes." Under any other circumstances, Evan might have noticed the brittle edge to his mother's voice, but she had hung up before he could register it.

They sat silently in the alcove, and when Kayleigh felt Evan's hand cautiously touch hers, she held it tightly, afraid that it would be the last chance they would ever have to be this close.

* * *

The old Toyota drew up to the movie theater's exit and the pair of them got in. In a heavy silence, they drove on through the night, Evan in the passenger seat next to his mother and Kayleigh in the back. Andrea hadn't said anything when she'd arrived to find the two of them there alone, and Evan had mumbled something about Tommy "finding his own way home", which was more or less true.

How did things get so complicated, Evan asked himself? It seemed nigh impossible for him to grasp it. The idea that one choice, just a small this-or-that, here-or-there decision had gone the wrong way and now everything in his life was coming apart. What had they done out there? What could have been so wrong? The problem was, with his memory locked behind an impenetrable mental wall, he had no way of knowing. Lenny couldn't answer his questions, Tommy would surely try to rip his throat out if he saw Evan again and Kayleigh... Kayleigh was never going to open up while she still had that rat bastard of a father ruling her life.

Evan thought hard about telling his mother what he'd seen, describing to her the bruises on Kayleigh's body; but even if he did, what could she do? If the police got involved, Evan could be sure he'd never see her again. Kayleigh and Tommy would become wards of the state, put up for adoption even—and the thought of losing her as well was something that made his gut feel hollow and cold.

If Evan had been less wrapped up in his own concerns, he might have paid more attention to Andrea's silent, watchful manner. If he'd been looking, Evan would have seen his mother studying Kayleigh in the rearview mirror, probing and searching for her own answers. When she broke the dull silence in the car, the two teenagers almost jumped with surprise.

"So how was the movie, Kayleigh?" Andrea said without preamble.

The girl hesitated before casting off a noncommittal lie. "Okay, I guess. I don't like horror movies…"

Evan's mother watched her for a lengthy, calculated interval. "Were there any exploding mailboxes in it? Stuff like that?" Her chatty voice was labored and fake.

Before he could stop himself from making such an obvious connection, Evan's head snapped back to shoot a look at Kayleigh; the girl recoiled visibly from the question, as if it had been a physical blow. Evan and Kayleigh exchanged glances. Oh my God, she knows!

"Wha-what do you mean?" Kayleigh tried to cover her reaction and failed utterly, guilt coloring her ashen complexion.

Andrea abruptly pulled over and brought the Toyota to a halt. For a second, Evan thought she was going to turn on them and deliver a stinging tirade, but his mother remained silent. Kayleigh blinked and realized that they had arrived outside the Miller house. She grabbed at her coat and exited the car as fast as she could, desperate to be away from Andrea's accusing stare.

"Goodnight," Evan's mother said to the air. She stared at her son, but Evan kept his gaze locked straight ahead, out through the windshield. After an uncomfortable pause—to Evan, it seemed like excruciating hours—Andrea put the Celica in gear and drove on.

Once or twice Evan drew in a breath and opened his mouth, fully intending to say something to his mother, to come up with some kind of explanation; but each time the words failed him.

When she spoke to him again, it was with two words that told him the entire story: that she had found out about the Blockbuster, about the planting of it at the Halpern house, and Lenny's tragic role in the whole affair. Two words that crushed his heart in a vice.

"We're moving," said Andrea.

Evan had hoped it was just some sort of vague intimidation on his mother's part, a shaking-fist warning of the kind that parents always offer up whenever a child does something off the board. Just you wait. You'll learn. You're going to regret it. But Andrea Treborn had never been one for idle threats; as a single mother, Evan had discovered the hard way that she was twice as strict as she had to be to compensate for the absence of a father. The day after the fight at the multiplex—which, to his surprise, hadn't trickled out into the neighborhood gossip circuit yet—Evan had begged and pleaded with his mother to reconsider. From shouting to crying and all points in between, he tried everything in his power to sway her.

She refused. Andrea stonewalled everything he said with cold and unbending surety of purpose, and by the end of the week there was a garish "For Sale" sign hammered into the front lawn, courtesy of Sunnyvale Realty. His mother had started packing their meager possessions into cardboard boxes scavenged from the Pay & Save, and she even had a new place picked for them, across the state border and close to a big town. They had a new hospital there, Andrea told him. They'd offered her the chance to transfer a month ago and she'd turned it down. The post was still open and she'd taken it. Now they were going, and Sunnyvale would be put behind them.

Evan sat in the living room on the sofa, the only piece of furniture left in the house that didn't have a plastic sheet taped over it to keep it safe for when the movers came. The room had been stripped bare of everything that made it part of his life, taken down and boxed away in hours. It was a mirror for everything else in Evan's world, all swept away and changed by forces beyond his control. He felt like he was in the eye of a storm, a hurricane that was systematically ripping his world to pieces around him.

He heard the front door slam and watched his mother walk out toward her car, the sunlight gleaming off the brilliant white of her nurse's uniform. She was going to give in her resignation today; in her hand she had the envelope with the letter in it.

Evan waited for the sound of the engine to fade away as the Toyota reached the end of the block—then he leapt to his feet and snatched his coat off the hook. Jamming his house keys in his pocket, he ran out into the drive, slamming the door shut on his empty home.

EIGHT

Evan had taken a big risk by calling the Miller house—and was ready to slam down the receiver on the payphone the moment he heard anything that sounded remotely like a male voice at the other end—but he was rewarded with Kayleigh's muted, hesitant tones.

"Kayleigh, it's me. Can you talk?"

"Evan?" It took a second for her to overcome her surprise. "Sure, yeah. I'm on my own. Tommy's gone out, he left the house before breakfast. Dad never came home last night, he went out with a bunch of his buddies from the tennis club." She paused; the raw need to get out of the house leaked from her voice. "Are you… okay?"

"I want to see you. Can you meet me? Mom said Lenny will be released this morning and I figured we could go visit."

"Yes." She jumped at the chance to see Evan again. "Where?"

"The tree on Elm Street?"

* * *

He spotted Kayleigh waiting for him at the corner of the street where they usually met on the way to school, doing her best to make herself invisible in the shadow of a nearby oak tree.

She fell in with his hunched, too-quick gait, exchanging a watery smile. "Hey."

"Hey," he echoed.

"Where's Crockett?" Kayleigh asked. "Don't you usually walk him around now?"

Evan shrugged. "He ran off last night and he hasn't come back yet. He does it sometimes, it's nothing unusual. He'll come back eventually."

She gave a dry, humorless chuckle. "Like my Dad."

"It's going to be tough for him to adjust, when we leave," Evan added. "He's not going to like being taken away from here."

Kayleigh nodded and looked away. "Yeah. I'll miss him too."

They walked for half a block before she spoke again. "Evan, are you sure it's okay for us to be visiting Lenny?"

"He's back from the hospital today," Evan looked at her. "You don't want to see him?"

"No, it's not that..." Kayleigh mumbled. "It's just... What if Tommy finds out? If he sees us together, or someone tells him we were—"

"To hell with your brother," Evan broke in, with less bravado than he had hoped. "He's not the boss of me."

"He's getting worse," Kayleigh looked away. "He had a big fight with my Dad. I heard him yelling that he was going to kill anyone who tried to touch me. He told me that you were going to get it first."

Evan's mouth felt arid. "I can't believe Tommy's still pissed at me. He knows I'm moving away, right?"

She nodded. "I don't think he cares. He's been acting real strange lately... Since, well, what happened. He won't even look me in the eyes anymore," Kayleigh hesitated. "I'm scared of him."

The broad shape of Janet Kagan's station wagon turned the corner at the far end of the block, and Evan tugged at Kayleigh's sleeve. "Here they come. Let's duck in here."

The two teenagers crouched in a clump of bushes as the car slowed and pulled into the driveway of the Kagan's house.

"Did your mom say if Lenny was... okay?" Kayleigh whispered.

"He must be, they're letting him go, right?" Evan sprang up to his full height with a bright smile in place and dashed over to the car. He gave a jaunty rap on the passenger window. "Hey, Lenny! Welcome home!"

Inside the station wagon, Lenny jerked back from the glass as if the greeting had been a gunshot, a look of abject fright on his pale, round features. His mother wound down her window and fixed Evan with a hard eye. "I think your little homecoming is in very bad taste," Mrs Kagan said icily. "Why don't you hooligans just go away and leave him alone?"

The smile fell from Evan's face. "I'm sorry?" Behind him, Kayleigh hovered with her hands in nervous bunches. "I just wanted to say—"

"Lenny has been through a hell of an ordeal, no thanks to you." Acid dripped from every word.

Evan felt useless and guilty as the car continued on up the drive, and under the automatic garage door. As it slid shut, Evan saw Lenny throw them a worried look, like an animal afraid that it could not outrun its predator.

"That didn't go very well," Kayleigh noted. "What now?"

Evan chewed his lip. "We can't just leave. I gotta talk to him."

"There's no way his mom is going to let us see him. You heard what she said."

"Well, we won't ask her, then." Evan studied the outside of the Kagan house, a plan forming in his mind.

Lenny sat carefully at the workbench in his room and felt himself gradually relax. The nightmare of the clinic was gone now, and all he wanted to do was let it fade away and fill his time with the perfect, private world of his airplanes. All of his tools and paints were laid out exactly as he had left them, the tiny files and plastic clippers next to the brushes and squeeze tubes of glue. The model kit before him was unfinished, wings and bits of propeller still connected to the plastic sprue next to a half-painted fuselage in matt silver. With deft and studied movements that belied the appearance of his chubby fingers, Lenny worked at the parts of the model kit and the form of a Bristol Bulldog biplane slowly began to come together under his hands. He loved losing himself in the models, imagining them as real flying machines. Lenny wanted to live in his own tiny museum, populated with prop planes, jets and helicopters, where nothing could ever disturb the flawless, airstream lines of his dreams.

When the noise came, he almost crushed the fragile model in a frightened reflex. Someone tapped hard on the glass of his bedroom window. Lenny looked up to see Evan and Kayleigh smiling in at him. He blinked. They had to have been standing on the very edge of the wooden ivy trellis outside.

"Welcome home." This time Evan whispered instead of yelling. "We thought you might like some fresh air for a change."

"Hi, Lenny," Kayleigh said with genuine warmth. "It's good to see you. You look okay."

Without being conscious of it, Lenny's eye ticked and he began to twitch ever so slightly. "Uh, is Tommy... is Tommy with you?"

Evan gave him a solemn shake of the head. "He's not here. It's cool."

Lenny glanced back at the biplane, still unfinished, crying out for completion. If he stayed here, he could have it ready by dinner, and then he'd be able to start on the F-80 Shooting Star his mother had bought him as a get-well gift. But there was Kayleigh, and Lenny was afraid that if he turned her away, he might never speak to her again.

"I'll be out in a minute," he told them. "I'll meet you at the corner."

The three of them skirted the far edge of the woods, an unspoken pact between the teenagers that agreed to steer well clear of the area near the Halpern's house. Down towards the southern end of town, the woodland was more ragged and ill-treated. Some of the older kids would use it for impromptu tailgate parties or make-out spots, and on rare occasions a car would be dumped by joy-riders and torched. Bracken and trees were joined by a junk pile or other collections of human-made debris. Evan slipped around the skeleton of a spring mattress and fell in step with Kayleigh and Lenny.

"So, what did you do in there?" she asked gently. Evan was content to keep quiet and let Kayleigh draw Lenny out of his shell. "Is it like you see in those movies?"

"It was awful," he said, and he seemed to be happy that he could actually open up about the experience. "You can't sleep at night 'cause everyone's screaming all night long…" He paled. "I never want to go back."

"I'm glad you're better. We were both really worried about you."

Lenny looked at his feet. "Doctor says I'll never really be well. He said it could come back if I let it. I just have to be careful."

Evan tried to think of something supportive to say that didn't sound trite, but came up empty. He was about to settle for a friendly pat on the back when a sound came to him; a thin, strangled yelp caught on the wind. A dog in grief. Crockett? Somehow he knew that it wasn't just any dog crying out there; it was his.

At the same moment, Kayleigh raised her arm and pointed in the direction they were headed. "Look! Do you see that?"

The boys followed her gaze. At the very edge of the woodland was a sprawling junkyard that bordered the railway lines. On a weekend day like today, it was empty, but from Monday to Friday it was a hive of activity, crushing cars and stripping vehicles for spares. Evan remembered his mother getting a cheap new fender there once, after a milk truck had backed into her Toyota.

A black column of smoke was snaking up from the junkyard, its source concealed by a wall of compacted old motor bodies. It was like a grim finger, lancing down out of the sky. Evan heard the hollow, terrified yelp again and instantly broke into a run, with Kayleigh at his heels. Behind them, Lenny made nervous rocking motions before he finally took off after them, following his friends through a torn vent in the chain-link fence and into the maze of rusted, dead cars.

Evan and Kayleigh rounded a tower made of flattened Pintos and skidded to a halt in shock. Tommy wheeled around to face them, his eyes bright with menace. In the clearing near the car crusher, a small, dirty fire built from oily rags and twigs had been started. Evan caught the tang of lighter fuel in the air, spying a yellow can in Tommy's hand.

Kayleigh's brother roared and kicked at the dirt in fury. "You!" he bellowed at Evan. "What the hell are you doing here? I'm not done yet!"

A muffled yelp of distress came from behind Tommy and something writhed on the ground near the fire. It was an old, discolored gunny-sack, a knot of heavy cord wrapped around the open end. A black probing nose tried to push itself through the tiny gap, and Evan saw Crockett's eyes, wide and terrified.

"Crockett!" he cried out. "You son of a bitch, what are you doing to my dog?"

Tommy's answer was to squeeze the can of lighter fluid and douse the animal in the sack with the thick yellow liquid. He showed his teeth in a feral grin. "Who wants a hot dog?"

Evan and Kayleigh raced forward, but Tommy was ready for them and he dropped the can, sweeping up a heavy wooden plank in one long arcing movement. "Back off, shit-head!"

"Watch out!" Lenny called from behind them, as Tommy went on the offensive.

The plank cut through the air toward Evan like a scythe blade and he ducked at the last possible second, the rush of the wood passing him with a whoosh of displaced air. Tommy couldn't halt the momentum of the plank in time, and to his horror, the very edge of the wooden slat clipped Kayleigh's temple with an audible snap.

Kayleigh's eyes rolled back into her head and she dropped to the ground like a puppet with its strings severed. Lenny, a few feet away from the melee, stood rooted to the ground, blinking furiously and trembling; his legs had become lead, heavy and immobile.

"Look what you made me do!" Tommy raged, spittle flying from his lips. "Now you've done it!"

"What is *wrong* with you?" Evan shot back, desperate to find some reason in Tommy's eyes; but there was none, only incoherent anger and dark malevolence.

The plank swung around for another pass and Tommy advanced on Evan, turning to strike his head. Evan twisted aside, but too slow to realize that Tommy had feinted the move. Instead, Tommy brought the wood down hard on Evan's right kneecap and the impact knocked him off his feet. Evan rolled away from his attacker, clutching at the firestorm of pain from his knee.

With precise motions, Tommy let the plank fall from his fingers and picked up the discarded can of lighter fuel from where it had landed. He looked over at Lenny and let out a short grunt of laughter. "Pay attention, fat ass," he spat. "I don't want you to miss any of this."

Lenny stood unmoving, the only movement the trembling of his lips.

Evan tried and failed to get up, agony lancing up his leg as he put weight on it. His eyes darted to Kayleigh's unconscious form, the comma of blood written across her pale forehead, then back to the sack where his dog cried and yelped, trapped inside the fuel-soaked cloth. "No, Tommy!" he yelled helplessly. He shouted out to Lenny. "Come on, man, snap out of it! Help her!" The other boy gave no sign of hearing him, and stood mutely watching the events unfold.

Evan spat in disgust and rolled over. Drawing up every last scrap of his strength, Evan grabbed at an overturned oil drum and propelled himself back on to his uninjured leg. Dragging his hurt limb behind him, Evan loped over to Kayleigh's side, reaching down to her. "Kayleigh! Wake up! Oh, please wake up!"

The girl lay still, her breathing shallow. She seemed fragile as glass, and Evan was afraid to touch her.

"Why don't you just fucking kiss her, Prince Charming?" bellowed Tommy. Squeezing the bottle hard, he sent a jet of fluid out to the smoldering fire and drew it across to the trembling form of the dog. The flames licked at the liquid fuse and rushed out toward Crockett.

Evan's vision fogged red and he charged at Tommy with his fists clenched, the singing pain in his kneecap forgotten—

And his body suddenly contorted as the muscle-memory of running shot through him. Evan's arms and legs gave a spastic jolt and he writhed, aware an instant later that he was flat out on the ground. Carefully, he rolled over and sat up. His face was tight with blossoming bruises and his ribs felt like they had taken a pounding.

"Another blackout..." Evan wheezed to himself. "How long was I out?" he followed in a louder voice.

Lenny stood nearby, his expression and pose unchanged, stock still and blank-eyed; Evan would get no answer from him. There was no sign of Tommy, but Kayleigh sat in a rough heap by the gutted cars, her knees drawn up to her chest. She was weeping, her face streaked with sooty dirt and bright tears. Evan tried to stand up, but a wave of dizziness enveloped him in a woolly fist and shoved him back to the ground.

It was then that the smell hit him. It was sickly sweet and rich with smoke, a mélange of musk from burnt hair, crisped flesh and spent chemical fuel. The smoldering, flash-burned shape of the gunnysack sat a few feet away from him, and inside lay the ruined, heat-bloated corpse of Crockett. His guts knotted with disgust.

A moan of anguish escaped Evan and he buried his head in his hands.

By the time the ambulance had arrived, a small crowd of people from the neighborhood had gathered around the edges of the Kagan's property. Everyone in this part of town had heard something about why chubby little Lenny had been sent up the hill to the clinic. When the sirens cut through the lazy afternoon air, they'd all got an inkling that the Kagan boy was going back to the booby hatch, perhaps for good this time.

"Such a shame," said one woman. "So awful for Janet."

"It's that Treborn kid's fault," snapped a man. "He's a rotten apple just like his dad. Not right in the head, I'll say."

A nod of agreement. "And those Millers aren't much better, that nasty little bully and his wastrel of a sister. They're all trouble. That poor young boy fell in with the wrong crowd and look what it got him. If you ask me, they ought to send the lot of them to Juvenile Hall."

Evan struggled to shake off a sense of terrible déjà vu as the paramedics loaded Lenny into the back of the ambulance. He took two steps toward the vehicle, hand outstretched, as if he could will it to stop and set Lenny free. As if keeping him here would make everything better. He flinched as a sharp bolt of pain sparked under his kneecap.

Janet Kagan shouldered past him and mounted the ambulance, pausing for an instant to turn back and face him. "Do you know what you are?" she said, in a low, glacial voice. "You're a monster."

Before Evan could even try to find a response, Mrs Kagan slammed the ambulance's door in his face and the vehicle roared away. Evan watched it go, biting back tears. The others were right, and the realization of that tore at Evan's heart.

It was his fault. All of it.

The last day came without ceremony or fanfare. There were no good luck messages, no farewell cards or going-away presents. None of the Treborn's neighbors came to wave them off or wish them well. After the incident with Lenny Kagan and the boy's committal, mouths were flapping all over Sunnyvale and the gossips were putting two and two together. Andrea and Evan had become pariahs in the neighborhood, ignored or dismissed as a bad element. People wanted them gone, and the Treborns were happy to accommodate them. It would only be a matter of time before somebody pointed the finger of blame at Evan for the mailbox blast, and mother and son were sure that nobody in town would be sorry to see them go.

Nobody but one.

Evan screwed up his eyes and tried very hard not to cry as he sat there in the passenger seat of the U-Haul truck, the accumulated weight and baggage of his entire thirteen years reduced to tape-sealed shipping boxes amid dismantled beds, chairs and kitchen appliances. Andrea got in the cab and keyed the ignition, awkwardly pulling away from the curb in small jerks of motion; she wasn't used to driving something so large.

Kayleigh stood by and watched the truck nose out into the road, standing as the lone sentinel marking their departure, out of Sunnyvale and out of each other's lives. Tears were spilling shamelessly down her cheeks as she watched them go.

Evan matched gazes with Kayleigh and tried to pour all his thoughts and feelings into one look, desperate to translate how he felt to her; but he was just a boy, and nothing he could do would be enough. With a flash of inspiration, Evan twisted in his seat and tore open the cover of a large cardboard box behind him. Inside were dozens of journals, some dog-eared and care-worn from his younger years and others more recent, still with empty pages. He grabbed at his current book and uncapped the pen he habitually carried in his pocket, scribbling a sentence in big, black letters.

As the truck pulled on to the road, Andrea pushed down on the accelerator and the U-Haul powered away. Evan slammed the open book into the window glass where Kayleigh would be able to read what he had written. He watched her jog after them, waving and crying. He returned the gesture, tears stinging his eyes.

For one small moment, Kayleigh kept pace with them; then she fell back, dropping away as the truck turned the corner, heading toward the freeway junction and the interstate. Kayleigh faded, a sun-bright afterimage on Evan's mind; there, then blurring with distance. Gone.

Evan shrank back into his chair and let the exercise book fall into his lap, the pages flapping open to where his message was composed in an urgent, desperate hand. Andrea looked over to see what her son had written and gave a rueful sigh.

I'll come back for you.

Evan stared at the words, as if he were burning them into his memory. He then uncapped his pen once more and began to write furiously, channeling his emotions into the flood of words.

"I'm sorry," said his mother.

Evan did not answer; he just wrote, and wrote.

NINE

And with that, another part of my life was gone, the pages ended, the book closed. This journey has taken me to places and shown me things that no man should ever see; but the moments that stay with me the most are the innocent ones. For the longest time, all I could see when I closed my eyes was Kayleigh's heart breaking as we left her behind. She's still there now, hidden in a snapshot of memory, frozen in that moment of sorrow.

We settled in a new town, a new home. We lived in a new neighborhood where nobody knew who we were. The first few months were the hardest. I entertained the idea of running away from home back to Sunnyvale every day, and I threatened it often, but I could never bring myself to do it. One particularly hard Christmas Eve, after we had argued each other into a rage, I took off on my bike for the bus station. Mom found me there, shivering in the cold, waiting for a Greyhound to take me back to Kayleigh. She cried as much as I did that night, and that was when I knew I had to stay. Mom needed me, and I needed her. We were all the family we had.

I had told Kayleigh I would come back for her, and I had meant every word of it; but the distance between us made that promise seem more and more illusory with every passing moment.

Things improved over time. Mom did well at her new posting and got promoted, junked that trashy old Toyota and got a better car. I settled into a new high school and with none of the baggage of our pasts to hold us down, we both found the freedom to excel. I graduated and was accepted into a good college; I channeled my energies into my studies, and the more I learned about the human mind, the more I wanted to find out the secret of my own missing time.

Neither of us wanted to admit it to the other, but leaving Sunnyvale behind was the best choice either of us had ever made—well, at least that's how it seemed for a few years.

I kept writing, kept telling the story of my life, and began to look forward to the future.

But the past had not finished with me. Not by a long way.

The answers came easily to Evan, flowing from the tip of his pen as quickly as he could write them. He paused before completing the final sentence in his essay, admiring it in the same way a carpenter would contemplate a finely turned piece of wood, or a painter as he was about to finish a masterwork. Just one more thing. There.

Evan scribbled a coda and sat back, a cocky grin blooming on his face. He closed the blue cover of the answer book with a soft slap of paper and glanced at the clock. Perfect.

"And that is time, ladies and gentlemen!" Professor Carter's voice called out across the lecture hall, his voice like the peal of a bell. "Put your pens and pencils down, and please stop writing. Place your blue books on my desk before you leave."

Evan noticed a couple of other students still frantically scratching away at their papers and spared them a look of pity. Psychology wasn't exactly a subject you could coast through and a lot of his classmates didn't seem to have the same level of dedication to it as he did. But then, he thought, none of them have a personal stake in it like I do. He stood, grabbing his textbooks from under his chair, and ambled down the gangway to the professor's desk at the front of the auditorium. Evan caught a snatch of conversation from two sorority girls as he passed them.

"Don't know what the hell half of that garbage was about."

"Why did we even take this dumb class?"

"You said it would look good on Beauty Pageant applications..."

Evan chuckled to himself and placed the blue book in Carter's waiting hand. "Mr Treborn," the professor said with a smile. "You're looking decidedly confident. If I might ask, how did you do, Evan?"

He pulled a mock-confused face. "Gee, professor, I'm not sure. I might have got some stories mixed up…" Evan made a play of scratching his head. "Did Pavlov condition his dogs to lick his nuts?"

Carter snorted with laughter and shook his head. "You know something, Evan? You're a typical psych major—a complete wise-ass!"

He shrugged. "What can I say? It's a gift."

The two sorority girls slipped past, dropping their blue books like they were hot to the touch. One of them gave Evan a sneer, and as she walked away he heard her say something about "that stoner geek" in a whispered giggle.

The teacher gave his paper a cursory look. "So, how's your big project going? Are you still planning to change the way we humble scientists view memory assimilation?"

Suddenly Evan didn't feel like smiling anymore, and Carter caught it too, mirth falling from his face. "Hey, I got no choice."

Carter nodded solemnly. Evan's condition had come up in conversation when the professor had been giving him some additional tutoring, and he'd come to realize the reason behind the seriousness with which his student attacked his studies. "Don't worry. I'm sure it's going to be a blockbuster."

Evan nodded a goodbye and left. If Carter's accidental choice of words registered with him, he gave no sign.

Biking across the quad, Evan tried to recover some of his good mood and partially succeeded. The college grounds were lightly populated at this time of the day, just a few knots of students in groups on the grass or hanging out by the kiosk. The muffled thuds of a hip-hop baseline blared from a boom-box nearby, and his fingers caught the rhythm, tapping it out on the handlebars. Evan took a corner at speed and the rush of air over his face seemed to buoy him up; he flashed over a shallow set of steps, and shot through the chicane made by two book-laden freshmen coming the other way. They yelped and swore at him, but he was already gone.

He poured extra power to the pedals as he cut around the porches of two fraternity houses. Evan could never bother to remember their names—he'd mentally labeled them the Phi Beta Whatevers and the Theta Something Somethings.

There were a bunch of Thetas, each of them in their cookie-cutter blue and yellow jackets, screwing around and laughing loudly as he passed. One yelled an obscenity. The jock pitched a beer bottle at Evan's bike and he deftly avoided the missile. "Get lost, you grungy slacker dick!" shouted another.

Evan rolled his eyes. Assholes would be a better name for them, he reflected. Didn't those self-important losers realize that Animal House frat boy bullshit just wasn't funny anymore?

A block or two later, Evan skidded to a halt in front of the main dormitory and docked his bike under a corrugated iron bicycle stand. He retrieved his daypack from the basket and tossed it over one shoulder.

"Ah, home, sweet, home," he said aloud, with wry humor. The dorm block was a bland brick rectangle four storys high, utterly characterless on the outside and always full of moving bodies on the inside. One of the students in Psych 101 had dubbed the building's architecture as "Early Moron Gothic." For Evan Treborn, this had been his residence for the better part of the semester.

Evan shared Room 404 with one other guy and his occasional female conquests. As he stepped up to the fourth floor from the stair-well, the sounds of creaking bedsprings and some athletic lovemaking echoing down the corridor signaled that he had company. Evan graciously gave them a moment to conclude, stopping at the vending machine for a drink before barging in.

Room 404's interior was sweaty and dark, with the window blinds pulled closed and the lights off. Evan walked through to his half of the cluttered double, dropping his textbooks on the bed. He did his level best not to look at the pale, half-naked girl on the other side of the room as she gathered herself together, although he couldn't help himself stealing a quick look at her pert breasts.

"Whoa," he sniffed the air like a wine connoisseur examining a rare vintage. "Smells like patchouli and ass in here."

Evan popped the blind and opened the window, ignoring the grunts of annoyance from the girl and his roommate. With shards of light penetrating the darkness, Evan's dorm revealed itself as a boxy little compartment with pale blue walls, most of them hidden on both sides of the room by head-shop posters and promo one-sheets for Goth bands. The posters changed on a regular basis, and most of the groups were ones that Evan had hardly heard of. His side of the room bore a similar, but more muted decorating scheme.

From under the blankets of the other bed came a fleshy arm and a leg, and presently Evan's roommate Thumper emerged like a rhino rising from slumber. Thumper was a big guy and no mistake. A year younger than Evan at nineteen, his dark, punked-out hair and drawn face made him perfect Goth material, all of it parked atop his three hundred pound frame. His real name was Wendell, but Evan had only made the mistake of calling him that once; the polystyrene ceiling tiles still had the dent where Thumper had bopped Evan's head against them in anger.

Without any aura of self-consciousness, Thumper began wiping his sweaty groin and torso with a fold of black cloth, simultaneously handing the girl a tattered lacy dress. "Cricket," he announced to her. "Meet my well-mannered roommate, the esteemed Evan Treborn."

Evan threw Cricket a non-committal "Hi," over his shoulder and went back to concentrating on his psych project. He'd constructed a simple maze out of heavy card, with a small saucer of soggy corn flakes at one end. At the other end of the puzzle was a Petri dish populated by a writhing colony of flatworms. "Hello, boys," Evan said to them under his breath. "Any of you feeling smart today?"

Cricket gave Evan an arch look and slipped her dainty feet into a pair of Doc Martens boots, completing her off-the-peg Goth Princess outfit. "Yeah, I know you. You're the one who fucked up the bell-curve on my Anthropology Final." She threw her lover a cursory glare. "Later, Thumper."

Evan watched her go. "Nice to meet you, too." He smiled at his friend. "Love is fleeting, eh?"

Thumper rolled the black cloth into a ball. "Ain't that the truth." He tossed it to Evan, who caught it by reflex. "Here, bro. I found your Sisters of Mercy T-shirt."

Evan held up the offending piece of laundry and his face soured. "Thanks. You're a real class act, Thumper. You know that?"

Thumper grinned as he rolled over and stole a sip from Evan's drink. "That's why the ladies just can't stay away…"

Tossing the soiled shirt into the overflowing laundry bin, Evan ran his fingers along the bookshelf over his bed, flicking past a small personal library of volumes on amnesia, hypnotism, memory loss and fugue states. From in between copies of *How to Get Dates Through Hypnosis* and *Contemporary Studies in Post-Traumatic Stress Disorder,* Evan removed a journal and opened it to the current entry.

His inkling about the date had been right. It was today, the anniversary of the last incident. The revelation made him smile and replaced the book with a decisive flick.

"Get dressed, Thumper. Me and you, we're celebrating. You're taking me out for my birthday?"

Thumper raised a quizzical eyebrow. "Birthday? I thought you were a December baby—"

"This is bigger," Evan interrupted. "Seven years to the day. No blackouts."

Thumper nodded with serious intent and rooted under his bed. He pulled out the discolored cylinder of his bong and shook it a little. "Let's do this."

Evan laughed. "I was thinking of something a little more sporting."

Every college town has a Dirty Hank's Bar. It's not always called that, and it doesn't always have the same surly bartenders or music blaring out of an aging jukebox, but everything else about it is identical. It's never that well illuminated. The bathrooms always smell like they haven't been cleaned since last semester. The music is always too loud, but in a good way; and most of all, the people serving the thin domestic beer never bat an eye at the taking of dollars from under-aged students for pitchers and pitchers of it.

Dirty Hank's was popular with most kids on campus, and Evan had marked it as part of his territory ever since he started studying at State. He liked hanging out there with Thumper, but if pressed he would have found it hard to come up with any singular incident that made him fond of the place. In all honesty, the only thing he found objectionable about the bar was the fact that it attracted as many of the frat boy community as it did of the outsider crowd. The truth was, most of his nights spent in Dirty Hank's ended up fogged by beer and weed, so all Evan had to go on was a kind of generalized warm disposition towards this low-end dive. It was the kind of place that a generous critic might have called "rustic".

At one of the pool tables in the back, Evan threw his roommate a sideways glance that communicated a whole lexicon of young male signals, most of them to do with sex and the possibilities of scoring. He and Thumper had carefully maneuvered themselves into playing a doubles game with a pair of girls in order to hold the table. Thumper had already locked his sights on Kristen, the taller of the two, who watched the game unfold with a cigarette in her hand and a coolly disinterested look on her face. Thumper liked girls like that; he went for long skinny girls like a shark after blood in the water.

Evan was trying not to be too obvious that he was eyeing-up Heidi, Kristen's partner. She was quite gorgeous in a local girl kind of way, with her ripped jeans and casual lack of any make-up. Evan liked what he termed "natural girls", ones with no hang-ups about their looks. As he watched her, she smartly deflected the eleven ball off the rail and sank it. For their part, the two girls seemed willing enough to play against the two boys. The only other alternatives for some male company were three wasted Phi Betas clustered in a corner and a meaty-looking trucker with a rapacious look in his eyes.

Kristen seemed confident that she and Heidi would retain control of the table. "So…" She took a puff from her smoke. "Which of you two is the one with the pet worm?"

Before Evan could answer, Thumper proudly stepped forward and grinned. "That's *worms*, plural." He did his best to make the sentence sound lascivious.

Kristen pulled a face. "That's so gross. Can't you have, like, a normal pet?"

Thumper instantly pointed at Evan. "Hey, talk to him about it, he's got the fetish."

Heidi put down another ball and gave Evan a strange look. "So, you got worms?"

Evan ignored the joke; it was only about the millionth time he'd heard it. "Actually, they're for my psychology class project. It's a study on memory." he explained. Neither girl seemed very convinced.

The next shot was a difficult one positioned off the rail, and Heidi hooked it with too little power down the angle. She frowned and passed the pool cue to Evan, then stifled a yawn. "Shit, you better explain before all the excitement gives me a heart attack."

Evan walked to the far side of the table to chalk the end of the cue. Just a few feet away were a couple of jocks from the Thetas, drinking and making noise. Evan saw them from the corner of his eye. They liked to call themselves "Greeks" after the Greek letters in their fraternity names, but Evan would bet good money that the nearest any of those morons had ever got to that ancient culture was eating a kebab. He leaned down to the table and sank a ball with one swift shot.

"Look at that fat loser," one of the Thetas was talking to a simpering girl sat on his lap. Her name was Gwen; Evan remembered her from his political science classes.

"He's a whale!" said the other.

Evan flicked a glance at Thumper, but he seemed to be oblivious to the Theta's words.

"Well?" said Heidi. "The worms?"

"It's an experiment with flatworms and a maze. You take a flatworm and you run it through the maze until it's memorized it." Evan orbited the table, searching for a better angle to shoot from. "Then you put a new flatworm in the maze. It's clueless, banging into walls, getting lost."

"Like Ozzy." Thumper nodded thoughtfully, ignoring a piece of popcorn that one of the jocks pitched past his head.

The dark-haired Theta, whose jacket bore the name "Spencer" over the breast, laughed and sipped his beer as his pal tossed more popcorn at Evan's roommate. "Hey, Hunter. Ten bucks says he eats it off the floor."

Hunter, the barrel-chested jock with Gwen, gave a high-five to his buddy. Evan was pretty sure that he was the guy who'd thrown the beer bottle at him that afternoon.

The three ball fell with a solid thunk against the rim of the pocket. "You chop up the smart flatworm and feed it to dumb one and presto," Evan continued, "the dumb flatworm suddenly knows the maze inside out." He moved past Heidi to line up his next shot, squeezing between her and a wall. His hand touched her shoulder as he stepped around, and she didn't seem to mind. Evan began to entertain the idea that he was going to get laid tonight.

"Just by absorbing the first worm into its cellular structure, it receives all of the other worm's memories." He punctuated the statement by sinking another ball.

Thumper tapped a finger on his chin, as if he was ruminating on some subject of great import. "That's probably why Hannibal Lecter's so smart." He barely got the words out before a whole fistful of popcorn hit him in the chest.

Kristen made a disgusted face and Heidi looked to Evan, doing her best to ignore the jeering chorus of the two Thetas. "So what's the point of doing this experiment, then?"

Evan carefully set up his next shot to bring the eight ball into play; he was into endgame now, just a matter of moments before the girls lost the table. "Maybe if I can figure out how the memories of a simple worm function, it'll help me understand the complexities of the human brain."

"Oh yeah," Kristen said. "You sound like the guy on the Discovery Channel. They did a show on that. Like, brains and stuff."

Another barrage of popcorn, this time thrown by Spencer and Hunter together, bounced off Thumper's leather jacket and pooled at his feet. The big youth's hand tightened around the hilt of his pool cue and for a second Evan thought he might react. However, Thumper meekly shuffled away to the opposite side of the table from the cackling Greeks.

Heidi leaned in a little closer to Evan. She was definitely interested in him now. "So are you planning on becoming a doctor or something?"

He gave her a semi-serious look in return. "No, I just don't want to lose my mind."

Thumper tapped him on the shoulder and whispered, "My shot, bro, okay?"

"Sure…" began Evan, making way for Thumper to line up the eight ball. It was a sweet angle, an easy win for them both.

Thumper winked at him and then struck the cue ball with a jolt of power. The ball flew across the green baize and connected to the eight, which in turn rocketed up from the table and described an arc across the room in a black streak. The eight ball landed with perfect aim directly in the pitcher of beer before the Thetas; glass shattered and an amber fountain of liquor sprayed all over them.

Irate and soaked, Spencer and Hunter pushed back their chairs and made to stand up, but Thumper twirled the cue around in his strong fingers and smashed it down on the rim of the pool table with a heavy crack of sound. He let out an innocent whistle, smiled warmly but none of the affability was reflected in his eyes. The two Thetas hesitated and sat back down, brushing pieces of glass from their jackets and grumbled. Gwen, her top slick with beer, had already left in an angry huff, followed by a trail of catcalls and comments about a wet T-shirt contest.

Kristen casually wrapped her arm around Thumper's waist and smiled at him; he returned her affection with a grin and a "no big thing" act of machismo. Evan, meanwhile, had to work to stop from bursting out laughing, and instead he turned a smile on Heidi.

"I think that's your game," he said.

Heidi licked her lips and gave him a playful smile. "How about a little one-on-one rematch?"

TEN

It was way past midnight when they burst through the door of the dorm, wrapped around each other, kissing and laughing, drunk on beer and arousal. Heidi whooped as she almost fell from Evan's arms and he guffawed as he tried to pull his door keys from the lock. After a couple of half-hearted attempts, he finally released them and flipped the keys around his finger in victory. Heidi applauded his manly efforts.

"I think," he declared, "I think I may be a little bit drunk." They'd polished off another six-pack of beer between them before making back to the dorm block.

"Really?" she replied. "But not too drunk." Heidi gave him a boozy wink.

"Oh no, not too drunk," Evan said with a grin. "I'm a guy. We never get too drunk for—"

She silenced him with a quick kiss. "For what?"

Evan laughed and pushed the door with his foot and slammed it shut. She tugged at his belt and drew him across the room. Heidi's hand snaked inside the buttons of his shirt, her fingers skipping lightly over his nipples, and he let himself overbalance. They tumbled on the bed and kissed some more.

After a moment, Heidi broke off and unbuttoned his top. She started to stroke his chest and paused, sniffing the air. "It smells like sex in here."

Evan dutifully reached up to the window and opened it a couple of inches. "Thumper had a busy afternoon," he said by way of explanation, nodding at the other bed in the room. It was still an unkempt snarl of sheets and blankets.

"You're kidding?" Heidi raised an eyebrow. She'd found it hard to grasp Kristen's interest in Evan's chunky roommate. "He's so... big."

Taking a few unsteady steps to the mini-fridge by the door, Evan retrieved two frosty bottles. "Charisma and black eyeliner go a long way with some girls, I guess."

Thumper's patented allure—which Evan had tagged as the "Hefty Goth" look—had certainly worked on Kristen, and Heidi's roommate had taken him back to their dorm, while Evan had got to play the home game. He dangled a longneck in front of Heidi. "Wanna beer?"

"Thanks." She took the bottle and swigged a hefty draught from it, then without explanation, she flipped over on the bed and peeked under the mattress. Heidi tugged at a pile of papers she found there.

"What are you doing?" Evan asked between sips. "Looking for the last girl I brought up here?"

"Most guys tuck their porn under here. You can tell a lot about a guy by what kind of skin magazines he reads," Heidi looked up. "But all you have are composition books."

He sat down next to her. "Yeah, I've been keeping journals since I was seven." Heidi leaned closer, intrigued, and Evan grinned.

She is so into me.

"Wow, that's cool," Heidi had always held a secret fascination for people's diaries, peeking at those of her sisters as a girl, and even her roommate's. "Hey, would you read me something?"

He snaked an arm around her waist and blinked, wondering how to edge her back towards more kissing. "No way," he slurred. "I'd be too embarrassed." Evan was feeling alert, but also quite wasted in that way that only drunken people can.

She teasingly ran her fingers over his bare torso, and Evan felt a little thrill of sexual energy. Her voice turned husky. "Then keep drinking, Worm Boy, you're too uptight."

Evan stiffened and waved a hand in front of her face like a cop at a stop signal. "Freeze!" he grated, with exaggerated seriousness. "Let's get this straight right now. I don't want to hear any worm gags from you. No 'Worm Boy', no 'Doctor Worm', no 'Worm-Master General'. Once you get a nickname like that you can't shake it, and I don't want everyone thinking I've got tapeworms coming out of my ass or something, okay?"

Heidi started laughing. "It's a deal. Now, read me something." She pulled a book out of the pile at random and handed it to him. The cover bore the title "Age 13". "This one, come on, I wanna hear your most intimate thoughts!"

Evan flipped it open and started to read aloud, the words coming out of his mouth before he had any clue what it was he was saying. *"It's like my mind refused to believe what it was seeing. Hearing Crockett make those awful screams…"* He found himself blinking and struggling to keep his attention fixed on the book. Evan felt a slow pressure building in the back of his head, like a heavy cold. *"Just writing about it gives me the shivers."*

The color drained from his face in a frigid rush as Evan suddenly realized what he was reading. He broke off and looked at Heidi; the beer sat badly in his stomach and he gasped. "I don't want to do this anymore—"

She planted a dainty kiss on his lips. "Come on, go on…"

He narrowed his eyes and fought down a surge of nausea. *"It was like Tommy was possessed or something. There was a hate in his eyes that I couldn't really call human—"*

Evan felt like the world was slipping away from him, the atmosphere in the room becoming thin and actinic. Around him, the dorm began to quiver at the edges of his vision, the walls, floor, Heidi and everything around him vibrating like a struck tuning fork. The girl seemed oblivious to it all.

Evan heard his own voice becoming distorted and scattered, as new sounds began to echo around him, old noises and snatches of speech rising up from the depths of his brain. He tried to stop speaking, but his tongue felt numb, his body distant and out of his reach. The pressure in his head felt like a rushing, thundering tidal wave, building and building and building—

And then the world shifted.

Without warning, without pause, Evan was abruptly flooded with strange sensations that were totally out of place. He had been sitting on the bed, in the dark, at night. Now he was on foot, running in bright daylight. His body felt strangely different, smaller and less powerful. Evan stumbled as his nerves reacted to the change and he fell heavily to his knees, his face kissing the dirt with a juddering impact.

Evan looked up and saw Tommy there. He was standing over Evan's prone form, his face fierce with red rage. But this Tommy was just a kid, a gangly teenager spitting curses at him through gritted teeth.

A terrible sense of disconnection washed through Evan and he looked around, utterly confused by this blunt transition.

"What the hell is going on?" he gasped.

Evan registered his surroundings in a second, the recollection of them as fresh as a new wound. He was in the old junkyard in Sunnyvale, with fat little Lenny shifting from side-to-side in tightly wound apprehension, Evan's stricken dog Crockett yelping through a gasoline-soaked sack, the crackling flames and Kayleigh unconscious and bleeding on the ground.

Why don't you just fucking kiss her, Prince Charming?

The memory struck Evan like a bullet. Somehow, impossibly, he was there. He was thirteen again, facing Tommy's insane rage amid the scrap and the flames.

"This can't be happening to me..."

He heard a growl of effort and tried to turn away. Tommy Miller smiled at his good fortune and swung the heavy wooden plank in his hand at Evan, striking him hard in the face. Evan went sprawling backwards, blood fanning out over his forehead. As if playing a cruel sport, Tommy came after him and sent one, two, three savage kicks into his ribs, laughing at his victim. Agony shot through Evan and he coughed up a gobbet of spittle streaked with blood.

He heard Lenny calling out to him over Crockett's pitiful cries. "I can't undo the rope!" Lenny pulled ineffectually at the tied gunnysack, his fingers slipping off the rope where the lighter fluid had made them slimy and slick.

Tommy spun around to face him and flashed Lenny a terrible grin. "Drop it or I'll slit your mother's throat in her sleep!"

Lenny let the rope fall from his fingers and backed away, cowed. His eyes glazed over in abject terror.

Summoning up whatever strength he could, Evan grabbed at Tommy's ankle and pulled hard, trapping Kayleigh's brother like a snare. "I got him, Lenny! Help Crockett!"

But the other boy just stood and stared, motionless. Evan's heart sank as he recognized the same dull expression he'd worn after the fateful prank at the Halpern house. Tommy brutally yanked his leg back from Evan's grip and he turned to tower over him. Tears of frustration, born out of anger and years of suppression, gathered at the corners of Tommy's eyes. "Listen to me good, Evan," he grated, gesturing at Kayleigh. "There's a million other sisters in the world. You didn't have to fuck with mine!"

Evan tried to retort, but nothing came out except a thin wheeze of air from his bruised lungs. Tommy brandished the lighter fuel can in front of Lenny's frozen expression and laughed. "You ready for this, fat ass?"

"Tommy, no!" Evan saw the bright glitter of the liquid as it arced into the flames of the campfire, then the sudden dash of orange fire as it raced across the dirt toward the sack. There was a bright flash of combustion and the dog let out a terrible, tortured scream that chilled the blood.

Evan's vision turned into an inky blackness.

Heidi's harsh slap sparked bright flares of light behind Evan's eyes and his body went rigid. "Oh my God, no! No!" he yelled, panic overflowing inside him.

He twitched, almost falling off the bed. Evan blinked away sweat from his eyes; he was back in the dorm room again, as if nothing had happened.

"Jesus, no! Crockett! I was right there!"

"Wake up, idiot." The girl rolled her eyes, every fraction of her seductive manner gone. "It was just a dream. Get a grip." Heidi got up angrily and snatched her jacket off the chair where she'd thrown it. "Shit, you're such a drama queen."

Evan struggled to stop himself from trembling. "It so felt real... It didn't feel like a dream..."

"Maybe because they never do." Heidi gave him a gimlet-eyed look. "So, Don Juan, do you pass out on all your first dates? You really know how to make a girl feel special," she added, with leaden sarcasm. When he didn't respond, she made a disgusted sound.

Heidi's words registered only peripherally with Evan, as he struggled to make sense of what had just happened. It had felt just like one of his blackouts, but different somehow, more visceral, more intense. Confusion warred with fear inside him; this couldn't have been a mere dream—the power of it had been enough to shock his body into instant sobriety—and his blackouts were always just that, moments of missing time. This had been recall, a raw moment of memory that had previously been denied to him. It had seemed so absolutely real...

"Hey, Evan," Heidi snapped. "Are you still on this planet, Worm Boy?"

He didn't hear her. Evan paused until his thumping heart and irregular breathing calmed, then snatched up his car keys and coat. Heidi watched him run out the door, dumbfounded.

The sun was rising up over the horizon by the time Evan had reached his destination. Without any kind of conscious thought, he'd just climbed into the car and started to drive. It was a route that he'd never taken before, although it was one he'd committed to memory when he was still a boy. But now none of that seemed to register as he drove past the sign at the edge of town that read "Sunnyvale Welcomes Careful Drivers".

Somewhere out here was Kayleigh, a distant, voice reminded him, and Tommy too, he added. He shivered. He wasn't ready to see her. Not yet.

Evan drove his battered blue Honda into the driveway of the Kagan house and paused. He ran

a hand over his face and felt a few day's growth
of beard. He was exhausted, from the episode
with Heidi and the lengthy drive, but whatever
compulsion had brought him here had to be
answered.

With slow and measured steps, Evan walked
up the front door and rang the bell. Looking
around, he spotted the wooden trellis that
climbed up the side of the house and remembered clambering up it with Kayleigh. It was
dense with ivy now, but other than that, little
seemed to have altered here in the past seven
years. He tried not to remember the last time he
had stood here, as the ambulance had roared
away with Lenny's catatonic form inside.

The door opened the width of the chain-lock
and Janet Kagan's jaw dropped at the sight of
Evan's face. Instantly, she recovered and her
expression froze over with hostility. "What do
you want?"

He forced a smile. "Hello, Mrs Kagan, long
time no see. You're looking very well." In truth,
she was like the house; no different to how she
was seven years ago, except for where the passing years had made her a little grayer and a little
fatter. "I was just in town and I... Well, I was
wondering, if I could speak to Lenny? For old
time's sake?"

For a second she considered slamming the
door in his face, and Evan saw it in her eyes and
the twitch of her fingers. "Lenny doesn't have
many friends over," Mrs Kagan said in a flat,

emotionless voice. Evan couldn't be sure if that was a brush-off or just a sad statement of fact. But then she opened the door wide. "Come on in then, if you're coming."

Mrs Kagan led him up the stairs with soft footfalls. "Lenny's such an early bird," she said offhand. "He's always up with the larks." On the landing, she indicated a door with a small ceramic plaque that read "Lenny's Room". "Don't upset him!" she hissed, then knock-knocked on the door before pushing it open.

"I've got a surprise for you, Lenny. You'll never guess who's here…" Her voice was cheerful, but her eyes glared at Evan with barely concealed enmity. "I'll be right outside!" she hissed.

Evan stepped into the room and gaped. Lenny Kagan's bedroom was identical to the way it had been the last time he had seen it in 1995. There were the same posters on the walls of the US Navy's Blue Angels aerobatics team and the panoramic shot of Yankee Stadium at night, the same boxes of comic books and Star Wars action figures on the shelves. The only difference were the models. There were hundreds of them now, a massive air show in miniature dangling from the ceiling on fishing line or crowding one another on racks along the walls.

Lenny sat at the same chair, hunched over his work desk with dozens of plastic parts arrayed in a careful, regular pattern. He had kept the plump, overweight figure of his youth and his clothes were pressed and regular. He still looked as if his mother dressed him, just as he had when they were kids. Lenny looked up at Evan with a slightly confused expression, but it quickly faded and he returned to his project.

"Hey, uh, it's me. Evan."

Lenny frowned in concentration as he threaded a pair of particularly small pieces together, but said nothing.

"So," Evan pressed on. "What's that you're making there, a model?" The moment the words left his mouth, he groaned inwardly at the lameness of his own question. Spotting a twin-tailed jet fighter on a shelf, he carefully picked it up and tried a different approach.

"Hey, this is like the plane they flew in *Top Gun*, right? What do they call it?" When Lenny still didn't answer, Evan replaced the model and sighed. This had been a bad idea. What had he expected to find here, some sort of instant answer? He decided to make his excuses and leave.

"Well," he turned back toward the door. "You look busy, so maybe I should make this quick. I'd totally understand if you didn't want to get into this right now, but that day in the junkyard... Could you help me remember what happened? Any details?"

Silence.

Evan reached for the door handle. "Okay then—"

"It's an F-14 Tomcat," said Lenny. "The airplane is called a Tomcat."

"Oh, right." Evan was startled by his soft tone. He picked up the model again. "It's a real beauty."

Lenny turned to look at him. "I couldn't cut the rope."

For a second, it was almost as if he was hearing Lenny's voice coming to him from across the years. Excitement began to build in Evan. "Yeah, good, and what else do you remember?"

With a dark glint in his eyes, Lenny said "Drop it or I'll slit your mother's throat in her sleep." The cadence and inflection mimicked those of Tommy Miller's words perfectly.

Evan dropped the model to the desk in surprise. "Jesus Christ," he breathed. "It really happened." Lenny's gaze drifted to the window and the morning sunshine. Evan was galvanized by the revelation, and rubbed his hands together. "This could mean... What if I can get back all the memories I've lost with my journals—"

The attack was wild, lightning fast and all the more terrifying for the sheer unexpectedness of it. Lenny sprang from his chair, the seat spinning away, and shoved Evan into the wall with unstoppable force. The impact dislodged entire squadrons of hanging aircraft from the ceiling, sending them spiraling down to the carpeted floor. Lenny's foot ground a helicopter into plastic fragments as his fingers clamped around Evan's shoulder, each one like an iron rod.

"Make one peep and I swear it'll be your last, motherfucker." Lenny's words were delivered in a dead monotone.

Evan's heart was in his mouth; Lenny was twice his size and he wouldn't find it difficult to hurt him very badly if he chose to. Evan found his eyes flicking towards the modeler's knife on Lenny's desk and he prayed that his former school friend wouldn't reach for it.

But then, as if nothing had happened, Lenny gently released his inflexible grip on Evan and he returned to his chair. Carefully, he grasped a pair of thin tweezers and set to work cementing a propeller blade into a nose cone. Lenny was a million miles away again, lost in the world of his airplanes. Evan took in a shuddering breath. Lenny's behavior had left him speechless and shaken.

The door burst open to reveal a red-faced Mrs Kagan. She shot a look at her son, then the smashed bits of model on the floor, then Evan.

He straightened himself up, ignoring her accusing stare. "Well, thanks for seeing me, man." Evan circled around Lenny's mother and threw him a farewell wave. "I shouldn't have waited so long…"

Before he could say anymore, Mrs Kagan snapped the bedroom door closed and hustled him back into the hallway, and then out of the house, and this time, she did slam the front door on him.

Alone in his room, Lenny gripped the incomplete fuselage of the model Mustang fighter plane between his twitching, pudgy hands. The plastic contorted and bent, before finally breaking in two with a loud, concussive crack.

ELEVEN

Standing in front of the dorm's only mirror, Thumper paused between jetting blasts of hairspray over his stubby Mohawk and gave Evan a serious look. "So you really think this Lenny character wanted to kill you? That's wild."

Evan was pulling book after book from the collection of journals under his bed, glancing at the covers of some, discarding them, flipping through the pages of others. "It felt like that to me. I was scared he was gonna run that model knife through my throat." Evan tugged his shirt down to show off his shoulder. The skin was red and bruised. "Look at this. His hand was on me like a vice."

"Nasty. Stabbed to death by some autistic airplane nerd. There are better ways to check out," Thumper shook his head. "But seriously dude, you are better off away from that butthole of a town you grew up in. You shouldn't have gone back there. It's asking for trouble."

"I had to," Evan said in a small voice. "I had to be sure about what happened."

"Well, I hope it was worth it, because after whatever little head-trip you had last night, you can be sure you have totally blown it with Heidi." He squirted out a little more spray. "She was very pissed off. She told Kristen you were some kinda mental case."

Evan looked up. "And you know this how?"

"She came into their dorm just as I got her room-mate's bra off." Thumper smiled. "Hey, you didn't think I was getting dressed up for your ugly ass, did you? I have a date tonight with Kristen, we're gonna go clubbing. Gaunt's Ghosts are playing at Redwing's tonight and I got me some tickets."

"Well, at least one of us scored."

His roommate's face turned sympathetic. "Look, Evan, why don't you come with us? You could try and patch it up with Heidi or maybe scope out some other tail? Come on, forget about this blackout shit."

Evan shook his head. "Thanks for the offer, man, but I can't. What happened to me last night was real. All I know is that I might be able to unblock some of my repressed memories with these." He gestured at the pile of journals.

"Hey, it's your call," said Thumper, "but know this: I'm bringing back some company tonight, and I don't want to have you spoiling the mood with some psycho spaz fest."

"I won't." He made a dismissive gesture. "Now go on, get out of here. I need some peace and quiet for this."

Thumper grabbed his leather jacket and ambled for the door. He paused before closing it. "Just be careful, Ev. You scramble your brains and I got nobody to steal lecture notes from."

Evan waved him away and returned to the books. Once in a while, he would find a page that was important. He peeled off a Post-It note and marked the place, scribbling the word "Blackout!" on the tab in large letters. Little by little, he began to form a small pile of journals to one side.

He drew out an "Age 13" book and put it on the bed. The journal automatically flapped open at a place where the spine had been bent. Evan looked down at the open pages and felt a sharp chill. There was no entry, just a single sentence written across the double-page spread, in hasty, nervous script.

I will come back for you.

The words lay there, a mute accusation in his own handwriting. A blunt stab of guilt cut into Evan's chest, and he looked away, closing the book firmly.

He hardly noticed the passing of the hours, and the vague silence that began to fall over the dorm as the students in the neighboring rooms dozed off to sleep or went out. Evan replaced the last of his books under the bed and looked back at the five journals he had separated from the rest, each with a yellow slip of paper peeking out from their pages.

He selected the book on the top of the pile; it was another 'Age 13' volume. At the marked entry, he started to read the words to himself. After a second he blanched and slammed the journal shut, a slow, creeping fear edging into his eyes. Thumper's warnings echoed in his mind. Perhaps his roommate was right, maybe this wasn't such a good idea after all. Evan noticed that his hand was twitching, his nervous energy radiating out to his fingertips.

Ignoring the racing beat of his heart, Evan took a shuddering breath and opened the book again. Forcing himself to act without hesitation, he began to read the entry aloud, his tense words hanging in the quiet air.

"The last thing I remember before the blackout was holding my hands over Kayleigh's ears."

It began almost at once; the dense, thick sensation of pressure against the back of his eyeballs, the resonance of some deep echo inside his skull. He felt himself gag, as if he would choke the moment he stopped speaking.

"I think I was more focused on her hands on mine than the mailbox across the street..."

The words on the page seemed to jump and flicker before Evan's eyes, his vision blurring and altering through a ghostly lens. The vibration was surrounding him, growing stronger,

reverberating across the floor, the walls. Noise
came then, strange and unearthly sounds torn
from his memory colliding with the present. It
was as if some huge vice had clamped around
his head, turning and turning—

And Evan's viewpoint shifted as if it were made
of flowing mercury.

His eyes widened; there was the same peculiar sense of dislocation, of difference in his
body. Lenny was behind him, huffing and puff-
ing with spent effort. Kayleigh was there in
front of him, a smile playing on her lips as she
pressed his flat palms over her ears. To one
side, Tommy shot them a venomous look, but
he then snapped back to staring at the
Halpern's mailbox like the rest of them. He
was back in the woods, as clear as if it were
taking place at that very moment.

Evan gaped, unaware of the lit cigarette that
dropped from his lips. He'd made it happen
again. It was really happening!

"Maybe it went out," Lenny whispered, pointing at the mailbox. "It should have gone off,
right? Should someone check it?"

"Yeah, why don't you do that, Lenny?" Tommy
said dryly. "Moron!"

The cigarette nestled in the folds of Evan's
shirt, smoldering there as it burned through the
thin material. He was utterly unaware of it, his
thoughts racing out of control. It's like I'm really
here! I'm reliving the moment when we set the

Blockbuster, not as a dream, but as reality! The experience was so real, so vivid that it thrilled him into stunned silence.

There was the growl of an engine, and a car pulled into the driveway of the house across the street from them. The driver emerged and began to approach the mailbox. Mrs Halpern! Evan almost choked on the sudden memory. Mom had always talked about her. She looked confident and poised.

Lenny twitched and started forward, his nerve breaking. "We gotta—"

Tommy's hand shot out like a striking snake and grabbed the chubby teenager's shoulder, his fingers boring into the fleshy skin. "Make one peep and I'll swear it'll be your last, mother-fucker."

The other boy's words made Evan's heart grow cold in his chest. The dull, hateful monotone was the same as the one Lenny had used when Evan had confronted him in his bedroom. His fingers strayed to his shoulder, where the bruises had been… or would be.

Lisa Halpern was almost at the mailbox when a thin wail cut through the air, and she turned and walked back to the car. Unbuckling the latches on a child seat, Mrs Halpern gathered up her baby daughter and the child's cries began to soften. "Don't cry, angel!" she smiled.

A flare of pain struck Evan and he glanced down at his shirt, flicking wildly at the curl of ash the cigarette had burnt into his clothes.

Swiping it to the ground, he pulled up his shirt to reveal a livid red wound on his belly. He ground his teeth in agony, glancing up as Tommy cursed quietly: "Shit, where's she going?"

Mrs Halpern's voice carried across the street to them. "How's my sweet girl?" she cooed to the baby. "Aww, you need a change, don't you honey?"

A wash of relief came over Evan as the woman walked straight past the mailbox and up the porch stairs, unlocking the front door. That's it, he thought furiously, willing her to keep walking, go inside, go inside! Beside him, he saw the same trepidation slackening on the faces of Lenny and Kayleigh.

But then Mrs Halpern turned and doubled back. "Shall we get all the mail for Daddy?" she smiled. The baby made a happy gurgle.

Only Tommy was smiling now. Evan, Kayleigh and Lenny were struck dumb, their faces etched in mounting horror.

Mrs Halpern held up the child to the latch of the ornate mailbox. "You want to open the door, honey?" Evan opened his mouth to yell, to scream, to say something, as the baby fumbled with the handle.

When the detonation came it was like the sound of the sky splitting open. The noise drove a needle of pressure into Evan's ears, blanking out everything around him into long whistling, shrieking seconds of deafness. Acrid smoke blossomed in a thin cloud, the breeze carrying it to them along with the smells of combustion, spent dynamite and burnt flesh. As much as he wanted to tear his eyes from the awful, bloody ruin that reeled away from the burning remnants of the mailbox, he couldn't look anywhere else. *What did we do?*

Splintered pieces of wood and what might have been strips of clothing began to fall from where the Blockbuster's blast had thrown them, and a searing black discoloration settled on the hood of Lisa Halpern's car. Evan found himself grateful that the explosion had robbed him of the chance to hear her scream.

Tommy scanned the road for approaching vehicles, but saw nothing. The only reaction was the barking of neighborhood dogs and the bleating of car alarms for blocks in every direction.

"Come on!" he snarled at the others. "Run!" They had only a few moments before people would come looking for the cause of the discharge.

Evan and Kayleigh backed away from the site of the blast in shock, as they both turned to run back into the woods. They'd taken a few hurried steps after Tommy when he looked back and shouted out. "Lenny, come on!"

Lenny stood as rigid as a statue, his hands clenched into tight balls. Lenny's blank eyes were fixed on the spray of crimson across the Halpern's driveway, the terrible sight burnt permanently into his brain. Doubling back, Evan

grabbed one of his arms and tugged at him,
while Tommy took the other.

"Move it, you stupid retard!" yelled Tommy. "If
you don't get your fat stinking carcass in gear,
we'll leave you here for the cops!"

Evan tried to push Lenny into a run, but his
feet pulled limply through the undergrowth,
clumsy and unguided. Tommy boosted Lenny up
by taking his arm and Evan followed suit, the
two teenage boys half-dragging, half-carrying the
third between them.

They ran on blindly, the trailing branches of
trees catching them as they rushed headlong,
desperate to get away from the destruction
behind them.

"Oh no," Kayleigh's hoarse voice seemed to
come from inside Evan's head. "Oh my God. Oh
my God... No—"

The spasm of agony rippled up through Evan's
entire body, from his feet to his head, and the
shock of it made his back arch. Before he could
even get his bearings, he found himself bolt
upright on the bed in his dorm, his stomach
knotting. On reflex, he lurched over the side of
the narrow cot and vomited violently on to the
floor. Searing acidic bile clogged his throat and
nostrils. A weak, incoherent sound of denial
escaped him and he twitched.

The interior of the dorm room was hot and
squalid, the stink of fresh puke mixing with
musty sweat and spilled beer. Evan caught the

rhythmic sound of creaking bed springs from Thumper's side of the room. He coughed and gagged on the stale, acrid taste in his mouth.

Something vague flickered at the very edge of Evan's recall and he glanced down, running a hand over his chest and stomach. His fingers found a discolored disc of scar tissue on his belly, exactly in the spot where the cigarette had burned him during his traumatic flash-back.

"What the hell?" he said aloud. "But that never happened to me... I didn't burn myself when I blacked out, I know it!" Evan studied the mark for a moment; it was old, as if it was a wound he'd suffered years in the past—but until tonight he had never seen it before.

Thumper's head rustled up from under his blankets and he called out. "Hey, roomie!" Evan looked over, glimpsing the naked shape of a girl—who wasn't Kristen, he noted—in bed with him. Thumper pointed his chin at where Evan had thrown up. "Christ, man, you wanna clean that up before I lose my appetite here? You're ruining the romance."

Evan ignored him and snatched up the journal he'd been reading from where it had dropped by his feet. He pulled a pen from a shelf above him and began to write in a frantic, desperate rush, scribbling notes in the margins of the page alongside the words of his thirteen year-old self.

As he wrote, he thought about the wound. Something had changed; he had made it change by being there, actually being there in the past. The scar was evidence, and the ramifications of it made him giddy with dread.

Evan couldn't face another road trip out to his old hometown again, and after Lenny's previous behavior, he wasn't sure if it would be safe for them to meet again. But that was only part of the reason he didn't want to go back there. The images from his freshly revived memory of the fatal mailbox prank were bright and new in his mind, and suddenly the thought of going any-where near the scene of the crime in Sunnyvale filled him with fear and repulsion. Evan swal-lowed hard and pushed his dark musings to one side, straining to hear the ringing of the tele-phone on the other end of the line. No answer.

He leaned in close to the payphone, pressing one finger to his free ear to drown out the noise from the dormitory lobby. The corridor had been brightly decorated with strings of colorful party streamers, a few clumps of limp balloons and numerous banners. All of the garish décor was in honor of the college's annual Parent's Weekend and some of the posters tacked up on the notice board by the phone announced special events, presentations and shows. None of that was for Evan, though. He had a much more personal day planned to spend with his mother, as far away from the college as he could make it.

The phone was still ringing, and Evan glanced up at the clock; he hoped that the woman would be home. The lobby was full of students, some gruff and disinterested in the hoopla, others carefree and happy, trailed by awkward-looking moms and dads laden with shopping bags and other treasures brought from home. The elevator nearby chimed, disgorging more students into the mix. One of them was a Goth girl, her hair wild and spiky, dressed in a black vest and jeans combo that matched her pale skin and kohl-rimmed eyes. Her only adornment was a gold Ankh on a chain around her neck; Thumper's latest love interest threw Evan a sultry wink as she passed him.

"How does he do it?" Evan asked aloud, just as the receiver at the other end clicked on.

"Yes?" It was a lady speaking, in one of those prim and telephone-perfect voices that older people always used.

"Yes, hello, uh, Mrs Kagan?" he began hesitantly. "This is Evan Treborn—"

"What do you want?" The tone went frosty. "Haven't you made enough trouble for Lenny? You upset him very much with that visit of yours!"

"I know, I'm sorry about that, but I really need to speak with him—"

"I don't think so!" Mrs Kagan snapped. "Don't come around any more. You're not welcome in this house, you hateful young man!"

"But—" The dial tone hummed tunelessly at him down the line. "She hung up..."

Evan had barely digested this when a hand suddenly grabbed his shoulder. In tense reflex, he slammed the payphone receiver down. He turned, afraid of whom he might find behind him—Lenny? Tommy? or worse?—and came face to face with Professor Carter.

"Whoa!" Carter beamed. "I didn't mean to scare you there, Evan!" He nodded at the phone. "Bad call?"

He blew out a breath. "It's okay, professor. I'm feeling a little highly strung today."

"I told you, cut down on the caffeine! Listen, I just wanted to know how the flatworms project of yours was coming. I'm looking forward to seeing the final results."

Evan gave him a non-committal nod. "Oh, fine, I guess. It's been kind of crazy lately with my Mom coming up and everything, so I haven't really—"

The professor smiled and held up a hand. "I know, I know. Who can think about the brain functions of worms when your libido is in full swing, right?"

Evan shrugged and forced a smile; he liked Carter's no-nonsense honesty. "I suppose so."

"But do me a favor," the teacher said, a little more seriously. "Just don't drop the ball, okay? You're a smart kid, Evan. Try not to get distracted from that. You've got a great future ahead of you, I can see it."

"I won't let you down, Professor Carter."

"I know you won't." Carter patted him warmly on the shoulder and walked on, waving to another student and her parents.

Evan sighed and studied the clock in the lobby again. He had time to get changed before he met his mother for dinner. But once again he found himself turning over the traumatic events of the recovered memory, trying to slot them into the gaping void that had been in their place for seven years. He'd already made up his mind not to tell his Mom about the flashbacks for the moment. As far as she knew, Evan's blackouts and memory losses were a thing of the past and he didn't want to give her something new to worry about. But still, something she had told him as a child had bubbled to the surface: a snatch of conversation from a visit to the Sunnyvale Clinic and that doctor, What was his name, Redfield?

They had been in the doctor's office. "That's why I brought you here, Evan," Mom had said. "Doctor Redfield already has a background in problems with memory loss."

Evan remembered his question. "My dad has a bad memory too?"

He'd never got the answer he had wanted that day, and now with all that had happened to him, he found himself wanting it more than ever. Until he decided otherwise, Evan made a decision to keep his strange new experiences to himself and study them in careful detail, like the flatworm project. Whatever they were, flashbacks, post-traumatic recall or some kind of lucid dreaming, Evan was determined to get to the bottom of it.

He walked away with a sense of fresh determination, unaware that his hand had strayed to the spot on his stomach where the smoldering cigarette had left a burn scar.

TWELVE

The restaurant felt like a world away from the shabby halls of Evan's college dorm, friendly and inviting with a hubbub of gentle conversation wafting from every table. Italian food had always been a favorite in the Treborn household—after all these years, Evan still thought of Wednesday evenings as "pasta night"—and dining out in an upmarket place like Giotto's was a welcome oasis of calm in the midst of the tension elsewhere in his life.

Andrea dabbed at her lips with a napkin and smiled. "Mmm, that tiramisu was delicious. Fattening, but delicious." She took a sip of mineral water. "Where did you find this place? It's not exactly Evan du jour."

"This is where I take all my special dates," her son gave a wry smile. "Believe it or not, Thumper worked here in the summer as a dishwasher. He got the leftovers sometimes, and they tasted great." He indicated his own empty plate. "They make good lasagna here—but not as good as yours, of course."

His mother grinned, brushing a curl of graying hair over her ear. "Flatterer. Just for that, I'll get the check." As one of the waiters cleared the dishes, she reached forward and took the bill.

"Ah, Mom, you don't have to do that."

"Buying you dinner is the least I can do for my genius son. Besides, you need all your money to pay back your student loans." She signed the bill, and then on impulse, leaned over and kissed Evan on the cheek.

He colored a little. "Please, Mom," he said, a little embarrassed, "People will talk!"

"I can't help it," she said warmly. "I'm just so proud of you." Evan smiled sheepishly as she continued. "You've got the highest grades in all of your classes."

Evan looked away for a second. Questions had been dancing on the tip of his tongue all night long, and every time he had come close to voicing one, his nerve had stalled. His mother was in such a good mood, and Evan felt torn about leading her into a conversation that could spoil the evening for both of them. He knew the last thing his mother would want would be to rake over the old coals of the past they'd put behind them; but to say nothing would leave him without any of the answers he so desperately wanted. He took a careful draw on his coffee and gave her an even look.

"Did my Dad..." The word almost choked him as he said it. "Did, uh, Jason get good grades at school when he was younger?"

For the smallest of instants, a flicker of concern crossed Andrea's eyes and then was gone. "Please," she smiled. "He always got straight 'As' without ever having to cram or touch a textbook, while the rest of us struggled over every page. That was the one area where his memory never failed him." Try as she might, Andrea couldn't keep a wistful note from entering her voice.

"Mom," Evan pressed on, the words sounding hollow and forced. "I was just wondering about him. About what happened to him, and all. Did he ever say that he figured out a way to recall a lost memory, years after he blacked it out the first time?"

The smile on his mother's face faded away. "Why do you ask?"

Evan tried to keep his tone light. "No, it's just weird, with him being such a brain and all, I just wondered if he was ever able to remember stuff that he'd forgotten."

Andrea gave him a cautious look. She wasn't ready to dissect her late husband's behavior with Evan—especially in the middle of a crowded restaurant—but something in his eyes, some innocent longing, made her keep talking. "When he was around your age…" She halted in mid-sentence, considering for a moment. "In fact, when Jason was almost exactly your age, come to think of it, he said he had figured out a trick to remember the past." As she spoke, she could see her husband's face reflected there in her son's, the same thoughtful eyes there as he watched her with steady interest.

"A trick?" Evan repeated, forcing himself not to give any sign of the building excitement he felt. "What did he mean by that?"

"I'm not sure," said Andrea. "He said he could do it, but I couldn't tell if they were his real memories or just phantoms." She eyed him. "You know, he might only have thought he actually remembered those things. They might have been delusions."

"Sure," Evan prodded. "Go on."

The next words were pained and difficult for his mother to articulate. "And then, well... Just before it got so bad that he had to be committed, he said that he could..." She drifted into silence, her eyes darkening.

"What? What could he do?" Evan's pulse was racing. I have to know!

Andrea shook her head, as if she were dismissing some ridiculous notion. "Forget it, it's nothing." She sighed. "He was far too sick by then."

Evan realized she had said as much as she was willing to say on the subject. He nodded slowly, the need to know still gnawing at him.

"Why are you asking me this now?" she said. "Is something wrong?"

"No," he replied, a little too quickly. "He was just on my mind, you know? Dad, and Sunnyvale, Kayleigh, the past and everything..." It was a lame attempt to deflect her and he knew it.

His mother's jaw hardened. The conversation was veering on to thin ice, and places where she definitely did not want to go. "That's all behind us now, kiddo," she said briskly. "You need to concentrate on the future. I've got a new post opening up for me in the oncology department at the hospital and you, you've got the chance to really make something of yourself."

"I know, I know," he replied. "But still, sometimes I wonder about it. I think about Kayleigh…"

"Evan, there's no point to this," she said flatly, her previous good mood starting to evaporate. "You haven't seen Kayleigh in what, six or seven years? You probably wouldn't even recognize her now. You've moved on in your life and so has she."

"Do you know what happened to her?"

Evan's mother took a long moment before answering. "I think she moved to Ridgewood," Andrea shrugged. "Look, the point is, all of that is over and done with. Dwelling on the past only brings up more regrets," she said mournfully. "Don't spend your life looking back, Evan. Your father did and it destroyed him. I couldn't bear it if that happened to you."

He reached out and tenderly touched her hand. "It won't, Mom. I was just asking, that's all."

Evan was surprised how easily the lie came to him.

Thumper propped himself up on his bed with one arm and watched his roommate's progress back and forth across the dorm room. He watched him dig through teetering piles of paperwork, yellowing old pages of lecture notes and dog-eared magazines, frowning when he couldn't find what he wanted. Thumper made a dismissive tutting noise with his tongue. "Dude, you're starting to worry me with this obsessive-compulsive thing you've got going on. Sit down and take a chill pill."

Evan threw him a blank look but said nothing. Finally, he found what he was looking for, a dozen of his journals held together with a rubber band. Snapping it off, he began to thumb through them.

"Seriously, Evan," Thumper added. "I'm starting to think you're going to go all Klebold on me. I can see myself on the evening news saying 'Yeah, I knew Evan Treborn. He was such a quiet guy...' after you've gone postal with an AK-47 in the chemistry lab."

"Shut up, Thumper," Evan said, and pulled a particular volume from the pile and turned to a marked page. He cleared his throat and began to read the entry aloud. "*I never wanted to be in the movie anyway and it was so cold so I wanted to wear my clothes but Mr Miller took my shirt off—*"

"What the fuck are you doing?" Thumper broke in, leaning up, a look of growing revulsion on his face.

"I said shut up!" Evan snapped. "I need to have quiet for this."

Before he could continue, Thumper had already rolled off the bed and vaulted to his feet. Evan barely had time to blink before the big Goth snatched the journal out of his hands. Thumper held it up high, keeping Evan at arm's reach like a basketball player holding on to the ball. "Are you utterly stupid or what?" he grunted. "Do you have even the first clue about what you are messing with?"

"What? Give me back the damn book, Thumper!"

"Why? So you can screw with your head some more? No way man, ain't gonna happen."

Evan made a grab at the book and failed to reach it. "What the hell are you talking about?"

Thumper pantomimed a confused expression. "Shucks, golly gee, I dunno. But maybe there's a good reason why you've repressed the one day when some sicko old lecher had you in your tighty whities, damn it!" He shot a glance at the open page Evan had marked and began to read. Thumper laughed bitterly at what he saw there. "Shit yeah, man. I'd think twice about reading this if I was you. You could wake up a lot more fucked up than you are now. Believe it."

"That's my choice! Now give me the damn thing back!" Evan spat.

There was a moment when Evan thought Thumper was going to throw the journal out the window, but then his roommate shrugged and tossed the journal to him. "Look, man, we're friends and all so it's your choice, but I gotta tell you I think you're on a one-way express to the insane asylum with this regression crap."

"Thanks for the advice, Doctor Freud." Evan retorted, without conviction. Opening the book to the page, he took a deep breath and began to read again, silently sounding out the words in his mind. Evan's fingers felt tight along the edges of the pages, and a tremble shot through them. The journal quivered in his hands as Evan's heartbeat throbbed loudly in his ears, threatening to overwhelm him with the sound.

With a sudden jerk of the wrist he snapped the book closed, and dropped it to the floor.

"Shit, I can't do it," he said quietly.

"You say that like it's a bad thing," Thumper shook his head. "You know what you should do?" He stabbed a thick finger at the books. "You should go downstairs to the incinerator and burn those fuckin' things. Get rid of them, be done with it."

"I can't," Evan said with force. "You don't know what it's like to have a hole in your head, to not be able to remember anything at all about a certain day!"

"Are you kidding?" Thumper gave a harsh laugh. "I've done so much weed, there are plenty of days I can't remember!"

Evan ignored the flippant rejoinder. "If there's a way I can fill in that missing time, I've got to try to find it."

"What, and send yourself gaga in the process? The price is too high," Thumper retorted. "You're a psych major, dude. You know about all that brain stuff. You push yourself with this shit, Evan, and you'll end up like your old man." He made a winding-up motion at his temple. "Mui loco."

"I have to try," he said, quietly.

Thumper sat heavily. "Then there's gotta be an easier way to get in touch with your past..." He gave an airy wave. "Talk to someone who was there. Your Ma, she's not going to give up anything—"

"Keep her out of this," Evan broke in.

Thumper nodded, "Okay then, so you can't talk to Mommy and you sure as hell can't go back to your old pal Lenny, 'cos he's out to lunch, big-time. What about your grade-school girlfriend? What was her name, Katie?"

"Kayleigh," Evan corrected. "I couldn't see her. We haven't talked since we were thirteen. I left her there..."

"Well, here's your ideal opportunity to make it right with her. You know where she lives, right?"

"Ridgewood. It's just outside of Sunnyvale, not much more than a couple houses and some stores." Evan thought back to what his mother had said.

His roommate spread his hands. "Cool. Shouldn't be that hard to find her then, should it?"

Evan stared at the marbled cover of the closed journal in silence; then with a sudden flurry of movement that startled Thumper, he snatched his car keys from where they lay and left the dorm in a rush.

Thumper called after him: "That'll be twenty dollars an hour!"

He drove through the afternoon, stopping at a gas station along the highway to make a couple of calls. It was surprisingly easy for him to track Kayleigh down. Part of him had hoped that she'd be impossible to locate—to give him the excuse to turn around and come home—but he felt his heart rise when he realized that she was there, that she was still alive, and he was actually going to see her.

Evan spoke with a friendly woman at the Ridgewood Sheriff's office under the pretext of locating alumni for a high school reunion, and then an acerbic old gent who served as site manager at "Woody Acres", a trailer park where Kayleigh rented a place. She was out all the time, the old guy told him, usually working the afternoon-to-midnight shift. He'd be able to find her just outside of town, at a truck stop off the interstate called the Ridgewood Diner. Evan scribbled the address down on a scrap of paper and drove on into the evening.

The closer he got to Ridgewood, the more his gut tightened and his nerves frayed. He looked up into the rearview mirror and got a good look at himself as a passing truck illuminated him in its headlights. He looked haggard and frail, the tension in his jaw making his teeth clench and grind. Evan tried to shake his worrisome mood away but to no avail and he ran a hand through his hair, wiping greasy locks out of his eyes. He pressed harder on the accelerator and gripped the steering wheel tightly, as if the speed would somehow enable him to outrun the aura of fear and churning emotions that surrounded him.

Night had fallen on Ridgewood when Evan finally pulled off the road and into the car park of the diner. It was a desolate little island of dulled chrome and dirty glass in the middle of a wide asphalt wilderness. Aside from Ridgewood itself, a good few miles back along the interstate, there was nothing but featureless countryside stretching away in both directions. He turned off the engine and sat there for a minute. The place felt lonely and desperate, although Evan couldn't be sure if he was projecting his own inner feelings on the building before him.

The diner threw out a thick, oily light that pooled around it like melted wax from a candle, and a flickering sign in hot pink neon glowed overhead, letters buzzing on and off in random pulses. He watched shapes moving around inside, indistinct blobs of people sitting in booths or at a long counter. Now and then, a lightly colored shape moved in and out of them, back and forth along the length of the diner. A waitress?

Kayleigh worked here. Evan tried to make that thought fit with all his memories and impressions of her, all his recollections of sad, lovely Kayleigh and her cruel, unfair life. The diner's doorway banged open and disgorged two truckers, a pair of overweight guys in dirty flannel shirts and baseball caps.

"Why the fuck do we stop at this shit hole?" one of them grunted in a hoarse voice. "The food stinks."

The other trucker shrugged. "Only place for eats for fifty miles. You're right, though, the grub tastes like re-fried puke."

The two men laughed rowdily and continued to talk, their voices growing indistinct as they passed around the rear of the diner and into the truck park.

Evan's heart sank. He thought of all the places he'd hoped to find her—maybe somewhere fancy, somewhere where she was valued and well paid—and compared them to the harsh reality of the Ridgewood Diner. I'm to blame for this, he told himself. I could have helped her get a better life.

Two trucks roared past him in sprays of gravel, as they caught the diner's grimy silver siding with their taillights. He saw the light-colored shape move again, glinting for a split-second as if it were a bright butterfly glimpsed through the dingy windows.

"What the hell am I doing?" Evan said aloud. "Am I just going to sit here and stalk her, or am I going to go in and say something?" Forcing a confident smile to his lips, he got out of the car and made for the diner. As he walked, he ran through what he'd say to her, just as he had a million times before. *I was just passing… What a coincidence that you just happen to work at this diner… I came looking for you*, and… All the words fell flat. I'll just talk to her, he decided. That'll be enough.

The door complained as he opened it and entered. Inside, the Ridgewood Diner matched the unappealing look of its exterior. The run-down roadside café was busy with a mix of indolent townie types from Ridgewood and Sunnyvale, along with a large percentage of truck drivers wolfing down plates of fried food or giant mugs of poisonously strong coffee. The air was stale with a haze of cigarette smoke and every surface was drab with grime.

He had a foot through the doorway when the hatch to the kitchen banged open and Kayleigh burst through, laden down with far too many plates of food for one person to carry. She was wearing a careworn pink and white waitress uniform that appeared to be a throwback to the 1950s, and it was filthy enough to have been dragged over twenty miles of dirt road. Her hair fell in ragged fashion over her pale, sweaty face. She seemed drawn and sickly thin.

The swinging door to the kitchen bounced back at her like a pinball flipper and caught her hip, the shock of the impact sending a plate piled high with chilli crashing to the floor.

"For the love of—" A strident male voice bellowed out at her. "Can we get through one goddamned day without you breaking something?"

Evan ducked back behind a stand of payphones, out of Kayleigh's line of sight. He watched her turn bright red with embarrassment as she bent down to clean up the spill. Her humiliation was clear and it made Evan's fists clench in response.

A bald, bull-necked guy in soiled cook's whites tore open the door and glared at her. "Don't just stand there, get that mess off the floor and get back to work!" He prodded her in the chest, "There's a hundred other trailer trash queens like you who'd get on all fours for a job like this, so just you watch your ass!"

Kayleigh didn't reply; she just meekly went about her work. Evan wanted to step in and say something, but he hesitated. He couldn't just blast back into her life like some white knight and probably get her fired in the process. He needed to speak to her alone.

She gathered up the spilled food and broken plates, edging up to the kitchen door with her load. One of the customers, a fat guy in a Mack cap and trucker's garb, pinched her backside with a raucous cackle. Evan recognized him as a face from the bar at Dirty Hank's.

"That's good eatin'!" he grunted, showing a mouth full of broken teeth. Evan studied her response to the offence; hate flared in her eyes, but she flashed the guy an uncomfortable smile and went on her way.

Kayleigh's unease was mirrored in Evan's expression and he hesitated, before turning around and walking out.

He sat in the car and waited, watching the glowing green numbers of the digital dashboard clock creep slowly toward midnight.

THIRTEEN

The night had turned cold and starless by the time Kayleigh left the diner. She'd been ready to finish her shift dead on twelve, but her boss had pulled the same stunt he did every other night and made her stay on another hour. She had had her coat on and her hand on the door, not like that mattered to him.

"What?" he grated, like it was her fault she wasn't going home. "You ain't got no kid or no man to get back for, what the hell are you bitchin' about? You can give me another damn hour."

The one occasion Kayleigh had brought up the word "overtime" he'd just laughed in her face. When Selma, the night shift girl, had finally arrived forty minutes late, she'd disappeared into the back with him and come back five minutes later with her hair mussed and her blouse unbuttoned. Kayleigh had got into the habit of turning on the radio to blank out the noise they made.

Kayleigh let the door to the diner slam shut behind her and took a deep breath. "I hate this place," she said quietly. It was a ritual she performed every day, the only affirmation she could give to herself that this place would not grind her down.

She pulled the shabby coat tight around her shoulders and fiddled with the zipper; the damn thing was cheap and nasty, and it never caught the first time, jamming halfway. She cursed under her breath—and then something in her peripheral vision sent a warning signal to her brain. Kayleigh caught the movement of a man-shaped shadow near one of the cars and her hand automatically went for the lipstick-sized canister of pepper spray she kept in her pocket. She hadn't liked the way that asshole had grabbed her ass, and if he had waited around looking for some action, he'd get a face full of Capsicum. It wouldn't be the first time Kayleigh had left a would-be rapist clawing at his eyes and screaming like a stuck pig.

But when Evan Treborn stepped out of the shadows Kayleigh stopped dead in her tracks. She recognized him instantly, even through the unshaven facial hair and the serious look in his eyes. He wore his maturity well, but with it he seemed to have kept the same boyish good looks.

"Evan?" she managed, her mouth catching up with her brain.

He gave her a friendly grin. "Hey, Kayleigh."

She did something then that she hadn't done in a long while: she smiled, and meant it. Evan stepped up to her and they hugged gingerly.

Evan broke away first and studied her. She looked tired and worn, and she smelled like cheap tobacco and fried grease, but he still found himself enchanted by her. Kayleigh still had the same sheltered beauty she'd had when they were children, and he was drawn straight to it.

"God, Evan, I never thought I'd see you again," she said. "How have you been?"

He gave a halting shrug. "Oh, you know. Same old, same old."

A brief laugh. "No, Evan, I don't know. It's been a long time. Fill me in."

"Well, I'm going to State College now, and things are going okay, I guess. My Mom is doing pretty good…"

Kayleigh threw a glance over her shoulder. Selma was peering through the window at them and suddenly she felt exposed. She nodded to Evan and they started to walk out along the road, back towards town.

"That's great," she said, for lack of anything else to add. Kayleigh's head was still spinning, knocked off kilter by Evan's surprise appearance. She produced a packet of cigarettes and offered him one. "Smoke?"

Evan shook his head. "Nah. I haven't touched them, not since we were kids."

Kayleigh lit one and took a deep lungful, savoring it. "I've stopped a hundred times. Never quit."

They walked on, both of them searching for avenues to continue the conversation. "So," Evan asked, "how's Tommy?"

She took another long drag, then blew out the smoke like she was discharging something negative from inside her. "They kept him in Juvy for a few years, after... y'know, what happened. Now he works over at Dale's Auto Body in town." Kayleigh shrugged. "I guess he likes it. He gets to beat the hell out of fender panels all day long."

Evan nodded and studied her carefully as he phrased his next question, even though he already knew the answer. "And you, do you still live with your dad?"

A slight tick of irritation jerked in the nerve under her eye. "No," she replied, in an even, rehearsed voice, "I emancipated myself when I was fifteen."

"Wow!" He couldn't keep the surprise from his voice. "That must have taken courage."

She shook her head and sneered. "Not if you remember my Dad..."

"So why did you end up here? You didn't want to go down to Florida with your mom? She lives in Orlando, right?"

Kayleigh shook her head with genuine regret. "No. She had a new family. Not enough space for me there. She said I should have moved in with her when we were kids, but..." The rest of the words fell away from her. "Whatever," she finished.

Silence hung between them for a few more footsteps before she spoke again, shaking off her own bleak thoughts. "So, why are you back in this dismal place?"

"Actually, Kayleigh, the reason I came back to town was to talk to you."

Despite herself, Kayleigh's heart suddenly leapt with adolescent joy. Her face brightened. "Me? Are you kidding? Why?"

"Well, it's kinda weird. Do you remember when I was a kid I had all those blackouts?"

She nodded. "Of course. Do you still get them?"

Evan made a negative gesture. "No, it's not like that. It's just that, well, lately some of the memories have begun to come back and I'd kind of like to talk to you about one of them in particular." He took a breath. "It'd be a big help to me."

Kayleigh was a little confused now about where the conversation was going, unsure as to where Evan was leading her. "Well, sure, I'll try to remember. Shoot."

He pressed on. "Do you remember when we were kids, when we were both seven... Your dad had a video camera and he was making a movie in the basement... It was Robin Hood, or something?"

The warmth in Kayleigh's eyes guttered out and vanished like a doused flame. "What do you want to know, Evan?" Her voice was brittle, as cold as the night sky.

Evan tried to frame his query, but the words that came to him were clumsy and tactless. "It's just that... Did he..." He frowned. "What happened in the basement?"

"It was a long time ago," she said tonelessly. "I was only a kid."

"I know that, but—" Evan's reply was cut dead by the icy look in Kayleigh's eyes.

"Is that why you came all the way back here?" she grated, her temper rising. "To ask me a lot of stupid questions about Robin Hood?" Kayleigh's brief moment of happiness at seeing Evan again was now a dim echo, and her heart was hardening over again with the armor she habitually wore.

"No," Evan tried to mollify her. "But I think something really bad might have happened to us that day."

Kayleigh took the stub of her cigarette and threw it to the asphalt in an angry flourish. She ground the orange ember under the tip of her heel. "Is there a point to any of this?" she asked angrily.

The questioning look in Evan's eyes gave way to tenderness and he stepped closer to her. She flinched a little as his hand came up to touch her face. For a second, he thought Kayleigh would back away, but she stood still and silent.

"Whatever happened in there, it wasn't our fault, you know." His voice was calm and soothing, and she wanted so very much to believe him. "We couldn't have stopped it."

Evan felt Kayleigh's cheek tremble beneath his fingers, and her eyes overflowed with soundless streams of tears. "Evan, I—" she choked.

"Look, Kayleigh…" he said carefully, "This may sound like bullshit coming from a guy who hasn't spoke to you in seven years, but you were just a little girl and there's nothing you could have done to deserve—"

Kayleigh pulled away from him abruptly, various emotions that contradicted one another etched on her face. She wiped her eyes with fierce, irritable strokes. "Just shut up, Evan. You're wasting your breath." Kayleigh's voice was weary and defeated.

Evan's jaw hardened in determination. "Kayleigh, you're a good person. You can't go through life hating yourself just because your dad is a twisted freak—"

"Shut up!" she screamed as a truck roared past them, her voice mingling with the blare of the horn. "Who are you trying to convince, Evan? You came all the way out here to stir up my shit just because you had a bad memory?" She thrust an accusing finger in his face. "You never came to see *me!* You want me to cry on your shoulder and tell you everything's all better now? Well fuck you, Evan!" Her voice peaked into a shrill snarl. "Nothing is gonna be all better, okay? Nothing ever gets better!"

Before he could respond, she shouldered past him and broke into a run, racing away towards the lights of Ridgewood. Apologies, excuses, explanations flew from him, leaving Evan alone and speechless as she fled from his touch.

She skidded to a halt and turned to face him. "If I was so wonderful, Evan, why didn't you ever call me?" Years of hurt filled her words. "Why did you leave me here to rot?"

Kayleigh turned away and ran, leaving Evan rooted on the spot, the empty hollow of guilt inside sickening him to his very core.

The day turned into a blur of morose contemplation for Evan. He sat on a shaded grassy knoll at the edge of the college quad and watched the world pass him by, blanking out the voices and faces of the students who moved through his line of sight until they were nothing but white noise, tuned out by his preoccupied mind. He let his classes come and go, cutting a handful of lectures, and drifted. After the gut-wrenching confrontation with Kayleigh the night before, Evan's concentration could go nowhere else. He sat, one hand idly tracing the line of the cigarette burn on his chest, staring into space.

Hour after hour, he picked apart what he had said to her, what she had said to him, his tone of voice, his manner, desperately trying to understand how the whole thing could have gone so utterly wrong. He had been too busy thinking about his own problems, too wrapped up in the events of the past few days to consider what her feelings might have been. Evan gave a heavy, dejected sigh. It had been so good to see her again, and it had felt so right for him to be with her, almost as if no time had passed between them and they were happy, laughing kids again. When they had been younger, Evan's world had always seemed to light up a bit brighter when Kayleigh walked in the room. He'd never imagined life without her around, but that had changed after the prank.

Then she was gone, and eventually, out of sight and out of mind. Kayleigh's brilliant smile had faded and sank into the depths of his childhood past. Evan had believed that he had forgotten her, but the opposite was true. The moment she looked into his eyes outside the diner, the exact instant that warm recognition flowered on her face, Evan Treborn had fallen in love with Kayleigh Miller all over again.

And in one moment of self-obsessed stupidity, he had destroyed whatever chance he might have had to reconnect with her again. How could I have been so damn stupid? he railed at himself, time and again. He had been so focused on getting the truth out of her about the past that he'd walked all over any future they could have had together. I ruined Lenny's life and now I've ruined Kayleigh's as well.

A bright yellow Frisbee spun past his head and bounced off the tree behind him. Evan focused to see a Theta—that asshole Hunter from the bar—approaching to recover it.

Hunter picked up the disk and gave Evan a sideways look. "What are you looking so sad about? Did your boyfriend choke on a reefer and die?"

"To hell with you." It was almost too much effort to argue.

The jock considered another insult, then thought better of it and left Evan to his black mood.

By the time the college day had ended and the last of the students filed past him, Evan had made a choice. Thumper had been right; he was going to go back to the dorm and burn the journals.

His past was over, and no matter how much it hurt him, Evan had decided that the only way forward was to leave it behind.

His roommate looked up from a cross-legged position on Evan's bed as he entered the dorm. Thumper was sucking furiously on a gurgling bong, nursing the cylinder of liquid like a mother cradling a baby.

Evan gave him a disgusted look. "If you're going to do that crap, sit on your own damn bed."

"What put the bug up your ass?" Thumper gagged out the words in between tight coughs. "You're welcome to share, man." He nodded at the telephone in the corner of the room. "Some dude left a message for you."

The red "message waiting" lamp was blinking on the answering machine and Evan acknowledged it with a cursory glance. He grabbed a towel and rolled it into a tube. "You know you can smell it all the way to the bathroom down the hall," he added pointedly. "Least you could do is open the window." Evan laid the towel against the door-jamb to block the outgoing odor.

Thumper grinned and made a choking sound that might have been an agreement.

Evan thumbed the "play" button on the tele-phone keypad and leaned close to the speaker. "You have. Two. Messages," it told him in clipped digital English.

"Hi, Evan, this is Professor Carter." Evan pulled a face. One of the lectures he'd missed today had been for his psych class. "I just won-dered why you didn't hand in your essay this afternoon. I was a bit concerned. Call me, and we'll schedule a make-up for it. Don't forget what I told you."

Thumper looked up from the bong and gave Evan a comically magnified look of stern disap-proval. The machine gave a strident beep. "Next message."

The words came out in a fevered, snarling rush, and they made Evan's blood run cold. "What did you say to my sister, you mother-fucker?" Although he hadn't heard him in seven years, Evan knew Tommy Miller's voice instantly. "Last night she cried on the phone for over an hour to me." He heard heavy, angry breathing, as if Tommy were champing at the bit to rage at him, to do some damage. "She said you came and saw her last night... What the hell were you doing, messing with my sister again?

You broke her heart once, wasn't that enough?" He shouted so hard that the words became garbled. "Why couldn't you just stay the fuck away?"

The bellow startled Thumper and he accidentally tipped over the bong, spilling the water within all over Evan's bed. His roommate grabbed the towel from under the door and started to dab fruitlessly at the blankets.

Evan was unaware of anything else except Tommy's voice. Miller gave a sound that was like a sob or a growl; it was hard to tell them apart on the playback. "Kayleigh... She... she fucking killed herself tonight! She's dead!" he spat. "And so are you."

His knees turning to water, Evan stumbled back a step and collapsed to the floor, his head jerking in tiny shakes, his mouth open and wordless, dumbstruck.

Behind him, Thumper was oblivious. "Whoa, bad news, bro," he said, indicating the stained blankets. "I don't think this is gonna come out."

Evan didn't hear Thumper speak; his senses were filled with sound of his world coming apart around him.

By chance, he had kept the telephone number of the old guy at the trailer park, so it was just a matter of some hollow, sympathetic words that got Evan the information that he needed. He ignored five messages from his mother that day and instead turned out the only clean shirt he had, and drove all the way back to Sunnyvale in a numbed haze. It wasn't until he parked at the edge of the cemetery that he realized his father was buried in this place as well, somewhere over in the southern corner, close to the highway. Evan picked up the bouquet of roses he'd bought that morning and slowly approached the knot of people clustered around a soft-spoken priest.

An image from his childhood prickled at the back of his mind: Kayleigh, reaching out to hold his hand as he watched his dad's casket drop into the ground. The recollection left an aching trail of emotion behind it. He could barely bring voice to the idea that she was gone, as if it were a concept too big for his mind to contain. Closer now, and the cleric's words were coming to him on the afternoon breeze, a gentle whisper about death and rebirth, ashes to ashes, dust to dust. Evan saw an older woman flanked by a smartly dressed guy in a suit, now and then her eyes flashing daggers at one of the other mourners. Kayleigh's mother, he realized, and her new husband.

She was staring at George Miller, and at his side, Kayleigh's brother, Tommy. The sight of the two of them made Evan stop in his tracks, and his hands tensed, the thorns from the roses piercing the wrapping as he gripped them in tight fury. For long, uncomfortable moments, Evan hesitated, torn between the need to say his goodbyes to Kayleigh, and the certainty that

Tommy would attack him the moment he showed his face.

No one had seen him approaching, and with regret, Evan turned his back on the funeral and returned to his car, watching the rest of the ceremony unfold in silence from the driver's seat.

Father Byrne gave a small, practiced smile of sympathy to the last of the mourners as they filed away, following them to their cars. The poor girl's mother gave him a tearful "thank you" and stalked away, pointedly ignoring the wary young man and his father. As he often did after such a day, the priest found himself wondering if young Kayleigh's life might have been so much longer and richer if her parents had spent more time on their daughter than on the spite they threw at one another. The father turned his back on the grave, leaving only the brother to give the plain, simple headstone a last, lingering look before he too went on his way. Evan watched them go, knowing that if ever there was a family that could have used some guidance, it was the Millers.

He turned back to the gravesite and was surprised to see a young man there, perhaps the same age as the deceased girl's brother, his face dark and troubled. Father Byrne approached him, watching. The young man gently laid a bunch of roses—a large, expensive bouquet, he noted—on the casket, then glanced around to see if any of the mourners were in sight. The priest was certain now; this person hadn't been part of the Miller's funeral party, but clearly Kayleigh had been someone very important to him. Byrne nodded to himself, and stood back. He understood all too well that some people needed a private moment to say their farewells.

At last, the young man placed something down by the headstone and turned on his heel, walking away without looking back. When he had gone, the priest stepped up to take a closer look. There, next to the flowers, was a folded piece of writing paper, and Byrne picked it up.

The five words written there conveyed the same raw sense of regret as the look on the man's face had. He studied the writing with reverence and then carefully put it back.

I'll come back for you.

FOURTEEN

You have to understand that history is not a just matter of dates and of places, of dusty old names in textbooks and museum vaults; it is a matter of choice, for every one of us.

Every decision we make sends a ripple of probability racing away from us, a wake of "what might have been" and "could have happened" veering away from our path, like jagged cracks in the snow pack before an icebreaker. Everyone looks back on their life at one time and asks, "What if I had been here instead of there, if I had bet on red instead of black?" You play with these thoughts until you tire of them, but there are some thinkers who claim that for every choice we make, the ones we don't choose break off into their own history, isolated but somehow parallel to ours. I'm not sure what to make of that. If every decision you make is played out somewhere, does anything you do really matter? You could go crazy trying to answer that question.

What I do know, what I am sure of, is that choice breeds life—and often, death. I used to wonder what I would have done if I hadn't had the journals, if I hadn't had this accursed talent. Would Kayleigh have lived? Would we have found some semblance of a life together, or would my world have slowly crumbled without her in it? If there are answers to these questions, I don't want them; not any more.

There's a line in a William Shakespeare play—I forget which one it is—where someone says, "Time shall unfold what plighted cunning hides." That turn of phrase has always spoken to me; meshed in those words are meanings that can play both ways, but had I heard it after Kayleigh's suicide I probably would have read it as an encouragement to do what I was going to do. The reality is, those words are not meant to comfort. They are meant as a warning.

I have to take a pause for a moment here to contain my feelings about what took place on that day. Looking back from where I stand now, with all the scars and the dreadful experiences that my arrogance brought me, I cannot imagine any other decision in my life made more wrongly than that one. How could I possibly have had the stupidity to think that I would be able to bend history to my own will? Causality, time, fate or whatever the hell you want to call it, it flows downhill like a raging river, from birth to death, from the Big Bang toward Entropy. I thought that perhaps I could step out of the stream, wander back down the bank and try to change the course of it to fit my choosing—but if you dam a river, eventually it will overflow, eventually it will flood, and woe betide anyone who has built their house upon the reclaimed ground below it.

I did this: I turned away the passage of the past and sent it in a new direction, convinced that history would accept my alterations and rumble on, unconcerned. And for a time, it did. For a time, I cut myself a perfect little world, an ox-bow lake on the river—but I pushed the past, and the past pushed back.

And it pushed. And it pushed.

This, then, was the moment when things began to fall apart, and by the time I realized that I was on the same downward spiral as my father, I was so far over the line I had crossed that I couldn't even see it any more.

You're asking yourself now, "Why did he do it? What drove him to such recklessness?" The answer to those questions is as clear as glass, and although it shames me to say it, if I had that choice again now, even knowing what I would wreak, I am sure that I would take that road once more. God forgive me.

Why did I do it? Why risk everything, not just my future, but those of everyone I had ever known? Why?

Because I loved her.

Thumper had wisely opted to find somewhere else to be that day, so Evan had returned from

Kayleigh's burial to find the room empty. He was
thankful for his friend's consideration. Thumper
was awkward and inept around situations such
as these, and although Evan had a lot of goodwill
towards the big Goth, there were times when he
needed his own space. The shirt he wore felt
constrictive and tight and it was a relief to get
out of it; tossing it into the laundry bin, Evan
caught a whiff of roses, the scent captured on the
sleeve, and fought down a roil of sadness. In the
mirror, his eyes strayed again to the cigarette
burn on his chest, and he resisted the temptation
to finger it. The healed wound lay there like a
perverse brand, or the scar from a tribal rite. For
a time, his mind turned on everything the burn
represented, on the dark possibilities of changing
the past.

In the muted silence of the dorm, Evan
watched the last rays of sunlight fade. On the
bed in front of him were all the journals, a
cardboard box full to the brim with them. He
had almost gone through with it—he had
picked up the container and walked to the
elevator. He had hit the call button, staring into
the middle distance and trying not to think too
hard about what he was going to do. At that
moment, Evan was ready to go to the furnace
in the basement and pitch the entirety of his
writings into the flames. Once they were ashes,
there would be nothing he could do and no
more harm that he could cause. He would not
be swayed from his course.

But then the elevator door opened on his floor and a pretty blonde girl was waiting in the car. She glanced up at him and for a heart-stopping second Evan thought she was Kayleigh.

"Hello," The girl gave him a questioning look. "Are you going down?"

"Sorry," Evan's voice seemed to come from very far away. "No." He walked back to the room, holding the box tightly to his chest.

And now, resting there in the half-dark, Evan made a choice.

Upending the box on to the blankets, he poured the books into a pile and began to sort through the journals, hunting for a certain volume. He found it close to the top; the cover bore a yellowing adhesive label that read "Age 7". It was the oldest one of them all. Taking up a pen, he thumbed through the dog-eared and ink-stained pages until he found the entry he wanted. Evan then began to write a stream of fresh wording, cramming it sideways into the thin margins. The compact, intense text of his writing contrasted sharply with the careful, bookish hand of his younger years.

It's been said that a person's life is little more than the sum of his experiences, he wrote, his thoughts moving freely on to the paper. *If that's true, then I'm not sure I really know who I am anymore*. Evan blinked back a surge of sorrow. I definitely never knew Kayleigh.

He finished there and turned over the page, his eyes darting to the paragraph he had marked earlier. Taking a deep breath, Evan began to read the entry, silently mouthing the words to himself.

The pressure inside his skull came once more, folding out of nowhere like a thunderhead forming from a clear sky; but now it was familiar to him, and Evan tried not to struggle against it. Like a swimmer at sea, he let the motion of the waves take him where they wanted to go. His head lolled forward as he forced himself to relax and just let it happen. He felt the distortion radiating outward, as if he were at the center of a ring of ripples, expanding and warping everything around him. The room began to vibrate and blur, and from nowhere a peculiar resonance of an older man's voice filled his hearing. He could feel it coming now, the shuddering disconnection from the present and the merging into the past. Evan's world jarred—

And shifted, drifting like oil moving over water.

In the bright atrium of the living room, George Miller glanced out from behind his new video camera and shot his complaining son Tommy an acid look.

"Shut up, moron." he grated. He turned back to Evan and his daughter Kayleigh, watching the two kids giggle and smile at one another. "Now, get in your costume, Evan. And you have to promise, your bestest super-duper promise, that this will be our little secret." With a slurp, Mr

Miller drained his glass of Scotch. "Think you can do that?"

Evan shifted, unsteady on his feet, as if he were out of practice walking on them. The boy nodded slowly and began to strip out of his clothes in a clumsy, uncoordinated fashion.

Mr Miller rewarded himself with a secret, predatory smirk as he put aside the tumbler, snatching a peek at Evan as he undressed. "Hey kids, you know what?" he said in a falsely genial manner. "I've got a great idea. Let's go downstairs into the basement. It'll look more like a dungeon down there."

Kayleigh clapped her hands and grinned. "That'll be cool! Just like a real castle!" She seemed unaware of Evan's sudden change in manner, the seven year-old boy's smiling face now sullen and muted.

Her father made a waving motion at them and followed the children down the stairs with his camera gear. Kayleigh danced around in little twirls that made her costume dress billow out. "I am Maid Marian," she announced, in a regal voice.

Mr Miller had Evan unfold a pair of dusty lawn chairs and place them in front of the tripod as he remounted the bulky camera. "Okay, here we go..." he said. "You two sit down here and—"

A creak from the staircase made him jerk around. "What are you doing up there?" he snapped. At the door to the basement, Tommy was watching them with hooded eyes. "What did I say about keeping that door closed, stupid?"

Tommy made a face of childish petulance. "But I wanna see!"

"You're gonna see my fist in about two seconds unless you do what I tell you!" grated his father. "Now get lost and close the damn door!"

"I don't wanna be in any stupid film anyway." His lip curling in a sulk, Tommy slammed the door shut. Mr Miller watched it for a second to be sure the boy had left, then he turned back to Kayleigh and Evan.

"Okay, actors, are we ready?" Mr Miller's voice was conspiratorial and chatty. "Now, in this part of the story, Robin Hood just got married to Maid Marian and they have to kiss and stuff, just like grown-ups do."

On the word "kiss", Kayleigh stifled a giggle and winked at Evan; the boy looked back at her father with a skeptical expression.

"So take your clothes off, Kayleigh," Miller added flatly.

The little girl's happy mood evaporated instantly and she looked at the floor. A blush began to rise in her cheeks. The video camera clicked into life as Mr Miller hit the record control. "And rolling!" he quipped. Evan kept silent, watching him steadily.

When Kayleigh didn't react straight away, Mr Miller let the angry tone he'd used to frighten off Tommy creep into his voice.

"Come on, it's just like when you take a bath. Don't make a big deal out of it." He glanced around the viewfinder, zooming out to frame both the kids. "You too, Evan," he added abruptly.

The basement fell quiet, save for an anguished rush of breathing from Kayleigh trembling lips and the whir of the video's porta-deck. "Let's go!" Mr Miller added.

Unnoticed by any of them, the basement door above silently came open, revealing a wide-eyed Tommy, his face rapt with mounting horror and perverse fascination.

Kayleigh's father was about to snap out another angry order when he caught Evan's eye; the boy's brow was furrowed with fury. Without any trace of hesitation or self-doubt, Evan walked behind Kayleigh and cupped his hands over her ears.

"What time is it?" Evan asked innocently.

Miller blinked in surprise; he wasn't used to snot-nosed little brats of seven disobeying him. "What time?" he repeated. "It's time for you to stand where the hell I told you to."

A smile crept on to the boy's lips and he gave a shake of the head. "That's the wrong answer, fuckbag." The swearword caught Mr Miller off-guard and his mouth dropped open. Evan continued in metered, even tones. "Let me tell you what this is. This is the very moment of your reckoning. In the next thirty seconds you're going to open one of two doors. The first door—

the wrong door—will forever traumatize your own flesh and blood."

Mr Miller's mouth worked but no sounds came out. He was completely unprepared for the surreal nature of the mature speech issuing out of Evan's childish mouth, and his gaze flicked around the room as if he were the butt of some sick joke, searching for an explanation. "What's happened to—" he blurted in stunned disbelief. "How are you doing that? Who told you to say those things? Did someone put you up to this?"

Evan continued, his voice rising. "What you do today will change your daughter from a beautiful child into an empty shell, whose only concept of trust was betrayed by her own sick, pedophile father." George Miller gasped at the damning words. "Ultimately, it will lead to her suicide." Evan gave him a hateful stare. "Nice work, daddy."

"Who—"Miller whispered, his throat suddenly dry and hoarse. "*Who are you?*" Suddenly he was very, very afraid of the child.

The boy removed his hands from Kayleigh's ears and made a dismissive gesture, as if Miller's question was beneath his notice. "Let's just say that you are being closely watched, George. Your other option is to get your porno off the rack and treat Kayleigh like…" Evan paused for effect. "Oh, let's say, like how a loving father should treat his daughter. Sound okay to you, papa?"

"Y-yes…" The reply was a strangled choke.

Evan's cold smile broadened. "Listen closely,

then, fuckbag. You screw up again and I swear I will flat out castrate you, you sorry son of a bitch."

George's hands closed protectively over his crotch and he nodded nervously.

"There's just one last thing." Evan leant down to whisper something in Kayleigh's ear. She looked away at the floor for a long moment, before raising her head to look her father in the eye. She shivered and glanced at Evan for support.

"Go on," he said, "Don't be afraid. Tell him."

His confidence brought a new boldness to her face and she turned back to George. "Don't you ever touch me again."

"I-I won't."

Kayleigh's newfound courage rose and she got up, gathering her costume dress. "I'm cold, and I'm putting on my clothes."

Evan grinned and beckoned Miller closer. "You know something, George? If you want to do some good, what you need to do is exercise some discipline on your son, Tommy, because that kid is one sadistic pup."

Hiding at the top the stairs, Tommy's face went white when Evan spoke his name and he recoiled, his fingers fumbling at the door. The boy grabbed at the first thing to hand—one of Kayleigh's dolls—and nervously began to twist the plastic head around and around.

Evan's viewpoint suddenly blurred and shivered—

* * *

He awoke in bed, a broad smile lining his face as he drew himself up from the aftermath of what had happened; but the smirk froze on his face as daggers of pain suddenly flashed into his head. This time it was different. Before, after the first two flashbacks, Evan had come to with a few lingering aches in his skull and a queasy sensation in his gut. This was far worse; now he felt like his brain was being pulled in two different directions. Behind his eyes was a maelstrom of sounds, colors and smells all shifting and merging into a storm of chaotic, broken memories. They trailed through his mind like film clips, one after another in blink-fast order.

Childish laughter as he pulls Kayleigh around the Kagan's yard in a little red wagon...The two of them playing in the ball pond at a family restaurant...Pushing her on a tire swing in the middle of a warm summer evening...

There was nothing he could do to stop it, to stem the sudden tide of flash-frame images and swirling recollections. Trapped inside a roller coaster of emotional feedback, Evan was deluged by a storm of memories that forced itself into his mind, ejecting all the history he had lived through for the past thirteen years.

Tommy glares at them, he turns to attack the teen in the movie theatre... A sudden spear of pain as a flaming sack lies in a junkyard, the stink of burnt hair and meat... Mom driving the truck away from the house, a rip of anguish leaving home behind... Then, love swelling as

Kayleigh leaps down from a Greyhound bus and she falls into his waiting arms... Mingled excitement and joy as he rides with her across the handlebars of his bike, passing his mother in the garden...

The effects of the changed events in the Miller's basement resonated out to the present like a shock wave. Evan saw Kayleigh in his mind's eye with the same brilliant smile he'd always loved, but now she was different, carefree and happy without a trace of the self-conscious insecurity that had always colored her.

A picnic on a rowboat, the sun splashing across a perfect day... Her lips on his as they embrace under New Year's fireworks... Kayleigh resplendent in her dress, watching the sunrise with him after the Senior Prom...

It ended abruptly, the storm of memories breaking with a visceral impact that made Evan tense all over. He groaned in pain, every inch of his body cramped and alive with aches. His upper lip felt wet and he reached up to touch it. Blood was there, fresh and bright, streaming out of his nostrils in a broad fan.

He tried to rise and felt a sleepy arm tug at his shoulder.

"Evan?" came a drowsy woman's voice. "Honey, are you all right?"

With the snap of a switch, the room illuminated around Evan and his mouth dropped open in shock. The grimy little dorm room he shared with Thumper was gone. Instead, Evan was half-out of a bed decorated in pink and white, and around the walls were a mirrored cabinet, a hope chest and scores of other typically girlish trappings.

"Evan? What's wrong?"

His head turned to see who had spoken. Kayleigh stared back at him from the bed with alarm and concern. The sight of her transfixed him.

"Oh my God, Evan!" she gasped. "You're bleeding! Look at you!"

"Kayleigh," was all that he could manage. She was, without any doubt, the most beautiful thing he had ever seen.

FIFTEEN

"Am I dreaming?" Evan muttered. "I must be dreaming…" He was almost ready to believe it, too, but then Kayleigh's hand came up to touch his face and her fingertips traced over his lips with a thin scrap of tissue.

Her perfect blue eyes were colored with concern. "Oh, baby, are you okay?"

Evan blinked and got out of bed, still unsteady on his feet. "I gotta…" He lost his train of thought as he looked back at her, the soft glow of morning through the windows illuminating her as if she were some rare and delicate piece of porcelain. "Jesus, Kayleigh, you look incredible."

She purred and arched one flawless shoulder. "Mmmm, you give good compliment, handsome. Do you feel all right?"

"I… I guess so." Evan touched his upper lip; the nosebleed seemed to have stopped as quickly as it started.

"Good, then clean up and come back to bed." The glint in her eyes made no secret about what she wanted from him, and despite his strange circumstances, Evan let a chuckle bubble up from his chest.

He sat on the end of the bed and accepted another tissue from her to dab at his nose. Like almost everything else in the room, it was pink, matching the rest of the preppy décor from the sorority plaques on the walls to the lace-edged pillows and beaded lampshade. He caught sight of a plump plush teddy bear with its arms spread wide and the words "Evan Loves You This Much!" embroidered on its chest. There was a framed photograph of the two of them nearby, grinning into camera with the Statue of Liberty rising up over their shoulders.

Evan registered the rest of Kayleigh's bedroom in only the most peripheral sense of the word. He could barely stand to allow his eyes to stray from her, the flawless sculpture of her face, the gold cascade of her hair over the white sheets. This wasn't the Kayleigh that Evan had grown up with, dogged by her own imperfect confidence and continual self-doubt—this Kayleigh was all that she had aspired to be, poised and beautiful. The wounded, broken girl who had taken her own life was gone.

It worked, Evan told himself. My God, it actually worked!

He groped blindly behind the bed for his clothes and dragged up a crumpled sweatshirt. Evan's face creased in a frown as he unfolded it; it was a Greek-lettered top, the kind that those obnoxious

Theta dicks wore all the time, and under it lay an expensive-looking brown suede jacket. "Who does this belong to?" He cast around for his habitually worn T-shirt and jeans. "Where... where are my clothes?"

Kayleigh gave him a grin. "In your hands? Those are your clothes, silly."

Evan gave the sweatshirt a distasteful look and picked up a towel instead, straightening his boxer shorts as he ambled towards the bathroom. Bathroom, part of his mind asked? But I've never seen this place before—how the hell do I know where it is? The question seemed to nudge the last remaining licks of pain in his head and he shied away from trying to formulate an answer. Thinking about it too hard seemed to make his head hurt. It was all too much for him to take in at once. Evan decided to just roll with it for the time being and see where this changed world would take him.

At the sink, he washed off the blood from his face and took a good look at himself in the mirror. The haunted, drawn expression he always saw reflected back there was gone. Evan smiled again; he looked happier—hell, he looked better all over. "This is just too amazing," he said aloud. "This is un-fucking-real!"

A hissing shower in the glass stall nearby cut out with a spatter of droplets and a girl responded. "I wish I could get so excited about a nosebleed." Evan turned to see an athletic brunette step out of the shower. She was naked, and she didn't seem even the slightest bit embarrassed about letting Evan look at all of her.

"Whoops!" He turned away. "Sorry! My bad..." He blushed and turned back to his reflection—but rather than step out of his line of sight, the girl stood right where he could see her and began to dry herself, flashing him a series of flirtatious looks.

Evan suddenly realized that he knew her. She was in one of his classes, and she'd been at Dirty Hank's that night Thumper and he had played pool. "Hey, you were with those assholes who threw popcorn at Thumper..."

"Who?" she asked. "That wide-load Goth loser? You know him? Since when did you hang out with the black trenchcoat crowd?"

A last, departing jolt of pain lanced through his temple as Evan searched for the memory of the incident; it was there, but it was hazy, like a faded photo in an aged family album. "And your name is... Gwen!" he finished.

Gwen wrapped the towel around herself with a bored look, aware that her vamping was not having the effect she wanted. "Seriously, Evan, if I were you, I would lay off the blow. It's making you into an idiot." Before he could react, she patted him on the backside and padded out of the bathroom.

Evan splashed his face with a handful of cold water, just to be sure that he was really, genuinely, actually awake. He shook his head incredulously. The day before, he'd woken up to the sound of

Thumper's industrial strength snoring and today he had woken up to find two naked girls in the same room with him. Things had definitely improved.

The fraternity sweatshirt and the jacket felt strange on Evan as he walked, with Kayleigh's arm around him, crossing from the sorority house and down to the college quad. She was wearing a flowing silky skirt that reminded him of her child-hood Maid Marian outfit and a red sweater that hugged her tightly. Evan was acutely aware of how many other guys' heads turned as she passed them by, and it raised ambivalent feelings in him. He loved that she looked so good, and that she was his girlfriend, but he also felt the sting of jeal-ousy. The men whose eyes lingered on her a little too long got a hard, steely glare from him.

"You know, I think Gwen may finally have given up on you," she chimed.

"Oh?" Evan said, clueless as to what she meant.

"Yeah, that 'just out of the shower' trick is her last-ditch tactic. I think she's upset you didn't try something."

He blushed. "Uh, look, I didn't know she was in there—"

Kayleigh laughed, and she made Evan grin when she did. "I know! Gwen always tries to land any guy I like—"

"Any guy you like?" Evan said with false seri-ousness. "Have there been many others before me, then?"

"Oh, lots," she said airily, slipping him a wink. "I use men up and wear them out, don't you know. I'm a very demanding woman."

"I see," he nodded. "I think you might just have met your match, though."

She halted and took his hand. "Is that so?" Her eyes sparkled. "And that would be you?"

"Yeah," Evan's voice lowered to a husky whisper. "You see, none of those other guys could ever love you as much as I do."

"I love you too," she said, and kissed him.

They broke off as someone called out Evan's name. The voice wasn't one he recognized, and he turned to see the source. A freshman sped past on a bicycle, waving. "Hey Evan!" he called. "Great game on Saturday, man! You gonna kick County's ass this year?"

"Uh, yeah!" Evan replied lamely. "Sure thing."

Kayleigh hugged him. "My hero. A genius and sports star. You're the big man on campus, Evan Treborn."

"Okay," he said carefully. "That's nice..."

Kayleigh began to talk about an upcoming test, making little moves with her hands to illustrate points as they walked. Evan tried his best to concentrate on her, but more people, students he'd never even seen before, were coming up and patting him on the back, waving as they passed or giving him friendly nods of acknowledgement. It seemed as if the whole world had taken on a different aura. Before today, everything in Evan's life had been underscored with grim reality, but now it seemed like a dark lens had been removed from his eyes and he was free to see things as they really were, bright, sharp and vibrant.

She tapped him hard on the shoulder. "Hey, Evan. Are you even listening to me?"

He grinned. "I'm sorry, angel. It's just…"

"Just what?"

He kissed her on the cheek. "It's just that I'm so damn lucky to have someone like you in my life."

She returned the smile. "You're still not bored with me after all these years?" she asked playfully. "Even though we've known each other since we were kids?"

"That could never happen." Evan shook his head, and then something in her words gave him pause. "Hey, uh, I don't want you to go freaking out on me over this, but do you remember when your dad first got his video camera?" The question raced out before he could stop it and Evan's body tensed, dread rising in him at the thought of upsetting Kayleigh all over again.

But she simply shrugged. "Well, I remember he had one…" She gave it a moment's thought. "But he, like, put it away after the first day. I don't think he could figure out how to work it. Why would that freak me out?"

Relief surged through him. "I dunno… I'm just being weird."

Kayleigh gave him a playful kick and then put on a butter-wouldn't-melt face, feigning innocence. "You're such a goofus. I'll see you tonight." She gave him a quick, intense kiss on the lips and walked away, waving to a group of other girls by the entrance.

Evan stood there for a second and just basked in the glory of the moment. "I," he announced to himself, "am the happiest son of a bitch on Earth."

He was so happy that he was completely unaware of the person who had been following him since he left the house with Kayleigh, and had no idea his every move was being watched.

The morning flashed by in a blur, and at first Evan felt well-disposed to the world—but by the afternoon, something began to nag at him, an irritating thought at the back of his mind that itched like a stuck splinter. Doodling on a piece of paper in study hall, he found himself drawing lines and whorls, musing on the ebb and flow of things and the abrupt changes in his life. He tried to shake it off, wave it away like some sort of bad smell in the air, but the tiny seed of a black mood threatened to grow into something larger.

I need to be sure, he told himself, and I need to know that everything is okay.

Someone thrust a leaflet in his face and he took it automatically. "What's this?"

"There's gonna be a memorial service tomorrow," said a girl. Evan recognized her as one of Thumper's many conquests—what was her name, Cricket?—and nodded. She looked little different than she had last time he saw her, except now her dark hair had bright blue tips. She continued: "For Heidi and Kristen? The ones who died?"

Evan blinked in shock and looked again at the poorly photocopied flyer. There were yearbook pictures of the two girls he and Thumper had picked up at Dirty Hank's that night, complimented by a block of tightly typed text. "Holy shit, someone murdered them?" he breathed.

"What?! Have you been in bed for the last week?" Cricket sneered. "It was all over the news. Some trucker picked them up at that crummy bar out on Route Fourteen and raped them. Slit their throats from ear to ear." She mimed the cut with callous relish. "They caught him, though, at some diner near Ridgewood."

"When?" Evan said. "Wh-what day?"

"Last Saturday night."

He shook his head, "No, that's not right. I was there, we took them home…"

Cricket gave him a cold look. "Are you stoned? Or is this some sick joke? You weren't there, you were at the basketball game with your frilly little girlfriend and the rest of your jock pals." She snatched the flyer back from him. "Forget it, I'm sorry I even spoke to you. Later, dickhead."

Evan didn't notice her leave, the tight knot of fear starting to unravel inside him. He tried to focus on Heidi and found that he couldn't quite do it. *If that has changed, then what else?* Snatching up his bag, he ran from the room and made for the payphones in the lobby.

For one nasty moment he thought he had no coins, but then his fingers closed around a lone quarter in his pocket and he thumbed it into the slot. Evan punched out his mother's telephone number and waited, his heart pounding in his ears as the ring tone throbbed out a steady rhythm.

"Come on, Mom," he fretted. "Be there!" It would be just his luck to have Kayleigh back in his world, but for everything else around him to be taken away.

The telephone pick-up clicked and he blurted out a question. "Mom?"

"Hi there," said her voice, hissy from the answering machine's recording. "Andrea,"

Then he heard himself say: "And Evan,"

"And Chuck," This one a warm male voice Evan had never heard before.

"Aren't here right now," they chorused. "You know what to do, so please leave a message."

"Uh, hello Mom," Evan began, knocked off guard by the recording, "and, uh, Chuck. I was just calling to say hi and well, call me." He replaced the handset and relief washed over him; at least that part of his life was still untouched. More or less.

Evan pulled up his sleeve to check the time. He had Professor Carter's class next period and he wanted to get there early, but the watch he usually wore was gone. His eyes narrowed. His mother had bought him an expensive diver's wristwatch when he turned sixteen and from then on not a day had gone by when he didn't wear it. But now as Evan tried to picture the brushed steel-strap and the blue face, he found the image of it ephemeral and ghostly, almost as if he'd never had it at all.

He looked up and a familiar face caught his eye. "Hey, Thumper! What time is it, man?"

The Goth paused and gave Evan a distasteful look. "Whasamatter, preppy? You lost your Rolex?"

"Huh?" Evan blinked. "Thumper, man, it's me. What's up?"

Thumper sneered in derision at him. "Fuck off, frat boy." Before he could say anything else, Thumper shouldered him out of the way and walked on, making a spitting sound at the back of his throat.

He doesn't even know me, Evan thought, as the clock tower in the quad struck one and signaled the end of lunch.

Evan entered the lecture hall at a run to see a line of other students picking pencils out of a box on Professor Carter's desk. He bounded down to the end of the queue, giving a couple of preoccupied nods to other guys who called out his name. Evan gave an involuntary shiver. At first, the idea of all these people knowing who he was had seemed cool, but now as the day wore on it began to seem invasive and creepy.

"Can I have your attention, ladies and gentlemen?" Carter announced from his desk. "Please, everyone remember: it's only two weeks until your science projects are due! I'm not going to allow any latecomers!"

Evan stepped up and took a pencil, leaning close to the teacher. "I still owe you an essay from last week. Is there any way I could get an extension?"

The professor gave him a measuring look, without any inkling of familiarity about it. "I'm sorry, and you are?"

His shoulders sank in disappointment. "Evan Treborn."

"I see. Well, welcome to the class, Mr Treborn. I'm glad that you decided to finally grace it with your presence. As for your question, the answer's no." He pointed at the chairs with a pen. "Now take a seat, the exam's about to begin."

"Exam?" he gulped, turning away to find a vacant chair. Evan sat heavily at a free seat just off the aisle. His butt had barely touched the cushion when an arm snaked around his neck and tightened.

"I gotcha, dickweed!" said a voice.

Evan twisted wildly in the grip, turning to go face-to-face with Hunter, the Theta that Thumper had doused with beer at Dirty Hank's—or at least, that's what had happened before things had changed.

"Leave me alone, asshole!" Evan snapped. "I didn't lay a hand on you, okay?"

Hunter released him and burst out laughing. "Evan, you're hysterical. Weird, but hysterical."

He gave him a meaty slap on the back. "You study for this crap, buddy?"

Evan looked down at the test paper before him. "I guess we'll find out soon enough," he said awkwardly.

"Nah, me neither!" Hunter snorted.

He opened the exam to the first page and began to read. The subject matter was still Psychology 101 but the set up was completely different from what Carter was—or had been—teaching. Evan floundered, flipping through the questions to find something he could answer and came up empty. "I'm screwed," he whispered.

"Not quite," said Hunter. "I gotcha a little something." The jock reached into an inner pocket of his fraternity jacket and removed a folded page of paper. "Here ya go. Never say your old buddy Hunter lets you down."

Evan smoothed the page out before him. It was a hastily made copy of the scoring matrix used by the college examination board. "You've got to be kidding me. Are these the answers?"

Hunter made a shushing gesture as Evan's words attracted the attention of some other students. "Damn, Evan. Keep it on the DL. Carter finds out about this and we'll get busted."

Despite himself, Evan let a grin of relief appear on his face. "Wow, thanks, man." He concealed the paper under his desk and set to work skipping through the answers. After a moment, he gave Hunter a look. "Hey, uh, buddy," he began.

"I want to do something really special for Kayleigh tomorrow night."

Hunter nodded appreciatively. "Oh yeah. She's a fine piece of ass, that one."

Evan ignored the comment. "So, if I said I needed some help from you and the rest of my fraternal brothers—"

"I'd say blow me," Hunter broke in. "Unless she got friends for all of us, you can get the damn pledges to do it."

"Pledges," Evan repeated. "Right." He'd never been all that clued up on the workings of the whole fraternity thing, but he'd seen *Animal House* and *Revenge of the Nerds*, and he had a rough idea of the basics. The pledges were just the wannabe frat boys, the lowest rungs on the collegiate ladder and thus open to use and abuse by seniors like himself and Hunter.

"Come on, man," Hunter added. "Let's ace this thing and get outta here."

Evan nodded and set to work. He'd be able to cut through the exam in half the time and get to Kayleigh that much earlier. And she is all that really matters, right, he told himself, shuttering away the doubts and fears in his mind with a near-physical effort.

SIXTEEN

That night Evan and Kayleigh made love with all the passion and desire of two newly found soulmates. As they moved together and he felt Kayleigh's supple, flawless body against his own, Evan found himself lost in her, his whole world drawing in to just the two of them. She filled his sensorial state with the soft caress of her skin, the indefinable scent of her hair and the pulse of her heart in his ears. Finally, they lay curved around one another, and Evan coiled his arms over her chest. He wanted to envelop Kayleigh and protect her, to keep her shielded from all the darkness beyond them. There, in the afterglow, Evan floated in absolute peace.

Breathless from lovemaking, Kayleigh turned away from him for a moment to give a lengthy sigh. A satisfied smile played over her lips. "Oh my God, that was good," she husked. "You are full of surprises. Where did you learn all those new tricks?"

He fumbled for an answer. "I, uh, read the Kama Sutra one time…" Evan watched her; the sense of discomfort he'd felt earlier in the day was returning to him now. "So it didn't feel weird?"

She sniggered. "Yeah, if you call multiple orgasms weird." Kayleigh snuggled in to him tightly, her affection as bright as her smile.

Evan wanted to feel calmed by her closeness, but his somber mood threatened to engulf him and it hovered at the edges of his awareness. The telephone on Kayleigh's bedside table rang once and Evan answered it without thinking.

"Y'ellow," he drawled. There was dead silence on the other end of the line and Evan listened carefully for any sound of breathing. "Hello? Anyone there? Who is this?"

Kayleigh shrugged. "Fuck 'em."

Evan smiled and nodded his agreement, replacing the handset. "What the hell was that all about?"

"Probably one of Gwen's toy-boys on the prowl for her. She's got a million of 'em, you know."

"Uh-huh," he said, and added with mock gravity: "Poor girl. She doesn't have the same fabulous relationship that we do…"

Kayleigh made a wordless, cozy noise of agreement.

"What do you think it is about us that makes us so perfect together?" Evan went on. "Do you ever wonder?"

"Not really," she murmured. "We just are."

"Like, looking back to when we were teenagers, what ever gave you the nerve to sneak out and visit me after I moved away?"

Kayleigh gave him an amused glance. "Sure, as if my Dad could have stopped me from seeing you. What was he going to do to me?" She threw off the suggestion like it was the most ridiculous notion she'd ever heard.

Evan took this in without comment and hugged her a little tighter to his chest. "You think we'll always be together then?"

She drew away and gave him a curious look. "That is the plan, right?" she said with a tinge of concern. "The two of us together, come Hell or high water? That's what we've always talked about."

There was nothing else she could have said that would have made Evan feel any better than he did right then, and, for the moment, his black mood receded. "I was just making sure."

Kayleigh smirked. "Good. Then come here and give me some sugar."

The sorority house dated all the way back to the 1950s and it had been built in gentler, less paranoid times. The northern corner of the building adjoined the far edge of the college quad, but the opposite side faced a road dotted with tall, broadly spread trees. The canopy was thick and lush by the summer months, and like it was now, the heavy branches full of leaves would sometimes crowd out the street lamps on the sidewalk. It was an ongoing bone of contention between the student body and the town council, with each claiming that the other should foot the bill to have the trees trimmed—but so far, nothing had been done. As a result, when night fell there were patches of street where shadows were deep and black as ink, and, by another fluke of poor civil planning, the telephone booth a few hundred feet down the way sat squarely in the middle of a lightless area.

The lamp inside the booth had been broken for a long time, and most of the glass was clouded with obscene graffiti from rival fraternities. For a casual outside observer to spot anyone standing inside it, they would have needed a night vision lens. The figure in the phone booth rested one hand on the receiver and another on the dirty glass pane. For this vantage point, the sorority house was clearly visible, with the soft glow of light flickering downstairs as someone watched television, and the occasional spill of illumination from an upper window. Kayleigh's room was one of those that faced the road, and its sole window was a dark rectangle. The fingers around the payphone handset tensed, as the watcher considered calling the number again; but no. It made no sense to warn them any further. It had been a mistake to call her number the first time. Yes, now was the time to plan a little payback.

A few minutes later, the headlights of a passing car threw bright white light on to the dark, empty interior of the phone booth.

Evan sat cross-legged on the lawn chair and fanned himself with a sheaf of photocopied paper, watching a gang of junior pledges dart about the unkempt yard picking up broken beer bottles, pizza boxes and other sundry items of garbage. He gave them all a pitying look. Each one of them was in some sort of disarray or another, their clothes covered in flecks of dirt, crusted pieces of food and what might have been vomit. One particularly gangly fellow had been labeled "Miss Theta" by Hunter and was forced to wear a threadbare evening dress, a ginger wig and a plastic tiara. Evan shook his head ruefully as they scampered to and fro. He found it hard to understand how anyone could be willing to undergo the kind of pointless ridicule and moronic hazing that was required to join a fraternity—all that crap they had to take just so they could learn a stupid secret handshake and join a boy's club full of beer-swilling assholes. He smirked. At least if he'd had to go through all this, it had happened to some other Evan and not him.

He took a deep breath and yelled at them: "Hey! Quit that! Drop whatever the hell you are doing and get your worthless butts over here!" Evan tried to sound like an army drill sergeant, but he was hard-pressed to keep from laughing at them.

The pledges did as they were ordered and clustered around him. "Hail, hail, Theta Chi—"
began the guy in the dress, in a half-hearted bari-
tone.

Evan snatched up a wooden spoon from where
it lay on the grass and waved him into silence, like
an orchestral conductor. "Shut up, dingus. I'm
talking here." He banged the spoon on a metal
salad bowl that one of the other hapless pledges
wore like a hat. "Order, order!" he demanded.
"Here, each of you take one of these and read it."
Evan handed out the pages to each of them.

Miss Theta studied the paper with intensity.
"This is our next task?"

Evan nodded. "That's right. So, do all of you
rushees know what you've got to do for me?"

Salad Bowl Hat raised a questioning hand.
"Uh, we're 'pledges', Sir Brother Evan Sir, not
rushees."

"Pledges, rushees, same difference," Evan said
airily. "Now pay attention, because this is a one
time deal. You do all this," he stabbed at the
paper with the spoon, "and I'll never give you
shit again. I promise."

"On your honor?" said Salad Bowl.

Evan theatrically put his hand on his heart. "I
swear on my honor as a Brother of Theta Chi
Whatever. Have we got a deal?"

A ripple of excitement ran through the pledges
and Evan was rewarded with a sea of nods.

"But where are we gonna get these outfits?"
Salad Bowl whined.

"Anything's better than this flea-ridden thing," Miss Theta shot back, pulling at his dress. "I'm in."

"What are you all dolled up for?" Gwen said sourly, as she applied a liberal layer of hot wax to her leg. "Is Mr Wonderful taking you out for a cheeseburger?"

Kayleigh blew a raspberry at her roommate and finished pulling up the zipper on the back of her dress. She gave an experimental twirl, watching herself in the full-length mirror. "Does my butt look big in this?" she asked.

Gwen snorted. "Kayleigh, honey, your butt wouldn't look big if you stuffed a beach tire in the back of your panties. I hate that about you, you're so damn toned."

"Plenty of sex, that's the key," Kayleigh retorted.

"Please!" Gwen threw up her hands. "It's bad enough having to listen to the two of you every night." She faked a breathless falsetto: "Oh, Evan, take me now…"

Kayleigh threw a cushion at her and the two girls broke up into raucous laughter. "So what about you and Hunter?" she asked. "Or is that off-book now?"

"Way off," said Gwen. "He's handsome and all, but he's as dumb as a brick and his idea of being gentlemanly is to uncap beer bottles with his teeth."

"A real charmer."

"Yeah…" Gwen tore the wax strip off her leg and swore explosively. After a moment, she gave Kayleigh a more serious look. "You know Evan really loves you, don't you? The guy is absolutely crazy about you."

Kayleigh took this in with a smile. "I know."

"So what's bothering you, then?" Gwen asked. "I know something's up. Come on, spill. He'll be here any minute."

The smile on Kayleigh's face became brittle. "It's just… I don't really know how to explain it, you know, but something about him has changed…"

"In a bad way?"

She shook her head. "Well, no, but I'm not sure—"

Kayleigh never got to finish the sentence, as a jaunty knock-knock reverberated off the door. "Paging Miss Kayleigh Miller," Evan's voice issued out. "Your gentleman caller has arrived."

Gwen flashed her a big grin. "Go on, then. Don't keep him waiting. He's in a house full of girls, and you know men and their short attention spans."

Kayleigh pushed aside her concerns and opened the door. Evan stood there, smartly turned out in a dinner jacket and a black bow tie. "Wow!" she grinned. "You look like James Bond."

Evan waggled his eyebrows and faked a Sean Connery accent. "Thish way if you pleash, Mish Moneypenny."

She wasn't sure what to expect, and as Evan led her out of the house she wondered if there would be a limousine waiting to whisk them off to some high class restaurant uptown; but instead he took her hand and walked her down the street, towards the Theta's building. He refused to be drawn on what he had planned, and after a couple of attempts to get him to open up, Kayleigh realized he wasn't going to say a word.

They walked through the entrance of the fraternity house and up the stairs. For a second she thought he was taking her to his room, but they wandered right past it and up the next flight to the attic hall.

"Are you going to tell me what this is all about?"

"Keep up now," he said with a smile.

"I don't understand, where are you taking me?"

Evan threw her a wink. "You'll see. Trust me, you're going to love it."

They came to a wooden door in the arched roof and he opened it with a flourish, gesturing for her to step through. "After you, my dear."

Kayleigh stepped out on to the roof and her hand came to her mouth in surprise. "Oh my!" she breathed.

The entire roof of the house had been painstakingly decorated with strings of softly blinking fairy lights, the bulbous forms of paper Chinese lanterns and what must have been hundreds of

candles. The set-piece of the display was an ele-
gant table with a dinner setting for two, and
either side of it stood two ranks of six young
guys in formal servant's dress. All of them stared
respectfully ahead, exuding an air of utmost
class.

Evan gave the nearest one of the pledges a nod
and he snapped his fingers; two more immedi-
ately pulled out their chairs for them. "Sir,
madam," said the tall teenager—who looked
much better in men's clothes—"if you'll come
with me, your table is ready."

Kayleigh clapped her hands and laughed with
delight. "I don't know what to say. It's beautiful."

"Go on, sit down," Evan said.

She took a step toward the table and from out
of nowhere a shower of rose petals began to fall
around her. Kayleigh looked up to see two more
elegantly-dressed pledges on step-ladders, tossing delicate handfuls of petals into the evening
air.

She sat, overwhelmed by Evan's intricate
romantic gesture. "Why are you doing all this for
me?"

Evan took the other chair and gave her a warm
smile. "It's a question of simple math," he
replied. "When I woke up this morning and I
saw you smile at me... I knew right then that I
wanted to spend the rest of my life with you."

Their hands met over the table and Kayleigh
gripped his with fierce longing. She tried to

find some way to spell out how she felt but mere words failed her. Evan seemed to know this and he read in her eyes what she felt in her heart.

The air tingled with the electricity of the moment and Kayleigh felt her spirit rise out of herself, buoyed up into the starlit sky above. They leaned in to one another for a kiss, the instant so timeless and perfect that it could have been their first.

But in the next second the pure, frozen perfection of it shattered as someone crashed madly up the attic staircase and barreled on to the roof.

Evan got to his feet, a pained retort on his lips as Hunter and Kevin, one of the other senior brothers, gate-crashed his romantic evening. The look on their faces was enough to warrant a pause. "You better have a damn good reason for this."

"Evan!" Hunter snapped between breaths. "We been lookin' all over for you, man!"

"It's your car, dude," said Kevin. "Someone trashed your car."

The moment between them gone, Evan and Kayleigh exchanged worried looks. "Where?" Evan growled.

With Hunter leading the way, Evan raced after him, Kayleigh struggling along on high heels, trying to keep up. Charging over the fraternity house's front lawn, they dashed down the hill to where Evan had parked his weather-beaten

Honda. His previous cheerfulness suddenly collapsed into one of seriousness and confusion.

"Shit," he breathed. "What the hell is this?"

The car had been ruined in a very careful and considered act of vandalism. The Honda was surrounded by a halo of broken glass, each window smashed in and the wing mirrors both shattered into pieces. The wheels sat low on the ground where all four tires had been viciously slashed into chunks of torn rubber, and the seats sported clumps of foam peeking out from cuts across every surface. The hood was on the road beside the car and Evan could see that every lead or connector on the engine had been severed. The steering wheel sat on the roof, bent into an oval. Liquid pooled on the asphalt where oil and brake fluid were spilling from split pipes.

He peered inside. The dashboard instruments and the radio were a mess of wires and smashed components. Something caught his eye and he reached in to snag it. Like some insane ornament, dangling there from the cracked rearview mirror was a spiked leather dog collar. It was brand new, and Evan felt his gorge rise as he turned it over to read the word engraved on the nametag. "Crockett," he whispered.

He whirled around; a crowd of people was gathering to see what was causing all the commotion, other students spilling out of their houses to come and take a look.

Evan turned on the closest one of them, a fat guy in a hockey jersey. "Did you see who did this? Did you see anyone?"

The fat guy threw up his hands. "Not me, man." Evan's eyes ranged over the spectators, but drew nothing more than shrugs from any of them.

Hunter spat on the curb in barely controlled anger. "You know who I think it was? I reckon it was probably them Pika fuckers. We ought to step up and kick their asses right now!"

Kayleigh took the dog collar from Evan's rigid fingers and looked at it with a mounting sense of horror. "Oh no," she breathed. "It's not him, it can't be…"

"Who else?" Evan grated, stepping closer to her and lowered his voice to an angry hissed. "Who else even knows that I had a dog called Crockett? Tommy did this!" He flashed a look back at the ruined vehicle. "Your psychotic big brother sneaked right on to campus and tore apart my goddamned car!"

She stared at the leather collar in fear, and then her eyes darted around the scene, scanning over the faces of the onlookers. "Evan," she warned, "I think he might still be here—"

Evan didn't hear her as he stepped away. "How could he get away with this?" he snapped at Hunter, "Was everybody in the street asleep? He trashed my car right in front of the goddamned frat house!"

Kevin jogged closer, and at his words, gave Evan an angry look. "What did you just say,

Treborn? Frat house? It's a fraternity, you prick! Hey man, would you call your country a 'cunt'?"

Evan waved off his vulgar, loutish comment with a sharp gesture and walked back to where Kayleigh stood fretting over the collar. Suddenly, the pointless, barbaric stupidity of it all made him want to rail at the world. "I've had enough of this," he told her. "Come on, let's get out of here." The girl shuddered, her bare shoulders trembling despite the warm air of the evening.

Evan took off his dinner jacket and went to put it around her, but Kayleigh stepped away as he approached, her face pinched with worry. "Don't," she said, glancing around nervously.

"What?" he asked, following her gaze around the street. "What is it?"

"He's probably watching," she said, with quiet anxiety.

"I don't care!" Evan snapped. "What? Do you think I'm going to let that asshole dictate the way we live our lives? Fuck him!"

But Kayleigh shied away from him and shook her head. "Please, Evan, can we just go? I don't want to stay here anymore. Just take me home."

Evan saw the defeated look in Kayleigh's eyes, and at once all the fight left him. "All right," he said, "but I need to go get something first. Just in case he is still hanging around."

SEVENTEEN

Evan led Kayleigh into his room in the Theta Chi fraternity house and shut the door hard, leaving Hunter and Kevin outside to chew over what plans they had to take revenge on the Pikas. Evan hadn't bothered trying to correct them; Hunter embraced any reason for a fight and this was just the excuse he'd been looking for to target the rival fraternity. If Tommy Miller was prowling around out there, Evan knew that Kayleigh's brother would be something he would have to deal with on his own.

Unbidden, all the old feelings towards Tommy burst to the surface, the hatred Evan felt for the cold-blooded murder of Crockett and the ruthless way he had bombed the Halpern's mailbox. He hated him with sudden, hot intensity for daring to turn up now, now when everything seemed to be going so right for him. Evan felt his hands tense into fists. His perfect life with Kayleigh would never be safe while Tommy was there to ruin it—all Evan wanted now was for Kayleigh's brother to be gone, by any means necessary.

He dropped to one knee and took a quick look under the bed; there was nothing there but a few discarded clothes and a box or two of his journals, no room for someone to lie under there in waiting for them.

"What are you doing?" Kayleigh asked.

Evan frowned. "Just checking." He locked the door as an afterthought, then moved to his desk and began rooting through the drawers.

"I never thought..." Kayleigh couldn't look him in the eyes. "It... it's my fault," she began. "I should have told you. He was released a few weeks ago, but I never would have thought he'd do something like this."

"Might have been nice to have some warning," he grunted. Evan's fingers closed around a stubby metal cylinder concealed underneath a dozen pairs of gym socks and he pulled it out. It was a canister of pepper spray, the high-intensity capsicum kind that police officers and security guards used. He studied it for a moment. "Huh. Like this is going to do any good. Maybe one of the frat guys has a gun I could use."

Kayleigh's eyes widened. "Please, Evan, don't even joke about that."

He glanced at her. "What makes you think I'm joking, Kayleigh? Or did you forget all about Tommy swearing that he wanted to kill me? After what he did to my car I think I'm well within my rights to defend myself."

"He wouldn't hurt you," she insisted. "He's just trying to scare you away from me."

"Yeah, right, tell that to Crockett." Evan gave the pepper spray can a shake; it was full. "Your brother's got a head full of bad wiring, Kayleigh. He burned my dog alive, he doused a dumb animal in lighter fluid and caught it alight just to make a point. That's not what someone does just to scare a person."

Her voice was hushed. "It's not his fault, Evan. You know how bad he had it when we were kids—"

"Stop making excuses for him!" Evan snapped, cutting her off in mid-sentence. "He may be your flesh and blood, but he's a mental case! And don't give me all this Oprah book-club bad upbringing shit, because you turned out fine."

"Things were different. My father never laid a hand on me," she said guiltily. "It's like the prick saved it all up for Tommy. He never stopped hounding him."

Evan's throat tightened as he remembered what he had said to George Miller in the basement. *If you want to do some good, what you need to do is exercise some discipline on your son, Tommy, because that kid is one sadistic pup.* A cold trickle of realization moved through him. What if it had been his fault? What if Evan's alteration of events on that day had led Miller down a different path, turning his abuse on Kayleigh's brother, molding Tommy into what he had become? The sudden possibility that Evan was just as responsible for Tommy's twisted behavior as he was for rescuing Kayleigh sat badly with him. He looked into Kayleigh's eyes and saw a pleading there, a desperate entreaty for compassion.

"Please, Evan," she begged. "He's sick. Don't hurt him. Just take me home."

He hesitated, contemplating her words. Anything else he might say could drive a wedge between them, and the last thing he wanted to do right now was force his girlfriend to choose between him and her brother. "Fine, then," he said after a moment. "We'll let the campus security deal with him."

Evan opened the door for her and followed Kayleigh out into the street, all the while keeping one hand close to the pepper spray jammed in his jacket pocket. If Tommy was out there, he would be ready for him.

They walked on into the evening. The night had seemed so open and welcoming a little earlier, but now it had turned threatening and oppressive, with each pool of shadow a place where Tommy could be hiding, ready to leap out and strike at them. Evan felt paranoid and tense, like the darkness itself was pressing in on him. He walked close by Kayleigh, ready to pull her to one side at a moment's notice—and he almost grabbed her when he caught a noise from the path up ahead—but relaxed when he realized it was a wayward student retching into the bushes, too drunk to stumble home to their dorm.

They crossed the college quad in silence, and as they passed under a lamp post she shot him a sideways glance.

"What?" he said flatly.

"Are you okay?" she asked.

Evan let out a soft snort. "Yeah, aside from having my car turned into a modern art sculpture and being wary of every shadow, I'm fine." A flicker of hurt crossed her face and he instantly regretted the flippant retort. "I'm sorry, Kayleigh. What do you mean?"

"I'm not talking about the car." It seemed like she was having difficulty finding the right words. "It's just… You've been acting kind of strange recently, you know?" Kayleigh recalled her earlier conversation with Gwen, the same vague sense of unease returning to her.

Evan kept his face neutral. "Strange?" he repeated. "Like how?"

Kayleigh's brow furrowed. "I don't know, it's just that you seem… different. You make weird jokes, your accent's changed, you don't even walk the same."

"I walk differently?" He gave a fake laugh and tried to brush her comments off. "I'm still the guy you've always known, Kayleigh." The words rang hollow as he said them. "I haven't changed." From Evan's point of view, he was telling the truth; it wasn't him that had changed, it was the rest of the world.

"I can't put my finger on it, but everything's a little bit off," she continued. "Even the dinner tonight. It was beautiful, but…"

Evan felt his chest tighten, afraid that he might lose her if he didn't head off this train of thought before it could continue. He took her hand and gave it a squeeze. "Look, I know that maybe I've been acting a little different lately, but it's just that…" Evan took a breath and told her the only honest truth that he could: "I don't want anything to happen to us. I want to be the best boyfriend I can, Kayleigh. I love you."

She returned a fragile smile. They reached the corner of the quad and turned, giving the poor sick guy a wide berth as he vomited explosively again. Evan and Kayleigh both instinctively averted their eyes from the drunk, but then Kayleigh did a double take and glanced back at the bent-over form of the ill student.

"Wait," she said, pointing at him. "Something's not right… That guy, isn't that your jacket he's wearing?"

"What?" said Evan, suddenly alert, turning to follow her direction. Instantly he saw what she meant. There was his brown suede coat, as clear as day on the back of the drunk. "But I left that in my car—"

The words were barely out of his mouth when the crouching form of the guy suddenly sprang to his feet, whirling around to face them both.

Kayleigh saw his face and went white with shock. "Tommy!"

"Surprise!" he said, with cold malice. "Miss me, sis?"

Evan's blood turned to ice at the sound of Tommy's name and for a second he stood frozen in fear, his hands rooted in his coat pockets, and his feet rigid and immobile.

Tommy shrugged off the suede jacket with a sneer and favored Evan with a hateful glare. He had changed a lot in the seven years since Evan had last seen him. He had grown taller and more menacing, and the lean cast to his face made him appear to be starved and dangerous. His hair was short and greasy, and the edges of tattoos peeked out along the collar of a camouflage T-shirt he wore under faded, oil-stained denims. But what hadn't changed at all about him was the thuggish spite in his eyes. Tommy let something angular and metallic drop out of his sleeve and into his right hand: a tire thumper—a small steel bat that truck drivers used on the wheels of their rigs. Tommy gave the club a threatening, experimental flick, making no secret of what he intended to do with it. "We're gonna have us a little class reunion," he growled.

"Leave us alone, you sick fuck!" Evan shouted, finding his voice. He stepped in front of Kayleigh, one hand gripping the pepper spray.

Tommy rolled his eyes; on anyone else, the gesture might have been comical. "Get this 'us' shit!" he grated. "As if I was gonna lay a hand on my own dear little sister. I wouldn't dream of it!"

Tommy spat into the bushes. "You've done nicely for yourself, Evan. I bet you think you're the big man now, huh, with your nice clothes, nice friends, nice life, not to mention you're fucking my sister." He gave her a leering appraisal. "She's not a bad piece of ass, if I do say so myself."

"Shut up, Tommy!" Kayleigh yelled. "Just shut up!"

He put on an overstated pout. "Aw, hey now, sis. That was a compliment." Tommy eyed Evan and made a few wide practice swings with the tire thumper; the heavy, bulbous head at the end of the bat made a low hum as it cut through the air.

"What the hell are you doing?" barked Evan, gaining enough confidence to take a step forward. "What do you want from me?"

Tommy gave a bitter chuckle. "What do I want, man? I want my seven fucking years back, you son of a bitch! I want to take it out of your ass in payback!" He angrily shook his head. "You play high school hero while I'm holed up in that stinking zoo for all of my teens, and then I come out to find this? It wasn't enough that the whole damn world loves you, but you had to take away the last person on Earth who didn't think I was a piece of shit!" Hatred and pain surged through his words.

"That's not how it is. No one thinks you're a piece of shit, Tommy..." Evan began, fighting to suppress the panic he felt.

Tommy snorted derisively. "Sure, right, Evan. I believe you just called me a 'sick fuck' a second ago."

"Listen, Tommy—" Whatever else Evan was going to say was lost as Kayleigh's brother suddenly surged forward with the tire thumper and brought the steel club over and down on him. The stubby bat hit him on the shoulder and he stumbled back. Evan's knees buckled under the shock of the impact and he went down, face-first into the grass.

"Stop it!" Kayleigh's shriek was thin and piercing, but it did nothing to halt her brother's assault.

Tommy looped the tire thumper around his hand and weighed it there for a second, considering where he was going to strike next. "You know what? I'm going to cave your pretty face in," he spat, "and then we'll see how handsome you are!" In a savage swing, Tommy brought the club down toward Evan's head.

Evan reacted and jerked aside from the blow, bringing up the pepper spray can. He squeezed the trigger button and a jet of searing liquid caught Tommy squarely in the face. Kayleigh's brother let out an incoherent bark of anger and reeled backward, clutching his free hand to his reddening face. Evan got to his feet, the pain singing through his shoulder blade, and circled Tommy, the spray canister held out at his attacker. Tommy blinked through streaming eyes and tried to rush Evan again, but this time he was ready. Evan sidestepped and hit him again with the spray.

"I'll kill you!" Tommy made a blind swing that sang past Kayleigh, and she screamed. He blundered forward like a charging bull, making fast motions with the tire thumper, flailing madly at the air in hopes of hitting Evan again.

Evan went on the offensive and charged into Tommy, as all the rage and anger that he'd held aside broke free and overtook him. Evan's vision hazed red. Suddenly, all he could hear was the blood rushing through his ears, the dying screeches of his dog, and the terrible, unending echo of the dynamite blast. Tommy was to blame for it all, and Evan hated him with every fiber of his being. He ripped the tire thumper out of Tommy's hand and emptied the pepper spray into Miller's open mouth, choking him on a near-lethal dosage.

"Evan, stop!" cried Kayleigh. "You're going to kill him!"

"He's a fucking maniac!" Evan bellowed. "I have to stop him from hurting anyone else!"

Tommy made a feeble, poorly directed punch at thin air and Evan replied with the steel bat, smacking him down with the blunt end. Thin vomit drooled out of Tommy's inflamed mouth and he coughed harshly.

Kayleigh grabbed at Evan's jacket, trying to pull him back, but he slipped from her fingers and planted a violent kick in Tommy's ribs. "Stop! Evan, stop it!"

"He ruined Lenny's life!" raged Evan, out of control and irate. "He killed Crockett!" He kicked him again. "He murdered that woman and her baby girl!" Ribs splintered under another blow. "And he's trying to kill me, Kayleigh! He's trying to fucking kill me!" Before he could even understand what it was he was doing, Evan had the metal club in his hand and brought it down on Tommy Miller's twitching, broken form with a horrific wet crunch of breaking bone.

A thin, final gasp of air escaped from Tommy's bloated lips and he lay still, eyes unblinking, open and clouded with tears.

A klaxon cut through the air and Evan turned to find the source. Kayleigh stood close to a Blue Light lamppost, her hand on the alarm switch box. The posts were dotted all over the college grounds, and setting one off would bring the campus security guards running in moments.

He looked back at Tommy's beaten, swollen and bloody face, and a new terror gripped him. The gore-stained tire thumper fell from Evan's fingers to the grass, and the inhuman, uncontrollable rage that had blinded him ebbed away, draining from his body in a wake of agony and burning tension.

Kayleigh ran back to her brother's still form and stumbled to a halt as she laid eyes on what damage Evan had wrought. He took a step toward her, tears of sorrow streaking down his face, but Kayleigh backed away, her hands

coming up to hold him at bay. "No!" she
screamed. "Stay away from me! Don't touch me!"

"Kay-Kayleigh?" Evan tried to speak but words
failed him. He felt like he was being torn apart, as
if his heart were ripping itself asunder inside his
chest. I didn't mean to. Didn't want to. Evan's
legs turned to water and he dropped to the
ground. He couldn't bring himself to look upon
Tommy's body, and instead he buried his face in
his hands and wept.

The wailing of the police sirens filled his ears
and Evan let the sound of them overwhelm him,
flattening out every other sensation. When they
picked him up and led him to the squad car, he
was only dimly aware of it, as if it were some far
off event happening to someone else. It was distant, faint and dreamlike.

A dream. It all had to be a nightmarish dream.

The bus skipped over a pothole in the road and
Evan's head jerked up on reflex. He leaned as
close to the window as he could get and tried to
make out something of the passing scenery
through the thick metal grille over the glass.

"Homesick already?" said the guard, with a
snide look. "Ain't that a pity?"

Evan looked away and found the guy in front of
him watching his expression with boredom. He
was a few years older than Evan, with a broken
pug nose and snake tattoos all over his exposed
neck. "Hey," he husked, leaning closer. "You got
any smokes, dude?"

Evan shook his head.

Snake shrugged. "I oughta give up anyhow." When Evan didn't respond straight away, he pressed on. "You look like you're new to the orange suit. What you in for?"

In spite of himself, Evan glanced down at the prison fatigues he wore, the scratchy denim overall dyed in dirty international orange. The words "State Correctional Department" were stenciled across the chest. "I killed a guy." Evan replied, finding a weak voice.

"Oh," said Snake with disinterest. "Just one?"

"What?" Evan's eyes narrowed.

"Did you like it?" the other prisoner said mildly, showing yellowed teeth.

Evan shrank back as much as the restraints on his seat would let him. "Fuck you, man, no."

Snake laughed. "Piece of advice for you, dude," he chuckled. "Don't be such an easy mark inside or else you'll end up in shreds."

He looked away, ignoring the other prisoners, and watched the thin slice of the world going by through the grill, clinging to it like it was a life preserver.

The events since that fateful night on campus were a blurry mess of images and dark, desolate emotions. There had been witnesses to the whole scene on the quad—a pair of sorority girls from the house across the street who had seen Evan take out his bottled-up anger on Tommy— and even without them there would have been no way for him to ever have escaped arrest for the murder. The local news station picked up on the story as a piece of juicy local scandal and ran with it, blazing the tale of the college sports hero turned killer across the television. Overnight. Evan was torn down and made a scapegoat by the faculty. He was going to be hung out to dry in order to save the reputation of the college, and almost all the other students stood up and closed ranks on him.

But Evan only cared about what one person thought of him. He did not see Kayleigh again until she had appeared on the witness stand at the hearing, and she had stared straight ahead across the courtroom, never once looking Evan in the eye. George Miller had been there that day, too, and he'd spat at Evan and cursed him for killing his son. Hunter and Kevin had stood up for him, for all the good that it had done, and even an impassioned delivery from Doctor Redfield citing the chances of hereditary mental problems had fallen on deaf ears. They wanted him in prison, and justice had been swift and harsh.

A whole rat's nest of things had been stirred up by the murder: connections were being made to Tommy's juvenile record and arrest, including the explosion at the Halpern house. Evan's distracted public defender had told him that the prosecution were looking to link the two cases together, attempting to prove that he had killed Tommy to keep him silent about what happened all those years earlier. His trial would begin in earnest in the next few months, but the conclusion was already pre-ordained. Evan's life seemed destined to end, like his father's, behind locked doors and barred windows.

The prison bus turned sharply off the main highway and rumbled through a perimeter gate, rocking the inmates from side to side. As the wire gate rolled closed behind them, Evan had to stifle a sob in his throat. In all his life, even on the day that his father had died in front of him, he had never felt so alone and so dispirited as he did at this moment.

The guard banged on the grill with his nightstick and waved it at them with barely concealed menace. "This is the end of the line, ladies," he sneered. "Welcome to your new home from home. The State hopes you enjoy your stay." The guard liked to say that at the end of every trip; it was a lame joke, but it made him laugh, especially if the cons got uppity and gave him the chance to swat one or two.

Evan looked forward and saw the arching metal doors of the prison proper as they yawned open; above them was a sign in dark blue letters: *Mavis Penitentiary*.

The bus lumbered in through the doors, and Evan shut his eyes as they slammed closed behind it, locking him off from the world.

EIGHTEEN

They did their absolute best at the prison to dehumanize Evan and the other convicts from the moment they stepped off the bus. In tiny, awkward baby steps, the ten of them were herded into the processing center, their ankle cuffs jangling and clicking together. Evan did his best to keep up, watching the way that Snake walked with the restraints, but a couple of times he misstepped and it earned him curses from the rest of the chain gang.

"See you around, fish." That was the last remark Snake made to him, and then they were split up, stripped naked and sent through stringent chemical showers. Evan's soft, city-boy skin went red under the harsh detergent soap and when he dressed in his new prison fatigue—a dark blue denim outfit a size too large for him—he felt like he'd been rubbed raw all over.

A bored guard peered owlishly at him from behind a pair of thick glasses and scrutinized his file. "Tree-born, Evan." He lingered over the name. "Your identity number is 1138. Take your bedding from the stores and get going. Cell 14, Block D, General Population."

Evan wasn't sure if he was supposed to answer, so he gave a sullen nod and gathered up the blankets that the quartermaster thrust at him. Along with a couple of other convicts from the bus, he was hustled through the corridors of the processing area and out past the exercise yard. Evan caught a glimpse of men in the middle of a rough basketball match before his attention was drawn to the guard towers. He saw more warders there, some of them cradling shotguns or rifles in deceptively lazy stances.

The door to Block D opened automatically, controlled by a switch located somewhere else in the building, and the guard made a sharp gesture for them to enter. The instant the three of them crossed into the hall beyond, a chorus of vicious taunts and catcalls began to rain down on them.

"Hey, hey! Pretty boy!"

"White fish! Gonna roll you in broken Coke bottles, man!"

"You wanna be my bitch, sweet cheeks?"

"New meat!"

The other two cons seemed to take this in their stride, and Evan desperately wanted to follow suit, but it was all he could do to hang on to what little composure he had. He felt like he had nothing to draw on now, no bravado, no strength.

Block D comprised of two facing walls of cells on three levels, lit from above by hanging florescent lamps and whatever faint sunshine made it through the dirty skylights. Every surface was painted concrete, except for the thick steel bars that formed one wall of each cell. At either end of the massive, echoing chamber were glassed-in observation rooms where warders sat watching the ball game or leafing through confiscated pornography. On the very highest level was a mesh catwalk where overseers could look down on the entire population of convicts.

Evan looked up and caught the eye of one of the men leaning over on the second tier. The inmate was a huge, muscular man with a shaven head; his jacket was open and the sleeves had been torn off, showing huge biceps and a barrel chest beneath. A cluster of other men, all of them white skinheads, was crowded around him. Evan could clearly see they all sported Klan symbols or swastikas tattooed across their bodies, along with scars and disfigurations they wore like battle honors. The big man blew Evan a kiss and winked at him, much to the amusement of the other skinheads. They watched him like eager predators as he walked out of sight.

"In here," said the guard and he pointed to an open cell door with his nightstick. "Hey, Carlos," he rapped on the bars. "Gotta new playmate for ya."

Evan swallowed hard and stepped into the dim interior. The smell of burnt shoe polish made him cough as he entered the tiny space. Cell 14, like all the others in Block D, sported a double bunk, a metal sink and toilet. All across the walls were pictures of Jesus Christ and various assorted saints, some of them hand-drawn on yellowed paper, others torn from the pages of books or magazines. None of them were the soft, kind-faced religious images that Evan remembered from childhood days at Sunday school—these were icons of pain and anguish that promised damnation and wrath to the unfaithful. Over the sink, cans of polish flickered with sooty flames as makeshift candles for a gloomy little shrine.

Evan's new cellmate looked up at him with a measuring gaze. Carlos was a Hispanic man in his mid-thirties with a worn, distant look in his eyes. He was broad across the shoulders and topless, allowing Evan to see the faded tattoos across his chest. Just like the skinhead's Nazi icons, the pictures drawn over Carlos's skin were "jail tats" done by other inmates with needles and Indian ink. Across his flesh was a representation of a crucified Jesus in agony. When he didn't speak, Evan took his cue and began to make up his bed on the stained bare mattress of the upper bunk.

Carlos kept up his disinterested stare. "First time in the joint?" he said at last.

Evan gave him a glum nod.

"You gonna find it hard." His cellmate looked away. "You'd best not bitch up. Wind up someone's luggage that way."

Evan felt lost and alone. "Can… can you protect me?" he said desperately, praying that Carlos might show him a shred of compassion, the grinning leers of the convicts still preying on his mind.

The big man shook his head. "Jesus himself couldn't make me take on the Brotherhood."

"Brotherhood?" Evan repeated. "Those skinheads?"

Carlos nodded. "That big fucker Karl is the boss. They're Nazis, you know. They like to play with the new meat. When they come, you just put your mind in another place, man. Be somewhere else."

Evan felt sick with fear and he closed his eyes, shutting out the accusing stares of all the saints.

A dull buzzer sounded through the hallway and Carlos got to his feet. He left the cell without another word, and Evan scrambled after him.

The prison cafeteria was a throng of men in blue denim fatigues, pushing and jostling one another along the chow line. Evan tried to keep in sight of Carlos and paid attention to the convict's movements, but other prisoners routinely shoved past him in the line-up, pushing him back and back along the line. Eventually, he managed to get to the server and his efforts were rewarded with a bowl of thin soup, a few flaccid vegetables and a hank of meat that had been boiled until it was gray. Evan's gut clenched but he took what he was given and made for a table. Carlos indicated an empty chair with the smallest of glances and Evan took the gesture like it was the most generous thing in the world.

He'd barely sat down when the rest of the inmates around him stabbed their forks into his food and stole almost everything from the tray. Each of them guarded their food jealously, like dogs gnawing at bones. Evan collapsed into the chair and toyed with the watery soup, glancing at Carlos. The convict gave him a non-committal shrug and offered him a gritty roll.

"Thanks." Evan accepted the bread and drained the soup bowl as quickly as he could, before he could have that nourishment taken from him as well. Amid the clatter of utensils and the rough murmur of conversation, Evan drew inward, silent and afraid.

Andrea came to see him a few days later. Evan's heart leapt when he saw his mother through the four-inch-thick Plexiglas wall—a barrier that prevented them from embracing. He sat at one of the alcoves and picked up one of the monitored handsets, his leg twitching with directionless, nervous energy. "Mom?" his voice quivered.

"Hey Evan," she began. He couldn't remember ever seeing her look so drawn and haggard. Her hair was the dirty straw color of a bottle-blonde and her skin was pale under the harsh lights. In her free hand she was twirling an unlit cigarette between her fingers, back and forth, back and forth.

"You started smoking again?" he asked; it was the first thing that popped into his mind.

Andrea eyed the No Smoking sign on the wall and gave a curt nod. "It's nothing. Not important," she sighed. "So, I wanted to tell you that I spoke to your new lawyer about the appeal. He says he's sure he can get you off on a self-defense verdict, so if you're patient—"

"How long will I be in here?" he broke in. Her words seemed to barely register. "This place is a nightmare."

She chewed her lip, a reflex Evan knew was shorthand for stalling. "I don't know," she said carefully. "These things take time."

He gave a weary nod. "How's Kayleigh doing? Is she all right?"

Andrea didn't need to say anything in reply—the sorrowful expression in his mother's eyes told Evan everything he needed to know—and that he would have to look for hope elsewhere. He smothered the emotions that Kayleigh's name stirred in him and continued. "You got my message, though? What about my journals, Mom? Did you bring the ones I asked for?"

She nodded and held up two of his composition books, one labeled "Age 7" and the other "Age 13". For the first time since he had entered the prison, Evan felt a flicker of hope. If he had the journals, there was a chance to change things. "Where are the rest?"

"I found these," Andrea said, "but the rest of them are still in storage—"

Evan's fist thudded on to the Plexiglas. "Damn it, Mom! I told you, I need them all!"

She flinched from his sudden angry snarl, and one of the guards raised an eyebrow at Evan's outburst. "Fine, fine," Andrea said, trying to mollify her son. "You'll get them, Evan, but it'll just take me a while. I think it's far more important to focus on your case right now..."

For a moment, Evan seemed like he was ready to argue the point and disagree, but then he closed his mouth and nodded slowly. "Sure, Mom. You're right, you're absolutely right. Just try to tell Kayleigh that I'm sorry."

Evan looked away and the warder signaled him, tapping an impatient finger on his wristwatch. He frowned; his time was almost up and he'd wasted it on fretting over the books. Evan looked back into his mother's eyes and saw the worry and the fear there, not just at seeing her son in prison but at the tiny, lurking possibility that he was following Jason Treborn's downward spiral into insanity. He wanted to promise her that everything would be fine, that he'd fix all the mistakes in his life—if only he had the journals!

"I'm not going to lose you, kiddo," she said, her voice catching. "Promise me you'll hang on, Ev."

"I will. I love you, Mom."

Andrea's eyes began to mist. "Love you too."

Evan slowly lowered the phone and replaced it, but his mother kept her handset pressed to her ear, as if she were waiting for some other message of hope.

He held the two journals to his chest like a drowning man would hang on to a raft. It was a fitting image, as Evan knew that there would be something in the books that would get him out of this shit hole, undo the damage he had done and reorder things. The journals could save his life. He just needed time and a quiet place.

Walking a few paces behind Carlos, Evan was so wrapped up in his own thoughts that he didn't notice the group of skinheads loitering in the shadows. One of them spat an insult at the Hispanic but the convict ignored him and walked on. From out of Evan's line of sight, Karl suddenly materialized and reached a meaty paw out in front of him. He clutched Evan's crotch in his palm and gave his genitals a hard squeeze.

The skinheads laughed in chorus as Evan turned white with rage. "Shit on my dick or blood on my knife," Karl hissed into his ear. "Your choice, pretty boy."

Evan stood rigid, stunned and unsure how to react. One of the other skinheads slapped at the books in his hands and sent them flying. Life sprang back into Evan and he rushed for the journals, desperate to grab them back. The thug caught the books at the same time and the two of them started a fierce tug-of-war, the covers tearing as they pulled in different directions.

"Get 'em, Rick!" snorted Karl. "Get the fucker's stuff!"

"Let go, they're mine!" Evan shouted.

"Let go, they're mine!" Rick mimicked him. "Not any more, shit weasel!"

Evan tried to hold to the journals without damaging them, but Rick could not have cared less and he swiped them from Evan's grip and tore them into pieces. His hands closed on a scant two or three pages in Rick's grasp and Evan's fury broke free. "Motherfucker!" he spat, and he sent a swing at the skinhead's grinning face.

Rick dodged the haymaker easily and threw a punch back, narrowly missing Evan's chin. Around the walls of Block D a cheer erupted as the inmates saw the fight begin.

"It's on!" yelled Karl. "Get the new meat, Ricky! Fuck him up!"

Rick lunged for Evan and the two men collided in the middle of the concrete footway, wrestling in a tight knot and trading short, blunt punches to the gut and the chest. The journals, forgotten in the melee, were trampled and split, pages fanning out across the floor.

The convicts' shouting reached a crescendo, but cut off suddenly as the sound of rifles cocking and shotguns pumping up rounds issued into the air. Rick and Evan released one another and looked up—on the upper gallery, a dozen wardens trained rifles on them, and more men in the observation rooms stood looking on with shotguns at the ready.

Evan froze in place, but Rick stepped quickly away. Before Evan could register what he was doing, the skinhead had scooped up the torn journals and walked off.

The adrenaline rush of the moment dissolved, leaving Evan shaky. Karl favored him with a callous grin. "We'll be comin' for you tonight, sister."

Evan caught his breath and looked down at the few scattered pages lying here and there on the floor. One by one, he gathered them all up and smoothed them out.

When he returned to the cell, Carlos gave him a rueful look. "You're some kinda fool to be crossing those loco skins. They gonna cut you, man."

"They had my books..." said Evan.

Carlos shook his head. "Books, man? You wanna take a shiv in the ribs just 'cos of some books? Maybe you gotta death wish or something."

He climbed up on to the upper bunk and began to leaf through the ragged sheaf of pages, searching for an entry that he might be able to use. "These are important to me." Evan's heart sank; there was nothing in the remnants he had that he could use.

"Ain't no book worth your life, esse."

He peered over the edge of the bunk. "What about your Bible? Would you have let them take that?" Evan tapped a finger on a worn photo of a little girl fixed to the bedstead. "Or how about this? Your daughter, right?"

The words hit home for the convict. Carlos said nothing for a long moment, then handed Evan a roll of duct tape. "Here. You wanna keep those papers you got, you better tape 'em up there."

Evan accepted the tape with a depressed nod and began to fix the pages to the ceiling above him, the writings of his seven year-old self giving him little comfort in the gloom of the cell.

Carlos broke the silence by removing the picture of the girl and holding it up to show Evan. "My little Gina," he said, and for the first time Evan saw the hint of a smile on the convict's face. "You're right. I would kill a man who tried to take this from me. It's all I got of her."

"She's pretty. Does she ever come visit you?"

He shook his head and returned the photo to its place. "Her mother, she won't see me. I was a car thief, see, but I got caught. Three strikes, man. My wife, she told me she didn't want her child growing up with a daddy in jail. She told Gina I was dead."

Evan felt a surge of sympathy. "I'm sorry."

Carlos gave a weary shrug. "At least I still got Jesus. And sometimes, that's almost enough."

He avoided Karl and his crew for the rest of the day until the inmates were ordered outside the cellblock and into the yard for afternoon exercise. Evan kept his eyes averted as he walked past the corner of Block D the white supremacists called their own, trying not to flinch when other convicts brushed past him. Every muscle in his body was wound tight and tensed for the inevitable attack.

As he passed, Karl stepped out from behind a pillar with one of Evan's journals in his hands. He read aloud from the book like a television evangelist quoting scripture. "Today I found my grandfather's death certificate. He died in a nut house, just like my father. Mom denies it, but she thinks I'm gonna end up the same way."

Rick brayed with laughter. "What a fuckin' nut job!" he called after Evan. "Hey freak! Hey psycho!" The other skinheads joined in and made chicken clucks as he rushed away from them.

Out in the yard, Evan found Carlos and sat next to him on the bleachers that bordered one end of the exercise area. Before them, a handful of inmates worked out on barbells, and close by Karl's skinheads hovered in a tight group, sizing up the other gangs in the yard and throwing cold stares at Evan.

As he watched them, Evan caught a glimpse of Rick passing something to Karl, a long object with a makeshift handle of white surgical tape. He looked around to see if any of the guards had noticed, but none of them were paying attention.

"I'm running out of time," he said, voicing his thoughts. "That bald bastard is going to put a shank in my back the first chance he gets."

"You better learn to stay awake all night, then." Carlos said, nursing the last inch of a cigarette.

Evan shook his head. "I gotta think. I can change this. I can use the pages that I have... I just have to figure out how."

Carlos gave him an arch look. "What are you saying? Those books of yours are gonna be worth nothing when you're dead, man. There's no way your little schoolboy diary is gonna get you out of shit with the Brotherhood, and if you reckon it will, you're as crazy as they said you are." The inmate turned his back toward Evan. The tormented figure of Jesus stared back at him from the middle of a hellish montage of punishment and pain.

Evan thought for a moment about the entries he'd been able to save and considered Carlos's words in the cell. "You're a religious man. You believe that bit about 'the Lord works in mysterious ways', right?"

He finished the cigarette and tossed the butt away. "Straight up."

"I ask you that because I think He sent me to your cell on purpose. I think the Lord wants you to help me."

Carlos shook his head. "Shit, I knew you were crazy."

"I ain't bullshitting," Evan said, leaning closer. "Jesus speaks to me in my dreams."

"Sure. Whatever." Carlos scoffed.

"A pack of smokes says I can prove it to you."

Something about the tone in Evan's voice made Carlos pause, and the convict found himself nodding, suddenly intrigued.

NINETEEN

Evan watched Carlos's eyes glaze over as he tried to explain how the flashbacks worked. He found himself using his hands to indicate places and times, but the more he got into it, the less his cellmate seemed to follow the logic. He stopped for a moment, and peeled one of the tattered pages off the ceiling of the cell and gripped it tightly. Carlos was the closest thing to an ally Evan had in the prison and if he started to tune him out, he might lose everything.

"Look, when I do this, it's like I'm in a trance, or something." He held up the paper for emphasis. "You see people do that in church, right?"

Carlos gave a slow nod. "Like the Rapture." He was still unconvinced, and only the lure of winning a carton of cigarettes was keeping him interested.

"So, when I'm out, I need you to watch my face and hands closely."

The other man studied him. "You know what I think? I think you need to see the prison shrink, man."

Evan gave an exasperated sigh; it was clear that Carlos would only accept proof that he could see.

Both men paused as the mail cart rolled past the open door of their cell and Evan was surprised to see Snake pushing it. "Hey," he said expectantly. "Anything today?" If his mother had managed to get some other journals to him, then his attempts to coerce Carlos could be forgotten; but Snake shot down that hope with a thin smile.

"Yep. Just not for you."

Evan didn't bother to mask the disappointment on his face, and he turned back to Carlos, holding the worn page firmly in his fist. "Look, will you do this for me? I need you to watch my back while I'm under... I don't want Karl slitting my throat while I'm out." When the convict didn't reply straight away, Evan tapped the unopened packet of smokes in his pocket. "Come on, man. What have you got to lose?"

"I guess. So what should I do?"

Evan rested himself against the wall and flattened out the paper on his lap. "Just tell me afterward, if anything weird happens."

"Weirder than this?" said Carlos, watching him doubtfully.

"There might be something on me, marks or scars, I dunno. Anything could happen, I guess. You ready?"

"Go on then," Carlos folded his arms. "Go talk to Jesus."

Evan swallowed hard and studied the page before him, silently reading the words written there in a labored child's hand. *On wensday I got in trouble for a drawing that I didn't do. Mommy won't let me see it.*

It came instantly now, easy and free; the pressing sensation across the inside of his skull, moving and vibrating with hollow echoed resonance. His vision fogged, and as it blurred and changed he saw the bars of the cell begin to deform and shiver. Carlos's face studied him with concern and then it too began to slip and alter, falling away from him. Evan heard the sound of children's voices, growing louder, filling his senses as his consciousness detached from his body and snapped back through the years. The cell trembled around him—

And it was gone, fading like a mirage.

Evan's head jerked like a poorly worked puppet's and he shook off the aftershock of the shift. He blinked, held up his hands before his face and he wiggled the little podgy fingers. "I'm here," he said aloud. His body felt strange, weak and shrunken.

"So am I!" said a child, and he glanced at the speaker. Kayleigh's seven year-old smile beamed at him from the next desk over.

He glanced around. Evan's first grade class was just as he had remembered it, the chattering hordes of kids all hard at work on sprawling pictures, some of them gluing pieces of paper together or sprinkling glitter over wet paste. He looked down at his own piece of construction paper that was blank save for a scribble of words at the bottom left corner of the page: *Evan Treborn, Age 7*.

"What… what are we drawing?" he asked, his words sounding strange in the high-pitched voice of a little boy.

Kayleigh worked at her paper and answered without looking up. "We gotta draw what we want to be when we grow up."

Evan nodded and looked back at the blank paper, wondering how he could turn this flashback into something that would help him in the future. For a brief second he considered writing a note, something explaining what would happen in thirteen years time but rejected the notion just as quickly. Sure, like anyone would take some little kid's wacko scribbling seriously…

The teacher wandered past, raising an eyebrow at him but said nothing. Evan watched her go. Boswell. That was her name, Mrs Boswell. He'd never really liked her as a child, but as he watched her circle the classroom, Evan found himself re-evaluating her with an adult's eyes—she was actually quite attractive, in an older woman, prim and proper kind of way.

He made a few experimental lines on the paper with a black crayon, then discarded it. Evan reached for a box of colored pencils, but another boy snatched at them first and he jerked back.

"I'm using these!" said the boy.

"Tommy?" Evan managed.

"What?" snapped Tommy Miller, giving him a combative stare. "Find your own pencils, Evan!"

His heart thumped in his chest as he looked at the child who would grow into the man he had killed, and Evan felt his stomach turn over. Tommy spilled the pencils out across the desk and started to draw, pausing to elbow Lenny Kagan when the portly kid crowded him a little. After a moment, Tommy glared at him.

"What? Why are you staring at me?"

"No-nothing," Evan said, tearing his eyes away. "It's nothing."

"If you copy my picture, I'll pound you!" he threatened.

Evan got up and stepped away from the desk, his mind a whirl. There had to be something he could do here, something he could do that would resonate through from now to the cell in the future. He shook his head. It was hard to try and keep it all in perspective, to manage all the shifts in time and place. He glanced at the teacher's desk and spotted a pair of paper spindles, the sharp metallic spikes pointed straight up skewering report cards and other paperwork.

Evan thought of the scar that had appeared from the cigarette burn before and studied the needle-bright spindles with serious intent. His small hands bunched and he took a step toward them.

Out of nowhere, a strong grip clamped around his shoulder. "No monkey business, Evan." said Mrs Boswell. "Sit still and finish your drawing." Firmly but gently, the teacher turned him around and steered him back to his chair. Feeling defeated, Evan let himself be pushed over to the desk; if he made a fuss or argued with her, he might lose any chance he might have to alter things.

Mrs Boswell handed him a new box of pencils and Evan took one at random. It was dark blue, the exact same shade as the denim fatigues at the prison.

"That's great, everyone!" the teacher called out. "Just imagine anything you want to be, there are no limits. Draw whatever you'd like to happen when you're older."

Evan twirled the pencil in his hand and with a sudden flash of inspiration, he started to rough out a sketch across the page. You want to see what future I want? he thought to himself? I'll show you what I want to happen.

A stark and uncompromising image began to emerge on the paper, forming into a representation of all the anger and hatred that Evan had stirred up in himself since he'd arrived at the prison. He drew Karl and Rick and their whole skinhead crew as dead and bloodied corpses, torn open and ruined by a vengeful depiction of himself. When he'd finished, he studied it with a cold smile of satisfaction. If only I could take this with me.

Evan grabbed the drawing and sneaked around to the front of his teacher's desk, catching her unawares. "Oh, Evan?" she blinked. "Are you finished already?" She took the paper from him and her face went white with horror.

Standing up on his tiptoes, Evan stretched to the full height his seven year-old self could attain and leaned over the front of the desk, where the paper spindles sat.

He gritted his teeth and called out to her in a musical voice. "Oh, Mrs Booossweeell?" Her shocked gaze met his just in time for him to slap his hands palms downward toward the sharp points of the two spikes.

"No!" she shrieked, the word drawing out into a long, echoing shudder of sound. Evan felt a millisecond of blinding sharp pain in his hands and then his vision went white—

Evan choked like a swimmer breaking the surface and jerked forward, banging his forehead off the metal frame of the bed with a dull ring. The noise of screaming children vanished from around him like the last fragments of dream, slipping between the cracks of wakefulness, gone like wisps of vapor. He became aware of his surroundings. He was still in the cell, still trapped in a dark, dismal present.

Carlos stared at him with wide eyes and new-found reverence. The convict crossed himself. "Oh sweet Jesus!" he breathed. "It's true… You weren't lying to me, it's a miracle. A true miracle!"

Evan blinked as the aftershock released him. "What? What did you say?"

"Your hands!" Carlos took his palms and turned them over. "You have the stigmata!" There, in the center of each of Evan's palms, were two circular scars. He turned them over. Identical marks were on the back of his hands too, where the spindles had pierced right though them.

"What did you see?" Evan asked. "What did it look like?"

Carlos laughed. "It was amazing, man! The signs of the Lord, they just appeared out of nowhere!" He shook his head. "I thought you were loco, but it's true! God really speaks to you!"

Part of Evan felt wrong about taking advantage of his cellmate's deeply held beliefs, but it was clear to him that if he didn't have Carlos on his side, any chance he had of surviving inside Mavis Penitentiary would quickly drop to zero. "So you believe me, then?"

"Amen," said the inmate, and handed Evan a packet of cigarettes.

He held up a hand to refuse them. "No, you keep them. You'll need them if you're going to help me."

Carlos nodded with absolute seriousness. "Anything, man. If Jesus works through you, then I'll do whatever you want!"

* * *

The last thing the members of the Brotherhood had expected to see was Evan. They'd been planning what to do with him for the past few hours, cooking up schemes and making heartless fun of how they would leave him busted and broken— if he was lucky. Karl had entertained them for a while by picking out passages from his stolen journals at random, but after a while that had paled. The skinheads were much more interested in shedding blood, and Rick in particular was looking forward to cutting his name on Evan's soft belly, as payback for daring to stand up to him.

One of them spat on the floor as he approached and blocked his path. "What the fuck do you want, bitch?"

"I want to make a deal." Evan replied nervously.

"Is that right?" snorted the skinhead. He inclined his head at Carlos, who was mopping the floor further down the corridor. "Wassamatter, you get sick of being dicked by the wetback?"

The crew of Aryans shared a rough laugh at Evan's expense and they crowded around him, itching to kick off and lay into him. Another one of the skinheads made discreet eye contact with Karl, who watched from the door of his cell; the Brotherhood's leader grinned and signaled. "Let the meat come on over. We'll get all friendly like." The skinheads parted and Evan stepped through, fighting down the reaction to turn tail and run.

Karl shared his cell with Rick, and it was almost identical to Evan's—but instead of pictures of saints adorning the walls—there was a mix of pornographic pictures and clippings from Neo-Nazi publications. In pride of place over the bunks was the reproduction of a German World War II recruiting poster for the Waffen-SS, and nearby was a bookshelf on which sat Evan's ripped journals. The two men watched him enter with expectant, predatory smiles, relishing the fearful silence.

Evan wrung his hands. "Look, I'm new to all this but I think I get how things work around here. You gotta join a gang or else you end up dead meat, right?"

Karl said nothing, content to let Evan keep talking.

He let a snarl enter his voice. "Well, I want to be with a crew and it sure ain't gonna fucking be with no niggers or spics."

The moment the racist slurs left his mouth, the skinhead's interest was caught. "Is that right?" Karl said coolly. "What about your buddy, the Jesus freak?" He jerked a thumb at Carlos out in the corridor, as he mopped over the area in front of the bars.

"Fuck him," Evan spat. "I don't want to share a cell with that trash." He hesitated, turning pale. "So, look, how do we do this? I know you gotta work your way up, and I'm the new guy..." He coughed self-consciously. "So... should I... I mean, do I suck your dicks right now?"

A silent look of understanding passed between the two inmates. "Is your blood pure?" said Karl. "Are you an Aryan son?"

Evan's tone turned angry. "I ain't no fucking kike, if that's what you mean."

The retort was obviously the right answer, although each of the bigoted insults left a bad taste in Evan's mouth. The skinheads got to their feet, towering over him in the cramped confines of the room. "Let's see what you got," Rick smiled. "And watch the fuckin' teeth or you'll be leaving without them."

Reluctantly, Evan dropped to his knees as Karl and Rick unbuttoned their prison-issue trousers, rolling them down to their ankles. Evan held a miserable expression for a moment, hovering there before doing the deed. He glanced over his shoulder, and caught the eye of Carlos.

"What are you waiting for, bitch?" Karl snapped. "Get to work!"

With his attention elsewhere, Karl didn't see Carlos move until it was too late; without any warning, the convict threw the mop aside and dove through the open door of the cell. The Hispanic man's broad form forced Karl into the wall and the skinhead screamed as Carlos jammed a shank into his crotch.

Rick jerked forward to rush Carlos, but the clothes around his ankles caught his legs and he tottered over. Evan was ready for him and helped Rick on his way, planting a savage kick on his face as he went down.

"Carlos!" Evan shouted. It had only taken seconds, but now the rest of the Brotherhood was scrambling towards them. Evan's cellmate dropped Karl's writhing form to the floor and pressed his broad girth against the cell door, physically blocking the entry of the other skinheads.

"Hurry, man!" Carlos yelled, weathering punches and kicks from the snarling, shouting Aryans.

Evan grabbed at the journals and flipped them open, frantically running past page after page, desperate to find what he was looking for.

"You… You piece of shit!" croaked Karl. "You're dead men!"

There! Evan ignored the thug's words and located the entry he wanted, focusing on the words. He had no idea if this would work as every other time he had tried to make the shift, things had been quiet and calm. Now, if what he tried failed, Evan and Carlos would be gutted by the Brotherhood and left for the guards to find.

He had no choice. It was this, or nothing.

Evan began to read aloud, running through the writing like it was a chant, spilling out the words as fast as he could. "We took the woods behind the junkyard just to make sure that we wouldn't bump into Tommy, but we hadn't seen the smoke yet."

On the page before him, the letters began to flex and merge, warping like an image seen through rain-slicked glass. The pressure blew into life behind his eyes, pulsing as the agitated cries of the skinheads mingled with a shrill stream of animal shrieks, coming together in a jagged profusion of sound. Evan heard the shuddering echo of new voices and a panicked yelp, as the cell became a quivering, frenetic blur—

Everything shifted once more.

Evan almost lost his footing and stumbled, nearly tripping on an exposed root. He forced himself to come to a halt and looked around, bright sunlight suddenly piercing his eyes.

A smile crossed his face and he sniffed the air, a new exhilaration coursing through him. He'd made it. "Rot in hell, you fucking animals," he said with venom.

A few steps behind him, Evan's sudden comment made Kayleigh and Lenny stop dead in their tracks.

"What did you just say?" asked Kayleigh, confused by the outburst.

Evan looked around, getting his bearings. He was thirteen again, out in the woods behind the Kagan place. "Nothing," he told her. "Just kidding around."

She didn't seem convinced, but Kayleigh decided not to press the point.

"So, uh, where are we going?" Lenny said in a flat monotone. "I'm not supposed to go far."

For a moment, Evan weighed things up in his mind. In the next few seconds he'd be taking Kayleigh and Lenny into something that would twist their futures on to a different course once more, toward an incident that could scar them all. Did he really have the right to meddle in their personal histories as well as his own? His one attempt to set things straight had already sent him on to a collision course with murder and a sordid death in prison, and he had no guarantee that what he would do now would be any better. But if he did nothing, that future was sure to come to pass, and Evan would not be able to stop it.

He held up a hand to halt the others. "Wait, before we go any further…"

"What is it, Evan?" said Kayleigh.

On the breeze, he caught the faintest smell of burning and the distant cry of an animal in agony.

TWENTY

Kayleigh heard the indistinct canine screech on the breeze and she stabbed a finger and pointed. "Look! Do you see that?"

Evan didn't need to see what she had seen, as the memory of the incident came trickling back into his mind, but he turned anyway, watching Lenny do the same with an open-mouthed expression of incomprehension. Sure enough, there was the junkyard and the railroad beyond it, and hanging above it, the thin black pillar of oily smoke marking the place where Tommy Miller was preparing to murder a defenseless animal out of spite for Evan.

"We've got to—" For the first time since he had shifted, Evan looked at Kayleigh and really registered her. What he saw made him hesitate; she had changed. His recollection of the junkyard incident, of the first time he had lived through these events seemed hazy and indistinct now. The Kayleigh that had been with him then, she was how Evan had always remembered her from their childhood—an awkward and unkempt tomboy in loose and unflattering clothes, her hair a mess and her eyes permanently downcast. The girl who stood before him now was different. She was a vibrant and feminine teenager, radiant and pretty in a fashionable dress. "You look great..." he breathed, forgetting himself for a moment.

A hollow, terrified yelp cut through the air and suddenly the spell was broken. Evan's purpose came back to him with a pulse of adrenaline, and he glanced around, spying the junk pile they had passed a few moments earlier. "I've got to get something!"

Kayleigh called after him, concerned. "Evan? What's going on? Maybe we should call the fire department or—"

"No!" he snapped. "We have to do this!" He began to root through the mound of trash, tossing aside broken pieces of wood, old papers and rags. Kayleigh and Lenny looked on, each of them disturbed and concerned by Evan's sudden manic behavior. "We need something to cut open the sack!" he called out.

"Sack?" Lenny murmured. "What sack is he talking about?"

Something sharp pricked Evan's palm and he pulled at it, dragging a bent piece of metal out of the rubbish pile. It was part of a discarded office chair, a flat blade-like shape around two feet long; where it had come loose from the frame the metal had snapped off to give it a razor sharp edge. Evan nodded to himself. This would do.

"Evan, you're scaring me..." Kayleigh started.

He ignored her for the moment and offered the metal scrap to the other boy. "I want you to take this, Lenny. Trust me on this."

Lenny eyed the fragment and a brief, dark emotion clouded his face. "I... I shouldn't be here..."

"Listen to me," Evan said intently. "Today is your day of atonement. I know how guilty you feel about that woman and her baby—"

"Evan, stop it!" Kayleigh broke in. "Don't torment him! It's not the time—"

"Now is the only time!" he retorted frantically. "Lenny, today you get a chance to redeem yourself, to make it right. You can start over with a clean slate, a tabula rasa—"

Lenny's face creased in confusion. "Huh? What are you talking about? I don't understand..."

"You're acting crazy!" cried Kayleigh.

Desperation filled Evan's words. "Lenny, please. If you have ever trusted me before, then trust me on this one." He placed the shard of metal in the other boy's hands. "Cut the rope."

Lenny nodded jerkily and clutched the piece of scrap to his chest.

Evan threw an apologetic look at Kayleigh, and in return she showed him a confused, worried expression. "Come on, we don't have much time." He broke into a run, and after a moment Kayleigh and Lenny took off after him toward a gap in the chain-link fence of the junkyard.

* * *

Things happened so fast that Evan found himself racing to keep up, as events began to unfold all over again, just as they had before. They came across Tommy in the clearing near the car crusher with the raging little pyre he had built, the air thick with smoke and the stink of spilled lighter fuel. The other boy spat and snarled when he saw them. "You! I'm not done yet!"

Evan's dog whined and he saw the quivering shape in the soiled gunnysack "Crockett! You son of a bitch, what are you doing to my dog?"

Tommy drenched the trapped animal with the fluid and then attacked with the plank; this time Evan didn't need Lenny's warning shout and he ducked clear as the piece of wood swung at him.

"Kayleigh—" Evan called, but he was seconds too late, and Tommy's wide strike hit his sister instead, sending the boy into a rage.

"Look what you made me do!"

Evan held up a hand to halt him. "What is wrong with you?"

Tommy went for him again, clubbing Evan to the ground. Blinking back bright flashes of pain, Evan looked around for Lenny but the other boy was nowhere in sight.

He called out to Kayleigh, but the girl lay silent and unmoving on the dirt. "Kayleigh! Wake up! Oh, please wake up!"

"Why don't you just fucking kiss her, Prince Charming?" Tommy yelled, pouring more fuel on the fire. With his free hand, the teenager grabbed at the plank again and swatted Evan. The blow sent him flying and Evan felt hot blood spatter over his face. Before he could recover, sharp kicks struck him in the ribs and belly. Evan coughed and spat out a thick blob of blood-laced saliva.

He tried to focus. Tommy stood over him, tears in the other boy's eyes making him blink and twitch. "Listen to me good, Evan—"

There's a million other sisters in the world. You didn't have to fuck with mine! Evan heard the words before Tommy could say them. He wheezed out a breath. "Tommy, wait. Just listen to me. I'll do whatever you want." Rolling over, Evan fixed him with a hard, unflinching stare. "If you don't want me to ever see Kayleigh again, then fine. Just let Crockett go."

Tommy wavered—this wasn't the response he'd been expecting, and it caught him off-guard.

"Besides," Evan continued, "you kill my dog now and they'll stick you in Juvy for sure. You'll be there until you're twenty, man." He searched Tommy's eyes for understanding, and to his surprise, he found it. "You don't want that. I know you'd never leave your sister alone with your father. You just want to protect her."

Evan's words struck home and Tommy's face softened, the violent tirade of anger gradually dissipating as comprehension took its place. Evan saw the first flickers of true, honest gratitude emerging there. "I…"

Tommy knelt by the sack and started to untie the rope; and without warning, the air was split by a keening scream of hatred. Evan turned to see Lenny bolt out from a hiding place behind a rusted Volkswagen, brandishing the shard of metal like a short-sword. Tommy looked up with surprise and shock in time to see the makeshift blade bearing down on him.

"Lenny!" Evan cried, but the other teenager was heedless and blinded by rage. With all the force he could muster, Lenny fell on Tommy and jammed the scrap fragment into the soft skin of his throat, piercing his neck and running him through.

Tommy could not scream. Bright arterial blood sprayed out of him and he gagged, clutching at the jagged metal, choking and suffocating as the gore filled his lungs.

"Oh fuck, Lenny, no!" Evan felt sick with horror as he watched Tommy collapse in a heap, his throat a red wreck of torn flesh. Lenny fell to his knees, clawing up handfuls of dirt to wipe away the blood, his watery eyes hollow and black.

Evan tried to get to his feet and stumbled, the agony of Tommy's kicks knocking him down. Close by, Kayleigh stirred and came to, rising from the ground.

"Tommy?" The single word was flooded with shock, horror and panic. Feeble, dying spurts of blood from her brother's punctured throat jerked into the air and she let out a shriek of wild hysteria.

From the corner of his eye, Evan saw the dog shake free of the sack and run away—but he couldn't sway his gaze from Lenny, who sat there staring at the damage he had wrought, with Tommy's blood spattered across his clean white shirt and his slack, expressionless face.

Silhouetted by the sky, Lenny seemed to shudder and vibrate, and then Evan's vision clouded—

The shock of awakening was like a violent electrical discharge across his whole body, and Evan's arms and legs quivered with tension, kicking off the blankets from where he lay. He had a moment to glimpse his surroundings—the dorm room he shared with Thumper, but the beds were reversed—and then a thunder of sharp, sparking agonies wracked his brain. Evan yelled out a wordless cry of pain and his hands flew to his temples, pressing into the skin as if they could somehow stifle the torment.

Just as before, when he had changed things in the basement of the Miller's house, the aftershock assaulted him with a torrent of clashing images as storms of memory and recollection collided and coalesced. Before, the experience had been horrific; it was now ten times worse.

"Oh Christ, help me!" he yelled, his voice seemed thin and scattered, as if he were hearing it from a million miles away.

Kayleigh, lying there before him, beautiful, resplendent... The pink, girlish interior of her bedroom at the sorority... Gwen and her smiling flirtations... The fresh apple blossom smell of Kayleigh's favorite perfume...

The memories bubbled to the surface of Evan's consciousness in bright colors, hanging there for a moment, but then they began to fade, darkening and growing pale. He tried desperately to hold on to them, but they shrank away from him, becoming nothing but faint ghosts of themselves.

That perfect night at the Theta house, the fairy lights and the lanterns... Kayleigh looking more beautiful than he had ever seen her... Then the sudden fear confronting the vandalized hulk of his car... The creeping threat of Tommy's mad anger...

Like sun-bleached photographs, the immediate, real texture of the events became shadowy, disintegrating into phantoms and fragments, breaking apart.

Carlos and his intricate tattoos, his watchful face... The oppressive gray walls and the razor-wire fences of the prison... Karl's hate-filled, leering eyes... The blood-hungry smiles of Rick and the skinheads...

Almost gone now, the recall dissipating, Evan felt a queasy surge as something new and strange forced itself into the echoing void in his mind.

Thumper grinning at him as he hands him a textbook... The two of them splitting a six-pack in the dorm room... Following girls across the quad...

And then from the eye of this storm of images, a single bright memory pressed forward on to Evan's reeling senses, impaling him on it, burning itself across his mind like a brand.

Lenny, his eyes blank and soulless... Limp and ragged, the boy being forced into a straight-jacket... Cornered there in a padded room, Lenny's round moon face lax and his gaze as dark as a deep-sea predator's...

Trembling, Evan fell back into the sweat-soaked sheets as his body tensed with spastic convulsions, his eyes rolling back into his head and showing bloodshot whites.

"Dude, I got beer—" Thumper began as he came in through the door, but the words died in his throat the second he saw Evan's twitching body. The paper sack full of beer cans fell from his fingers and he jumped back in horror. "Holy shit!" Thumper scanned the corridor outside for anyone he could call to and one of the lab geeks from room 408 caught Thumper's eye as he fumbled for his door keys. "Hey, you!" he bellowed. "Call 911, right now!"

Evan tried to croak out something but his words were a jumble of gasps and half-breaths.

Thumper went to his bedside and cradled his head, using a discarded towel to stem the flow of blood streaming from Evan's nose. "Oh, man, what happened to you?"

"Thuh-thuh—"

"Easy, Ev," Thumper said, forcing himself to be calm. "Just be cool, man. Thumper's here, buddy, I gotcha. You're going to be okay. Help is coming." He looked up and shouted as loud as he could: "Hey! Where the fuck is that ambulance?"

By the time they were arriving at the Sunnyvale clinic, Evan was cogent and lucid, demanding that they take him back to his dorm and that nothing was wrong with him—but by then it was too late. Thumper's quick reactions had got Evan picked up before he could recover enough to protest, and as they rolled him out on a gurney, he saw that his mother was already there, in anguished conference with Doctor Redfield.

Andrea raced over to him and jogged alongside as they ferried him into one of the examination rooms. Her eyes were brimming with tears. "Oh, Evan, are you all right?"

He gave her a brave grin. "I'm fine, Mom. Just a nosebleed or something. I passed out. I've probably been working too hard."

She didn't believe a word of it, but she forced a fragile smile in return and grasped his hand. "The doctor says they're going to run a scan for head trauma."

"It's just a CAT scan," Evan heard Redfield's voice say from behind him.

Evan smirked. "Oh yeah. The mission to Mars."

The orderlies turned the gurney into the exam room and Evan glimpsed the doctor as he passed him. "Try to relax, son. We'll get to the bottom of this soon enough." Redfield looked worn down and tired—the years clearly hadn't been easy on him.

They placed him on the bed beneath the massive mechanism of the scanning device, and the machine drew him in, turning probes and imaging panels toward his skull, searching for flaws and imperfections.

When they were done, a nurse brought him a wheelchair and took him along the corridors to Redfield's office, refusing Evan's request to let him walk. He sat in silence for a moment, then glanced up at her with a question. "Hey, you still look after people with mental problems in here, right?"

She nodded. "Over in the other wing. We have quite a few residents."

"Do you—" He hesitated. "Do you have people here who are like, you know, psycho? I mean like the criminally insane, that sorta thing?"

The nurse frowned. "We don't call them that. Those people are sick, they're not criminals. They can't help themselves with what they do."

"But you do look after them here?" he pressed.

She sighed. "Yes." They turned a corner and she nodded toward a heavy security door with a barred window of reinforced glass. "We have a secure unit for residents who are... high risk."

Evan took this in and said nothing. The nurse opened the door to Redfield's office and wheeled him in. Evan's mother shot him a worried glance from a seat by the cluttered desk.

"Thank you, Joanne, I'll take it from here." As the nurse left, Redfield rotated a monitor screen on his desk so Evan could see what he had been showing his mother. The display showed an oval cross-section of his brain; Evan was reminded of a rounded coral formation he'd seen in a National Geographic magazine.

"Okay, Doc," he said breezily. "What's the damage? How much time have I got?"

"That's very cute, Evan," said his mother in a voice that told him she thought that it was anything but.

The doctor gave a weak smile. "Uh, well, you can rest assured you're not dying... But this, this is a little bit complicated." He tapped the screen with a pencil. "I haven't seen results exactly like these before. Frankly, I thought the scanner was out of alignment for a moment, but the base readings check out fine, so it's not a glitch. This is new to me; I've never come across anything like this."

"Are you sure?" Evan asked, serious now. "Not even with my father?"

Andrea and Redfield exchanged looks. "Well, actually these tests were not available twenty years ago, when your father was a patient."

"So what did you find?" said Andrea.

The doctor used the pencil to point to the outer edge of Evan's brain, where the gray mass met the inner wall of the skull. "This is where we're finding most of the irregular trauma, the hemorrhaging. The outer lining of the cerebral cortex."

"What does that do?"

"Let me guess," Evan broke in before Redfield could answer. "Would that be the part where memories are stored?"

"That's right, yes." The doctor stared at the display, mesmerized by it. "I have to be honest, I've never seen anything like it." He tapped a few keys and the image was joined by a second CAT scan, almost identical to the first. "This is from the scan that was performed on you last year—"

"Last year?" said Evan.

Redfield gave him a sideways look. "Yes, after that car accident you had?"

"Oh. Right. Of course," Evan nodded. It was peculiar to hear of something that had happened to him, but not happened to him; another example of how time had jumped tracks and reordered itself.

The doctor continued. "I've compared your scan today to the ones taken last year and there's evidence of severe hemorrhaging and massive neural reconstruction."

Andrea stared at Redfield blankly, considering his words. Evan felt nervous energy in his fingertips and channeled it out, pushing at the spokes of the wheelchair and popping impatient little wheelies.

"Reconstruction?" asked his mother.

Redfield nodded. "Yes, we sometimes see this in head trauma victims. People who've been shot in the head, for example. Sometimes they lose a portion of their brain functionality, but the tissue reconstructs itself and they recover. It's like rewiring an electrical circuit to bypass a blown fuse."

"But what does that mean for Evan?"

"He's saying that it's like forty years of new memories have been jammed in my brain since last year," Evan interrupted. "Overload City. Is that about the gist of it, Doc?"

The doctor gave a slow nod, struck by Evan's effortless interpretation of the scan's conclusions. "I suppose so…"

Evan snapped the chair back on its wheels and stood up purposefully. "Mom, do you mind if I go wait in the car? The lighting in here bugs my eyes."

She nodded and handed him the car keys. "I'll be along in minute."

He shook Redfield's hand and flashed him a quick smile. "Well, it's nice seeing you again. But, you know, I've got people to see, books to read…"

Andrea gave the doctor an apologetic look for her son's sudden reluctance, and as he made for the door, Evan collided with a coat hanger and knocked Redfield's jacket to the floor. "Whoops! I'm sorry!" He gave a contrite shrug and re-hung the coat, then left closing the door behind him.

In the corridor, Evan smiled to himself as he examined the bunch of keys and the smart card he'd palmed from the jacket and weighed them in his hands. With care, he made his way around the corner and walked towards for the security door.

TWENTY-ONE

Evan wound his way back down the maze of corridors inside the Sunnyvale Clinic, retracing the steps of the nurse who had wheeled him to Doctor Redfield's office. He was careful to avoid making eye contact with anyone who passed him by, concentrating on looking deliberate and focused, as if he had every right to be where he was going.

He made it to the door of the secure unit unchallenged, and swiped the doctor's smart card through the scanner by the entrance. A red light on the electronic lock blinked green and the magnetic latch snapped open. Evan was in and glanced back through the armored glass window in the door to see if anyone had noticed. No alarms began to sound and no challenging voices were raised.

So far, so good. He pocketed the card and drew out the bunch of keys, sorting through them as he walked. The corridor seemed faintly familiar to Evan—had he come this way as a boy on the day his father had died? It was hard to tell. Parts of the clinic had been redecorated and altered since he was a kid, and it was possible that it was different in other ways, thanks to the changes he had made in the past.

Evan came across an unmanned nurse's station and leaned over the desk—sure enough, there was a patient register and a single name leapt out at him. *Kagan, Leonard.* He moved from room to room, peering in through pillbox-style slot windows, searching for his friend. Some of the locked cells were empty, but others were home to people who stared blankly into space, or who sat in curled balls in the far corners. One man looked directly at him as he surveyed the room; he was thin and raggedy, like a loose cloth doll modeled on a person. Evan's heart skipped a beat as he realized he knew him—he'd seen this patient before, thirteen years ago. Someone said something indistinct, a woman, and Evan realized that a nurse was on her way, probably doing her rounds. He had little time, so he moved on, searching.

In the next room he found what he was looking for. Evan tried a couple of wrong keys before he unlocked the door, and managed to get in before the nurse could see him. He pressed himself flat against the wall as she passed by, and when he was sure she was gone, Evan allowed himself a breath and took in the interior of the cell.

Like most of the clinic, the room was slightly decrepit, with peeling paint on the ceiling and fixtures that dated back to the 1950s. There was a single window of marbled reinforced glass in the far wall, surrounded by a cage of bars, and no other furniture except a heavy metal bed made of gray angle iron. There lay Lenny in a shapeless set of disposable paper clothes. He was thinner and more gaunt, as if life had been drained out of him by this place. Evan took a careful step toward him.

"Uh, hey, Lenny. It's me. Evan."

There was no response, and for a moment Evan thought he might have been sleeping, or perhaps medicated into quiescence. The only movement of Lenny's body was the slow rise and fall of his chest. Evan saw that his ankles and wrists had been secured to metal loops on the side of the bed frame, held there by thick leather restraints. Why would they need to do that? What kind of person has Lenny become?

Evan studied the dulled appearance of his friend and felt his chest contract. Lenny's face sported a dark patina of unkempt stubble and his face was fixed in something that might vaguely have been referred to as a grin. It was a sinister countenance, malicious and cold with haunting, unblinking eyes. Evan thought of Lenny—poor little Lenny who had grown up as the victim of Tommy's incessant abuse—and tried to connect that to the man he saw lying before him, this silent figure who seemed to radiate hate and murderous intent. He suppressed a shiver and spoke again. "Is there anything you need? Anything I can get for you?"

Lenny didn't respond; he seemed neither surprised nor upset by Evan's secretive arrival, almost as if he were completely unaware of anyone else in the room. He just lay there, staring upward, breathing silently.

Evan made a gesture at the high, airy ceiling. "Hey, what about the models, man? Your airplanes? I'd bet you could get a shit-load of models up in here."

He waited, and still Lenny did not speak or even acknowledge his presence. Evan sagged; he wasn't sure what he had expected to find here, but the moment that searing memory of seeing Lenny committed had burned itself into his brain, Evan had wanted to know it for himself, to be sure that it wasn't just a hallucination, a terrible fantasy concocted by his frenzied mind. His heart heavy, he turned to leave; there was nothing for him to see here except the evidence of his own failure.

"Okay, Lenny," Evan sighed. "I just wanted to say 'Hi'. So long."

His fingers were on the door handle when Lenny spoke. "You knew."

Evan whirled around. The voice was cold and distant. "Lenny?"

"You knew the whole time, didn't you?" It was an accusation, hateful and vehement. "When you put that blade in my hand, you knew something big was going to happen. Didn't you?"

Evan found himself nodding in shock. "Y... yes. I guess I did."

For the first time, Lenny moved; he turned his head just enough so he could look Evan straight in the eye and show him the raw, seething hatred that burned there. "Then you made this happen," he growled. "You should be where I am... You should be where I am!"

Evan fumbled the jangling keys into the lock and ran from the room, unable to blot the echoes of Lenny's words from his mind. Guilt tore into him, burning its way through his chest like hot acid.

He made it back to the car before his mother, pausing to drop Redfield's keys at the front desk when the duty nurse's back was turned. Andrea drove him over to the dorm, her manner falsely chatty and upbeat, taking care to assure him that the doctor had said that Evan would probably suffer no ill effects from his seizure. He gave her the vaguest of grunts as an answer and stared out of the window, trying to lose himself in the passing scenery and failing.

They drove in silence for a few miles after Andrea ran out of things to say.

"Do you miss Dad?" Evan asked without preamble.

The question caught her off-balance. "Well, sure..." she began hesitantly. "Yes, a lot of the time."

"Sometimes..." It was hard for Evan to say this. "I wish he was still here. There are things I wanted to ask him about. Questions."

"You can always talk to me," Andrea said tenderly. "About anything, Evan. I love you, you know that. I'm always here for you."

He turned to look at her and she saw his eyes were misted with emotion. "I know that, Mom. But there are things that… that only Dad could have known."

Andrea accepted this with quiet understanding. Finally, she squeezed his hand. "He loved you too, don't ever forget that. If you could talk to him now, I know he would be proud of the man you've become." She blinked back tears as the car halted outside the dorm block.

Evan kissed his mother on the cheek. "I have to go. I love you too, Mom." He stepped out of the car and gave her a brave smile. "Everything will be okay. Trust me, I'm going to fix things."

Andrea watched her son go, unsure of what it was he was trying to tell her.

The dorm room was empty, for which Evan was quietly thankful. He wasn't in the mood to field questions—no matter how good-natured—from his roommate. For a second, he stood in the middle of the room and tried to orient himself; he took a step toward what had always been his bed, on the right side of the door and stopped. The décor of rock band flyers and dog-eared movie posters was the same as it had always been, only now it was backwards. Thumper's stuff sat where Evan's used to be and vice-versa. He shook his head and sat on the bed—the left-hand side bunk—before reaching under the frame with a probing hand. His fingers touched cardboard and he tugged.

Relief surged through him as he produced a box full of worn Mead composition books, and he snatched up the one at the top of the pile. "Age 7," he read aloud from the label on the cover. Evan weighed the book in his hand and glanced around the silent room, considering. The gloom and the closeness of the stale dorm seemed oppressive to him, too reminiscent of both Lenny's sparse chamber at the clinic and the dark den of the prison cell he'd shared with Carlos.

Tucking the book under his arm, Evan left and quickly made his way to a sheltered corner of the quad. At first, he'd believed that somewhere quiet and calm was required for him to induce a flashback, but he'd put paid to that theory after his frantic reading in Karl's cramped cell. No, it was becoming clear to Evan that the more he tried, the easier it was becoming to simply push his mind into the words on the page and let his consciousness make the transition.

He sat under a tree, propping himself up against the trunk. Nearby, a group of Theta Chi pledges were clowning around with a Frisbee and making jokes. He recognized a couple of them from his romantic evening with Kayleigh, but they blanked him completely. And why not? *They don't know me. We never met, that never happened.*

Evan returned to his journal and worked through the pages until he found what he was looking for, an entry he'd written the morning of the day when his father had died. He began to read the words aloud, letting the memory come freely to him, almost chanting it like an arcane mantra.

"Today I get to mete my father," Evan let the tight, straining sensation behind his eyes develop, giving it freedom to expand outward in a wave and engulf him. "His name is Jason and he is crazy."

From the corner of his eye, he saw the kid who'd sported the salad bowl give him a strange look. The Theta pledge caught the bright yellow disc of the Frisbee in his hand and it seemed to vibrate like a struck gong. Evan kept reading, aware of the tree, the grass, everything around him on the quad starting to shudder.

"I hope he lets me call him Dad."

There was the dim echo of a man's voice and—

Evan was there, blinking under the blurry actinic glow of the fluorescent strip light.

"Son?" The word echoed off the bare metallic walls of the observation room, and Evan shuddered a little, riding out the moment of confusion that accompanied every shift into a younger, smaller version of his body. He looked up to see Jason Treborn watching him with a mix of warmth and concern. "You were saying something about your eyes?" he prompted. "Are you okay? You looked like you were somewhere else for a second, there."

There are things I wanted to ask him about. Questions. Evan's words to his mother came back to him with force and he straightened up. "Look, Jason... Dad," he said in a low voice. "I need some fast answers from you if I'm ever gonna fix what I've done."

For a second or two, dull confusion crossed Jason's expression; but then in the next moment shock and dire understanding flared in his father's eyes as he realized the reason for the sudden change in Evan's tone and manner. The blood drained from Jason's face, turning it as pale as paper. "Oh, no," he managed, his voice thick with anguish. "Oh God, no. Not you too. My poor boy. My poor, little Evan..."

"Jason, listen to me," Evan snapped. "I need you to focus."

The older man shook his head in grief. "You're part of it too, aren't you? I was praying that this curse would have ended with me."

Evan touched his father's arm. "But it didn't, and now I need you to help me. I need information about how I can make things right again, and you're the only one who can give it to me." He flashed a glance over his shoulder at the opaque glass screen, on the other side of which stood his mother. "You have to help me."

Jason's brow furrowed in frustration. "Make it right? There is no 'right'... You have to understand, when you change who people are, you destroy who they were. It's *wrong!*"

"Who is to say that you can't make things better?"

"Don't you think I tried?" Jason's voice rose. "Don't you think I tried and tried and tried? But every time I did, things just got worse!" He gripped Evan's small, child's fingers. "Listen to me: you have to stop it!"

"I can't," Evan insisted. "I just need to change one small thing—"

"There are no small things!" his father's lips trembled. "It's like ripples on a pond, echoes in a cave, ocean waves, falling dominoes, the butterfly effect…" His words trailed off.

Evan shrank back—Jason seemed to be babbling now, making no sense. "What? What the hell are you talking about?"

"Nothing happens in isolation, Evan. You make one tiny change in the past, but that affects something else, and that changes something else, on and on, bigger and bigger! A butterfly flaps its wings in China and shifts the air, and it ends up causing a thunderstorm in New York—do you understand?" His hands bunched, making the restraint cuffs around them rattle. "You can't play God, son! It must end with me. Just by being here, you may be killing your mother!"

"Bullshit!" spat the boy. "If you won't help me, fine. I'll do it on my own. I'll be sure to send you a postcard when I've made everything perfect again."

"I won't let you!" Jason growled, and he launched himself across the table, dragging his shackles with him. Even though he knew it was coming, Evan barely had time to throw up his hands before his father's vice-like grip closed on his throat. "I have to stop you!"

Evan's vision fogged as the breath was choked out of him, and Jason's florid, fury-red face shimmered and vibrated—

He came to with an explosive cough and grabbed at his neck. Evan gasped in a breath of air and probed at the skin of his throat; the sensation of tightness there gradually faded away to nothing.

"You okay, man?" said one of the pledges. Evan identified him as the guy who'd been forced by Hunter to wear a dress, in another version of things. "You dropped off there."

Evan gave him a weak nod and shakily stood up. "I'm... I'm fine, thanks." Glancing around, he saw nothing to indicate that anything had changed and he blew out a breath.

He felt loose and adrift now, directionless. Evan had pinned all his hopes on dragging something out of his father, some detail that would aid him, only to come back with nothing. He was dejected, heartbroken.

Jason's warning rang in his ears as he wandered away from the quad, and the words turned over and over in his mind, refusing to be silenced. Evan tossed the journal in the back seat of his beaten Honda and drove away from the campus, turning on the highway.

"I just need to clear my head," he said to the air. "I have to get things straight."

He let the roads take him where they wished until the sun began to fall below the horizon, and then when his stomach started to growl he pulled off the highway at the first truck stop he saw. It wasn't until he'd sat down at one of the greasy, worn booths that Evan realized where he was. The stained plastic menu announced the Blue Plate Special at the Ridgewood Diner as the tuna melt.

He ordered a cheeseburger and fries, and attacked it with savagery—suddenly Evan felt as if he hadn't eaten in days. Without being aware of it, he curled one arm protectively around the out-side of the plate, instinctively guarding his food.

"Anything else, honey?" said a waitress. "Top you off?" she gestured with a coffeepot.

"Nah, just the check," Evan replied, around a mouthful of food. He glanced at the woman's uni-form—it was the same dumb thing he'd seen Kayleigh wearing when he'd found her working here. The waitress's name badge read "Selma".

She tore off the bill and placed it before him. "Just get out, did ya?"

"Huh?"

Selma nodded at his arm. "Nothing. Just that my brother did a stint in the pen, and he used to eat like that."

"I come from a big family," Evan said defensively. "I'm not a convict."

She shrugged. "Didn't mean no offence." Selma turned to walk away.

"None taken," he added. "Hey, uh, I was wondering. Does Kayleigh Miller still work here?"

Selma gave him a confused look. "Kayleigh? Sorry, never heard of her. I've worked here for five years and we ain't ever had a Kayleigh."

Evan finished off his food and watched the night fall through the dirty window, the distant lights of Sunnyvale gradually brightening into a tight constellation low on the horizon. He watched the night draw in, and thought of Kayleigh Miller.

Kayleigh.

How many times does it come back to her? I've lost count of them. It might be hard for you to understand if you never knew her, if you never saw her through my eyes. For the longest time, I didn't really manage to figure it out myself, until one day it came to me. She was like my compass, you see, she was the star that I had steered my life by. Without her, I was lost. I had thought that I could get by without her, and there were times when we were apart, after Mom and I had left Sunnyvale, when I almost believed it.

Looking back at that time now, I can't understand how I got through not seeing her smile, not being able to sense her, touch her. Love is strange. These are the things that it does to you, and I won't pretend to understand them.

That day, there in the diner, I stood on the edge of an abyss even though I wasn't aware of it. My father had tried to warn me and I had ignored every word he had said. I was too far along the road by then, and I could not—I would not—turn around. I remember how the weight of it all pressed down on me, the terrible knowledge of what I had done. I suppose I had wanted Jason to hand me some kind of magic key that would let me bring things back into the lines I desired, but when I realized that would not happen, I was lost. Utterly, hopelessly lost.

And so, I went looking for my star, my compass. For Kayleigh.

TWENTY-TWO

The Miller's house had been one of the best-looking places on the block when they were children, but now as Evan approached it from the street, he saw that time had been unkind to the building. Dilapidated and ripe with neglect, the house was shabby where chips of paint were peeling off and decayed timbers had split and crumbled. The garden, which Evan remembered as the site of many childhood games with Kayleigh, was an overgrown mess of yellowed weeds. Lying in the undergrowth was the discarded frame of a lawnmower, rusted into an unusable heap.

The front porch sported two worn car tires and various other piles of nondescript garbage, along with a cracked plastic sign that warned hawkers that they would be unwelcome. Evan curled his lip at the state of the place and reached for a tarnished brass doorbell.

A man's shout came from somewhere in the back of the house. "Just shut the hell up, already!" Evan instantly recognized George Miller's voice. "Can't a man get a little goddamn peace in his own home?" Who or whatever he was yelling at remained silent.

Evan thumbed the bell and it let out a thin, reedy whine, as if the batteries powering it were on their last legs. He heard footsteps approaching. "Oh for Christ's sake, now what?" Miller griped as he came close.

He blinked at Evan as he opened the door, his slack expression making it clear that he had no clue whom his visitor was. "Who are you?" he snapped. "What the hell do you want, punk? I don't suppose you're here to sell cookies?"

"Good guess." Miller's manner instantly made Evan angry and he leapt forward, shoving the older man back into the house and up against a wall.

"Oh shit!" Miller cried out. "I got nothing! Leave me alone!"

"Shut up, fuckbag!" Evan growled, and the other man twitched with surprise. "Remember me now, George? We had a great little chat when I was seven."

Cold recollection crossed Miller's face and his eyes widened with horror. "Oh, no, please," he whimpered. "How did you…"

"I told you you'd be watched, didn't I?" Evan continued, enjoying the role he was playing, "Now you gotta do something for me."

"I never touched her!" George said desperately. "I never laid a finger on her, I swear it!"

Evan gave him a slow nod. "Good boy. Now I need you to answer one question for me, fuck-bag." He snarled in Miller's face. "Where can I find your daughter?"

"I'll tell you!" he blinked back tears. "I'll tell you, just please leave me alone!"

The address on the paper where Kayleigh's father had nervously scribbled it out for him was barely readable. Evan flicked his eyes up at the sign on a crossroads and turned the Honda right, past a line of gutted brownstones. He felt disgusted by his encounter with Miller. The person who had intimidated Evan and his own children so many years ago was now just a pathetic shell, a weak little man who had been all too eager to give up his daughter's whereabouts to save his own neck.

He saw the flickering neon sign showing the entrance to the Sunrise Motel and pulled in, parking the car close to the office. Inside, a bored-looking old woman with her hair in curlers glanced up from a magazine to study Evan for the briefest of moments before returning her attention to the gossip page. Evan walked around the car, avoiding two grimy teenagers who sat hunched beneath a sign that displayed the motel's fees for hourly rates. Evan could smell the toilet floor odor of speed on them and kept walking.

As he passed by the dark shape of a van he heard a sudden scrape of metal on metal and a male voice swearing in Spanish. A figure shied away from the driver's side door and came into the light. "This yours? Hey, I wasn't doing nothing…"

"Carlos?" Evan's jaw dropped. His cellmate stood before him in street clothes, trying to conceal a slim-jim—a metal bar used to release car locks—in his sleeve.

Carlos eyed him without recognition. "Who are you? You don't know me." He shoved past Evan and walked away. "You don't know me, man."

"Yeah, I do," Evan called after him, as a thought occurred. "I know all about you, Carlos." When he kept walking, Evan spoke again. "I know all about you, your wife and your baby girl, Gina."

Carlos froze in his tracks and whipped around. "What did you say?"

"Gina, your daughter. Dark hair, big brown eyes like her mom has. You want to be a good father to her, don't you?"

Confusion and anger mingled in Carlos's expression. "You ain't no cop. Who the fuck are you, man?"

"Jesus sent me, Carlos. He told me to tell you to quit stealing."

"You're a crazy man," snapped the thief, but with more conviction than he felt.

Evan pointed at his chest. "Those tattoos you got under that shirt, of Christ on the cross. You believe in him, don't you?" Carlos nodded, his face pale, and Evan continued, spreading his hands so the scars on his palms were visible. "Jesus believes in you too, but you gotta stop stealing, or else he won't be able to help you."

Carlos saw the stigmata-like marks and gasped. "Wh-what do you mean?"

Evan gestured to the van. "I know your future, Carlos. You steal a car tonight and you'll get arrested. That'll be three strikes for you, man, and you'll be in the joint for the long haul. Once they send you down, your wife won't let you see Gina anymore. Your little baby girl will grow up thinking her daddy is dead."

Carlos looked away, and Evan knew he'd hit a nerve. "She told you that, didn't she?" he went on. "She told you not to go but you went out anyway."

"I need money for them..." Carlos began lamely.

"Stealing's not the way, and you know it," Evan snapped. "Go get a job. Make a life for yourself. Be a good husband and father."

For a second, Carlos seemed like he was about to argue, but then a police cruiser rolled by, the watchful cops inside scrutinizing the two men as they passed. Carlos looked back at Evan—if he had broken into the van, he would have been halfway though hot-wiring it when the police had passed by. He would have been caught for sure.

"Do it for Gina," Evan added. "Let her grow up to be proud of you."

Carlos gave a slow nod of contrition. He then drew out the slim-jim, snapped it in two and tossed it into the shadows. "Thanks, man..." he said, looking back. But Evan had already gone.

He had to pick his way over a couple of passed-out bodies in doorways along the second floor corridor, stepping around what looked like a ragged burn hole in the frayed carpet. The floor smelled of stale urine. One of the doors had been hastily replaced with a piece of fiberboard, and Evan could still see the ends of yellow adhesive tape stuck to the frame, the kind that had "Crime Scene—Do Not Enter" written on them.

He found room 22 and knocked on the door, examining the piece of paper in his hand. There was a rattle of a chain and it opened. The face that stared out at him was haggard and strung-out, eyes ringed with thick kohl and cheekbones showing through the gaunt, pale skin.

"Kayleigh." Evan managed, the sight of her threatening to seize up his throat.

The dark eyes flashed with contempt and she put on an expression of studied disappointment. "Oh. A blast from the past," she sniffed wetly. "I thought you were my eight o'clock." Evan expected her to close the door in his face, but instead she let it swing open. "Make it fast. I'm expecting someone."

"Nice to see you too," he grated. "Can I come in?"

"Whatever." She took a quick look around the empty hallway, then waved him in. "Sorry about the mess," Kayleigh said with flat sarcasm. "If I knew you were coming, I'd have cleaned the stains off the sheets."

The door closed with a thud and Evan's gaze ranged around the squalid, soiled little room. It was dirty and sparse, a silent television showing a flickering, out-of-tune picture in the far corner, with a filthy bed and bare wood dresser. Evan saw an overfilled ashtray there, near a pile of greasy pizza boxes. Next to a purple handbag, he noticed a wide spoon with a charred bottom, yellowed cotton balls and brown-spotted squares of tin foil. Oh Kayleigh, he wondered, what's happened to you?

She sat down heavily in the room's only chair and lit up a cigarette with a disposable lighter, watching him. "You gonna stand there all day?"

"You live here?"

Kayleigh blew out a cloud of smoke. "It's not the fuckin' Hilton, but yeah, this is it. Sorry if you don't approve."

He studied her for long seconds; her hair, that beautiful, gorgeous golden hair that Evan had buried his face in, that had turned into a shabby knot of wiry, greasy strands across her shoulders and neck. She wore a brown leather jacket that seemed held together by patches, and threadbare enough to have been dragged behind a car for fifty miles. It barely covered a coarse, glittery tube-top that forced her pale, anemic breasts forward. Kayleigh crossed her legs, the fake vinyl snakeskin-pattern trousers she wore scraped together. She was a mess, a pale junkie parody of the girl that Evan had known.

"So what do you want?" Kayleigh asked as Evan sat on the dirty bed.

At first he couldn't speak, and Evan felt his eyes starting to water. He took a gasp of air and forced out a sentence. "I just needed to see... a friendly face."

Even with her dismissive manner, Kayleigh could not help but be touched by the sincerity in Evan's voice, and she softened by the smallest fraction. She flicked a glance at a wind-up alarm clock on the nightstand. "Well, time is money, Evan, so if you—"

He cut her off by pulling out his wallet and tossing it on the dresser. Evan saw the practiced glint of avarice in her eyes, but she made no move to pick it up.

Kayleigh shrugged and drew on her cigarette. "Well... I guess I can spare ten minutes for an old friend, right?"

Evan watched her, his face rigid and immobile; streams of tears, incongruous against his dispassionate expression, flowed down his cheeks.

"So, how's tricks?" she said sharply. "Oh, sorry. Occupational humor, y'know."

"I get it," he mumbled. "You can drop it now."

She stubbed out the cigarette in a puff of sparks, her face tightening with annoyance.

"Oh, I'm so sorry. Does my line of work make you uncomfortable, precious?"

He shook his head. "No. Just that you need to hurt me with it." He took a shallow breath. "I've been where you've been."

"Ha!" she spat. "Where's that, turning tricks for horny assholes on the street corner?"

"The bottom. When you're just a piece of meat waiting for the next attack. I know what that's like."

Kayleigh stared at him, weighing up his words and the hollow look in his eyes that told her he wasn't lying. "What happened to you?"

He gave a doleful shake of the head. "You wouldn't even believe me if I told you," Evan smiled mirthlessly. "I mean, people always say that, don't they? 'You wouldn't believe me,' but in this case it's not worth trying to explain it."

"That's so much bull," said Kayleigh. "I've seen some sickening shit, Evan, let me tell you. I don't even blink twice anymore." She paused and leaned forward. "Especially in your case."

"Why is that?"

"Something about you," she nodded to herself, "Because you're... different."

Evan shifted uncomfortably. "Different how?"

Kayleigh grabbed the purple bag and started rooting around inside it for another cigarette. She found one and lit it. "I knew it from when we were kids, something that was just off about you, Evan." She waved the cigarette though the air in front of her. "Let me ask you a question, just a little something that's been gnawing at me for all these years."

"Yeah?" He knew what she would say before she even spoke.

"In the woods. That day in the woods. How did you know that Tommy had your dog? That was no fucking hunch, you knew about it already."

Tell her. Evan felt all of it start to bubble up inside him, the terrible knowledge of the shifts and the flashbacks, the journals, all the changes and mistakes he had made—and suddenly, all he wanted to do was pour it out to her, to share the weight of it with another human being. "Do you remember when I was a kid, I used to have these blackouts…?"

She nodded. "Sure. Tommy used to say it was because you were sick in the head, like your old man." There was skepticism in her expression, but interest wavered there as well.

"He wasn't all wrong—" Evan's words were interrupted by a rap on the door.

"Open up, it's me," said a man's voice. Kayleigh frowned and went to the door, opening it a few inches. "Hey baby," the voice continued, "I got what you need…"

She glanced at Evan and then back at the unseen speaker. "Sorry, Chuckie, but we gotta postpone tonight. I got other plans."

The man turned angry. "What?" he snarled. "You little skank, you can't tell me to get lost—"

"I can and I will. Piss off, Chuck." She slammed the door in his face. Kayleigh gave

Evan a weary look. "So much for my john. Listen, if we're gonna talk, you can buy me something to eat instead, okay?"

"All right."

Down the block was a cramped little diner, empty but for a few late workers and night owls. They took a booth at the back and got food. Evan mostly talked and nursed a cup of jet-black coffee, while Kayleigh ate her way through a meal like she was fresh from a famine.

Evan gave it all to her, every single incident, every moment of what had happened since the night with Heidi and the first time he'd flashed back to their childhood. Most of the time, she listened with a sneer of derision on her face, but now and then she stopped cold as he described things like Tommy's murder and his ordeal inside the prison. He ran out of words after a while, and his story petered out into silence as Kayleigh pushed her empty plate aside and lit a post-dinner smoke.

"You're on something, right?" she said, after a long draw on the cigarette. "Did you, like, drop acid and watch a *Back to the Future* marathon on TV? 'Cause what you're saying is like some fucked up head-game bullshit."

"It's true," he retorted. "Every word."

She shook her head. "You were right back there in the room, Evan: I don't believe you."

"I never thought you would," he stared at her with fatigued, dull eyes. "That's why I've never bothered to tell a soul until now, and that's why I never will again."

"I'm the only person you told?" Kayleigh said in an arch voice. "Wow, that's a great line. Tell me, does that ever work? Do you ever get any with that, does that make other girls swoon when they hear it?" she sneered at him. "Do they actually eat up this bullshit you're spouting?"

"I couldn't give a shit if you believe me or not, and frankly, I'm too damn tired to prove it to you." Evan let the words out with weary effort. He felt drained and listless—even lifting the coffee cup to his mouth seemed like too much trouble.

"Oh, so there's proof now as well? This I have to hear."

"Shit, I dunno," he said, making a vague, tired gesture with his hand. "If I was lying, how would I know about the twin moles you have on your inner thigh?"

Kayleigh laughed harshly. "You'll have to come up with something better than that! Plenty of guys have seen them. Anyone with fifty bucks could tell you that!"

He leaned forward, marshalling his concentration. "Then forget that. How about..." Evan paused, running through his memories of Kayleigh. "How about you prefer the smell of a skunk to flowers?" She blinked and he went on. "You've always hated cilantro because, for reasons unknown to you, it always reminds you of your stepsister."

Kayleigh's jaw dropped open. "How could you possibly—"

"Oh!" Evan snapped his fingers as something came to him. "How about this? When you have an orgasm, your toes go numb. I'm pretty sure your clientele aren't privy to that bit of information."

She tried and failed to conceal the surprise in her eyes. Evan nodded to himself. "I came here because I wanted to tell you something. I just thought that you should know."

Kayleigh watched him carefully. "Know what?"

"That I didn't leave you there to rot."

She physically flinched as the words left his mouth. Any thin thread of confidence Evan had built up with her over the past hours snapped as Kayleigh's eyes filled up with distrust and contempt. "You're a sick son of a bitch," she said coldly, "and there's one major hole in your story."

Evan looked away. "Which is?"

She flicked her spent cigarette butt into her coffee cup. "There is no fuckin' way, on this planet or any other, that I was in some fuckin' sorority." Kayleigh stood up and pulled a twenty-dollar bill from Evan's wallet and threw it on the table. She weighed the billfold in her hand. "You sure you don't want this?"

He shrugged. "I don't think I'll need it where I'm going."

She gave him a scornful sneer. "What, you're off to change everyone's life again, is that it? Off to screw with history one more time?"

"I don't know if I can."

"Sure, whatever. Maybe this time, you'll pop up in some mansion while I wind up in Tijuana doing the donkey act, huh?"

Evan drew his hands over his face; the skin there felt flaccid and lifeless. "I'm over it. Whenever I try to help anyone, it all turns to shit."

Kayleigh picked up her coat and stuffed the wallet in her pocket. "Well, don't give up now, Slick." She made a mocking sweep of her hands, "I mean, just look, you've already done so much for me."

"I'm sorry," Evan whispered.

"I got an idea," she went on, ignoring him. "Hell, why don't you go back in time and do something that matters, be a hero and save Mrs Halpern and her baby? Then maybe that psycho Lenny wouldn't freak out and ruin my family?" She was walking for the door now, with purposeful, angry footsteps. "Oh, and here's another one!" Kayleigh threw the words over her shoulder at him. "Go back to when I'm seven and fuck me in front of Daddy's handicam, you know, straighten me out a bit..."

She threw the wallet back at him and slammed the diner door shut behind her.

Evan stared into his coffee cup, losing himself in the swirling black liquid—falling and yielding to the darkness around him.

TWENTY-THREE

It was dawn by the time Evan got back to the campus dormitory, and with the first orange rays of sunlight spearing in through the windows, he stalked through the passageways of the building like a ghost, slump-shouldered and gray. The corridors were empty this early, with many of the students sleeping off hangovers or late-night cram sessions. Evan felt weighed down with fatigue, as if the pressure and gravity of all the years he changed or caused to come undone were now bearing upon him, forcing him to stoop, slowly pushing him into the ground. Evan tried to remember when he had last slept, and came back with an unclear, fuzzy and fragmented memory of events. Do I even know what day it is?

He opened the door to his room and heard the familiar sound of Thumper's creaking bedsprings, and the gasps of some young co-ed on the verge of an orgasm. They ignored Evan as he entered, and he tore open the curtains and flooded the dorm with light.

"Get out," he said in a dead, toneless voice. "Both of you."

Thumper fumbled to a halt and stifled a whiny complaint from his bed partner. "Sorry, dude," his roommate said without abashment. "We're just, uh, you know…"

Evan fixed him with a hard glare that told Thumper no argument would be tolerated. "We just figured it would be okay to get together, what with you bein' sick and all…" he finished lamely. "Right?"

Anger flared in Evan's face, and he picked up a desk chair by the backrest and swung it around. Thumper blinked in surprise and flinched as Evan smashed it into the wall over his head. The girl beneath him yelped and shrank under his bulky chest.

"I'm not saying it again." Evan's words were ice-cold.

"Come on, Cricket," Thumper said quickly. "Let's give my buddy here a little space, huh?" He pulled the blankets up around him and stepped off the bed. The girl jerked as her naked body was exposed, and she dived for her clothes in the heap where she'd tossed them earlier.

"Shit, what is this?" she griped. "Thumper, you told me he was in the hospital, or somethin'. Why is he back so—" A frosty look from Evan silenced any more comments from her lips.

Thumper led Cricket barefooted through the door and shut it behind them, the muffled sounds of their argument fading as they walked away. Evan dropped to his haunches as if his legs had given way beneath him and sat hard on the floor. He rubbed at his face, trying to work away the exhaustion that seemed to be collecting around his eyes. He extended a hand and felt around under his bunk.

The box of journals was still there, and seeing them intact gave Evan what felt like the first relief he'd had in days. These were the only touchstones he had now, the only constants that remained no matter how much everything else in his life altered. The books were in a vaguely chronological order and he soon found the one he wanted, spotting the protruding flag of a sticky note poking out from between the pages. Evan sat there with it for a moment, his eyes not really focusing on anything.

A glitter of light from the encroaching morning attracted his attention and he looked up. There, on the shelf over Thumper's bed, was the happy brass face of a laughing Buddha statuette. Next to that was a large votive candle with a portrait of Jesus Christ on it—Thumper clearly wanted to cover his bases in a theological sense. Evan remembered Carlos's tattoos, but the smiling figure emblazoned on the candle was softer and gentler. He had never really been a great believer in religion, but at this moment, as weary as he was, Evan found himself reassured a little by the idea that something greater than him might be watching over things. He closed his eyes and mumbled—for what it was worth—an invocation.

"Lord, give me the strength and guidance I need to set things right."

In the diner, he had told Kayleigh that he was over it and that he was done with the books—but even as he had said it, Evan had tasted the lie. He gripped the journal firmly. This was as much his gift as it was his curse, and so help him, Evan knew he would have to see it through to the end.

It was becoming a formality to him now. First, a deep calming breath, and then a moment to clear his mind and ready himself. Next, the words, concentrating on them, letting them conjure the memory from the depths of his mind.

The last thing I remember before the blackout was holding my hands over Kayleigh's ears. I think I was more focused on her hands touching mine than the mailbox across the street.

His eyes slipped easily over the page. He had visited this event once before, and the second time around it seemed easier, like pulling on a pair of comfortable shoes.

Then came the sensation, the growing tension inside the bony cage of his skull, the subtle press against his eyes—then the flickering, jumping dance of his vision, as the sights around him started to shiver and quake. At last, the sounds, the weird backward echoes from some other time and place—

He let the world change and shift.

Evan was ready for the confusion of displacement and he blinked it away, the drained sensation he'd been feeling all day suddenly gone in a heartbeat. His hands were over Kayleigh's ears as she smiled, Tommy there to one side grimacing as he touched his sister, and Lenny panting like a dog after a run.

Evan spat the cigarette out of his mouth and drew back his hands. His fingers strayed to the place on his stomach where the burn scar was— would be, he corrected himself. But now I've dropped the lit cigarette, that will never happen, will it? He ground out the smoldering stick under the heel of his sneaker.

"That's one thing changed," Evan said under his breath, and Kayleigh gave him a curious look.

"Maybe it went out," Lenny was saying. "It should have gone off, right? Should someone check it?" He extended a chubby finger toward the mailbox across the street from them.

Tommy threw him a withering look for the idiocy his comments. "Yeah, why don't you do that, Lenny? Moron!"

Evan ignored the quizzical expression on Kayleigh's face and looked up at the mailbox opposite from their hiding place. Inside the tiny model house outside the Halpern home, the makeshift fuse he had created for the dynamite Blockbuster was slowly burning away, the seconds ticking away towards an explosion.

"We gotta—" Lenny tried to say something and floundered.

Outside the house, a car pulled up and a woman got out.

Lenny edged forward, but Tommy grabbed his arm before he could move too far. "Make one peep and I'll swear it'll be your last, mother-fucker."

A child cried out, and then Evan saw Mrs Halpern approaching the mailbox with her daughter held high. She was cooing to the baby: "Don't cry, angel!"

Lenny strained half-heartedly against Tommy's grip, as the other boy swore softly. "Shit, where's she going?"

"Aww, you need a change, don't you honey?" said the woman, oblivious the drama unfolding around her. "Shall we get all the post for Daddy?"

Evan bolted to his feet and launched himself forward, like a runner coming off the blocks at sound of a starting pistol.

"What the—" Tommy began, but Evan was already out of cover and sprinting across the road. "What is he doing? He's going to fuck it all up!"

"Lady, stay back!" Evan came roaring and waving his arms at Mrs Halpern. "Don't go near the mailbox! Stay back!"

The woman was startled by the sudden appearance of the boy, but she gave him a pained, skeptical look and continued to approach the container, holding up her child so that she would be able to reach the latch of the ornate mailbox. "You want to open the door, honey?"

"I mean it woman! Get the hell back!" Evan shouted at the top of his thirteen-year-old lungs, pounding over the asphalt of the road and up the grassy embankment of the lawn. She has to listen to me! he told himself. She has to!

Lenny bolted after Evan, and after a couple of seconds of indecision, Tommy shrugged at the reversal of events and came up after him.

"Tommy, what—" began Kayleigh, but her brother was already gone, a new plan forming in his mind as he tore across the road.

"There's a bomb in the mailbox!" wheezed Lenny, his voice high and panicked. "A bomb! Get away!"

At the word "bomb", the woman paused for a moment, rocking back on her heels—but then she shook her head and walked on, hefting her baby up into a cradled position.

"Dumb kids." she muttered. This wasn't the first time that teens from the neighborhood had played tricks on the Halperns, like knocking on the door and running, or the old 'burning bag of dog poop on the porch' gag. Her husband told her that it was because they were better off than most of their neighbors; like their parents, the kids were jealous of the Halpern's nice home and big car.

Behind Lenny, Tommy made a sour face at the other boy's idiotic confession. "Stupid fat ass," he said, under his breath. Tommy began to mentally compose the lie he would tell about how they had known about the Blockbuster—they'd blame it on older kids, maybe. Yeah. Or else say it was all Lenny's idea.

Evan skidded to a stop on the damp grassy lawn and interposed himself between the mailbox and Lisa Halpern. He spread his arms wide to block her way, waving them up and down. He called to her to back off, but she kept on approaching. "You've gotta keep back!" Evan insisted.

"Look," she said, with the pained and measured calm of an adult forced to deal with an over-active child. "What are you kids doing in my garden?"

Before Evan could answer, Tommy hove into view, running full-tilt at the woman and her child. "I'll save you, lady!" he cried, and hit her hard in a straight tackle, shoving her to the ground with a lot more force than was really necessary.

By reflex, Mrs Halpern clutched her baby daughter tight to her chest and took the majority of the impact, as Tommy flopped over her. She was down, and save for some bruises, unhurt. "Stay there!" Tommy added urgently.

The sweet release of tension ran through Evan like a wave, and he backed away from the mailbox, a grin forming on his lips.

I fixed it, for real this time!

He had perhaps one or two milliseconds of smug complacence, before the Blockbuster detonated. Lenny was close enough to be knocked off his feet, but Kayleigh was out of range and thanks to Tommy, Mrs Halpern and her daughter were safely away from the blast. It was Evan Treborn who stood alone, exactly in front of the mailbox, unwittingly in the path of the iron latch that shot off like a bullet when it blew open. The doctors would later dig the metal rod out of his spine, where it had lodged in a gap between his vertebrae.

The construction of the box was wood around a metal frame, and the curved steel shape of the inner structure channeled the force of the quarter-stick of dynamite outward in a flaming jet of superheated gas; for the briefest of moments, it would have been like standing underneath a rocket ignition.

The image of the shattering box burned itself into Evan's eyes, searing him with every tiny instant of the detonation. The little mailbox house suddenly bulged along all its seams as an explosive cloud of vapor blew out across the lawn in an orange fireball. The shock-wave deafened him instantly and swept aside Evan's teenage body as if it were a leaf caught in a hurricane, hurling him backwards into the road. Strings of bright crimson blood trailed out behind him like horrific streamers—

The blast echoed though his head, making every bone in Evan's body shake and tremble with tight agony. He gasped for air and writhed on the bed, leaning up as the hot kiss of the explosion faded away. The skin on his face felt tight

and warm, as if it were drawn taut over his
skull. Evan's gut flip-flopped and he fought
down an acidic pulse of bile as his stomach
threatened to eject the contents of his belly all
over the floor.

The dorm. He was back in the dorm room, as
the warm morning light flowed in through the
windows. Things were back as he remembered
them, the beds were on the right side once
more, the posters and the flyers all over the
wall—and even the familiar sounds of athletic,
frantic lovemaking came from Thumper's shapeless hill of bedclothes.

"I thought I told you two to beat it…" Evan
began, as the first licks of pain began to gather
in his temples, swarming together like fireflies.

"Huh? What?" The voice from the bed did not
belong to Thumper. "Hey, sorry, man. Did we
wake you?"

Evan grimaced as he tried to hold off the ache
building across his skin, but the next second
found himself stunned as a familiar moon face
emerged from under the sheets.

"You okay there, roomie?" said Lenny, his
complexion flushed and red from the effort of
sex. "You having bad dreams? You look a little
piqued, there…"

Confusion clashed with delight as Evan managed a tight smile. Lenny was here, not strapped
down to a bed in some psycho ward in Sunnyvale. "No, it's cool. Really cool." I've changed
things; it's changed again!

Evan yawned and brought up his hands to massage his temples. A blunt, fleshy stump pressed into his face where fingers and a thumb should have been.

Shock made his skin go live with prickling, electric heat and Evan bolted upright in bed, sending the cotton sheets around him into sprawling disarray. His limbs trembled as he stared at them in rapt, unblinking horror. Where two perfectly good working hands had been before, now there was nothing but a pair of featureless, bent stubs, the twisted and broken remnants of his arms. Evan tried to force out a scream, but the sudden tightness in his throat prevented it. He tried to move off the bed, but his legs failed to respond and he caught sight of the shapes of them under the sheets, contorted at sickening angles. He realized that he couldn't feel his toes.

"What happened to me?" he cried, as sparkling torches of white-hot agony ignited inside his memory. He tasted the lukewarm coppery tang of blood in his mouth as the tremors of new recollections forced their way into his patched, leaking psyche. Like a flood, the images and sensations engulfed him, dragged him and drowned him in their relentless undertow before he could stop them.

Kayleigh, drawn and skeletal, watching him with cold disdain... The cloying stink of spent heroin and stale urine in the motel room... The dark glitter of absolute evil in Lenny's eyes as he lay on the metal bed... The fear on George Miller's lined, worn face...

Like flashbulbs, the memories flared brightly and then burnt away, decaying into powdery remnants, fading and fading.

Doctor Redfield's careful platitudes and assurances... Mom's tight grip around his hands as she promises him everything will be all right... Thumper cradling his head in his arms, Evan's bright blood on his fingers... The taste of the thick, sour coffee at the Ridgewood Diner...

Suddenly, each sensation vanished, every one of them sending a hissing dart of pain into his brain as it departed. In some faraway place, Evan moaned as events started to reverse themselves and unfamiliar emotions came out of nowhere and hammered themselves into the cracks and voids in his mind. He heard sounds like some mad cocktail of laughter and weeping, wondering if it might be coming from his own mouth or some distant phantom voice of the past.

Flashes like fireworks bursting, a storm of snapshot days... A younger Evan looking at his own reflection in a hospital bed, his ruined arms swathed in thick bandages... Andrea's fingers through his hair as she cries, telling him he'll never walk again... Lenny and Kayleigh loading popcorn and drinks on to his lap as they push his wheelchair through the cinema lobby...

Evan tried to force the images away, praying that perhaps, if he could hold them back, then somehow these dreadful incidents would never have happened; but still the memories came, choking the hope out of him

His fourteenth birthday, his friends towering around him as he blows out the candles on a massive cake... Mom, Lenny, Kayleigh, Tommy, all of them clapping and smiling and happy... The swelling sound of hymns as Tommy wheels him into church on a bright, glorious Sunday... Alone and waving a stump at the other kids from the dock as they leap and frolic in the lake...

Evan screamed and for a fragmentary moment, the storm of memory released him to let him choke in a breath of tainted air.

"Oh shit, he's bleeding!" He was dimly aware of Lenny coming to his aid, pinching his nose shut as blood gushed out of his nostrils. "Help me!"

A girl scrambled out of Lenny's bed, pulling her sleep shirt down over her body, tearing a towel off a rack as she raced toward him. She had golden blonde hair that caught the sun, even in wild disarray as it was now, and the most beautiful eyes.

"Kuh. Kuh. Kayleigh?" Evan coughed, as his gaze met hers; the sight of her set off another strand of recall, popping open like a string of firecrackers made of sights and sounds.

On the lake, Evan sits alone in the gunwale of a rowboat while Lenny and Kayleigh hold hands... The hollow and bitter emptiness inside as he watches the two of them share secret jokes and the joy of each other's company... Burnt wood smell of the campfire, as Evan drinks from a beer cap, while Kayleigh and Lenny kiss in the moonlight… Trapped in the metal shackles of his wheelchair as they dance together at the Senior Prom…

"Evan, we've got you," Kayleigh said with tenderness and concern. "It's okay, Lenny and I are here."

"Don't touch me!" he shouted, and knocked them aside with his crippled limbs. "Don't touch me!" Shivers racked him and Evan's vision dulled, tunneling into a landscape of gray wool. "Don't…" he coughed, before finally, mercifully, he lost consciousness.

TWENTY-FOUR

Hanging there in the silent, blood-warm darkness of unconsciousness, Evan found a moment's peace, a brief respite from the cascade of events around him. When the first sensations of wakefulness returned to him, he wanted to shy away, to stay in the black where it was safe and sound instead of facing the new future he had unwittingly created for himself. But for all his hopes, he found himself being dragged back toward the light and noise of a harsh and uncompromising reality.

The sound of doors crashing open brought him the final few steps from sleep to awareness, and with them came needles of agony across the sides of his skull.

"Where…" he mumbled. "Where are we going?" The halls of the dorm raced past him as his wheelchair rushed headlong through the dormitory block.

Ahead, Kayleigh pushed open another set of fire doors with one hand, cradling what appeared to be a pair of heavy plastic gloves in the other. Evan's head lolled, and he caught sight of Lenny behind him, his friend's powerful hands pressing the wheelchair, rushing it forward.

"We have to get you to Sunnyvale. You're having one of your famous hemorrhages," Kayleigh puffed, holding the doors open. "Just stay calm, you'll be fine!"

"No!" Evan shouted, rubbing at the pain as it flared in his temple again. "Stop! Take me back!"

"Sorry, tough guy," Lenny said from over his shoulder. "No can do. Your mother would kill me—"

Evan drew together what little strength he could muster in his legs and torso, and forced it against the back of the metal frame. He pitched forward and spilled clumsily from the chair, landing on the floor in a heap. Lenny jerked the wheelchair to a halt before it could crush him.

"Shit, Evan." Lenny gasped. "Are you all right?"

He pulled at the dead, heavy meat of his legs, but no amount of effort Evan applied could even begin to move his paralyzed limbs. Kayleigh shoved her way though the edge of a forming crowd of students, who looked on with a mix of gawking faces and cruel snickers of laughter.

Evan ignored their jibes and stared at his roommate. "Take me back, Lenny!" he gritted through clenched teeth. "You owe me that much."

The demand made Lenny pause, and someone at the back of the crowd made a spiteful comment. Kayleigh turned to face the jeering students, eyes alight with anger. "What are you geeks looking at?" she spat at them. "Must be nice to be so goddamned perfect, huh? You fucking losers!"

Her retort had the desired effect, and the crowd began to break apart and dissipate. On the floor, Evan reached his arms up to the chair and tried to pull himself into it, falling short. He stared at the ground, his face flushed with embarrassment at the indignity of his predicament.

When he looked up, both Lenny and Kayleigh were offering him their hands, with expressions of concern and friendship.

They took him for a walk around the quad, against their better judgment letting Evan stay at college instead of whisking him off to the clinic. Kayleigh handed him the plastic gloves—they were prosthetic forearms and hands that worked by nerve induction—and as they circled the trees, Evan worked at the devices with only little success. They were gross, clumsy mechanical approximations of fingers that whined and clicked when he moved them.

As they walked, Lenny would wave to a passer-by or share a joke with one of the other students. He seemed so different now, any trace of his hesitant, inward-drawn self washed away by a new, vital personality alive with confidence. Lenny was clearly popular with just about everyone.

"Hey, Len!" called a dark-skinned girl as she rolled past on a skateboard.

"'Sup Sheila! We missed you at the party!" Lenny called after her. "Don't even think I'm giving you my lab notes, either! Think I like getting up for 'eight-thirties'?"

Evan felt disconnected from things as he watched Lenny's casual interplay. It was like watching himself from the outside, the circumstances playing out in the same way they had when he had been the "big man on campus". Kayleigh too was different, her persona changed back to the vibrant, attractive sorority girl once again, but with a new edge of melancholy hidden beneath it. He looked away and noticed Thumper and Cricket standing by the side of the path. Evan gave them a weak smile, but neither of them could look him in the eye, and their conversation stopped as he rolled by, both staring at their feet, uncomfortable at the sight of him.

They were not the only ones to treat him as if he were non-existent. Almost everyone who greeted Kayleigh or Lenny threw them a hello but looked passed Evan as if he were not there. Evan nursed a knot of anger and glared at the pavement before him.

"Hey, there's Tommy!" said Lenny, turning the chair off the path. "Let's go say hi."

The name made Evan flinch and his heart leapt into his mouth—the thought of facing Tommy

Miller in so vulnerable a state made his palms sweat with fear—but in the next second, that fear was overcome by surprise. At first, Evan didn't recognize Kayleigh's brother in this new, clean-cut guise, dressed well and smiling widely. He stood beneath a bright banner that read Campus Crusade for Christ. Tommy handed out leaflet after leaflet to all the passing students with a good-natured grin for everyone who took one. Evan saw a small silver cross pinned to his lapel, along with a badge that screamed "Ask Me about the Good News!"

The sight of Tommy was so strange and incongruous that Evan almost laughed at him. Tommy saw them approaching and his eyes brightened with genuine warmth as Lenny rolled Evan his way. "Hey, guys, how are you? We're doing great today, we're getting lots of sign-ups!"

"That's excellent, Tommy," said Kayleigh.

"Evan," he stepped closer and patted him on the shoulder. "I did what you said, man! We're pooling our student funds with Hillel House and we're going to have an Awareness Dance! Is that cool, or what?"

"Oh goody," Evan said, his black mood returning. "There's nothing like spinning my chair around to a techno remix of Hava Nagila until I puke."

Tommy frowned at the sour comment and exchanged a glance with Lenny who shrugged and nodded back at him. "Well, thanks for the idea, anyhow."

"Uh, well, we should be getting to classes now…" Lenny began, drawing back the wheel-chair.

"Forget it," Evan snapped. "What's the point of taking my Psych class now? Tomorrow I could wake up as some dirt farmer in Bangladesh."

The others looked at one another and an unspoken comment passed from Kayleigh to the other men. "You know what, Lenny, you go on. Evan and me are going to go for a stroll, okay?"

Evan didn't complain as Kayleigh took the handles of the chair and pushed him off in another direction, guiding him away to a more secluded part of the quad. Evan shivered as they passed by the spot where he had fatally confronted her brother, on that night that now seemed like a lifetime ago. He stared down at the prosthetic hands crossed in his lap and made them click open and closed like some weird kind of wind-up toy.

"So Tommy's really into this Jesus kick, huh?" he asked.

Kayleigh gave him a look that told him that this was something he should have already known about. "Well, yeah, you know he is. You know how spiritual he got after he saved Mrs Halpern and little Katie."

"He saved Mrs Halpern?" Evan growled. "Please. The twisted fuck," he added with venom.

They halted at a bench and Kayleigh sat, using her foot to turn his chair toward her. Kayleigh's pretty face was troubled. "Hungry?" she asked, fishing a candy bar out of her pocket. She broke it in half and handed him some.

Evan took the bar in his hand, but the plastic limb twitched under his inexpert control and crushed it to dust. Kayleigh seemed confused by the reaction, but she said nothing and instead fed Evan her remaining half of the bar. He took it carefully, trying to avoid looking directly at her.

"Is something the matter?" Kayleigh asked after a moment.

Evan looked at the prosthetics and clapped them together to brush the food fragments away. "Yeah, I think I gotta get these fixed or something."

"I've never seen you like this before," she continued, leaning closer to feed him the last bit of the snack bar.

Evan caught the apple blossom scent of her skin and it made his breath seize in his throat. "Kayleigh? Do you ever think about us? I mean, do you ever wonder if it could have been different between the two of us?"

She nodded. "Sure, Evan, why not? You know, you were the first person I ever really cared about."

The pure candor in her words made his eyes prickle with emotion. "I was?"

"That's why when I was little, I never went to live with my Mother when she and my Dad got divorced."

"I don't get it," Evan breathed.

Kayleigh delicately wiped a crumb from his lip. "When my folks split, they gave me and Tommy a choice of who we wanted to live with. I couldn't stand my Dad, but I knew that if I moved to my Mom's place in Florida, I'd never see you again."

Evan's heart pounded. "I never knew that," he said quietly, suddenly sobered by the consequences of Kayleigh's childhood decision. "So, then you still sometimes think of us... together?"

"It's crossed my mind from time to time. I wondered what might have been."

"And?" he prompted, his voice filled with futile hope.

She gave Evan the tiniest of sorrowful smiles. "Well, a lot of things cross my mind. I've always been a fast thinker, Ev. I can play out the movie of our entire lives in under a second." She took a breath. "Boom, we fall in love. Get married. Two kids, your keen analytical insight matched to my generous nature," she answered, to which Evan smiled. "Kids grow old as do we. Relatively stable relationships, matching burial plots, the whole bit," Kayleigh looked away. "It took a lot longer to spit out than to imagine."

"Then, you think it might have worked out?"

"Why not?" she replied. "But that's not how things wound up. I'm with Lenny. Lenny is your friend, and there it ends." Kayleigh looked into his eyes and gave him an almost apologetic shrug.

Evan felt like an abyss was yawning open beneath him, as hot tears began to brim over and roll down his cheeks. "Would it make any difference if I told you that no one could possibly love you as much as I love you?"

She shook her head sadly. "I have to go." Kayleigh stood, touching him once on the shoulder in farewell, and then walked away to where Lenny was waving to her.

As much as Evan wanted to look elsewhere, he could not tear his eyes from her as she embraced Lenny and the two of them drew together into a kiss.

His heart breaking, Evan finally closed his eyes and turned away, hoping that the darkness would come and engulf him once again.

Evan felt nothing as he turned on the bath's taps to full, his stump awkwardly pushing the silver handles open. He felt as if he was hollowed out inside, as if all his emotions and desires were gone, drained away to nothing. He just wanted it to end now, for the hurt to go away.

The chair clattered over on to its side as he hauled himself out of it, the wheels spinning listlessly as it capsized. Evan pushed off it with his body and slid fully clothed into the bathtub, the pooling water soaking through his trousers and shirt. He eased back and let himself slide down, finding what comfort he could against the hard, cool enamel. The gushing taps played against his knees and quickly filled the tub, up past his ankles and waist, covering his chest and arms.

Evan felt an odd kind of calm come over him, a strange peace that welled up from nowhere. If he had doubts about what he was about to do, they were gone now.

The water drew up to his neck, then his lips and nostrils. Evan inclined his head just enough to lift it out of the liquid and took a last, deep breath. He sank back into the bath and let himself go under. Lukewarm water spilled out over the edges in spatters.

The bathroom door opened and Tommy stood there, instantly grasping the situation. Air bubbled out of Evan's mouth as he tried to warn him away.

"You forgot to put the toaster on the edge. It doesn't work without that." With an almost casual air, Tommy twisted off the taps and reached into the tub, popping the plug out of the drain. The water rushed away, down Evan's soaked body to his mouth.

"But you, and Kayleigh and Lenny… You all like toast," Evan said lamely. "And that's all that matters now. Not me."

Tommy's face tightened with sympathy. "Ah, Evan. Everyone matters." He reached into the bath and gathered him up, putting him down on the wet floor. Without any hint of self-doubt or hesitation, Tommy held him, offering the only comfort he could. At first Evan bristled, his anger towards Tommy sparking to life, but then he realized that the Tommy he'd hated was not this man, not the kind and decent human being who had just stopped Evan from taking his own life.

"Thank you," he whispered.

Tommy nodded. "Come on, I'll get you changed. Visiting hours are almost up."

Tommy drove him out of the campus and across town to St Vincent's, a secluded hospital complex on the edge of a well-kept parkland. They arrived as evening fell, and Tommy unfolded the wheelchair with practiced ease and smartly deposited Evan in it. They rolled through the corridors, every now and then passing a patient or a doctor who gave Tommy a friendly hello.

"I do volunteer work here, remember?" he said, responding to Evan's questioning look.

"Oh, right," Evan replied. He looked around as they passed through a ward towards the private rooms. "So what are we doing here? Did my Mom get transferred to a different job again?"

The words died on his lips as Tommy pushed him into a private room and turned him to face the sole occupant. Evan found he couldn't speak.

Lying there on the bed, surrounded by a network of clear tubes and quiet machines, Andrea Treborn gave him a wan smile and beckoned them closer. Tommy leaned in and kissed her on the cheek, and she tousled his hair in return.

Evan tried to force out "Why?" but nothing came. His mother was connected to a forest of IV drips, a tracheotomy tube, the dull green torpedo shape of an oxygen cylinder and a respirator. Evan watched the machine's bellows opening and closing, breathing for his mother.

Tommy wheeled him closer to her and she spoke in a faint whisper, her voice hissing like a distant breeze through grass. "Looking. Good. Kiddo."

Evan's eyes flicked to the treatment regimen attached to a clipboard at the foot of the bed. "Lung cancer?" he gasped, the words bearing down on him.

Andrea and Tommy shared an awkward look. "Sorry, Mrs T. Evan's been a little out of sorts lately. Forgetful."

A flicker of concern crossed his mother's face as he looked at her, his eyes wide. "That's right…" he said cautiously. "You started chain smoking after I blew myself up…" The memory of it seemed ephemeral, but it churned up a sick guilt within him. "There must be a way to fix this."

"Fix?" It was painful for her to even whisper out the word.

"The doctors are doing everything they can…" said Tommy, but Evan ignored him, his mind racing along other lines.

"I just need to find the entry about the Block-buster!" he snapped, and Tommy stiffened.

"Evan, look, that was all in the past—" he warned.

"Wait, shit!" Evan continued, not hearing him. "No arms! There won't be any entry about it, because I never even got the chance to write it."

Andrea's face showed shock and a terrible, abrupt realization. "No," she breathed. "Not you." She gripped Tommy's arm and pulled him closer, laboring out a ragged whisper. "Is Evan... different?"

Tommy chewed his lip and tried to hide his reaction. "It's not... Well, he's just going through some tough times right now..."

Thin tears began to fall from Andrea's eyes. "Evan, no..."

Her son leaned forward on his chair and wiped them from her thin, bloodless cheeks. "Mom, don't cry," he said with certainty. "I can change this. I know I can."

"I, uh, think I'll go down to the chapel," Tommy smiled weakly, suddenly feeling uncomfortable for interrupting the mother and son. "I'll come back later."

Andrea grabbed at Evan's arm as soon as they were alone. "What... are you... doing?" she panted. "You're... acting... like your father."

Evan tried to make light of her fears. "No, no, it's nothing like that. Come on, Mom, just because Dad was my age when he started going crazy, that doesn't mean that I'm nuts too."

"How?" she said with shock. "How... did you... know that?"

"You told me on that Parent's Weekend, remember?" he said.

"I never... told you," Andrea grated. "Never."

Evan went cold; those events had happened in a different set of events, in a different time-line. "Wait, that wasn't me... Or you..."

With effort, his mother used her left hand to pinch off the air to the oxygen tube snaked into her neck and forced herself to speak in a sick, gravelly whisper. "Just... like... Jason."

Her eyes implored him not to go on, but Evan shook his head, a fresh new determination coming to him. "No, Mom. I'm gonna fix it. I have to see this through to the very end, no matter what." He patted her on the arm. The gesture was meant to reassure her but her reaction was anything but, her eyes tearing, head shaking. "To think, I could have drowned myself and left you to suffer through this for years. I'm not going to let that happen. Don't worry. I'm going to get you out of here. Trust me."

Evan flipped up the brakes on his wheelchair and rolled forward, out of the room and into the corridor. Andrea pulled in as much air as she could into her ruined lungs and forced out her loudest rasping scream.

"Stop him," she cried. "Stop him. Stop him. Stop him..."

Her son did not look back.

TWENTY-FIVE

Lenny groaned with exertion as he pulled the last of the weighty cardboard boxes down from the cupboard shelf. He dropped it to the floor alongside an identical container. Both had the word "Evan" written on them in thick black marker pen. Lenny nudged the box with his foot, pushing it across the frayed dorm room carpet toward Evan, who looked on intently.

"Okay?" Lenny prompted.

"Can you empty them out for me?" Evan asked.

"What is it you're looking for?" Lenny said, stealing a glance at the clock by his bed. He'd promised Kayleigh that he'd come visit her tonight, and he was anxious to get going.

"A composition book," said Evan. "Marbled cover, like the kind we used to have in grade school."

"Oh yeah, I remember," Lenny upended the boxes on to Evan's bed, pouring out a cascade of accumulated personal junk, the spent debris of

Evan Treborn's childhood. "Are you sure she even packed it in here?"

Evan nodded. "My Mom never threw anything away. She packed for me when I left for college. I think she sent everything I ever owned, so we'll see."

Lenny began to paw his way through the mass of stuff. "Look at this: books, photo albums..." He held up a crumpled picture showing two small boys in colorful paper hats. "Hey, check this out! It's us, at my fifth birthday party!"

"Yeah, cute," said Evan tightly, and Lenny continued.

"Report cards. Listen to this: 'Mrs Boswell says Evan is an enigma—"

"Lenny, please. Just the journal?"

"Oh right, sorry." He dropped the card back into the pile. "Shit, she even put your toys in here." Lenny dangled a die-cast jet fighter from his fingers. "Cool, an F-15 Eagle! I used to love planes when I was a kid..." His words trailed off as he saw the hard look Evan was giving him. "Right, right. The journal. I got it."

After a moment he dragged a thin booklet out of a pile of dog-eared old superhero comics. "Is this it?"

Evan's heart leapt as he saw the worn cover of the volume, with the words "Age 7" written there in his mother's clean, elliptical handwriting. "That's it, give it here!" He practically snatched it from Lenny's fingers, and used the clicking prosthetic hands to fumble through the pages.

"What do you need it for, anyway? All of a sudden you want to read your old diary?" He sighed. "I don't get you lately." Lenny picked up his jacket from the back of a chair.

"Duly noted," Evan said, glancing up at him. "Now I'm going to ask you for one last favor."

Lenny paused, one hand in his jacket sleeve. "Dude, I've... I've got a date tonight."

A momentary grimace shadowed Evan's face at the thought of Lenny spending the night with Kayleigh, but he shuttered it away. "I know, but this won't take long. I just need you to watch me."

"Watch you?" Lenny repeated, putting on the coat but sitting down. "What do you want me to do that for?"

"In case I have another seizure," Evan said off-handedly, coming across the page in the book that he wanted. "Here we go."

"Evan, look, you've been acting screwy ever since this morning. Kayleigh says you're forgetting stuff, and Tommy said you were weird at the hospital tonight. Now you're talking about seizures and stuff..." Lenny paused, chewing his lip. "Maybe you should go to see Doctor Redfield at the clinic. Just to be on the safe side."

"I'm not going there," Evan said with force. "Now be quiet. I need to concentrate on the Blockbuster if I'm going to destroy it."

"Destroy it?" Lenny's concern mingled with confusion. "That was years and years ago. Evan, you're making no sense."

His roommate leaned forward and Lenny felt the metallic grip of his artificial hand on his knee. "If I hadn't blown my arms off, Mom never would have started smoking in the first place," Evan's eyes flashed with intensity, "and she wouldn't be in that hospital, having to use a stinking machine to breathe! Now be quiet and let me concentrate!"

Lenny threw up his hands and stood. "That's it, you're officially off the deep end, buddy. I'm calling Kayleigh right now and we're gonna take you to the clinic."

"No! No!" Evan snapped, recoiling. He took a breath and calmed himself. "Look, okay, maybe you're right," Evan began again in a more rational tone of voice. "It's just that, this morning... It really shook me up, you know?"

Lenny hesitated, his apprehension clear.

"I'll go to the clinic with you tomorrow, okay?" said Evan. "But I just need you to do this one thing for me now. Please?"

His friend sat down again, still baffled by what was being asked of him. "All right."

Evan began to read from the book, his lips moving silently as he went over the words. From Lenny's perspective, his roommate's head seemed to sway slightly, and then without warning Evan went limp like a rag doll.

"Evan? Evan, can you hear me?"

There was a shimmering, oscillating shift and he was there, in the kitchen, thirteen years earlier.

"Evan?" He heard his mother's voice calling from another room. "Did you hear me?"

Something was clogging his throat, and Evan coughed explosively, sending a mouthful of soggy breakfast cereal across the kitchen table. He dropped the spoon into the bowl before him and shook his head to wave away the momentary distortion he felt in his body.

"Yes!" he piped, ignoring the change in the pitch of his voice. "It still works!"

In front of him was the open page of the journal he had just been reading, but here and now in the past it was clean and new, the ink still drying on the paper. *Today Mommy is takeing me to play with Kayley and Tommy,* read the entry, *I will mete there father and see what a real dad is like.*

The last sentence made Evan's boyish face twist in a very adult expression of mockery. George Miller a real dad? Yeah, right, and I'm Miss America.

He jumped down from the chair and flexed his hands—his real, flesh-and-blood hands. From under the table, Crockett watched him with wary eyes. The dog seemed to sense the change in Evan and shrank back from him, growling softly. Ignoring the animal, Evan glanced around the room. "Now, how do I destroy the Blockbuster?" His eyes settled on the cutlery drawer and he went to it, picking through the blades until his small fingers closed around the handle of a heavy kitchen knife.

Evan hefted the blade in his hand; it seemed ten times larger in his little-boy grip. This would do the job, but how would he get it to the Miller's house? He tried tucking it into his socks, but the thick metal would not fit. Evan let it dangle from his fingers while he racked his brain for another solution.

He heard a cry of alarm and the racket of keys falling to the tiled floor. His mother had appeared in the kitchen doorway, her expression one of shock at the sight of her young son wielding a butcher blade.

"Evan?" she said in a shrill, querulous voice.

He froze in place, unsure what to say or do. Andrea went pale as she saw the light glint off the knife in his hands, and Evan abruptly realized what must have been going through her mind.

With a visible struggle, Andrea added "Evan? Wh-what are you doing with that?"

When he tried to speak, Evan felt a flash of tension in the back of his head, and then a sudden flare of light—

"Evan!" Lenny patted his cheeks and he threw up a hand to stop him.

"I'm okay, I'm okay!" he insisted, wavering for a second or two as the aftershock's nausea faded away. "Well, that didn't work...

"You looked like you nodded off," Lenny began.

"Yeah, that's right."

"Oh. From what you were saying, you had me thinking something big was gonna happen…"

Despite himself, Evan snorted. "Like what? My head spinning around?"

Lenny frowned. "So, you're done?"

Evan turned over the page in the journal and studied the next entry. "Not yet."

His eyes narrowed as he read the words written there. *I never wanted to be in the movie anyway and it was so cold so I wanted to wear my clothes but Mr Miller took my shirt off.*

At the corner of his vision, Lenny's watchful expression seemed to tremble slightly, blurring as if a warped lens had come over Evan's eyes. A girlish giggle issued out of the air, echoing and reverberating—

And time shifted again.

"Now, get in your costume, Evan. And you have to promise, your bestest super-duper promise, that this will be our little secret. Think you can do that?" George Miller smirked. "Hey kids, you know what? I've got a great idea. Let's go downstairs into the basement. It'll look more like a dungeon down there."

"That'll be cool! Just like a real castle!" Kayleigh grinned.

Evan said nothing, letting events carry him on, down toward the basement. As Mr Miller set up the video camera on the tripod, Evan stretched his small body, wearing it like a familiar suit of clothes. The transitions were becoming seamless now, stronger and easier every time he did them.

George snapped an angry retort at Tommy Miller as Kayleigh's brother peeked in from the top of the stairs. "What did I say about keeping that door closed, stupid?"

"But I wanna see!"

"You're gonna see my fist in about two seconds unless you do what I tell you! Now get lost and close the damn door!" Tommy's sullen reply was lost in the slam of the door, and George threw Evan and Kayleigh a boozy wink. "Okay, actors, are we ready? Now, in this part of the story, Robin Hood just got married to Maid Marian and they have to kiss and stuff, just like grown-ups do."

Kayleigh giggled as Evan carefully studied his new surroundings. He caught sight of Tommy, surreptitiously watching them all, the boy's hands twisting the head of a doll around and around, mechanically wringing its neck.

In the far corner of the room, close to the cold grate of the fireplace, Evan saw what he was looking for. Partly concealed under some blankets was George Miller's old army footlocker, and somewhere inside that was the quarter stick of dynamite that Tommy would find when they were thirteen.

"Wait! I need my belt!" Evan said sharply, and he skipped past Kayleigh. Her father looked up with a puzzled expression, torn between centering the video lens on his daughter and Evan's sudden burst of movement.

Evan began to sing as he gently skipped from foot to foot, veering towards the footlocker. "Lou, Lou, Skip to my Lou," he chanted. "Lou, Lou, Skip to my Lou."

George Miller shook his head. "Dumb kid," he murmured, and bent back to the camera's eye-piece, fiddling with the focus control.

Evan saw his chance and took it. While Kayleigh's father was distracted, he reached down and flipped open the pressed metal lid of the footlocker. The first thing that caught his eye was a vintage 1982 issue of *Playboy*, the same one that Tommy had thrown—that Tommy would, he corrected himself, throw in Lenny's face. Beneath the magazine was the dull green cylinder of an Army-issue thermos flask, and Evan's face lit up when he saw it. "Paydirt!"

"Lou, Lou, Skip to my Lou." He kept up the rhyme as he quickly unscrewed the cap of the flask and shook it. The blocky shape of the dynamite stick dropped neatly into his waiting hand. Evan took the Blockbuster between his fingers and twisted it firmly, digging his nails into the paper coating; but no matter how hard he tried to crack it, his seven-year-old muscles could not muster the strength to do it.

George looked up, getting impatient. "Hey kid," he began. "Don't even bother with the belt..." Miller's jaw dropped as he turned to see Evan bang the inert piece of dynamite on the lip of a table. He went white with shock as he recognized what it was the boy held in his hands, and he took a warning step toward him.

Evan's finger shot out and pointed at his face. "Back off, fuckbag!"

Mr Miller froze, blinking and making fearful little gulping sounds.

Evan allowed himself a wry smile. "Amazing," he said. "That word never fails to make an impression on you, does it, George?"

Kayleigh watched the unfolding conversation with rapt attention, not quite sure what was going on, but fascinated by it. On the staircase, Tommy crept stealthily downward to get a better view.

George Miller took a slow, measured pace toward Evan, his hands raised in a calming, non-confrontational gesture. "Easy does it, Evan. Just pass that over and we'll say no more about it, eh? Don't be a bad boy or else I'll have to tell your mommy you were naughty."

"Oh, really?" Evan sneered, the expression looking odd on the face of a child of seven. "And I'll tell Child Protective Services about your kiddy porn endeavors! You come one step closer and I'll shove this up your ass!"

Kayleigh's mouth hung open in utter amazement. "Evan said bad words!" she thrilled.

He fished in the footlocker and came up with a box of strike-anywhere matches, the same kind that he used—Evan corrected himself once again—he would use when he was a teenager. He rattled the box.

"That's dangerous, you little moron!" Miller snapped, angry and worried now. "You could blow your hands clean off with that!"

Evan gave a callous shrug. "Been there, done that." Standing in front of the fireplace, he drew out a match and gave it a defiant flick with his thumb; the match head popped into flames and he touched it to the Blockbuster.

The short fuse fizzed and spat into life, making Evan blink while George pitched forward and dived at him, trying a sudden desperate grab for the dynamite charge. The two of them collided and Miller clutched at Evan's hand as they fell down on to the iron grate of the fireplace. The Blockbuster flew from the boy's grip and described an arc through the air, dropping and rolling across the floor. It came to a halt at the leg of the video camera's tripod and rested there, hissing.

"Just like a sparkler..." said Kayleigh, the glittering, luminous fuse dazzling her. She leaned down to pick it up, enchanted by the dancing orange flame.

"Kayleigh, noooo!" Evan couldn't be sure which of them it was that screamed out the warning—her father, her brother or him—but it came a heartbeat too late. As her finger touched the Blockbuster, the fuse lit the powder inside the dynamite charge and converted its chemical energy into instant, devastating, explosive power.

The shock-wave shattered every window in the Miller house and sent Evan's mind reeling, plunging into a burning void filled with the charnel stench of death—

He awoke with horrific violence, smashed out of unconsciousness with all the force of a body struck by a speeding car. Every muscle, bone and sinew in Evan Treborn's frame stretched to near-breaking point, and he coughed out a wet haze of bloody spittle as fluids streamed from his nose and mouth. Evan's back arched and he flopped back on to the bed sheets, thin croaks of pain and anguish coming to him as the terrible realization of what had happened took root.

"Oh god," he trembled, sick with dread. "Kayleigh..."

Then the pain surged anew, and this time it was so strong Evan was afraid that his skull would burst open like an overripe fruit. He clutched his hands to his head, part of him hoping that the agony of it would kill him for what he had done.

Police cars in the driveway, a coroner's wagon outside the Miller house... Tommy screaming and screaming and screaming... Andrea watching him as if he were something alien and deadly... The echoing crash of the judge's gavel in the courtroom...

Evan's eyes snapped open, taking in the dull horror of his surroundings, the sparse walls of the cell-like room in the clinic and the barred cage over the windows.

Nurses with plastic smiles handing him bland cake on his tenth birthday... Doctor Redfield comforting his mother from behind a glass screen as he scrawls on paper in the day room... An endless procession of inkblots passing before his eyes...

He tried to shift up, his muscles refusing to obey, as the grimy white enclosure pressed in on him. He was trapped, forced back into the rough embrace of the hospital bedclothes.

Redfield talks to him in his office, smiles robotically... Redfield shakes his head no as Evan rants and snarls... Redfield looks on as the CAT scanner sucks him in... Redfield closes his file with grim finality as he fails another test...

With a dizzying cerebral thunderclap, Evan felt the aftershock release him and he swayed there for a moment, buffeted by the passage of remembered time. In front of him there was a window, and through the white-painted bars that covered it Evan could see the far side of the Sunnyvale clinic, the office block where he had visited Doctor Redfield; that meant that he was deep inside the asylum proper, somewhere in the secure unit.

Thin streams of tears, turned to pink with the blood that leaked from his nostrils and lips, dropped on to his hands. His breaths became gasps, then sobs, uncontrolled and wracking wet gasps of air as Evan's misery overwhelmed him.

"Kayleigh, no..." he cried. "You can't die, not again! I won't let this happen!" The hard sting of anger colored his words. "I won't let it happen!"

Evan fought off the lingering pain and reached under the bed, his hands—intact once again—probing and reaching. "Where are they?" he demanded.

Wiping his face, he stood and pulled at the bed, tearing off the sheets, upending the mattress and finally, tugging at the frame where it was bolted to the floor. At last, spent and broken with despair, Evan felt to his knees and forced himself to look under the bed frame.

There was no familiar cardboard box there, no repository of all his effects and journals. He glanced around the room with watery, clouded eyes, desperately searching for any sign of his books.

"Where are they?" he repeated, unable to comprehend the terrible meaning of it. "My books! I can't change anything if I don't have my books!"

The fierce need gave Evan the strength he needed to propel himself up from the floor, and he lurched through the door of his room and into the corridor beyond, searching for answers.

TWENTY-SIX

Evan tried to outrun the fear. In his mind's eye he saw it come racing down the corridors after him, surging along like some malevolent wave of dark, an ink-black tide of terror that would stop his heart beating if only it could touch him.

He crashed past nurses and sent them falling like ninepins, shouldered his way through fire doors that crashed open against the walls. He left chaos in his wake as he ran, fighting to keep the fear out of reach, forcing away the tears in his eyes.

The glass-paned door to Doctor Redfield's office was slowly opening as Evan reached it, and he skidded to a halt, his hospital-issue slippers squeaking on the polished linoleum floor.

He caught a snatch of conversation. "Come see me again tomorrow, Anthony, and we'll talk some more about your mother."

Another patient was leaving, a large guy with a pinched, unhappy face and a waddle in his walk. Evan pushed past him, ignoring the irritable look he got in return, and rushed into the office. Red-field's sanctum was one of the few things that seemed to remain the same, he realized, no mat-ter where or when Evan visited it—the room still sported piles and piles of unkempt papers, moth-eaten chairs, bookshelves groaning with academic tomes on psychiatry, and the doctor himself in his worn leather chair behind the clut-tered desk.

Redfield looked up at Evan's frantic entrance with surprise and pushed his glasses back up his nose. "Hey, Evan. What's the big rush?" The doctor flicked a glance down at his day planner. "We don't meet for another hour."

Evan forced his hands together with a soft clap to stop them from trembling. The fear rose in him as he said the words. "My books!" he fumed. "Where are my goddamn books?"

"Books?" The doctor repeated. "Evan, any reading matter has to be left in the day room unless you have—"

"My journals!" Evan spat. "Where are they? What have you done with them?" His eyes ranged around the room with wild fright. "Are they in here somewhere? Have you got them?"

Redfield's face fell as he realized what Evan was looking for and he sighed, shaking his head. An orderly appeared at the door, red-faced and pant-ing with one hand clutching the hilt of his baton.

"Doctor," he wheezed, giving Evan a hard stare. "Is everything all right? This patient was running through the halls, causing havoc."

"It's okay, Mitch," Redfield said in a sad voice. "I'll take care of it."

The orderly and Evan locked eyes for a long moment, and Evan realized that a younger Mitch had been one of the men who had pulled his father off him all those years earlier. The door closed, leaving Evan alone with the doctor.

"I had thought we were finished with all this, Evan," Redfield began. "If you're starting to insist on these 'books' again, I'm concerned we might be seeing a slip backward in your condition, maybe even a relapse."

"What are you saying?" Evan's fingers knotted. "Just tell me where they are."

The doctor sighed and shook his head. "It kills me to have to go through this again, but you have to accept the truth. There are no journals, Evan. There never were."

Redfield's words hit him like ice water and Evan took an involuntary step backward, stunned by the admission. "No," he said weakly. "That's not right…"

"The books, they were part of the fantasy world that your mind created to cope with the guilt you felt for what happened. It was your way of getting past the responsibility for the accident. For Kayleigh Miller's death."

The sound of Kayleigh's name made his legs go weak and Evan sat heavily in a chair, his cheeks hot with emotion.

The doctor continued in a careful, calming voice. "Think about it, Evan. You borrowed from your father's psychosis, you invented a disease that doesn't exist. You created a fiction for yourself—time travel, alternate realities based on different events with colleges, prisons, paraplegia. The journals were the keystone of that delusion."

Evan tried to reply, but his voice was small and distant. "But I... I need those books. I can't make things right without them." He closed his eyes; the dark fear was in the room with him now, clouding and pulling at the edges of his vision. Evan felt heavy and warm, and his limbs began to twitch. "I need them."

Redfield frowned. "You remind me of your father. Do you know, when I was handling his case, he would always be questioning me about a book of family photographs? He screamed for that photo album even though he never had one. It was just a figment of his imagination. A phantom."

Evan's head lolled forward; Redfield's voice was dimming, becoming thick and woolly. "Photos..." he repeated.

"Evan?" The doctor said with alarm, approaching the chair. "Are you all right?"

"Photos," Evan said again; and then his eyes rolled back into his skull and he pitched forward, falling into a heap on the worn, dirty carpet of Redfield's cramped little office.

He drifted in and out of wakefulness like a wave lapping at a shore—steady and rhythmic as a heartbeat, flickers of consciousness coming to him in tiny little bursts, book-ended by moments of nothing, of a warm, senseless void. Evan saw a disjointed series of snapshots as things went on around him: Redfield calling Mitch back to take him speeding back down the halls, the brilliant glare of a penlight flicking into his eyes, and the plastic smell of the laboratory, the wheels of the gurney clickety-clacking over the smooth tile floor.

They put him inside the CAT scanner and ran the big machine through its paces, beaming into his skull to peel back the mysteries held in there, like rings in a tree trunk. The sensor heads of the scanner orbited around him in slow, languid loops, mapping every inch of his tortured brain. Evan watched them go around and around, and with them they brought brief kisses of pain, little butterfly touches of heat. At the corner of his vision, Evan saw the smallest of vibrations and the blink of a dead memory like a far off star burning out.

The taste of Kayleigh's soft lips...

Newly-baked waffles, sweet smelling straight from Mom's oven...

Anger, naked as flames, as his fist connects with Tommy's chin...

Lenny, chained to the bed frame...

Another Lenny, kissing Kayleigh...

Tommy grinning savagely...

Another Tommy smiling at him, warm and human...

Mom, blonde and frayed in the prison meeting room...

Another Mom, choking out a warning on the life-support machine...

The memories collided and bounced off one another, merging and changing, becoming a chaos of events half-dreamed, half-experienced.

Mom wielding the tire thumper, hateful...

Thumper, Heidi, Lenny, Snake, Hunter, Kayleigh...

Tommy crying like a child...

Kayleigh screaming at him from the bars of the prison cell...

Junkyard, movie theater, grade school, dorm room...

Redfield stabbing him with the steel spar...

Carter, Gwen, Mom, George, Jason, Kayleigh...

Jason waving at him from the end of a corridor...

Kayleigh, Kayleigh, Kayleigh, Kayleigh and Kayleigh ...

Evan let himself sink into the ocean of his own memories, as the scanner rumbled on, enclosing him like a mechanical cocoon.

He awoke later in his room, at some unknown hour of the night. In the dimness, he stared out at the dark rectangle of the window, the mirror of his face hanging there in pale, mute contemplation. Evan stared into his own eyes and read the emotions there, the utter loss of hope and the loneliness. Even in the most hellish moments of his time in the prison, or the helplessness of being confined to the wheelchair, Evan had still managed to keep hold of the smallest thread of faith. But now, for the very first time he felt totally and utterly trapped, locked in a world that he had brought upon himself.

Once in a while, the window would quiver a little around the edges, shimmering like a distorted television picture, and when it did Evan could be sure that he heard sounds like voices, echoing and reverberating from some other time or place.

After his performance the previous day, Evan found himself watched by Mitch wherever he went, the orderly's dour face never straying too far from him.

After breakfast, he looked up from the meal he'd barely touched and Mitch was waiting there. "Phone call," he said without preamble. "Come on."

In an office opposite the day room there was a bare table, a chair and a telephone. It was gray plastic, the kind that had a blank fascia instead of a dial or pushbuttons. The handset was off the hook, and Evan stared at curiously.

"It's for you," Mitch added.

Evan sat and picked it up. "Hello?"

"Oh, Evan," His mother sounded strung out and tearful. "Are you all right?"

Another blur vibrated at the edge of his vision, and he blinked it away. "I'm okay, Mom. I'm just… confused."

"I know," she sighed. "I wanted to tell you I'm coming to see you today. Doctor Redfield asked me to come in."

Evan felt relieved. "I'm glad. I want to see you, Mom. I want to get out of here."

A long pause. "I know you do, kiddo, but the doctor says that might not happen right away."

His hand tightened around the receiver and for a moment Evan had to fight down the urge to cry out in anger. He made his voice level, aware that Mitch was watching him closely. "He knows best. I just want to get well."

She made a sound, a strangulated sniff. "Can I bring you anything?"

My journals? But then, Redfield says I never had any, right?

"I... I'd like a picture. I miss you and all. Could you bring me a photo album, or something? I could put up some family photos in my room." In the back of Evan's mind, a plan began to form.

"Doctor Redfield said you might ask for that kind of thing," she sighed. "You were too young to remember, but your father, he... When he was sick, one night he burned them all. The only thing I managed to keep were the old cine films he made."

"Could I see those?"

"I'll have to ask the doctor." She sniffed again, holding back a sob. "I'll see you soon. I love you."

"Love you too, Mom."

* * *

Andrea paused outside the entrance to the clinic and shifted nervously, taking a long draw on the cigarette in her hand. A tickle in her throat made her cough and she choked out smoke in a wheezy burst of breath. Suddenly, the smell of nicotine sickened her and she dashed out the cigarette on the ground. She shook her head to clear it. She would need to be focused now, for her son's sake, not thinking about where her next smoke break would be. With determination, she reached into her handbag and ditched the cigarette packet and lighter she found there, slamming them into a waiting trash can. Andrea stooped to pick up the big cardboard box at her feet and walked into the clinic.

Redfield met her at the reception. "Hello, Andrea. You're looking well."

"I just quit smoking."

"Good for you. Shall we go to my office?"

She hesitated. "I'd like talk to my son…"

He took a measured breath. "He'll come and meet us in a few minutes. I think it's best if we go over the results of his new set of scans first."

"You've seen them?" Andrea tried to keep the anxiety out of her voice.

"Not yet. I thought we should review them together." He walked her through the clinic proper, skirting the day room and the nurse's station.

She nodded. "I spoke to Evan this morning."

"Yes, I was notified. Do you notice anything different about his behavior or speech patterns?"

"No. He seemed a bit upset. He said he was confused."

"That's to be expected after a seizure. We'll know more when I compare the CAT scan series." The doctor indicated the box. "You brought something for him?"

"He wanted to see some photo albums, but we don't have any," Redfield nodded and she continued. "These are Super 8 movies Jason shot years ago. I wasn't sure if I should bring them along, but you said it might be good for him—"

"That's perfectly all right, Andrea." They reached the office and he opened the door for her. "Those films are part of his life, and Evan's fixation with changing events that have already happened won't be broken until he comes to realize that history can't be altered." He sat and she did the same. "I'd like to review those films myself, and hopefully I'll be able to find something to convince him that what's past is past..." Redfield indicated an old portable cine projector on a nearby shelf.

"I don't want to lose him like I lost Jason," she said in a small voice.

The doctor looked uncomfortable. "Psychology has advanced a lot in thirteen years, Andrea. There are treatments we can provide for Evan that simply weren't available when your husband was with us." When she didn't reply, the doctor worked the keyboard on his desktop computer to bring up the CAT scan results.

"Oh." What he saw on the screen made him shudder. "Jesus, no," Redfield breathed.

Andrea fiddled with her fingers nervously, trying not to bite her nails. "No dances, Doctor," she said, unable to conceal her fear. "Just tell me."

Redfield had been a clinical psychologist and neurologist for more than twenty years, and he'd seen his share of patients who hadn't responded to treatment—people like Jason Treborn, who had lived out their last days trapped in insanity—but still he found each inevitable, damning diagnosis as hard as the first. Even with the professional distance he maintained with his residents, Redfield had grown to like Evan and he'd privately hoped that he would be able to bring the young man back to normality. But what he saw on the screen told him that would never happen. Large, dark clots of twisted matter scarred the cross-section of Evan's cerebellum, in torn tracks like tears across a cloth.

"The hemorrhaging…" he began tightly. "The neural damage in his outer brain tissue is massive. This kind of degradation is inoperable and irreparable." Redfield shook his head. "I'm frankly surprised Evan still has any use of his motor functions…" The moment he said it, the doctor regretted it, and he heard Andrea burst into tears. "I'm so sorry."

In the corridor outside the office, Evan stood with his back pressed to the wall, listening to the conversation. He'd managed to slip away from under Mitch's watchdog gaze and arrive in time to follow his mother to the doctor's office. As he listened to Redfield's prognosis, a hand strayed to his temple and rubbed the skin there. The Doc's not going to let me get hold of those reels, Evan realized. I've got to play this out and find another angle. With determination, Evan took a few quiet steps back, then walked forward again as if he'd just arrived, fixing a false, breezy grin on his face.

Redfield looked up as he entered, and the doctor registered the young man's gaunt, drawn features, despite the upbeat manner he displayed.

"Hey, Mom! Did you remember to bring those goofy old home movies we used to make?" Evan deliberately looked away from his mother, giving her a moment to wipe her eyes and regain her composure.

Andrea nodded. "Y-yes, they're here."

The doctor gave him a practiced smile. "Have a seat, Evan. Let's talk about how you're feeling."

Evan let Redfield speak and kept up his false front as there, on the desk before him, was the crumpled box his mother had brought with her. Evan tried not stare at it, as he turned over the possibilities it contained in his mind.

One last chance, he told himself.

It was night when Evan returned to the office; he knew the interior of the clinic like the back of his

hand now, and it was not hard for him to carefully avoid the patrolling nurses. With a swift
press from his shoulder, the weak door gave way
as he leaned all his weight on it and the lock
came open in a splinter of wood.

It was still warm in the confined box of Redfield's room from the lingering heat of the day.

Evan pushed the door closed and propped a
chair against it, then stealthily crossed the room
and picked up the box from where it still lay. *Treborn, E.* was written there on the flaps in the
doctor's brisk, imperfect scribble. Evan smiled a
little. Redfield's idea of filing seemed to be to
place everything in plain sight.

The smile jerked into a grimace as the wall
before him flickered suddenly, bringing an echo
of sound along with it. Evan screwed his eyes
shut and forced away the pain. Time and memory were starting to unravel around him.
Outside, an alarm began to ring and he glimpsed
staccato flashes of light from the flashlights of
the clinic's security guards. Someone called out
an order, the voice indistinct and unclear, and
the lights bobbed away.

Evan opened the box and felt his way through
the contents, a thrill of tension through his fingers as he laid his hand on a spool of cine film.
He hesitated for a moment as a figure ran past
the office door, and Evan noticed his reflection
in a picture frame on the far wall. The doppel-
ganger staring back at him trembled a little,
threatening to shift and drift away from him. A

black streak crawled out from his nose and
Evan saw dark blood trickle into drops down
his shirt.

He pushed the ache away and tried to ignore
the slowly increasing pressure inside his head,
the constant slow pulse of it like a vice screwing
ever tighter. Evan grabbed at a sheaf of paper
from Redfield's desk and retreated under the
wooden table with the box and a pen. He felt the
sudden need to document what he was doing,
perhaps on the off-chance that if he failed, then
maybe his Mother would have some small con-
solation in understanding why.

He spoke aloud the words as he wrote them.
"If anyone finds this, then I guess my plan didn't
work and I'm already dead, but if I can just go
back to the beginning of all this, I still might be
able to save her—"

The pain drilled itself back into his consciousness and more blood drooled out of his nostrils,
spattering across the paper. Evan's racing heart
drew panic along with it, and even as he tried to
ignore the ever-increasing spasms and vibrations
in the environment around him, he felt an icy
claw of fear tighten.

He studied the film rolls in the box and reached
in, taking out a single spool marked with a yellowed piece of tape as a makeshift label. Evan
recognized his father's writing there, and his
own name in black marker.

One last chance.

TWENTY-SEVEN

Doctor Redfield found Mitch and two of the security guards near the main entrance and waved them to him. He'd been on his way home, getting into his car when the alarm had blared. Some sixth sense made him come running back, and at the front desk he discovered that a nurse had found Evan Treborn missing and a window forced open in the nearby corridor.

"No sign of him in this block," Mitch panted. His age was catching up with him these days, and he was looking forward to finding the Treborn kid to put in some licks as payback for making him run his ass off around the asylum.

"He's not in his room," Redfield said. "Search the grounds!"

Mitch made a sharp gesture to the guards and they took off, out through the main doorway. Redfield watched them go, their flashlights stabbing out into the night.

He saw a familiar face approaching, her eyes narrowed in concern. "Harlon, what's the fuss this time? You left the barn door open again?"

"I hope not, Kate. It's Evan Treborn. He's made a break for it."

Doctor Pulaski shook her head. "Oh, Treborn, right. The delusional case. But that's off-pattern behavior for him, isn't it?"

He nodded in agreement. "I'm thinking this seizure he had has scrambled what healing we've been doing in the past few years. He's back to square one, or worse."

"How did he get out?"

"Window. Busted it in with a fire extinguisher."

She thought for a moment. "That doesn't track, Harlon. This Evan, you said he's a smart one, right? He's been here long enough to know how well the grounds are covered. Even if he got over the wall, he's got to know the cops will be waiting for him."

Redfield followed her reasoning. "He might not be rational, though."

"But what if he is?"

"You think the window was a diversion? He could still be inside, maybe?"

She shrugged. "The question is, would Evan have any reason not to run? Is there anything here that he'd want more than the chance to escape?"

Redfield's eyed widened with sudden realization. "Shit! The films!" He tore away from Pulaski, leaving her speechless. "Call the guards back!" he shouted over his shoulder. "He's in my office!"

Evan shifted the bulky projector off the desk and placed it carefully on the floor, aiming the lens at the underside of Redfield's heavy desk. He plugged the extension cord into a wall socket and took a moment to make sure that no light from the machine would spill out against the walls and the windowed door. Numbness at the tips of his fingers made it difficult for him to thread the Super 8 filmstrip through the spools of the projector, and twice he had to stop and start again. It took every iota of Evan's will not to succumb to the building panic in his gut.

He turned the aged projector's dial switch to *on*, and the device stuttered into life, the film rattling and clacking as it fed through past the blank strip of white leader. The sound of the old motor running seemed as loud as a machine gun burst to Evan, and he gave the door an apprehensive glance, convinced that someone would come through it at any second, drawn by the clattering of the sprocket holes. The still air inside the room became heavy with the tang of hot ozone and cellulose.

There was no speaker attached to the projector, so the flickering color pictures were silent, their only voice the tick and whir of the rolling film. The image wavered as the focus shifted in and out, softening and then hardening on the face of Evan's mother, sweaty and florid, racing away from him down a hospital corridor, clutching at her pregnant belly. The picture fluttered past, a sharp snap making him jump as the film stock changed. A different setting now—his mother's mouth moving silently as she holds up a tiny little child to the camera—then another snap and another scene, as Andrea wraps the baby Evan in a pale blue blanket.

He heard a sound out in the corridor, and it drew his attention away. A voice? Evan realized that his time was running out, perhaps even measured in seconds now, and he looked back at the flickering image, as the bright vista of a sunshine-filled day appeared there. Through the age spotting, grains and cracks, Evan could see Lenny Kagan's backyard and it brought a smile to his lips. The swing set, the tired old apple tree, the porch's peeling white paint over careworn pine.

A five year-old Lenny scampered into view, sheepish in front of the other kids at his birthday party, unsure of what to do as his mother brought him a pile of presents. As the camera panned around, Evan caught a glimpse of his younger self, and there in the washed-out colors of the background, Kayleigh Miller skipping in circles.

He heard a man call his name, but the voice seemed to be somewhere else, nowhere near where Evan was now. He let himself let go and allowed the vibrations and the pressure in his head to come freely. Evan's eyes filled with the dancing, blinking images of the party and he lost himself there, sinking into the captured frames of the past.

From all around him came the voices of chattering parents and laughing children, someone blowing poorly on a toy harmonica and a dog yapping excitedly.

Evan's world lost all definition as it shuddered uncontrollably and he fell—

Into a bright, summer day.

The world seemed immense around him, huge and out of proportion to the body Evan found himself in. The nausea of transition lasted scarcely a heartbeat, and he peered through five year-old eyes at the gaily-colored decoration strewn around the Kagan's garden.

A firm but gentle hand pressed into the small of his back and Evan let himself be prodded forward. "Go on, Evan, introduce yourself." He tottered forward on little legs, glancing up to see his mother—younger, more lively than he remembered—smiling down at him. "Say hello." Andrea pointed at someone and Evan followed her direction.

Kayleigh stood a few steps away, coyly staring at her feet, every now and then stealing a secretive look at him. When he took a slow step toward her, she smiled bashfully at him. Even as a child Evan saw the bright, vital glow of her personality dancing there, the earliest glints of the woman that he would fall in love with.

You were the first person I ever really cared about. Kayleigh's words came back to him with sudden force, the memory of it clinging to him. *When my folks split, they gave me and Tommy a choice of who we wanted to live with. I couldn't*

stand my Dad, but I knew that if I moved to my
Mom's place in Florida, I'd never see you again.

Evan's young heart tightened in his chest, as
the stark responsibility of her statement
became clear to him. He took a slow look
around the yard, taking in all the reality of the
moment, savoring the truth of his revisited
memory.

"He's not usually this shy..." he heard his
mother say. "Evan, don't be rude. Say hello to
Kayleigh."

There was no choice really, he decided, no
other route that he could take to make things
right. Evan leaned over toward Kayleigh,
almost as if he were about to kiss her lightly on
the cheek, but at the last moment he turned his
face and hissed a forceful little whisper in her
ear, never breaking the mild, guileless expression he wore.

"I hate you," he told her with venom. "If you
ever come near me again, I'll kill you and your
whole family."

Kayleigh drew back as if she had been stung
and her face screwed up into a mask of
absolute distress. Bursting into gales of tears,
she ran away from Evan and into her mother's
arms.

Kayleigh's mom gave Evan a scolding glare.
"What did you say to her? What happened?"

He ignored her, concentrating on Kayleigh as
she wept into her mother's shoulder, hoping for
one last gaze from her perfect eyes before she

was finally struck from his life. He felt tears forming at the corner of his vision and his breath caught in his throat.

I'm sorry, Kayleigh, I'm so, so sorry.

"Goodbye," he whispered to himself.

The pain was familiar now, and as Evan felt the shock of it release him, he tasted warm blood, a stream of it caught up in the unshaven hair on his upper lip. He registered only that he was lying in a bed before the agony of the change took over him once again, and Evan barely had the time to grab a pillow and wrap it around his head before the cascade began anew.

Kayleigh in her Maid Marian dress, fading... Kayleigh blowing him a kiss from across the college quad, vanishing... Kayleigh holding his hands on the roof of the Theta house, disappearing... Kayleigh dissolving, Kayleigh dwindling, Kayleigh gone and unremembered...

This time things went differently—instead of the flickers and merges of his other memory-storms—this change was like a flurry of strobe light images, the merest blink of an event, striking like a sucker punch, then gone.

Lisa Halpern and her daughter, the little girl growing up and playing outside the Treborn's house... Tommy Miller in an Eagle Scout uniform, serious and intent... Evan's father shaking hands with Doctor Redfield as he leaves the clinic...

Evan rode it out, taking in shuddering breaths, wondering where he would awaken this time, and what world it would be that he had forced into existence.

Evan and Lenny clowning around in class... George Miller proudly saluting his son as Tommy heads off to fight in the Gulf... Andrea cooking a pasta dinner for her new husband... Evan accepting the college scientific achievement award for his flatworms project...

And finally, it ceased. Evan dropped the pillow from his face and saw blots of blood and tearstains on the white linen—it was over.

"You all right?" asked a familiar voice. "You want I should call a doctor?"

Evan looked up and accepted the towel that Lenny Kagan held out to him, smiling with genuine warmth to see his old friend there. "Hey, buddy. You look good." Evan wobbled a little, taking in the sight of the dorm room around them. Little seemed different, save for a few posters here and there. It was oddly comforting in its own way.

Lenny grinned, reassured that Evan was all right. "Better than you."

"You wish." Evan studied his roommate. Lenny was right, in a way, he did look better than Evan had ever seen him before; fit and happy with no sign of the awkward self-consciousness that had plagued the other alternate versions of him.

"You're sure you're okay?" Lenny asked, still a little concerned. "You fry that big brain of yours and I got no one to poach my Psych test answers from."

Evan gave him a feeble smile. "I think I'll be all right this time," he said, and as the words left his mouth, he felt a new hope swell inside him. "I really do."

"Are you sure about this?" Lenny asked, as he shouldered open the door to the basement, peering over the lip of the cardboard box in his hand.

Evan followed him into the dimly lit room, carrying an identical box. "I'm sure." He dropped the container to the ground and gripped the crank of a thick metal lever. With a grunt of effort, Evan pulled the handle downward and the vent hatch to the dormitory's main furnace yawned open, sending a wash of heat out at them.

Lenny blinked and stared into the cauldron of flames inside. "Last chance to change your mind about this, Ev." He nudged one of the boxes with a foot. "What you are doing here, this is pretty radical. Are you sure you want to send all your history up in smoke?"

"I'm sure," Evan repeated, and without any hesitation he upended the first box into the furnace, sending bunches of paper, old photographs, the spools of home movies and yellowed school report cards into the flames. The furnace accepted them greedily, chugging out a puff of smoke from its open maw.

Lenny stepped back from the other box, aware that this was some kind of solemn duty for his friend, a rite of passage that only Evan could perform. Inside the second container were dozens and dozens of identical Mead composition books, their marbled covers catching the hearth light of the fire.

Evan pulled one out at random and flipped it open without looking at the age written on the cover. In among the tight scrawl of his handwriting was a vague, half-finished pencil sketch of a girl. The image seemed incomplete and ghostly, as if it had been based just on the idea of a face, and not on an actual person. Evan saw the dream of a teenage Kayleigh Miller there, and he closed the book with a snap.

Evan weighed the journal in his hand for what seemed like an eternity, and then with a flick of his wrist he sent it spinning into the inferno. Without pause, he scooped up all the other books and fed them to the fire, letting the pages crisp and blacken, the heat turning them into dark, featureless ashes.

After a while, Lenny spoke, his soft voice breaking Evan's reverie. "So, what now?"

"Now?" Evan let the question float there for a moment. "Now I get on with the rest of my life."

And with that, it was done.

No more books. No films, no pictures, not a single thing that I could use to remind me of years gone by. From that day on, I kept no diaries, no logbooks or records beyond the most basic notes. I made sure that I was always the one who took the photos when somebody waved a camera around, and I did my best to make sure that I never owned one myself. I grew older with my memories safely held in just one place: my mind.

You hear me say this and it seems cold of me; thoughtless, even, that I cut out a piece of my own history and left it behind, gone and forgotten, burned away in the flames. In one life, on one track of time, I had sworn to Kayleigh that I would come back for her, but the irony of it all was that I had to leave her in order to save her. Fate, if such a thing really exists, has a cruel sense of humor.

The truth of it is that Kayleigh was the greatest loss that ever came in my life. In the changed world that I came to rest in, nobody around me had any idea of who she was—some of them remembering the little girl I'd upset as a boy, but no one knowing anything of her beyond the day the Miller's divorce was final, when she packed up with her mother and went to Florida. The Kayleigh that I remembered, and the mélange of alternates from all the different versions of history were just phantoms now, vague possibilities of how she might have grown up in Sunnyvale. No one knew the woman that I had fallen in love with, because she did not exist. Like that picture in the burning journal, Kayleigh—my Kayleigh— was a ghost of some distant, other present.

So I went on with my life. I graduated from State College with honors and thanks to the help of Professor Carter, I found myself a path that led to my own practice in New York City. Things began to go my way, and, after a few years the wound in my heart for Kayleigh healed some. Soon, whole days would go past without me even thinking about her, then weeks, then months, and eventually, years. Time passed and passed and passed, ever forward, never backward.

But then one afternoon, as I was crossing 67th Street toward Central Park West, fate jerked my chain one more time.

I remember it so clearly. It is a lovely day. Spring, and it rained the night before so that cool, fresh feeling in the air is still around. I have a dataphone pressed to my ear as I weave through the crowds. I'm talking to my mother, just one more suit in the milling throng of thousands of New Yorkers going back and forth.

"Yeah, Ma," I say with a frown. "I'm running a little late for lunch. One of my patients had a breakdown." She says something sympathetic and I nod my assent. "Anyway, order some soup in the meantime. The French onion with celery is great there. I'll see you soon."

I sign off and fold the phone in half, and as random as you please, my eye line drifts over the crowds and snares on something. On someone.

She's crossing the street like I am, but coming the other way. She's dressed in some impeccable business suit that's cut to fit her like a glove, her face matured but still strong with that perfect spark that captivated my soul. The shock of seeing Kayleigh Miller is so powerful that it strikes me dumb, knocks me off my stride and I almost stumble as she passes by.

Her eyes linger on me for just a little longer than necessary, but there's no glint of recognition—and why should there be? She doesn't know me, not this Evan Treborn, not the man who fell in love with another her.

I came to a halt and stand there on the sidewalk, watching her drift away from me, gradually merging into the mass of the lunchtime crowds, her golden blonde hair and absolute poise growing ever more distant.

A million reasons why and why not flashed through my mind in that second, and in all honesty I had no answer to any of them. I thought of where I had been, of the broken threads of time that I'd traveled, and all of it came together into one moment of choice. That moment, in that place, at that time.

So I took a deep breath, turned on my heel, and I went after her.

ABOUT THE AUTHOR

London-born and bred, James Swallow's youthful love of science fiction led him into a career as a media journalist and author in his early twenties. Swallow has worked on a number of books, including the Sundowners quartet of 'steampunk' Westerns (*Ghost Town*, *Underworld*, *Iron Dragon* and *Showdown*) as well as short fiction for the *Silent Night* anthology and *Inferno!* magazine. The only British writer to have worked on a *Star Trek* television series, he created the story premises for the *Star Trek: Voyager* episodes 'One' and 'Memorial'. An itinerant writer of fortune, James Swallow has written about science fiction, games and oriental media for more than sixty different publications in seven languages around the world, including *SFX*, *Dreamwatch*, *Starlog*, *Manga Max*, and licensed magazines covering *Star Trek*, *The X-Files*, *Star Wars* and *James Bond*.